RAMAGE'S

DEVIL

Historical Fiction Published by McBooks Press

BY ALEXANDER KENT
Midshipman Bolitho
Stand Into Danger
In Gallant Company
Sloop of War
To Glory We Steer
Command a King's Ship
Passage to Mutiny
With All Despatch
Form Line of Battle!
Enemy in Sight!
The Flag Captain
Signal–Close Action!
The Inshore Squadron
A Tradition of Victory
Success to the Brave
Colours Aloft!
Honour This Day
The Only Victor
Beyond the Reef
The Darkening Sea
For My Country's Freedom
Cross of St George
Sword of Honour
Second to None
Relentless Pursuit
Man of War

BY DOUGLAS REEMAN
Badge of Glory
First to Land
The Horizon
Dust on the Sea
Knife Edge

Twelve Seconds to Live
Battlecruiser
The White Guns
A Prayer for the Ship
For Valour

BY DAVID DONACHIE
The Devil's Own Luck
The Dying Trade
A Hanging Matter
An Element of Chance
The Scent of Betrayal
A Game of Bones

On a Making Tide
Tested by Fate
Breaking the Line

BY RAFAEL SABATINI
Captain Blood

BY DUDLEY POPE
Ramage
Ramage & The Drumbeat
Ramage & The Freebooters
Governor Ramage R.N.
Ramage's Prize
Ramage & The Guillotine
Ramage's Diamond
Ramage's Mutiny
Ramage & The Rebels
The Ramage Touch
Ramage's Signal
Ramage & The Renegades
Ramage's Devil
Ramage's Trial
Ramage's Challenge
Ramage at Trafalgar
Ramage & The Saracens
Ramage & The Dido

BY ALEXANDER FULLERTON
Storm Force to Narvik
Last Lift from Crete
All the Drowning Seas

BY PHILIP McCUTCHAN
*Halfhyde at the Bight
of Benin*
Halfhyde's Island
*Halfhyde and the
Guns of Arrest*
Halfhyde to the Narrows
Halfhyde for the Queen
Halfhyde Ordered South
Halfhyde on Zanatu

BY A.D. HOWDEN SMITH
Porto Bello Gold

BY V.A. STUART
Victors and Lords
The Sepoy Mutiny
Massacre at Cawnpore
The Cannons of Lucknow
The Heroic Garrison

The Valiant Sailors
The Brave Captains
Hazard's Command
Hazard of Huntress
Hazard in Circassia
Victory at Sebastopol
Guns to the Far East
Escape from Hell

BY R.F. DELDERFIELD
Too Few for Drums
Seven Men of Gascony

BY DEWEY LAMBDIN
The French Admiral
Jester's Fortune

BY C.N. PARKINSON
The Guernseyman
Devil to Pay
The Fireship
Touch and Go
So Near So Far
Dead Reckoning

*The Life and Times of
Horatio Hornblower*

BY JAN NEEDLE
A Fine Boy for Killing
The Wicked Trade
The Spithead Nymph

BY IRV C. ROGERS
Motoo Eetee

BY NICHOLAS NICASTR
The Eighteenth Capta
Between Two Fires

BY FREDERICK MARRY
*Frank Mildmay or
The Naval Officer*
The King's Own
Mr Midshipman Easy
*Newton Forster or
The Merchant Servic*
*Snarleyyow or
The Dog Fiend*
The Privateersman
The Phantom Ship

BY W. CLARK RUSSEL
Wreck of the Grosvenc
*Yarn of Old
Harbour Town*

BY MICHAEL SCOTT
Tom Cringle's Log

BY A.D. HOWDEN SM
Porto Bello Gold

BY JAMES L. NELSON
*The Only Life That
Mattered*

RAMAGE'S DEVIL

by

DUDLEY POPE

THE LORD RAMAGE NOVELS, NO.13

MCBOOKS PRESS, INC.
ITHACA, NEW YORK

Published by McBooks Press 2002
Copyright © 1982 by Dudley Pope
First published in the United Kingdom in 1982 by
The Alison Press/Martin Secker & Warburg Limited

Cover painting by Paul Wright.

Library of Congress Cataloging-in-Publication Data
Pope, Dudley.
    Ramage's devil / by Dudley Pope.
        p.   cm. — (Lord Ramage novels ; no. 13)
    ISBN 1-59013-010-3 (alk. paper)
        1. Ramage, Nicholas (Fictitious character)—Fiction. 2. Great
    Britain—History, Naval—19th century—Fiction. 3. Great
    Britain. Royal Navy—Officers—Fiction. 4. Napoleonic Wars,
    1800–1815—Fiction.   I. Title
    PR6066.O5 R33 2002
    823'.914—dc21   2001007008

Distributed to the trade by National Book Network, Inc.,
15200 NBN Way, Blue Ridge Summit, PA 17214
800-462-6420

Additional copies of this book may be ordered from any bookstore
or directly from McBooks Press, Inc., ID Booth Building,
520 North Meadow St., Ithaca, NY 14850. Please include $4.00
postage and handling with mail orders. New York State residents
must add sales tax to total remittance (books & shipping).
All McBooks Press publications can also be ordered by calling
toll-free 1-888-BOOKS11 (1-888-266-5711).
Please call to request a free catalog.

Visit the McBooks Press website at www.mcbooks.com.

Printed in the United States of America

9   8   7   6   5   4

For the late Frank Casper,
sailor, navigator and friend

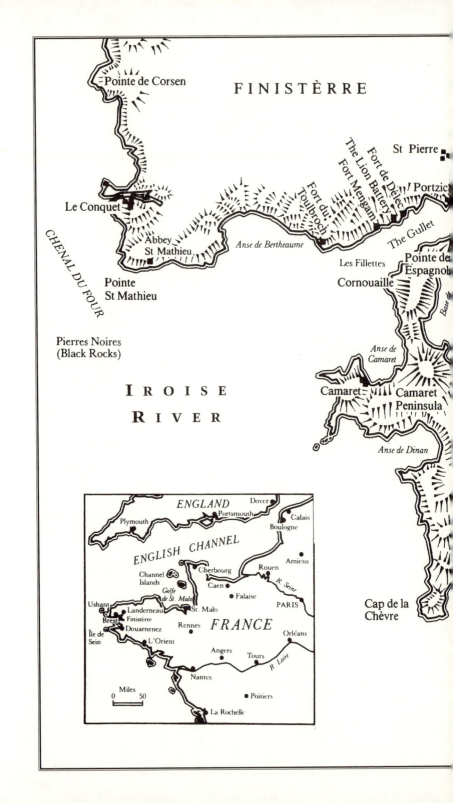

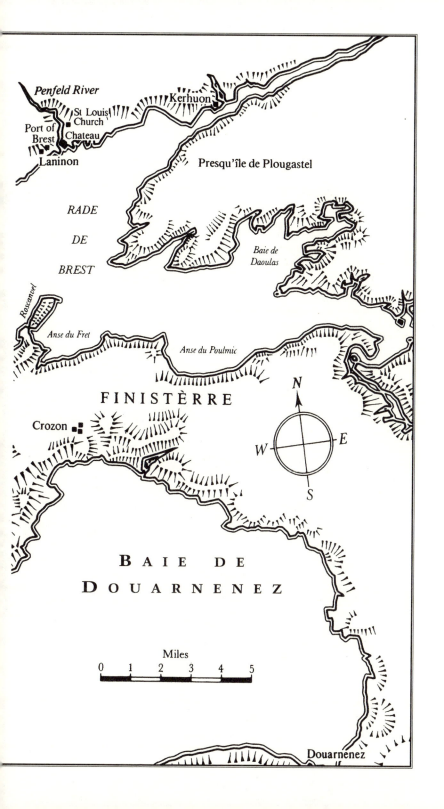

Penfeld River

Kerhuon

St Louis
Church

Port of
Brest

Chateau

Laninon

Presqu'île de Plougastel

RADE

DE

BREST

Baie de
Daoulas

Roscanvel

Anse du Fret

Anse du Poulmic

N

W — E

S

FINISTÈRE

Crozon

BAIE DE
DOUARNENEZ

Miles

0   1   2   3   4   5

Douarnenez

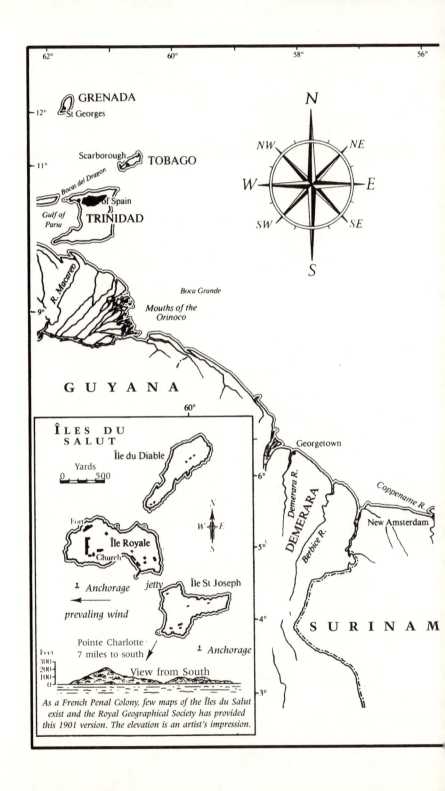

GRENADA
St Georges

Scarborough
TOBAGO

Bocas del Dragon
of Spain
Gulf of
Paria
TRINIDAD

R. Macareo

Boca Grande

Mouths of the
Orinoco

G U Y A N A

60°

ÎLES DU SALUT

Île du Diable

Yards
0   500

Fort
Île Royale
Church

⊥ Anchorage   jetty   Île St Joseph

prevaling wind

Pointe Charlotte
7 miles to south

Feet
300
200
100
0
View from South

⊥ Anchorage

Georgetown

Demerara R.

Coppename R.

DEMERARA

Berbice R.

New Amsterdam

SURINAM

As a French Penal Colony, few maps of the Îles du Salut
exist and the Royal Geographical Society has provided
this 1901 version. The elevation is an artist's impression.

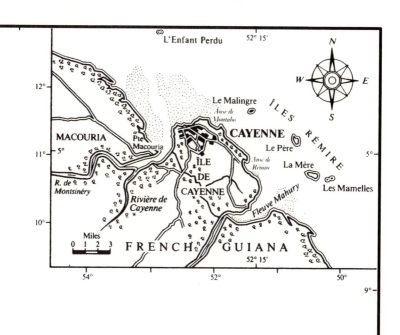

L'Enfant Perdu   52° 15'

12°

Le Malingre
Anse de Montabo

MACOURIA   Pte
Macouria

CAYENNE

ÎLES RÉMIRE

Le Père
La Mère   Les Mamelles

11° — 5°   5°

*R. de
Montsinéry*

ÎLE
DE
CAYENNE

*Anse de
Rémire*

*Rivière de
Cayenne*

Fleuve Mahury

10°

Miles
0 1 2 3   FRENCH   GUIANA

52° 15'

54°   52°   50°

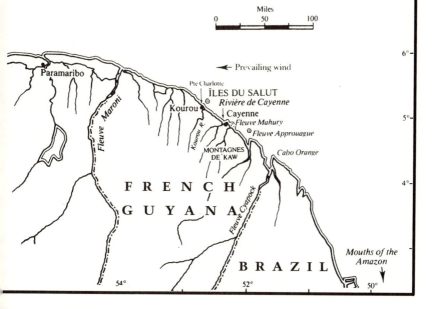

ATLANTIC   OCEAN

9°

8°

7°

Miles
0   50   100

6°

◄— Prevailing wind

Paramaribo

Pte Charlotte
ÎLES DU SALUT
Rivière de Cayenne

Kourou   Cayenne
Fleuve Mahury
Fleuve Approuague

MONTAGNES
DE KAW

Fleuve Maroni

Kourou R.

Cabo Orange

5°

FRENCH

GUYANA

Fleuve Oyapock

Mouths of the
Amazon

4°

BRAZIL

54°   52°   50°

CHAPTER ONE

THEY WERE both lying, propped up by an elbow, on the bristling carpet of short, coarse grass which was fighting for its life on top of the cliff, the roots clinging desperately to the thin layer of earth and finding cracks in the rock beneath. The browning leaves struggled against a wind which, although this afternoon little more than a brisk breeze, still whipped up a fine, salty spindrift from the swell surging on to the rocks below and sent it high like invisible smoke across the top of Pointe St Mathieu.

The Atlantic swell, from this height looking like slowly rippling wrinkles, swept in lazily from the west to hit first the barrier of tiny islands and rocky shoals stretching a dozen miles from Ushant, over on their right, down to the Black Rocks, which were in front of them and five or six miles to seaward. After surrounding each rock and islet with a fussy white collar of foam, the swells rolled on inshore to smash against the front of the cliffs sixty feet below with a strangely remote booming that they felt rather than heard, like the tiny tremors of a distant earthquake.

Above them the sky was strewn with white cottonball clouds which seemed to be looking down on the rollers and the cliffs, pleased at finally making a landfall after a long but boring Atlantic crossing. But to the two pairs of eyes long accustomed to the brilliant, almost gaudy sharpness of tropical colours, the sea and sky background seemed washed out, faded and without energy.

Gulls hovered like kites on the wind currents coming up the cliff face and sometimes wheeled over them, as though curious and wanting to see why this dark-haired man and young, tawny-haired woman should be there alone and just looking seaward, not tending cattle or sheep, their horses tethered by the reins to pieces of rock jutting like teeth. Close by, two brown and white cows cropped the grass with indifference, as though they were supposed to graze a particular area by nightfall, and knew that they were comfortably ahead of their schedule, moving so slowly that the bells round their necks only occasionally gave muffled clangs, apparently reluctant to interrupt the whine of the wind and the distant thunder of the waves.

The occasional contented sigh, the sudden indrawn breath, the gentle touch of a finger, the woman's occasional toss of the head to move strands of tawny hair that blew across her face and tickled, revealed an erotic atmosphere (though neither of them thought of the word) not entirely due to the splendid isolation of Pointe St Mathieu which, with one exception, seemed to be saying that up here, on a sunny afternoon, nature was pausing briefly at the second phase of the cycle of birth, love and death, and smiling.

The exception stood behind them, grey, stark, shadowed in the sun yet not menacing. The ruin of the old Abbey St Mathieu was still solid, the walls forming geometrically precise angles with the flying buttresses. It looked as though it had been lived in until some unpredictable giant or unexpected storm had lifted off the roof and hurled it away.

A couple of artillery batteries, one to the left and the other to the right, with their guns still in position, were the only other signs that humans had ever passed this way.

"Les Pierres Noires," Ramage commented, gesturing down at the handful of black shapes scattered in the sea below them like sheep crouching against the wind on a distant moor. "Known to the Royal Navy as the Black Rocks. It seems strange to be looking down at them from up here, from France. Having the French view . . . If these were normal times—wartime, anyway, because that's all I can remember—the French lookouts up here would be watching Ushant over there"—he pointed to the rocky island just in sight, the last in a series of smaller ones leading to it like enormous stepping stones—"making sure no English ships sneaked along the Chenal du Four inside that great shoal, or round the southern end to get into the Iroise river.

"How different it looks from a British frigate!" he added, the dreaminess leaving his voice. "There'd be the Black Rocks sticking up like ancient teeth and beyond you'd see this line of cliffs with the ruins of the abbey on top. And of course Le Conquet"—he pointed to the right—"and the other villages to the north, although from the deck of a frigate the cliffs mean you can only see church towers and steeples. Le Conquet's tall open steeple: I remember that well, a cone-shaped skeleton.

"And French and English alike are here just to watch the Gullet. That's the mouth of the river down there"—he pointed over the edge of the cliff to their left—"round the corner, as it were, and running up to Brest itself."

She nodded across to the other side of the Gullet. "What's that headland over there?"

"The Camaret Peninsula, forming the south side of the Gullet, with plenty of guns to keep out *rosbif* trespassers. The little town of Camaret is well inland. I remember seeing Camaret Mill once, but we had gone very close in and had a scare when the wind dropped on a flood tide."

Sarah said: "All this must remind you of Cornwall."

He paused, lost for a moment in memories. "Yes, because apart from the cliffs and hills the village names would be hard to distinguish, Delabole, Perranzabuloe, Scorrier, Lanner, Lansallos, Trelill, Lanivet, Lelant, St Levan—all good Breton names: could be within 25 miles of here!"

She nodded, and he added: "And in Cornwall—Portsall, Lesneven, Lanion, Lannilis, Crozon, Plabennec, Kerlouan . . ."

"It's extraordinary," she commented. "Still, I think one can distinguish the Cornish ones."

"Can you?" he smiled, eyebrows raised.

She nodded. "Oh yes, even though I'm not Cornish."

He laughed and leaned over to kiss her. "Don't be cross with your new husband because he's teasing you. The first names are Cornish—the ones you thought were Breton. All the second are here in Brittany!"

"But . . ."

"Just listen to these: St Levan and Lesneven, Lanivet and Lannilis, Perranzabuloe and Plabennec . . . the first of each pair are Cornish, the second Breton. I can forgive you for mistaking them! And Botusfleming, Lansallos, Lesnewth, Lezant, Trelill—they hardly sound very Cornish, but they are."

Sarah smoothed the olive green material of her dress, not bothering that the wind ruffled her hair. "Brest . . . the blockade of Brest . . . I've heard you and your father talk about it," she said thoughtfully. Her voice was deep; he reflected that he seemed to hear it with his loins, a caress rather than a sound. She was watching a bee circling a buttercup, thwarted as the breeze bent over the golden bell. "We can't see the port from here, can we?"

He shook his head. "Bonaparte's main naval base on the Atlantic coast is well up the Gullet. One has to sail in close under the cliffs (with these and other batteries pelting you if you're British in wartime) and usually there's a soldier's wind to let you run in. All the way up to Brest the Gullet narrows like a funnel and there are three forts on your larboard hand—if memory serves they're Toulbroch, Mengam and de Delec; we'll be able to see them on the way back—and one on the other side. Plus various batteries."

He half turned, resting on an elbow and looking across at the hills beyond Brest and at the ruined abbey in the foreground.

It was built many centuries ago and obviously had been abandoned for at least a hundred years, but he tried to think what men had quarried the rock and hammered and chiselled the blocks to shape to build a monastery on what is one of the bleakest spots in Europe. Here during winter gales it must seem the Atlantic was trying to tear away the whole continent. Were those monks of the Middle Ages (or earlier?) scourging themselves by establishing their home on one of the windiest and most storm-ridden places they could find? Did they think the harshness made them nearer to God? Were they seeking absolution from nameless guilts?

"This must be the nearest point in France to Canada and America," Sarah said.

He shook his head. "Almost, but Pointe de Corsen is the most westerly." He pointed northward along the coast. "Look, it's over there, about five miles, beyond Le Conquet. Hundreds, indeed thousands of English seamen know it because it's a good mark when you're working your way through the Chenal du Four, keeping inside of Ushant and all those shoals . . ."

He fell silent, looking westward, until finally Sarah touched his cheek. "Where are you now?"

He gave a sheepish laugh. "Running the *Calypso* into Brest with a south-west wind. Earlier I was beating in against a north-easter, with all the forts firing at me. I was scared stiff of getting in irons and drifting ashore."

"Southwick wouldn't let you do that," she said teasing.

Like Ramage, she remembered the *Calypso*'s white-haired old master with affection. She said: "I wonder what he's doing now?"

He shook his head as if trying to drive away the thought. "By now he and the *Calypso*'s officers and men will probably have the ship ready to be paid off at Chatham."

"What does 'paid off' really mean? I thought it was the ship, but it sounds like the men."

It was hard for him to avoid giving a bitter answer. "Officially it means removing all the *Calypso*'s guns, sails, provisions, cordage and shot (the powder will have been taken off and put in barges on the Thames before she went into the Medway), and then the ship, empty except for a boatkeeper or two, will be left at anchor, or on a mooring. They may take the copper sheathing off the hull."

"Why 'may'?" she asked, curious.

"Well, you know the underwater part of the hull of a ship is covered with copper sheathing to keep out the teredo worm, which bores into the wood. Now some peculiar action goes on between the metals so that the ironwork of things like the rudder gets eaten away. Not only that, but after a year or so the copper starts to dissolve as well, particularly at the bow: it just gets thinner. So when a ship is laid up she is usually first dry-docked and the sheathing is taken off."

"You still haven't explained 'may'—and there's a strange look on your face!"

He sighed and turned back to look at her. "Well, you know my views on this peace treaty we've signed with Bonaparte, and that neither my father nor I—nor most of our friends—believe Bonaparte truly wants peace. As a result of the treaty, he's already had more than a year to restock his arsenals and from the Baltic get supplies of mast timber and cordage, which we had cut off for years by blockading places like Brest. So now he's busy refitting his fleet: new sails, masts, yards. New ships, too. Now—or very soon—he'll be ready to start the war again."

"Yet all the French we've met in the past weeks seem happy with the peace," Sarah protested.

"We've only talked to two types—innkeepers, who smile readily enough as they take our money, and the monarchists who've returned to France from exile and have been trying to get back some of their possessions. They have to believe that Bonaparte really wants a permanent peace; otherwise they're admitting to themselves that they'll soon be exiles in England once again—only this time probably for the rest of their lives."

"You keep on saying Bonaparte will start the war again, my darling, but what proof is there? After all, the ministers in London aren't fools!"

"Aren't they? Have you met Addington or any of his cabinet? And Lord Whitworth, the British minister in Paris, can't have looked out of the embassy window—or else they're ignoring his despatches in London."

"The British government might be stupid and the French innkeepers greedy, but that hardly proves Bonaparte is going to war again!"

"Perhaps not, but we'll know for sure when we ride back through the port of Brest. Will the sight of men-o'-war being refitted in large numbers convince you?"

"Nicholas, why did you propose Brittany for the last part of our honeymoon?" she asked suspiciously.

"Don't you like it?" He was suddenly anxious, the picture of a nervous bridegroom anxious for his bride's comfort. "The weather is fine. Not much choice of food, I admit, but the inns are not full of our countrymen—they go directly to Paris!"

"You haven't answered my question!"

Her eyes, green flecked with gold, were not angry; they did not warn that she felt cheated or duped. It was obvious she would accept it if he gave the real reason. Only evasions or half-truths would upset her, although good food was rarely spoiled by being served on fine china. He leaned over and kissed her. "I have another wife," he confessed solemnly. "I married you bigamously."

She undid the top two buttons of her dress, recently collected from a French dressmaker using materials Sarah had brought with her from England. "The sun has some warmth in it, if you wait long enough, but not enough to tan. Yes," she said matter-of-factly, "I knew about that when you first proposed. Anyway, your mother warned me. In fact she used almost the same words. She said what a shock it had been for her as a new bride when she realized that her husband had another wife. She was very relieved that I already knew about you and your first bride, the navy."

"Well, we met under unusual circumstances."

She blushed as he reached over and undid the next two buttons of her dress, pulling back the soft material so that he could see her breasts.

"Bonaparte has done one thing for us—the French fashions help lovers," he said, and kissed a nipple, touching it with his tongue so it stiffened.

It was strange, she reflected, that you held your husband naked in bed; you even walked round the bedroom naked in front of him, and it all seemed quite natural. Yet out here in the sunshine, lying on the grass with bare breasts, she felt shy, as though this was the first time that Nicholas had unfastened a button. But how right he was about French fashions! Unlike in London, bare arms in the drawing rooms were commonplace here and very few French women of fashion bothered with corsets, although those sensitive of their plumpness wore narrow stays. And the flimsy materials! Often they were almost transparent, and most respectable women wore petticoats, but she had seen several women who passed for respectable wearing dresses that revealed their whole body when they stood against the light, and it was quite extraordinary how often they found themselves in front of a window. Still, anything was welcome that freed women from the constriction of corsets: why should women have to live as though squeezed in a wine press for the sake of fashion? Nevertheless, she pictured some women she knew and imagined them freed of corsets: it would be like slitting the side of a sack of corn!

She felt her breasts hardening as he pretended to inspect her nipples for the first time, commenting on their colour and size. Did he really like large nipples?

"Very well," she said, concentrating with great effort, "so the navy is your first wife and you are honeymooning in Brittany with your second on secret business. *What* business?"

"It's no secret," he protested. "Our *passeports* are in order: the French authorities admitted us—welcomed, almost—to the country, enchanted that we are on our honeymoon, so if I happen to be able to count up the number and type of ships being fitted out in Brest, and perhaps La Rochelle and L'Orient . . . well, that would be only the natural curiosity of a couple interested in ships and the sea. After all, you have only just completed a voyage to India and back, and you love looking at ships—don't you?"

"Of course, dearest," she said with a smile. "And having closely inspected my breasts, taken my virginity, counted the ships and returned to London at the end of your honeymoon, what do you report to whom—and why? Surely the Admiralty must know what is going on in the French ports?"

"If not what happens on nearby clifftops. No, the Admiralty as such is not the problem. The man who seems to be completely hoodwinked by Bonaparte is the First Lord of the Admiralty, Lord St Vincent. He's laying up ships of the line and frigates. That in itself doesn't matter so much because they could be commissioned again in a few weeks, but he's letting go all the prime seamen: they are being turned loose and are just disappearing like chaff in the wind, looking for work. You can commission all the ships again in a month and get them to sea—*providing* you have the seamen."

"But, dearest, surely an admiral like Lord St Vincent realizes all that?"

"Of course he realizes he needs trained seamen to commission ships and get them to sea. His mistake is he doesn't believe we need the ships. He doesn't think we'll be at war again with Bonaparte for another five years."

"Five years? Why not seven, or nine—or three?"

"He's attempting a complete overhaul of all the dockyards— to get rid of the theft, corruption and inefficiency which ranges from commissioners at the top to workmen at the bottom. It will take at least five years."

"So, my dear, do you think your honeymoon in Brittany will result in Lord St Vincent changing his mind and not paying off any more ships?"

The whimsical note in her voice took the sting out of the question, and he frowned as he answered. It was a fair question and hard to answer satisfactorily. "It's almost too late to stop him paying off ships: most are already laid up. No sooner had we arrived home in the *Calypso* than (as you well know) I had orders to go on round to Chatham and lay her up. That means all those men I've been collecting together for years, from the time of my first command, the *Kathleen* in the Mediterranean, will be turned out of the navy the moment the *Calypso* is laid up."

"And the commission and warrant officers—Southwick, Aitken and the others, yes and young Paolo—what happens to them?"

"Well, they'll join another ship if they can find a berth, but hundreds of lieutenants and masters will be after a few dozen jobs. Paolo should find another ship because my father has enough influence to arrange a midshipman's berth. There's virtually no limit on the number a ship can carry: it depends on the captain."

She sat upright to avoid the sun dazzling her and wondered if it could possibly tan her bosom a little. Her nipples were so large and brown. Did Nicholas prefer small pink ones, she wondered again. He seemed more than satisfied with them as they were, although she realized new husbands were unlikely to be critical.

"So you lose everyone once the ship is laid up again," she commented. "Supposing a month later—a month after you are back in London—the Admiralty commissions the *Calypso* again and gives you command?"

"I can ask for the officers, and for Southwick, and if they're not employed I'd probably get them. But the men—not one, unless they heard about it and volunteered, because they'd be scattered across the country, or perhaps serving in merchant ships."

"And if the war started again?"

"I still wouldn't get them back. They'd volunteer or be pressed and be sent to whichever ship needed men most urgently. I'd have to start all over again. My name is well enough known that volunteers would join, hoping for prize-money. But—well, you saw that I knew just about everything concerning every man in the *Calypso*."

"Yes, you seemed to be father confessor to men twice your age. Anyway, at least we're not at war," she said and touched his arm. "At least you're not away at sea and I'm not sick with worry in case you have been wounded. Killed even."

"That's a cheerful thought for a summer's afternoon!" he protested.

"Every time I hold you in bed, I feel a scar," she retorted. "Like knots in a log. You've been lucky so far, the shot or sword cuts have not damaged anything vital. Why, you've done more than enough already to be able to resign your commission and just run the St Kew estate."

"My mother has been talking to you!"

"Not really. She would like you to, and so would your father."

"He has no faith in the Admiralty or politicians."

"That's hardly surprising, considering what they did to him. If they hadn't made him the scapegoat so many years ago, he would probably have been First Lord now, not St Vincent."

Ramage shrugged his shoulders. "Perhaps—but I wouldn't have done so well."

"Why on earth not?"

"He would have been so determined that no one should accuse him of favouring his son that I'd probably still be a lieutenant commanding a cutter, probably on the fishery patrol off Newfoundland."

"So although you might complain about Lord St Vincent's policies, you've done well enough, thanks to him." Sarah was unsure why she was sticking up for St Vincent, who had always seemed taciturn, almost boorish, when she had met him.

"Thanks to his predecessor, Lord Spencer. He gave me my first chances in the early days—the chance to win my spurs, as it were."

"So you have a honeymoon task—to get enough information to persuade the First Lord and the Cabinet to change the country's policy towards Bonaparte!"

"Not quite," he said wryly. "Just to convince the First Lord to keep enough ships in commission. I—we, rather—don't *want* war; we just want to be ready because we think it is coming."

She buttoned up her dress. "Come on, let's get on our way. War *may* be coming, but it's certain we have only a few weeks of our honeymoon left and Jean-Jacques expects us for an early supper."

Sarah riding side-saddle brought a stop to the daily life in each village: women stood at the doors of their houses or shops, or came down the paths to the gates in response to cries from their children.

"We're probably the first foreigners they've seen since before the Revolution," Ramage commented, keeping a tight rein on his horse, which was nervous at the shrill cries and cheers of the darting children.

"They wonder what nationality we are," Sarah said. "There'd be fewer smiles if they knew we were English."

"Yes, they won't like the *rosbifs* here. Still, we could be Spanish, or even French: here in Brittany anyone from another province is a foreigner!"

"But we are obviously *aristos*," Sarah said quietly. "They probably think we escaped the guillotine at the Revolution and with the peace have returned from exile . . ."

Ramage shrugged his shoulders. "I am not very worried about that! It's more significant that Fort du Toulbroch, Fort de Mengam and the Lion Battery are still fully manned, as though the war was still on and a British squadron might sail up the Gullet any moment."

"I can see another fort ahead of us. There, just to the right of that church."

"Yes, the church is at St Pierre and the fort is de Delec, less than a mile short of Brest. This side of it, anyway."

"How many sides are there?"

He laughed and explained: "The port is built on both sides of the entrance of the Penfeld river, just where it runs out into the Gullet. From what I remember of the charts and from what Jean-Jacques said last night, the arsenal is this side, by the entrance to the river. Then as you go upstream there's the repair jetty, and a couple of dry docks and another arsenal. Then on the other side, to the east, there's the château with high walls: an enormous fortress complete with gate and towers. There are barracks further inland. The commander-in-chief's house is in the centre of town, the Hôtel du Commandant de la Marine, in the Rue de Siam, although why I should remember that I don't know! There's a naval college nearby. All along this side of the river are more quays, for another arsenal which is probably used for storing guns and carriages. On the road to Paris at the main gate, the Porte de Landerneau on the north side of the town, there's the hospital. I remember the map of the town in the Hydrographic Office at the Admiralty, drawn ten or fifteen years ago, noted that the pile of garbage from the hospital was polluting the water. And the cartographer was called St Nicolin. Strange how one's memory dredges up these odd items!"

"Look," Sarah said, "I can see masts. Like trees that have lost their leaves."

"Yes, there's just one more village, Laninon, before we reach the port. Ah, over to the right you can now see the ships at anchor in the Roads in front of the port. Yards crossed, sails bent on—why, it really does look as if Bonaparte is preparing a fleet. To send to India, the West Indies, the Cape? . . . Eight . . . nine . . . eleven ships of the line. Thirteen . . . fifteen . . . sixteen frigates. Four transports. And various others—corvettes, *frigates en flûte*—"

"What are they?" she interrupted.

"Frigates with most of the guns removed and fitted out as transports. And," he continued, listing what he saw, "they're anchored out in the Roads, ready to sail. I wonder what we will see along the quays once we get into the port . . ."

She shivered. "I don't like this, Nicholas. Supposing they stop us in the port and want to see your documents? You captured and sank enough French ships for them to know your name only too well. They could accuse you of being a spy."

"Hardly a spy," he protested. "My papers give my full name. There's nothing secret about our visit—we're on our honeymoon. I'm not writing down lists of ships . . . And remember, there's nothing to prevent a French naval officer visiting Portsmouth, or Plymouth—nor anywhere he wants in England. He could probably set up an easel in front of Southsea Castle and paint all the ships he saw riding at anchor at Spithead, and with half a dozen small boys and a sergeant of fusiliers watching him admiringly."

"Yes, but remember what Jean-Jacques said," Sarah reminded him.

"Dearest, poor Jean-Jacques is a stranger in his own country. He's lived in England as an exile since 1793. Nine years. A long time."

"He realizes that. Imagine leaving a château empty, except for vandals, for nine years . . . Still, I must say he's done everything to make us comfortable. Thank goodness he brought linen, crockery and cutlery with him from England. The place might be short of furniture but it's still more comfortable than the back of this horse!"

As they jogged along the lane skirting the coast and passing through the village of Laninon before reaching the Penfeld river, Ramage noted the state of the road. Apart from its width it was little more than a deserted track pocked every couple of yards with large potholes. Yet it was obviously the most important road for the defence of Brest because it was the only link (without going miles inland and swinging out again) with the three forts and the Lion Battery. The defences of Brest were between the port and Pointe St Mathieu, but quite apart from rushing out field artillery or cavalry, it was unlikely a company of soldiers could hurry along here on a dark night without a quarter of them spraining ankles in potholes. Yet summer was the time to fill potholes so that cartwheels and horses' hooves packed down the earth.

By the time they returned to the château, to be greeted by Jean-Jacques, they were weary, feeling almost stunned by the monotonous trotting of the horses. Jean-Jacques' valet, Gilbert, busied himself with buckets of water, filling the only bath in the house. This, a large circular basin about twelve inches deep, had been found outside—the Revolutionaries had used it for watering their horses. Now, with it sitting on a thick bath mat on the dressing room floor Gilbert walked back and forth from the kitchen stove with buckets and jugs of hot water. Finally, with six inches of hot water in the bath and some jugs of cold left beside it, he reported all was ready and left.

Those buttons! Being constantly in the company of a woman with a beautiful body (with a body, he told himself proudly, which delighted a French dressmaker who took pride in cutting and stitching her material to emphasize or take advantage of every nuance of breast and thigh), buttons took on a new meaning for him. Previously they were devices for holding together pieces of cloth; now they could be a gateway to ecstasies.

Slowly she undid the buttons of her dress, starting at the bottom so that finally with a quick shrug of her arms the whole dress slid to the floor, and as he started up from the armchair she said: "No, dearest: poor Gilbert has spent the whole afternoon boiling this water—let's use it while it is hot." More buttons, more shrugs, and she stood naked, pleased at his obvious pleasure in watching her. Yes, her breasts were firm; yes, her hips were generous without being plump. Yes, her buttocks had that pleasing fullness: so many Frenchwomen, she noticed, had the flatness of young boys.

She turned slowly, and then picked up the towel. "You bring the soap," she said, and he stood up and began to undress, thankful that while in France he found it easier to forget breeches, which the French seemed to associate entirely with the aristocracy, and wore the trousers which the *sans-culottes* had adopted as a garment and a slogan.

By the time they had bathed and dressed, Sarah wearing a pale yellow dress which was low cut in the latest fashion, Ramage was sure he would doze off at the dinner table. However, in the high-ceilinged dining-room, sparsely furnished with a table and five chairs, they found Jean-Jacques in high spirits. He had, he told them, just been able to trace some more of the furniture left behind and stolen by looters when he fled the Revolution.

Stocky, with crinkly black hair, a nose so hooked that in some lights he looked like a contented puffin, and dressed as though Louis XVI was still on the throne, instead of long ago executed by a revolutionary mob, Jean-Jacques wiped his mouth with a napkin. "Landerneau, out on the Paris road, that's where I found them," he said. "A dining table, twelve chairs, the sideboard and wine-cooler."

"Who had them?"

"The mayor. He was using the table and four chairs; the rest were stored in his stable. Luckily his wife was proud of the table and kept it well polished."

"What happens now?" Sarah asked.

"Tomorrow I am sending my bailiff and a couple of carts to collect everything. With plenty of straw to protect the wood."

"The mayor doesn't claim they're his?" Ramage asked.

"Oh yes, although of course he doesn't deny they were once mine. He claims the Revolution put an end to all private property."

"You had an answer ready for that!" Ramage could imagine the conversation.

"Oh yes. He had half a dozen silver tankards on the sideboard with someone's crest on them, so I said in that case I'd take three since he had no claim to them. His wife nearly had hysterics!"

"But you haven't made a friend—a mayor can be a danger-ous enemy," Sarah said.

"The Count of Rennes has few friends in Brittany after the Revolution," Jean-Jacques said grimly. "My real enemy is Bona-parte, so I need hardly care about the mayor of little more than a hamlet. And since Héloïse—well, stayed behind—when I went to England I have no sons to inherit the title or this château.

Rennes," he said quietly, as though talking to himself while he stared back through the centuries, "the ancient capital of Brittany. Two hundred years ago we were one of the half dozen most powerful families in the country. Now the last survivor is reduced to retrieving sticks of his furniture from the local thieves. Where are all my paintings, my silver, my gorgeous carpets, the Gobelins tapestry which ran the length of that wall?"—he gestured to one side of the long dining-room—"the Venetian glassware which has been handed down from father to son for generations? Being used by oafs.

"I don't begrudge oafs their possessions, but they are just as content swilling rough wine from pottery mugs. They get no pleasure from looking at and using a Venetian goblet; indeed, it just means they get short measure. To them, a Gobelins is a piece of cloth that keeps out a draught, or makes a good tarpaulin to prevent hay blowing off a rick. I could accept the local people stripping this château when the Revolution began if I thought they'd *appreciate* the treasures they stole. But . . ."

Ramage wanted to change the subject to cheer up the Count, whose grandfather had begun the family friendship with the Blazeys, but there was a difficult question to ask, and now was obviously the time to get the answer.

"Héloïse—have you seen her?"

"The Countess of Rennes, in the eyes of my church still my wife, though no doubt divorced by some new law of the Revolution? No, I last saw her here nearly ten years ago, when she refused to escape with me."

Sarah knew only that the Count had spent his exile in England alone while his wife stayed in France, and could not resist asking: "Why did the Countess stay?" A moment later she could have bitten her tongue.

The skin of Jean-Jacques' face suddenly seemed too tight for the bone structure, but he struggled to present an unconcerned smile. "She agreed with the aims of the Revolution, or at least she said she did. She was very young then. It goes back a long time: she hated her father, who was of course one of the King's favourites, and she imagined the King once snubbed her at Versailles. Hardly the stuff of revolution, one might think, but she brooded so that when the mob from Brest and Nantes and Angers came yelling through the gate, crying death to the King (and the Count of Rennes) she met them in old clothes and invited them in and served them my best wine. Meanwhile I escaped with my valet and my life. She was very beautiful. Still is, I expect. She is the mistress of one of Bonaparte's generals, I believe: a former corporal, who is not too proud to bed a citizeness who has an old title in her own right and another by marriage."

He signalled to one of the servants, indicating that the glasses were empty. "The candles are getting low, too," he said, and apologized to his guests. "Before long we'll be reduced to using rush dips."

Sarah said: "You know, all that riding has made me so tired . . . Perhaps Nicholas will give you your game of backgammon."

The Count stood at once, apologetic. "Of course, both of you must be worn out: how thoughtless of me to keep you up talking of sad yesterdays. Yesteryears, rather. But tomorrow perhaps we shall dine at a more suitable table—I must be the first Count of Rennes to entertain in his own dining-room with his guests seated round a scrubbed kitchen table."

Ramage laughed and turned to Sarah. "In Jean-Jacques' defence, I should explain that the house he bought in England was furnished with the finest English furniture he could find!"

"Ah, the house in Ruckinge. You know Kent, my dear? Not Ruckinge? I was fortunate enough to be able to carry jewellery with me when I left here for England and by selling some I could buy a house in Kent. Although I love that house, my heart is really here, even though the château is almost empty. I spent my childhood here. My father's father's father—so many forebears—grew up here and died of old age. The vaults in the chapel are nearly full. There'll be just enough room for me. Perhaps the original builder saw into the future and knew how many of us he would need to accommodate!"

"You seem to be full of gloomy thoughts tonight," Ramage said as he helped Sarah from her chair.

"Yes, and as your host I am appalled that I have to put you in a suite over in the east wing furnished only with a bed, two chairs, commode and a single armoire. And no curtains at the windows."

"You should see the great cabin of a frigate," Ramage said dryly.

The Count led them to the door and once out of earshot of the two servants said: "I met an old friend today. He lives at La Rochelle but travelled to Rennes by way of L'Orient to arrange some business. He was an officer in the old Navy and like me escaped to England. He says that five ships of the line and six frigates are being prepared at La Rochelle, and seven and eleven of each in L'Orient. How does that compare with Brest?"

"Eleven and sixteen," Ramage said grimly. "So 23 ships of the line and 33 frigates are being commissioned along the Atlantic coast. I wonder what's going on at Toulon?"

"I must admit that's a large fleet for peacetime," Jean-Jacques said, and then added, as if to reassure himself that there was a future: "But I am sure Bonaparte wants peace now. At least, he wants to—how do you say, to 'consolidate.' You've seen how he has sent most of his soldiers home to reap the harvest. There are many hundreds of miles of roads still to be repaired—thousands in fact. Today France is a whole country where reaping, plough-ing and sowing will take every available man this year if the people are not to starve. Already he is gambling on a good harvest—a bad one would topple him. People will go short in time of war, but with peace they want full bellies."

Ramage shook his head. "Ten bad harvests won't topple a man who controls the biggest army and the most powerful police force the world has ever seen."

"Still," the Count persisted, hope overcoming reason, "Bonaparte has concluded a peace with the Russians, and Britain is isolated. The world is at peace. I have no need to remind you that by the Peace of Amiens England has surrendered most of her colonial conquests—and in return Bonaparte has given up the deserts of Egypt. He has all he wants. You don't suppose he needs Spain, Portugal, the Low Countries, Scandinavia . . . ?"

"I do, but I'm probably in a minority," Ramage said. "Bonaparte has kept control of the Italian states and Switzerland."

"But he knows he can't beat the British at sea. Think of the Battle of Aboukir Bay—what a disaster for France! He is a soldier; he has created a great army. But he can't use it to attack England because the Channel is in the way. He realizes this. And that is why he sends his soldiers home."

"But why does he prepare his navy—the navy you say he knows cannot defeat the Royal Navy?"

Jean-Jacques held out his hands, palms uppermost. "Perhaps to make sure they are in good condition before he stores them away—or whatever you sailors call it."

"Perhaps," Sarah said, taking Ramage's arm. "You must excuse the bride for dragging her groom off to bed, but she is going to sleep standing on her feet!"

CHAPTER TWO

SHE WAS LYING on her side with her back to him, and for a moment he marvelled that the female body had been so shaped that in this position it fitted the male so perfectly. But sleeping alone in a swinging cot at sea—for him that would from now on be an almost unbearable loneliness. Quite why horses should now be galloping with harness jingling he did not know, and he opened his eyes to find the first hint of dawn had turned the room a faint grey.

Horses? Harness? Now, as he shook the sleep cobwebbing his head, he heard shouted commands coming from the centre of the château; from the wide steps leading up to the front door.

He slid out of bed and walked to the window, cursing the coldness of the marble floor but too impatient to find slippers.

A dozen men on horseback, blurred figures in the first light. Perhaps more. Now he could just distinguish that they were dismounting. Some were hurrying up the steps, sword scabbards clinking on the stone, while a single man held all the reins.

One man was making violent gestures at the great double door—presumably pounding on it with his fist. Then he heard more horses and another five or six men cantered past the window towards the others. Soldiers. Even in the faint light it was possible to distinguish them—and only cavalry would have so many horses.

She was standing behind him now; he could feel her breasts pressing into his shoulder blades. "What is it?" she whispered. "It's so cold. Why aren't you wearing a robe? You'll get a chill."

"French cavalry," he said briefly. "Quickly, dress in riding clothes. Don't try and light a lamp."

He hurried across the room and pushed their two trunks so

that, from the door, they were hidden by the armoire and commode. He then bundled up the clothes they had been wearing the previous evening and which they had been too tired to do more than drape over the chairs, and pushed them under the bed.

"What are you doing?"

"Hurry, darling. Something's happened and these soldiers aren't here on a search for army deserters. They look more like an escort for Jean-Jacques or me. The second group was leading a riderless horse."

"You don't think . . . ?"

"The mayor of Landerneau may be trying to keep his furniture by telling the *préfet* some tale. Don't forget Jean-Jacques is very vulnerable—he's only recently returned from exile."

She shivered as she sorted out underwear. "And he has the notorious Captain Lord Ramage staying in his house."

"That can't be a crime," Ramage said as he pulled up his trousers, but his voice was doubtful, so that what was intended as a statement sounded like a question. "Anyway, whatever they're up to I can't think the soldiers know anything about us. One spare horse . . . that's for Jean-Jacques."

"The officer in charge can easily leave two of his troopers behind, or have two of Jean-Jacques' horses saddled up for us. Or make us walk."

"Let's rely on them not knowing we're here!"

"The servants," Sarah said, ignoring her husband's attempts to reassure her, "can they be trusted? Will they tell the soldiers we are here?"

"If you hurry up, we won't be here, darling," Ramage said, reaching for his jacket. "We'll be hiding in another room, so if the French soldiers search our suite they won't find us."

"Dearest," she whispered, "do up my buttons." She turned her back to him so that he could secure her coat. By now, he noticed, it was getting appreciably lighter. He had been thinking that the first cavalry had passed only a couple of minutes ago, but he realized it was now nearer five.

"There—now, my lady, hurry up or—"

He stopped and listened to the gentle but persistent tapping at the door. Tap, tap, tap—and then a hissed "Milord . . . milord . . ."

He recognized the voice: Jean-Jacques' valet Gilbert, a tiny, almost wizened Breton who had gone to England to share his master's exile and then returned after the Treaty of Amiens.

Ramage hurried to the door and the moment he had opened it the valet slipped through and shut it again.

"Ah, milord—and milady, of course—you are dressed." Gilbert glanced round the room, noted the trunks and the lack of clothing and toilet articles lying about. "You are prepared, then: this suite looks deserted—they will say the English have flown, if indeed they know you are supposed to be here. Quickly, please follow—I take you to a small room where you must hide."

"But what—"

"I explain in a few minutes, milord: first, to safety!"

The valet shut the window ("No Frenchman would have a window open," he explained) and they followed him out of the room, along the corridor away from the main part of the château, down a staircase where it was so dark they had to grip the rail and feel for the next step before moving, until finally the valet opened a door.

"An old storeroom, milord," he explained. "No one would seek you here, and there's a side door leading into one of the gardens."

He extended a hand to Sarah. "There is a small step up, milady. I am afraid there are simply these old packing cases, but we hope you will only have to wait an hour or two before returning to your suite."

Ramage felt like a piece of flotsam swirling round rocks at the mercy of random waves, but before he had time to ask, the valet said: "I have a message from the Count, milord, and some information I—er, well, I happened to hear. I took the liberty of listening beyond the door.

"The message from the Count is that he thinks France is again at war with Britain and you must escape. That was all he could say before the cavalry officer and his men came in to arrest him."

"But you heard more?"

"Yes, sir, it is indeed war. The most important thing the cavalry officer said as he arrested the Count—on direct orders from Paris—was that Lord Whitworth, your ambassador in Paris, had left the capital on the twelfth of this month. He said this was close to a declaration of war. Then on the seventeenth the British authorities had detained all French and Dutch ships in their ports and issued commissions to privateers."

He paused a moment, pulling at his nose as though that would stimulate his memory. "Yes, then on the next day, the eighteenth, the British declared war on France and on the nineteenth ships of the Royal Navy captured some French coasting vessels off Audierne—almost in sight of Brest and, of course, in French waters.

"Then, according to the cavalry officer, on the 23rd Bonaparte issued an order to detain British men between the ages of eighteen and sixty who are liable to serve in the British army or navy."

Ramage glanced at Sarah. It was now the 25th of May. Britain and France had been at war for exactly a week. Yet yesterday when the two of them spent much of the day out on Pointe St Mathieu there had been no sign of police guarding the roads, no sign of a blockade; not a frigate on the horizon.

The valet seemed to have more to say, but whatever it was, he was not enjoying the prospect.

"Well, Gilbert, is that all?"

"No, milord, I regret it is not. You appreciate that my purpose in listening at the door was to obtain information to pass to you . . ."

"I am sure you were doing exactly what the Count would wish you to do, Gilbert, and we are grateful."

"Well, milord, the cavalry officer stressed that the Count was being arrested on the orders of Bonaparte but as the result of information laid by the Countess—the former Countess, I mean. And she had told the authorities that he was likely to have English guests staying with him. That was why I wanted you to leave your suite quickly."

"But they'll look in the trunks . . ."

Gilbert shook his head. "I doubt it, sir: the suite looked unoccupied when I came to you. Not only that, it is hardly where you would *expect* to find guests . . ." There was no mistaking Gilbert's horror at the choice of rooms forced on the Count by the Revolution. "The Count's own suite has even less furniture. Anyway, the soldiers will start their search in the kitchen—"

"The *kitchen?*"

"Oh yes, milord, straight to the kitchen—to look for wine. I sent Edouard there at once to make sure there was plenty readily available. Once the officer has taken the Count away and the soldiers start searching, they will be half drunk. I do not think it will be a careful search."

"They were taking the Count away at once?" Sarah asked.

"The officer gave him ten minutes to dress and pack a small bag, milady."

Ramage was conscious that what he did from now on would govern whether or not he was marched off to a French prison as a *détenu*, but he was much more frightened of Sarah's possible fate. A selfish thought slid in before he had time to parry it: being married did indeed mean you had given a hostage to fortune. Now he could understand Lord St Vincent's dictum, that an officer who married was lost to the Service. Quite apart from Sarah's own safety in a case like this (which was admittedly unusual), would a happily married officer risk his own life in battle with the same recklessness as a bachelor, knowing that he now had something very special to lose? And if he had children . . .

He looked up at Gilbert. "What will they do to the Count? Guillotine him?"

"It is possible, milord, but—if I may speak freely—I think the Countess, the former Countess rather, will probably make sure his life is saved. I thought they were happily married—until the Revolution, when she became caught up in the fever. Transportation is likely—I believe many Royalists who were not executed were sent to Cayenne, which I'm sure you know is a tiny island in the Tropics off the coast of French Guinea, in South America. Priests, masons, monarchists, indeed anyone out of favour with the Republic, are sent to Cayenne."

"What do you suggest we do now? Obviously we want to get back to England."

Gilbert nodded cautiously. "The first priority is to avoid you falling into the Republic's hands. The second is to get you back to England. If you will excuse me, I will go to see what news Edouard has. The soldiers will have been talking freely to him, I am sure; a good revolutionary always assumes a servant is downtrodden and sympathizes with him."

With that Gilbert seemed to vanish through the door, but Ramage realized the man was so deft and light-footed he could open a door, go through and close it again, with less fuss than most people reach for the knob.

Once they were alone, Sarah smiled affectionately and took his hand. "We should have been married a month or so earlier, then we would have been back home by now," she said. "Or had a shorter honeymoon. Anyway, now you don't have to worry about convincing Lord St Vincent not to pay off any more ships."

"No, it looks as though the Cabinet at last became suspicious of Bonaparte. Withdrawing our ambassador from Paris must have startled Bonaparte, who will have been full of his own cleverness in getting us to sign that absurd treaty last year. Now we've suddenly slapped his hand. No more than that, though, considering the size of his army."

"You'll have to fight him at sea, then!" Sarah said cheerfully, and then could have bitten her tongue for the second time in less than twelve hours.

"I'm hiding here," Ramage said bitterly, "and someone else is commissioning the *Calypso* in Chatham. He's the luckiest captain in the navy if the men haven't been paid off yet, because he gets the finest ship's company."

Suddenly she had an inspiration. "That means you are lucky. He will keep the men together, all ready for you to resume command when you escape."

"Providing I escape and providing the Admiralty are prepared to turn out a captain for me," he protested. "Neither seems very likely at the moment."

"If you are captured—I'm sure we won't be—they'll release you on parole. Then you can make for the coast and steal a boat, or something."

He laughed sourly. "My love, you have a simple approach to it all but the Admiralty doesn't share it. Parole, for instance."

"What is difficult about that?"

"Well, giving your parole means giving your word of honour not to escape, and you are freed to live outside the prison. You pay for your board and lodging, of course."

"There's bound to be a 'but,' though," she said gloomily.

"There certainly is. If you break your parole and escape to

England, the Admiralty doesn't welcome you. In fact they might send you back. They certainly won't employ you."

"Why ever not?"

"Because you gave the French your word of honour and you broke it."

"But there is a war on! The French killed their king. They guillotined thousands of innocent people."

"True, and probably will go on executing more, but the Admiralty's view is that you don't have to give your parole. If you do, then you must keep your word."

"So what on earth can a captured officer do?"

"Refuse parole. That means he stays in prison, but it also means that if he *can* escape and get to England, he really is free and can expect to be employed again."

"Do the Admiralty actually check?"

"I presume so. There's a French commissioner in London, you know."

"Not when we're at war, though."

"Oh yes. He's a fellow called M. Otto, Commissioner for the Exchange of Prisoners. Every now and again we exchange Frenchmen we've captured for an equal number of Britons that the French have taken."

"Let's not talk about prisoners," Sarah said. "We'll get out of this somehow. Gilbert—we can trust Gilbert. I fear for Jean-Jacques, though."

He shook his head. "No, I think Gilbert is right: that damned wife, or whatever she is, won't want him executed: it wouldn't do her reputation any good. The widow of a traitor. Transportation—yes, he could be sent to Cayenne, and that's one of the unhealthiest places in the world. But death there is not certain. Not as certain as being strapped down to the guillotine here."

"And what about us? I don't want to sound selfish but we

are foreigners in the middle of the enemy camp!" Her smile was wry; he was pleased to see that his new wife neither showed fear nor attempted to blame him for the fact they were caught in a trap.

"When Gilbert comes back we'll hear if the French authorities know we're here and if they're looking for us. I don't think Jean-Jacques registered us anywhere or reported to the authorities that we were staying with him. I think he should have done—at the *préfet*'s office, perhaps—but he wouldn't bother because he thought it was not the *préfet*'s business whom he chose to entertain."

"That attitude is all right in England, but I can't see Bonaparte and his merry men agreeing."

"No, but although the French know the names of every foreigner who has entered the country, unless they have their present addresses, it doesn't help. Remember," he said bitterly, "if the French are arresting all the visitors, it means they are breaking their word."

"In what way?"

"Well, everyone visiting France has to get a *passeport* from the French. That's a guarantee, a document permitting the foreigner to pass through the ports of France and travel about the country. Now, having granted these *passeports*, it seems Bonaparte is breaking his word."

Sarah nodded but said with casual sincerity: "Yes, that's true, but anyone—and that includes us—who trusts a man like Bonaparte or the government of France cannot complain if he is cheated. 'Honour' is a word that the French deleted from their vocabulary when they executed the king. Any nation that cheerfully executes a whole class of its people for just being born into that class is wicked and mentally sick. A Frenchman could be born an aristocrat but be poorer than the local gravedigger, yet

the aristocrat was dragged off to the guillotine, and the gravedigger went along to cheer the executioner."

"We shouldn't have come here on our honeymoon," Ramage
said wryly.

"Where else? Prussia isn't very appealing. The Netherlands
and Italy—Bonaparte will be arresting all foreigners there.
Spain—who knows. Anyway, we are really learning something
about the French."

She sat down on one of the packing cases. "What happens if
the French soldiers find our trunks in the suite?"

"Well, they won't find us. Don't forget they came at dawn,
so they'll assume we've escaped."

"That seems too good to be true," she warned.

"No, it's obvious when you think about it."

"Where do we go now? This storeroom is rather bare!"

"Back to our suite eventually, because it'll probably be the
safest hiding place in France."

"Our suite? But . . ."

"'It's been searched by the cavalry, so the *rosbif* and his wife
can't be there,'" he said, imitating the precise speech of an officer reporting to a senior. "They'll be searching everywhere else
for miles around."

There was a faint tapping at the door and Ramage opened it.
Gilbert slid in, a reassuring smile on his face. He bowed to Sarah.

"You must find that box uncomfortable, milady." As soon as
Sarah reassured him, he turned to Ramage and took a deep
breath.

"Edouard used his ears and eyes carefully, milord, and he
acted as a simpleton so that he could ask silly questions—and
sprinkled some shrewd questions among them.

"Anyway, it means this. As far as the Count is concerned,
because France is now at war with England again and the Count

spent all those years in England, he is regarded as an enemy of the state. He was denounced and the authorities in Paris sent orders to the *chef d'administration* in Rennes to arrest him."

"Where is he being confined?"

"Ah, that's my next piece of information. He will be confined in the château in Brest, the naval headquarters. He and many others not yet brought in."

"What others?"

"Landowners like the Count who returned from exile, people who in the past year or so have fallen out of favour with Bonaparte or the local *préfet* or even a local chief of police. Priests who have spoken out too boldly. People to whom some of those in authority owe money . . ."

"Why the château at Brest—to be near a convenient ship?"

Gilbert nodded. "They will be transported to Cayenne as soon as a ship (a frigate, the cavalry captain said) can be prepared."

"So the Count had how long—a year?—back in his home . . ."

"Eleven months, sir. Now, concerning you. The officer knew you had been staying here but Edouard was naturally a great supporter of the Republic and told the officer that you had received a warning yesterday evening and fled, leaving your trunks behind. This was confirmed by the Count, who was still in the room.

"The Count pretended anger—he said you were under the protection of *passeports* issued by Bonaparte. The cavalry officer just laughed and produced a handful of papers and read them to the Count—I think because he had some idea that the authorities could blame him for your escape.

"Anyway, the first was a letter from the *préfet* at Rennes addressed to you by name, milord, telling you of a decree dated a few days ago. It enclosed a copy of the decree that made you a prisoner of war, from the second *Prairial* in the eleventh year of the Republic, which is a few days ago. The decree was signed

by the First Consul, and with Bonaparte's signature was that of
M. Marot, the Secretary of State."

"And her ladyship?"

"No mention of wives, milord. Edouard had the impression
that the letter was simply a copy of one being sent to all foreign
males. He thought that women and children were not affected."

Ramage looked squarely at the little man. "What it means
now, Gilbert, is that you and Edouard and the rest of the staff
are harbouring enemies of the Republic. You could be guillotined.
We must go."

"I assure you Edouard and I are true patriots, milord; we are
not harbouring enemies of the state because this house has
already been searched carefully by a company of cavalry which
had ridden specially from Rennes."

Ramage held the man's shoulders. "Gilbert, thank you. But
there is too much risk for you."

"Sir, please stay. The Count would wish it. England gave me
a home, as well as the Count, when we were refugees. And there
is no risk now for you or us: the house has been searched. And
we are already making inquiries about their intentions for the
Count and to see if it is possible to hire a fishing-boat to get you
to England, or even the Channel Islands."

"Who is making inquiries?" Ramage asked.

"The second cook and her husband, Louis, a gardener, always
take a *cabriolet*, how do you call it—?"

"A gig."

"—ah yes, a gig. Well, they go into Brest each week to buy
fish and other things. The *gendarmes* at the Landerneau Gate—
that's where everyone has to show papers when entering or
leaving Brest—"

Ramage was curious and interrupted: "Is it possible to get into
Brest without papers? No one asked us."

"But of course, milord. You rode across the fields without

knowing. Otherwise you simply leave the road half a mile before the town gates and go round them through the fields. There are gates on the road but no wall round the town. The risk now the war has begun is being stopped later somewhere in the town by a patrol of *gendarmes.*"

Ramage nodded and glanced at Sarah, a glance noticed by Gilbert. "Ah yes, when it comes to getting you to the fishing-boat, you dress as a French married couple going to market—or travelling to visit relatives or looking for work. You will have documents—"

"What documents?" Ramage asked.

"Genuine documents, I assure you, milord. You will have French names of course, and your French accent, of Paris, will need modifying. Thickening, to that of the Roussillon or Langue-doc, for instance: you know both areas. We need to choose somewhere specific, a long way from here—where if the *préfet* in Brest wants to check, he knows it would take three or four weeks, so he is unlikely to bother. But if it was Paris"—he shrugged his shoulders expressively—"a courier leaves for there daily."

"You have been giving it all careful thought!"

"When we returned from England," the valet admitted, "I did not share the Count's optimism for the future in France. The Count thought we would have many years of peace. For myself, I thought the Treaty was like two prize fighters having a rest during a bout. I advised the Count not to leave England, but alas, the nostalgia for this château overcame the love he had developed for the house in Kent. Now I fear the Count will travel the road to Cayenne . . ."

"And you—what will happen to you?" Sarah asked anxiously.

"I took the precaution of supplying myself with papers—and of course, like Edouard and Louis and the rest of the Count's staff, it is well known how deeply we hate the *aristos!* We work for them in order to eat!"

"And your stay in England—how will you explain that?"

"Oh yes, the Count threatened me so I had to go with him. The *gendarmes* are always most sympathetic with those who have suffered at the hands of the *aristos* . . . They even congratulated me on persuading the Count to return to France at the peace . . . I think even then the *préfet* knew the Count (with many scores of other exiles) was walking into Bonaparte's trap."

Gilbert then struck the palms of his hands together like a pastry-cook dusting off flour. "We must cheer ourselves. I think it is safe for you to return to your suite and I will serve you breakfast. It will be safer if you eat there—not all my plans have worked."

Intrigued, Ramage asked: "What went wrong?"

"The cavalry suddenly arriving. I had paid out a good deal of money to make sure we had enough warning to allow the Count to escape."

"I should think the *préfet* received the orders about the Count from Paris during the night," Ramage said. "As soon as he read them he sent out the cavalry and at the same time hoped to pick us up."

Gilbert nodded slowly, considering the idea and finally agreed. "That would account for it. I do not like to think that I was cheated—or betrayed."

CHAPTER THREE

THE MEALS, Sarah commented, were superbly cooked, and although the choice was limited, the food was plentiful; their suite was large and airy, even though the furniture was sparse. The view from the windows was spectacular, if you liked the Breton landscape, harsh to English eyes accustomed to rich greens and unused to the great jagged boulders scattered here and there like distorted hay ricks. Her only complaint was that they had not been able to leave the rooms for three days.

Ramage pointed out that their plight hardly compared with that of Jean-Jacques: he would be in a cell at the château in Brest, a huge citadel both had agreed was cold and grim even when they saw it on a sunny afternoon only a few days ago (although it seemed a lifetime). Whereas Jean-Jacques at best could look forward to confinement for years in one of the unhealthiest places in the Tropics, the worst that could happen to them would be for Nicholas to be taken off to Valenciennes, where prisoners of war were held, while Sarah had to live with a French family for the rest of the war.

Sarah had declared that she would stay as near as possible to wherever her husband was incarcerated—they had all agreed that he would not give his parole. The unspoken agreement was that if they were discovered and captured, Nicholas would try to escape to England while Sarah would, if necessary, be left behind. She refused to consider that the French might punish her as a reprisal for her husband's escape.

The knock on the door was gentle but at the wrong time: Gilbert had taken away the dirty dishes only half an hour ago, and was not due to bring the first course of the next meal—Ramage took out his watch—for another four hours.

Gilbert slipped in and gave a dismissive wave with his hand as he shut the door and saw the look of alarm on their faces.

"The cook and gardener are back, milord. You would not have heard the horse's hooves because of course they came to the servants' entrance."

Sarah sat down again, realizing that the sudden tension made her feel faint and that Gilbert would be quick to notice if she went white.

Ramage raised his eyebrows, although not wanting to betray

impatience by asking a question, he noticed a curious tension in the Frenchman.

"You understand the word 'brig,' milord?"

"In English? Yes, it is a type of warship."

"Ah, so they did get it right," he said. "Now, the news of the Count is bad, but no worse than we expected: he has been sentenced to transportation to Cayenne: he and 53 other *déportés* are being held in the château and will sail in a frigate which is being prepared. The ship sails in about a week, the gardener believes: some of her guns, powder and shot are being unloaded to make room for prisoners."

"What is the name of the frigate?" Ramage asked.

"*L'Espoir*, so the gardener understands. She was pointed out to him. Boats are taking out provisions, and it was said that carpenters are building special cells. Not to imprison the *déportés* all the time; only when they are punished."

Ramage noticed that "when": Gilbert knew enough of the Republican way to know that no monarchist would reach Cayenne without being punished for something, however minor; an important part of being a staunch Republican was to show that one was a staunch anti-Royalist, and the most effective methods were to betray someone (an easy way of settling monetary debts in the early days of the Revolution was to accuse your creditor of being a secret Royalist: the guillotine quickly closed that account) and to cheer lustily every time the guillotine blade crashed down. A woman had become famous in Paris because she sat quietly knitting beside the guillotine day after day—in three minutes it could despatch a victim from him standing to his head rolling into a basket.

"We ought to find out exactly when *L'Espoir* intends to sail," Ramage said.

"You hope we can make an attempt to rescue the Count?" Gilbert asked hopefully.

Ramage shook his head. "You, Edouard, the gardener and me to capture a frigate? Four against at least a hundred, and the garrison of the château as well if you tried it in Brest?"

Gilbert nodded. "I grasp at straws, milord."

"It's all we have to grasp," Ramage said. "I had in mind only that if we can escape to England before *L'Espoir* sails, perhaps I might be able to warn the Admiralty so that a watch is kept for her. But Gilbert, you mentioned a brig. What brig?"

"Ah yes, that was just some gossip the gardener's wife heard. Not the gardener," Gilbert said tactfully, as though not wanting to cast any doubt on the intelligence of womanhood in Sarah's hearing, "he was at the meat market, and she heard about this at the fish market."

Gilbert was a splendid fellow, Ramage told himself, and his only fault is that for him the shortest distance between two points is a well-embroidered story. His listeners needed patience, and it was a defect in Ramage's own character, he admitted, that he had been born with little or none.

"Yes, the gardener's wife—her name is Estelle, by the way—overheard two fishmongers discussing a brig which had arrived in Le Goulet the evening before, escorted by a French corvette."

"Why 'escorted'?" Ramage asked.

"Oh, because the brig is English, milord, and with the war now resumed one would expect an escort, no?"

Ramage nodded and managed to avoid looking across at Sarah: he knew she would be hard put to avoid laughing as she saw him struggling not to snap at Gilbert, swiftly drawing the story from him like a fishmonger filleting fish.

"Anyway, this brig has a name like *Murex*. It seems a strange name, but Estelle was sure because one fishmonger spelled it to the other."

"Yes, it would be *Murex*," Ramage said, and remembered another ten-gun brig of the same class, the *Triton*, also named after a seashell (not the sea god, as many thought). She had been his second command, and she had stayed afloat during a hurricane in the West Indies but, dismasted, then drifted on to the island of Culebra. By now there would be very little of her skeleton left: the teredo worm would have devoured her timbers and coral would be growing on any ironwork while gaudy tropical fish swam through whatever was left of the skeleton.

"Were many killed and wounded when the *Murex* was captured?" Sarah asked.

"Killed and wounded, milady?" a puzzled Gilbert asked. "I don't think anyone was hurt. The captain and the officers, perhaps, but I doubt it."

Ramage had a curious feeling that he was dreaming the whole conversation: that he was dreaming about a fairy tale entitled "The Two Fishmongers." The time had come to be firm with Gilbert.

"Start at the beginning and tell us what Estelle overheard in the fish market. Now, she is in the fish market and she hears two fishmongers talking."

"Well, she was to buy salt cod. There was plenty of that. Then she wanted some halibut—but she could find none. What, she asked herself, could replace the missing halibut? Bear in mind she would be cooking it: the first cook, Mirabelle, refuses to cook fish: she says that a woman with her delicate pastry should not be asked to meddle with scaly reptiles—that's what Mirabelle calls them, milord, 'reptiles.'"

"The fishmongers," Ramage said patiently.

"Ah yes, Estelle was discussing with them what to buy in place of the halibut. She had the sauce in mind, you understand. Well, the second fishmonger joined the discussion, and while Estelle was thinking, asked the first fishmonger if he had heard about the English brig arriving.

"The first fishmonger had not, and the second—his name is

Henri, a Gascon, and he has trouble making people believe his stories: not for nothing do we have the word *'gasconade.'*"

"And then . . ." Ramage prompted.

"Henri then told how this brig had been sighted in the Chenal du Four by the lookouts now stationed on Pointe St Mathieu. Then they noticed the strange business about her flag."

Once more Gilbert came to a stop, like a murex (or a winkle, Ramage thought sourly) retreating into its shell after every few inches of progress. Dutifully Ramage encouraged him out again. "What about the flag, Gilbert?"

"She was flying a white flag above the English colours. Had she been captured? the sentries asked themselves. But why a *white* flag—one would have expected a *Tricolore* over the English.

"Anyway, they passed a message round to the château and a corvette which was anchored close by was sent out to investigate. She returned with the English brig following, only now the white flag had been replaced by the *Tricolore*.

"If you want my opinion, milord"—he paused politely until Ramage nodded—"the brig had already surrendered, but the corvette met her before she started coming into *Le Goulet* and put men on board and claimed to have captured her. That way they get a reward."

They must be optimists, Ramage thought. The British Admiralty courts were notoriously fussy and the agents corrupt when awarding prize-money, and he doubted if Bonaparte's navy even bothered with prize courts. The corvette had been sent out to check up on a vessel already flying a white flag which traditionally meant surrender or truce. He raised his eyebrows in another variation of prodding Gilbert to continue.

"This English brig now flying the *Tricolore* over the English colours, and with her guns still—how do you say, withdrawn, not in place for firing . . ."

"Not run out."

"Ah, yes. This brig is anchored in front of the château and many important men—including the *préfet maritime* and Admiral Bruix, the *commandant de l'Armée navale*—are rowed out to the ship. They stay about an hour, and then after they return the crew of the *Murex*—her name can be read from the shore you understand—are brought on shore and given accommodation in the château, while French sailors are taken out to guard the rest."

"The rest of what?"

"Well, the officers, and a few seamen," Gilbert said, clearly surprised at Ramage's question.

"But why are the officers and a few seamen being left on board? Who were the men brought on shore and lodged in the château?"

"Why, they are the mutineers, of course!" Gilbert said. "The officers and the seamen who did not mutiny are kept on board as prisoners of war. That," he amended cautiously, "is how Estelle understood it from Henri."

The ship's company of the *Murex* brig mutinying within a few days—almost hours—of the resumption of war and carrying the ship into Brest to hand her over to the French? Ramage looked at Sarah, as if appealing to her to assure him that he had mis-heard. She stared at the floor, obviously stunned.

Who commanded the brig? He could be a lieutenant—almost certainly would be. The *Murex* would probably have left Plymouth or Portsmouth before war began. Most likely she was based on the Channel Islands.

But what caused a mutiny? The mutinies at the Nore and Spithead had brought better conditions for the navy and he had heard no murmurs of discontent since then. There was occasional loose talk of malcontents among Irish seamen; a few captains also complained of the activities of the London Corresponding Society, which some had blamed for the Nore and Spithead affairs, but the subsequent inquiry had produced no proof.

A mutiny in a single ship, Ramage felt instinctively, was the captain's fault. Either he was too harsh (like the late and unlamented Hugh Pigot, commanding the *Hermione*) or he was too slack, failing to notice troublemakers at work among the ship's company. The troublemakers did not have to be revolutionaries: far from it. There were always men who genuinely enjoyed stirring up trouble without a cause and without a purpose, and they usually became seamen or Members of Parliament, depending on their background. Either way, they talked shrilly without any sense of responsibility, like truculent whores at a window.

The *Murex*. Ideas drifted through his mind like snowflakes across a window—and, he admitted sourly, they had about as much weight. He looked up at Gilbert and smiled. "Don't look so sad: now's the time to plot and scheme, not despair!"

The Frenchman shook his head sadly. "We need a company of *chasseurs* or an English ship of the line, milord," he said. "Three or four of us against Bonaparte . . ."

"Don't forget Bonaparte was alone when he sent the Directory packing! From being a young Corsican cadet at the artillery school he rose to be the ruler of most of Europe . . . Don't despair, Gilbert; come back in half an hour and we'll talk again. First, though, tell me who we can count on among the staff."

"All are loyal, sir. I mean that none will betray us. For active help: well, Edouard, Estelle and her husband Louis—who was a fisherman before becoming a gardener when the authorities confiscated his boat—will actively help. The others may not care to risk their lives."

"But those two men and the woman would?"

"Yes, because they all hate the new régime. Not that it's very new now, but they have all suffered. Estelle and Louis lost their fishing-boat and then had to sell their little cottage in Douarnenez: Edouard's father should be buried in the cemetery at Landerneau, on the Paris road, but instead the body is in a mass grave near the guillotine they set up in Brest."

"What did the father do?"

"A terrible crime," Gilbert almost whispered. "He was the Count's butler. He decided to stay here in France when the Count escaped to England because he could not see any danger from his own people for a butler. But he was denounced to the Committee of Public Safety as a Royalist."

"On what evidence? That he worked for the Count?"

"Milord, you do not understand. If you are denounced, you are not brought before the kind of court you are accustomed to in England. You are first locked up, and next day, next week, next month—even next year—you are brought before a tribunal, the denunciation is read out, and you are sentenced. You might be asked for your explanation, but no one will be listening to it. The sentence is the same, whatever you say—the guillotine."

"Does Edouard know who denounced his father?"

"No, but he knows the names of the three members of the tribunal."

"What does he intend to do?"

"We Bretons are like your Cornishmen, milord: we have long memories and much patience. Edouard is prepared to wait for his revenge. Nor is he alone: there have been many unexplained accidents in the last year or two, so I hear: farms catch fire, the wheel comes off a *cabriolet* and the driver is killed or badly hurt . . . it seems that a band of assassins occasionally prowl the countryside. It was only six months ago that members of tribunals stopped having armed guards at their houses. But now, milord, I will leave you for half an hour."

When the door had shut, Sarah patted the bed beside her.

"Come and sit with me—I suddenly feel very lonely." She leaned over and kissed him. "If I said what I felt about that, you'd blush."

"I'd like to blush. For the last few hours I've felt pale and wan."

"If you'd told Gilbert to come back in two hours, I'd lure you to other things."

"I had thought of that, but Gilbert will be expecting to hear of a plan worthy of Captain the Lord Ramage—one that frees Jean-Jacques and gets us all safely back to England."

She looked at him carefully, as though inspecting a thoroughbred horse at a sale. "A slight turning up at the corners of the mouth . . . a brightness in at least one eye . . . a jauntiness about the ears . . . Or am I mistaken?"

"You're in love," he said solemnly. "I can produce plans as a cow gives milk, but they curdle as soon as you look at them."

"What are the chances of rescuing Jean-Jacques?"

"You know the answer to that question."

"Yes, I suppose I do. What are the chances of us escaping?"

He paused a minute or two. "Better than they were, I think. It depends on how the French authorities regard the mutineers from the *Murex*. Yes, and what they intend to do with the officers and the seamen who did not join the mutiny and are still on board as prisoners of war."

"Why is all that important?"

He shrugged his shoulders. "I don't know. That's the worst of plans. Most of the time they're just ideas. Occasionally, if you're lucky, you can throw an idea at a problem and it solves it. That's how swallows make those nests of mud in odd places."

"And was doing that what made Captain Ramage famous in the navy for his skill and daring?"

"Captain Ramage is famous at the Admiralty for disobeying orders!"

"They do say," Sarah said, "that being too modest is another way of bragging."

"Well, skill and daring have landed Captain Ramage with a

wife in a château a few miles from Brest while his ship is at Chatham, which is only a war away."

"You make it sound as though you're sorry you married me."

He took her in his arms. "No, my dear, I'm blaming myself for not having married you sooner: then I'd be taking the *Calypso* out of the Medway and you'd be safe in London or St Kew, starting to write a passionate letter to me saying how you miss me."

Sarah sat up and patted her hair as there was a gentle knock at the door. Ramage realized with a guilty feeling that he had nothing to say to Gilbert. Well, maybe he could think aloud, but that seemed like cheating a man who trusted you.

CHAPTER FOUR

SARAH put the triangular red scarf round her head and knotted the ends under her chin. Then coquettishly she spun round a couple of times so that her heavy black skirt swirled out and up, revealing knee-length and lace-edged white cotton drawers.

Ramage frowned and then said judiciously: "Yes, there's a certain rustic charm, despite the revolutionary scarf. Your complexion is just right: you have the tan of a country wench who helps with the harvesting."

"You are a beast! You know very well this is the remnants of a tropical tan!"

"I do, yes," Ramage teased, "but I was thinking of the *gendarmes* you might have to charm."

"You don't think my accent is adequate?"

"Oh yes—thanks to Gilbert's coaching you are a true Norman from Falaise. Just remember, in case they question you, that William the Conqueror was born in the castle there, his wife was Matilda, and the Bayeux tapestry is very long!"

She walked round him. "You don't look right, Nicholas. That hooked nose looks far too aristocratic for you to have survived the guillotine, although I admit your hair looks untidy enough for a gardener. Those trousers! I'm so used to seeing you in breeches. Isn't it curious how the revolutionaries associated breeches with the monarchists? Personally I should have thought trousers are much more comfortable than *culottes*. If I was a man I think my sympathies would be with the *sans-culottes*. I'd cry *'vive les pantalons!* To the bonfires with the *culottes!'*"

She inspected his hands. "You have worked enough earth into the skin, my dear, but they still don't look as if they've done a good day's hoeing or digging in their entire existence. And there's something missing . . . Ah, I have it! Slouch, don't stand so upright! When you stand up stiffly peering out from under those fierce eyebrows, you look just like a naval officer dressed for a rustic *fête*. Ah, that's better."

"Now surely I must look like the henpecked husband of a Norman shrew."

"Yes," she agreed, "why don't you bear that in mind. Think of me as *la mégère*. With this red scarf round my head, I must say I feel the part!"

Gilbert slipped into the room after his usual discreet knock on the door. He excused himself and inspected Sarah closely. Finally he said: "The shoes, milady . . . they are most important."

Sarah gestured to the pair of wooden clogs. "And they are most uncomfortable!"

"Yes, milady, but you must wear them so that they seem natural. We are extremely lucky that Estelle had a pair which fitted you, even if those that Louis found for . . ."

"Even if Louis has enormous feet and I feel as though I'm wearing a couple of boats," Ramage grumbled.

"Yes, sir, but the socks?"

"The extra socks do help," he admitted. "I had to put on three pairs, though."

"But the coat and *pantalons*—perfect. You have adopted to perfection the, how do you say, the *stance,* of a man of the fields."

Ramage glared, defying Sarah to make a facetious comment.

Gilbert himself was dressed in black. The material of the trousers was rough, a type of serge; the coat had the rusty sheen denoting age and too much attention from a smoothing iron. He looked perfect for the role he was to play, the employer of a young couple who was taking them to market.

He was carrying a flat canvas wallet, which he unbuttoned as he walked over to the table. "Will you check through the documents with me, sir? From what Louis reports, we might have to show them half a dozen times before we get back here."

With that he took out three sets of paper and put one down on the table as though dealing playing cards for a game of patience.

"The *passeports*," he explained. "Foreigners need one type, and every Frenchman visiting another town needs a different sort: he has to get it from the local Committee of Public Safety, and it is valid only for the journeys there and back. Now, milady, will you examine yours."

Sarah picked it up. The paper was coarse and greyish, and at the top was printed the arms of the Republic. The rest comprised a printed form, the blank spaces filled in with a pen. She was now Janine Ribère, born Thénaud in Falaise, wife of Charles, no children, hair blonde, complexion *jaunâtre.* (*Jaunâtre?* She thought for a few moments, combing her French vocabulary. Ah, yes, sallow. Well, certainly Gilbert was not trying to flatter her!) Purpose of journey: multiple visits to Brest to make purchases of food from the market. She nodded and put the page down again.

Gilbert gave her another which had a seal on it and a flourish of ink which was an unreadable signature. It was smaller, had a coat of arms she did not recognize, but bore the name of the department beneath it.

"This, madame, is a certificate issued in Falaise, and saying, as you can see, that you were born there, with the date. And beneath the *préfet*'s signature is a note that you removed to the province of Brittany on your marriage. And beneath that the signature of the *préfet* of Brittany."

"All these signatures!" Sarah exclaimed. "Supposing someone compares them with originals?"

Gilbert smiled and took the sheet of paper. "If he does he will find they are genuine. *Préfets* sign these papers by the dozen and leave them to underlings to fill in the details."

"But how did you get them?"

"That's none of our business," Ramage said. "Where did we get them from officially?"

"Madame had this issued to her by the *mairie* in Falaise and it was signed in Caen (the *préfet* gives the name). Then she had the addition made at the *préfecture* here. The *passeport*, too, comes from the *préfecture* in Brest. I shall point it out to you."

He took a second set of papers. "These are yours, milord. The same kind of documents but you see there is one extra—your discharge from the navy of France. Dated, you will notice, one month before your wedding. The ship named here was damaged in a storm at Havre de Grâce and is still there. You were discharged and were making your way home when you met a young lady in Caen and you both fell in love . . ."

Gilbert tapped the paper which had the anchor symbol and the heading "Ministry of the Marine and Colonies" and, like the others, was a printed form with the blanks filled in. "You are of military age, so you will have to show this everywhere."

"And you? Have you the correct documents?" Ramage asked. "You aren't taking any extra risks by coming with us?"

Gilbert shook his head. "No, because I have all the necessary papers to go shopping in Brest. I am well known at the *barrières*. You have told madame about the difference between foreigners, and French people passing the *barrières?*"

"No. We've been busy making these clothes fit and I would prefer you to explain. My experience in Republican France is now several years old: I'm sure much has changed."

Gilbert sighed. "To leave the *ancien régime* and go to England . . . then to return to Republican France. Now it is the guillotine, the tree of liberty, *gendarmes* every few miles, documents signed and countersigned . . . no man can walk or ride to the next town to have a glass of wine with his brother without a *passeport* . . . few men dare quarrel with a neighbour for fear of being denounced out of spite, for here the courts listen to the charge, not the defence—"

"The *barrières*," Ramage reminded him.

"Ah yes, sir. Well, first there is the curfew from sunset to sunrise: everyone must be in his own home during the hours of darkness. To travel—well, one has the documents you have seen. You need plenty of change—at every *barrière* there's a toll. The amount varies, depending on the distance from the last *barrière*, because they are not at regular intervals."

"A large toll?" Ramage asked.

"No, usually between two and twenty *sous*. It wouldn't matter if the money was spent on the repair of the roads—which is what it is supposed to be for—but no one empties even a bucket of earth into a pothole. But luckily we have our own gig because travelling by postchaise is very expensive. Before the Revolution a postchaise from here to Paris was about two hundred and fifty *livres;* now it is five hundred. No highwaymen, though; that's one triumph of the Revolution!"

"Highwaymen!" Sarah exclaimed. "You mean that France now has none?"

"Very few, ma'am, and the reason is not particularly to our

advantage. We now have many more mounted *gendarmes* stopping honest travellers, and instead of money and jewellery they demand documents. Truly 'money or your life' has now become 'documents or your life.' So as well as the *gendarmes* at the regular *barrières,* there are ones who appear unexpectedly on horseback, so no one dares move without papers. But," he added, tapping the side of his nose, "there are so many different documents and so many signatures that forgery is not difficult and false papers unlikely to be discovered."

"How many *barrières* are there between here and Brest?" Ramage asked.

"Three on the road, and then one at the Porte de Landerneau, the city gate on the Paris road. We could avoid it by going in along the side roads, but it is risky: if we were caught we would be arrested at once."

"Whereas our documents are good enough to pass the Porte without trouble?"

"Exactly, sir. Now, if I may be allowed to remind you of a few things. As you know, the common form of address is 'Citizen,' or 'Citizeness.' Everyone is equal—at least in their lack of manners. 'Please' and 'thank you' are now relics of the *ancien régime.* Rudeness is usually a man's (or woman's) way of showing he or she is your equal—although they really mean your superior. Many *gendarmes* cannot read—they know certain signatures and have them written on pieces of paper for comparison. But don't be impatient if a *gendarme* holds a paper upside-down and "reads" it for five minutes—as if it has enormous importance. They are *gendarmes* because they have influence with someone in authority. Neither the Committees of Public Safety nor the *préfets* want illiterates, but often giving a job to such a man is repaying a political debt from the time of the Revolution."

Gilbert paused and then apologized. "I am afraid I am talking too much . . ."

"No, no," Ramage said quickly. "And you must get into the habit of giving orders to 'Charles' and 'Janine.' Lose your temper with me occasionally—I am a slow-thinking fellow. Poor Charles Ribère, he can read slowly and write after a fashion, but . . . even his wife loses her patience with him!"

A smiling Gilbert nodded. He found it impossible to toss aside the natural politeness by which he had led his life. Since he had been back in France, some Frenchmen had called it servility: why are you so servile, they had sneered: man is born free and equal. Yes, all that was true, but man also had to eat, which meant he had to work (or be a thief, or go into politics). Working for the Count was very equable: he lived in comfortable quarters, ate the same food as the Count and his guests, but in his own quarters without the need (as the Count often had) to let the food get cold as he listened to vapid gossip. But for these revolutionary fools he could have expected a comfortable old age with a good pension from the Count, and probably a cottage on the estate, here or in England.

"Servility"—yes, that was what these Republican fools called it. Elsewhere, particularly in England, it was called good manners. Please, thank you, good morning, good evening—according to the Republicans these were "servile phrases." A true Republican never said please or thank you. But he had never listened to the Count, either: the Count *always* said please and thank you and the suitable greeting every time he spoke to one of his staff. In fact, a blind man would only know who was servant and who was master because the Count had an educated voice: his grammar, too, betrayed his background of Latin and Greek, and English and Italian. Gilbert had once heard him joking in Latin with a bishop who laughed so much he became nearly hysterical. No Committee of Public Safety would ever understand that normal good manners were like grease on axles—they helped things move more smoothly.

"I think Edouard will have the gig ready for us by now," Gilbert said, making a conscious effort to avoid any "sir" or "milord." "We are going to buy fruit—our apples have been stolen—and vegetables: the potatoes have rotted in the barn. And indeed they have. We need a bag of flour, a bag of rice if we can buy some, and any vegetables that catch your fancy. I am tired of cabbage and parsnip, which is all we seem to grow here. A lot of salt in the air from the sea makes the land barren, so Louis says, but I think it is laziness in the air from the Count's good nature."

Gilbert gestured towards two wicker baskets as they reached the back door. "We take these to carry our purchases—you put them on your laps. I have all the documents here and will drive the gig, because your hands are occupied." He winked and then looked startled at his temerity in winking at a milord and a milady. Ramage winked back and Sarah grinned: the grin, Ramage thought in a sudden surge of affection, of a lively and flirtatious serving wench being impertinent. Impudent. Adorable. And what a honeymoon—here they were setting off (in a gig!) at the beginning of an adventure which could end up with them all being strapped down on the guillotine. So far, the Committee of Public Safety (though perhaps the Ministry of Marine would step in, but more likely Bonaparte's secret police under that man Fouché would take over) could accuse Captain Ramage of disobeying the order to report to the local *préfet* as an *otage*, because to call them detainees and not hostages was polite nonsense. Then of course he was carrying false papers and dressed as a gardener—proof that he was a spy. And he was lurking around France's greatest naval base on the Atlantic coast . . . Yes, a tribunal would have only to hear the charges to return a verdict. And Sarah? A spy too—did she not carry false papers? Was she not assisting her husband? Was she not also an *aristo* by birth, as well as marriage? *Alors*, she can travel in the same tumbril, and that valet, too, who was a traitor as well as a spy.

As he helped Sarah up into the gig and heard a disapproving grunt from Gilbert (husbands might give wives a perfunctory push up, but they did not help them), he thought bitterly that their luck had been unbelievably bad. First, that the war had begun again while they were on their honeymoon—after all, the peace had held for a year and a half. Then that they should be staying with Jean-Jacques. Admittedly they would have been arrested if they had been staying at an inn, but the point was that they were now involved with *L'Espoir* and trying to think of a way of rescuing the Count of Rennes. *Noblesse oblige.* He was becoming tired of that phrase—his first love, the Marchesa di Volterra, was back in Italy because of it, and possibly already one of Bonaparte's *otages,* too. An *otage* if she had not yet been assassinated.

So, heavily involved with keeping himself and Sarah out of the hands of the local Committee of Public Safety, trying to rescue Jean-Jacques, and getting all of them (including the faithful and enterprising Gilbert) back to England, it was not just bad luck, it was damnable luck which brought the *Murex* through the Chenal du Four and into Brest with a mutinous crew on board.

Or, he allowed himself the thought and at once felt almost dizzy with guilt, why did the mutineers not put the officers and loyal seamen in a boat and let them sail back to England? Why keep them on board and bring them into Brest, where the French had anchored the ship, landed the mutineers and left the officers and loyal men on board the brig with an apparently small French guard? Now every *gendarme* in the port would be on the alert in case one of the loyal men escaped from the *Murex;* every fishing-boat would be guarded—perhaps by soldiers—so that the chance of stealing one and getting back to England would probably be nil. Damn and blast the mutineers—and her captain, for not preventing the mutiny! He was not being fair and he found he had no *wish* to be fair: he wanted only to find someone to blame for this mess.

Lord St Vincent! The name slid into his thoughts as Gilbert flipped the reins so that they slapped across the horse's flanks and started it moving. Yes, if Lord St Vincent had not given him, as his first peacetime orders, the task of finding a tiny island off the Brazilian coast and surveying it, he would never have met Sarah. If they had never met they would never have fallen in love and from that it followed they would never have married or be here on a prolonged honeymoon through France. Which, he admitted, was as disgraceful a thought as any man should have so near breakfast.

The country round the château was bleak. Or, rather, it was wild: it had the harsh wildness of parts of Cornwall, the thin layer of soil sprinkled on rock, rugged boulders jutting up as though scattered by an untidy giant. The small houses built of tightly-locked grey stone, some long ago whitewashed, roofed by slates, a small shelter for a horse or donkey, a low wall containing the midden. Life here was a struggle against nature: crops grew not with the wild profusion and vigour of the Tropics—to which he had become accustomed over the past few years—but because men and women hoed and dug and ploughed and weeded from dawn to dusk.

Gilbert became impatient with the horse, a chestnut which looked as though it was not exercised enough and heartily resented being between shafts. Perhaps, Ramage thought sourly, it was a Republican and resented having to work (if jogging along this lane rated the description "work") for Monarchists.

"Pretend to be asleep—or sleepy, anyway," Gilbert said as they approached the first village. Ramage inspected it through half-closed eyes, and for a moment was startled how different it was from all the villages he had seen up to now. A few moments later he realized that the village was the same but his attitude had just changed. He had been a free visitor when he had seen all the other villages on the roads from Calais to Paris, south across Orléans and the Bourbonnais, among the hills of Auvergne, and to the north-west up towards Finisterre through Poitou and Anjou . . . Towns and villages, Limoges with its superb porcelain and enamels, the fourth-century baptistry of the church near Poitiers which is France's earliest Christian building . . . Clermont-Ferrand, where Pope Urban (the second?) sent off the first Crusade in 1095 (why did he remember that date?), the châteaux and palaces along the Loire Valley . . . Angers with the château of seventeen towers belonging formerly to the Dukes of Anjou, and no one now willing to discuss the whereabouts of the tapestries, particularly the fourteenth-century one which was more than four hundred and thirty feet long. And Chinon, on the banks of the Vienne, where Joan of Arc prodded the Dauphin into war. No, all these towns had been impressive and the villages on the long roads between them for the most part interesting (or different, anyway), but they had been at peace—with England, at least.

With England: that, he suddenly realized, was significant, and he wished he could discuss it with Sarah but it had to be talked about in English, not French, and it was too risky talking in English when they could be overheard by a hidden hedger and ditcher.

The French had been at peace with England but not yet with themselves. He had been surprised to see that the enemy for the people of all the villages, towns and cities of France was now their own people: the members of the Committees of Public Safety at the top of a pyramid which spread out to *gendarmes* enforcing the curfew and standing at the *barrières* demanding *passeports*, the old enemies denouncing each other in secret, the banging on doors in the darkness, when no neighbour dared to look to see who the *gendarmes* were bundling away.

Liberté, Egalité, Fraternité—fine words. They had stretched France's frontiers many miles to the north, east and south, but what had they done for the French people? Now every able-bodied young man would have to serve again in the army or navy, and there was no harm in that if they were needed to defend France. But France would be attacking other countries: earlier France was everywhere the aggressor, even across the sands of Egypt.

That was looking at the phrase in its broadest sense, yet the picture those three words summoned up for him was simple and one that fitted every *place* in every city, town and large village in France.

The picture was stark and simple: two weathered baulks of timber arranged as a vertical and parallel frame, and a heavy and angled metal blade, sharpened on the underside, sliding down two grooves. A bench on which the victim was placed so that his or her neck was squarely under the blade, a wicker basket beyond to catch the severed head. Weeping relatives and wildly cheering onlookers—that dreadful melange of blood and hysteria. Of the three words, the guillotine must stand for *fratenité* and *égalité* because *liberté* was represented by the other part of the picture. This was the rusted metal representation of the Tree of Liberty. Usually it was little more than an example of the work of a hasty blacksmith and always it was rusty. And sometimes on the top was placed a red cap of liberty, faded and rotting, rarely recognizable as a copy of the old Phrygian cap.

And the gig had stopped and Gilbert was getting out and saying something in a surly voice, using a tone Ramage had never heard before. Yes, they had arrived at the *barrière*. It was in fact simply three chairs and a table in the shade of a plane tree on one side of the road. Three *gendarmes* sat in the chairs and one had called to Gilbert to bring over the documents. Gilbert was carrying not just the canvas wallet but a bottle of wine.

Pretending to be asleep, hat tilted over his face, Ramage watched. Gilbert took out the papers—leaving the bottle on his side of the table, as though putting it there to leave his hands free—and handed them to the *gendarme,* who still sat back in his chair and gestured crossly when Gilbert first placed the papers on the table. To pick them up the *gendarme* would have to lean forward, and this he was reluctant to do. Gilbert put the documents in the man's hand, and the *gendarme* glanced through them, obviously counting. He then looked across at the gig and handed the papers back, holding his hand out for the bottle.

Gilbert walked back to the gig, resumed his seat, slapped the reins across the horse's rump and the gig continued its slow journey towards Brest. The other two *gendarmes,* Ramage noticed, had never opened their eyes.

Beyond the village, Gilbert turned. "You saw all that—obviously they are not looking for any escapers. That is the routine, though: two sleep while the other reaches out a hand."

"So our papers are not—"

The thud of horses' hooves behind them brought the sudden command from Gilbert: "Don't look round—mounted *gendarmes.* Pretend to be asleep!"

A moment later two horsemen cut in from the left side, then two more passed on the right and reined their horses to a stop, blocking the narrow road.

"Papers!" one of the men demanded, holding out his hand.

"Papers, papers, papers," Gilbert grumbled. "We have only just showed them back there, now the four horsemen of the Apocalypse want to look at them again . . ."

One of the *gendarmes* grinned and winked at Sarah. "We like to check up on pretty girls on a sunny morning—where are you going, *mademoiselle?"*

"Madame," Sarah said sleepily. "To Brest with my husband."

Her accent and tone of voice was perfect, Ramage realized.

The *gendarme* was flirting; she was the virtuous wife.

The *gendarme* looked through the papers. "Ah, Citizeness Ribère, born 22 years ago in Falaise. You look younger—marriage must suit you." He looked at Ramage. "Citizen Ribère? Off to Brest to buy your wife some pretty ribbons, eh?"

"Potatoes and cabbages, and rice if there is any," Ramage said with glum seriousness. "No ribbons."

The *gendarme* laughed, looked at Gilbert's *passeport* and handed the papers back to him. "You buy her a ribbon, then," he said, and spurred his horse forward, the other three following him.

"Was that normal?" Ramage asked.

"Yes—but for, er Janine, I doubt if they would have bothered to stop us."

They passed the next couple of *barrières* without incident, although at the second two of the *gendarmes* were more concerned with their colleague who was already incoherently drunk but unwilling to sleep it off out of sight under the hedge. He had spotted the bottle that an unsuspecting Gilbert had been clutching as he alighted from the gig and probably saw a dozen. Finally, while Gilbert waited patiently at the table, the other two dragged the man away, returning five minutes later without apology or explanation to inspect the papers.

As they jogged along the Paris road into Brest, Ramage spotted the masts of ships in the port. Some were obviously ships of the line and most, he commented to Sarah, had their yards crossed with sails bent on. The French seamen had been busy since the two of them had spent the afternoon at Pointe St Mathieu.

The five *gendarmes* lounging at the Porte de Landerneau, the gate to the port, were too concerned with baiting a gaunt priest perched on an ancient donkey to pay much attention to three respectable citizens in a gig, obviously bound for the market.

The road ahead was straight but the buildings on each side were neglected. No door or window had seen a paintbrush for years; the few buildings that years ago had been whitewashed now seemed to be suffering from a curious leprosy.

"This leads straight down to the Place de la Liberté and the town hall," Gilbert had explained in French. "Just beyond that is the Hôtel du Commandant de la Marine. Then we carry on past it along the Rue de Siam to the river. While we jog along the Boulevard de la Marine you'll have a good view of the river as it meets Le Goulet, with the arsenal opposite. Then to the Esplanade du Château. There we'll stop for a glass of wine under the trees and you can inspect the château."

He laughed to himself and then added: "From the Esplanade it is only two minutes' walk to the Rue du Bois d'Amour . . . in the evenings the young folk dawdle under the trees there and look down Le Goulet at the ships and perhaps dream of visiting the mysterious East."

"But now, the young men have to be careful the press-gangs don't take them off to the men o' war," Ramage said dryly.

"Yes, I keep forgetting the war. Look," he said absently, "we are just passing the cemetery. The largest I've ever seen."

"I'll keep it in mind," Ramage said in a mock serious voice. "For the moment I have no plans to visit it."

Gilbert finally turned the gig into the open market-place, a paved square, and told Ramage and Sarah to alight. Sarah looked at the stalls while Gilbert secured the horse and groaned. "Potatoes . . . a few cabbages . . . more potatoes . . . a few dozen parsnips . . . Louis may be right about the soil at Finisterre!"

There were about twenty stalls, wooden shacks with tables in front of which the sellers spread their wares and gossiped.

Gilbert said: "We'll walk to the end stall; I have a friend there."

Despite the lack of variety, the sellers were cheerful, shouting to each other and haggling noisily with the dozen or so buyers walking along the line of tables. The man at the end stall proved to be one Ramage would normally have avoided without a moment's thought. His face was thin and a wide scar led across his left cheek, a white slash against suntanned skin. His hair was unfashionably long and tied behind in a queue. He wore a fisherman's smock which seemed almost rigid from frequent coatings of red ochre, which certainly made it waterproof and, Ramage thought ironically, probably bulletproof too.

He shook hands with Gilbert, who said: "I am not introducing you to my friends because—to onlookers—we all know each other well."

The Frenchman immediately shook Ramage's hand in the casual form of greeting taking place all over the market as friends met each other for the first time in the day, and he gave a perfunctory bow to Sarah, saying softly: "The Revolution does not allow me to kiss your hand, which is sad."

"Now," Gilbert said, "I shall inspect your potatoes, which are small and old and shrivelled and no one but a fool would buy, and ask you what is happening in the Roads."

"Ah, very busy. The potatoes I have here on display are small and old because I have already sold twenty sacks to the men from the Hôtel du Commandant de la Marine, who were here early. Paying cash, they are. They tried buying against *notes de crédit* on the navy, but suddenly no one in the market had any potatoes, except what were on these tables."

"Why the navy's sudden need for potatoes?"

"You've heard about the English mutineers? Yes, well, you know the English exist on potatoes. All the mutineers are now billeted in the château and demanding potatoes. On board their brig there are still prisoners and their guards, demanding potatoes—it seems the ones they have are mildewed. And that frigate over there, *L'Espoir,* is leaving for Cayenne with *déportés,* and they want more potatoes . . ."

"Who had your sacks?" Ramage asked.

"Nobody yet. They paid extra to have them delivered—it seems that with so many ships being prepared for sea, with the war starting, they're short of boats. So I pay a friend of mine a few *livres* to use his boat and the navy pays me many *livres!*"

Ramage thought a moment. "Are you going to carry all the sacks on your own?"

"I was hoping my nephew would help me when he's finished milking."

Ramage glanced at Gilbert then at the man. "Two of us could help you now."

The Frenchman pulled at his nose. "How much?"

Ramage smiled as he said: "Our services would be free." He looked at Gilbert, seeking his approval. "We could carry the potatoes down to the jetty in the gig."

Gilbert nodded enthusiastically. "Then Janine can look after it while we go out to the *Murex.*"

"The loyal men who are prisoners of war in the English ship do not speak French," the man said pointedly.

"If I needed to speak to them, it would be in whispers."

The man nodded. "It would have to be," he said. "Much discretion is needed."

Gilbert walked away from the tiller and took a rope thrown down from the *Murex's* deck. As he turned it up on a kevil he shouted forward at Ramage in well-simulated anger: "Hurry up! Not so tight—you'll jam our bow into the Englishman. We want to lie alongside her, not butt her like a goat!"

"Yes, citizen," Ramage called aft in a remorse-laden voice. "These ships, I am used to a cart with wheels . . ."

Several French seamen lining the *Murex's* bulwarks roared with laughter and in a glance Ramage counted them. Seven, and the fellow at the end, probably the bosun, had been giving orders. Was that all the French guard, seven men? It seemed likely, though he would soon know.

"Here," a voice called down in French and the tail of another rope curled down. "Secure that somewhere there as a spring."

He saw that Gilbert was already making up another rope as a spring, so that the fishing-boat was held securely against the brig. A glance aloft then showed that some British seamen, prisoners, were working slowly and obviously resentfully under the shouts and gesticulations of a French bosun, who was becoming more and more exasperated that he could not make himself understood as he tried to get them to rig a staytackle to hoist the sacks of potatoes on board.

Again Ramage counted. More than a dozen prisoners, though some of the men reeving the rope through the blocks were officers. Obviously the French guards were practising *égalité*.

Another shout from the *Murex's* deck brought a stream of curses from Gilbert and the vegetable seller (Ramage had established his name was Auguste), and something landed with a thump on the deck beside him. It was a heavy rope net.

"Spread it out flat on the deck, then put two sacks in the middle," the bosun shouted. "Hurry up, or this ship will never sail!"

Ramage hurried with the net and found it easy to make the job last twice as long as necessary while appearing to work with ferocious energy. While he was untangling the thick mesh he slowly inspected the *Murex*.

She had been out of the dockyard for only a few weeks: that much had been obvious as the fishing-boat had approached because the brig was rolling at anchor enough to show that her copper sheathing was new, each overlapping edge of a sheet helping make a mosaic still bright and still puckered where the hammers driving home the flat-headed sheathing nails had dented the metal.

Her hull, a dark grey with a white strake, showed that her captain was a wealthy man: he had been prepared to pay for the paint himself, because the dockyard's meagre ration was black. Some captains who wanted a particularly smart ship paid for the gold leaf to line out the name on the transom, and pick up decorations on the capstan head. The captain of the *Murex* was one of them.

With the net spread out on the only flat part of the fishing-boat's deck, the tiny fo'c's'le, Ramage climbed down into the little fish hold and hauled a couple of sacks up to the coaming. The stench was appalling: whoever had to eat these potatoes would think they had been grown in Billingsgate fish market.

Auguste's lopsided face appeared over the edge of the coaming. "You are doing well," he muttered. "A clumsier oaf straight from the farm never set foot in a fishing-boat."

"How many guards, do you reckon?"

"Seven, but we'll know for sure when we get on board."

"Can we manage that?" Ramage asked.

"The knot I shall use to secure the net for the staytackle hook is almost impossible to undo—and I am an impatient man! Here, sling up that sack!"

Gilbert arrived to help haul the first two sacks to the net, and the two Frenchmen gathered up the four corners. Auguste produced a short length of rope to secure them together while Ramage played the simpleton with the dangling end of the staytackle, using it to swing on until one of the French guards quickly slacked it so that Ramage suddenly dropped to the deck with a yell of alarm. That established his position as far as the French guards were concerned: he was the buffoon, the man who fell down hatches and on to whose head sacks of potatoes dropped.

Auguste knotted the corners of the net, took the staytackle and hooked it on, and shouted up to the *Murex*'s deck to start hauling. There was a delay: the French guards were not going to haul sacks of potatoes aloft, but Ramage saw equally clearly that their British prisoners, tailing on to the tackle, would have the French bosun demented by the time the last sack was on board.

"Don't stand under the net," he warned Auguste and Gilbert, and a moment later the net and two sacks came crashing down on the deck again, making the little fishing-boat shudder as it caught the forestay a glancing blow and set the mast shuddering.

Auguste sent up a stream of curses and warned the French bosun that he, the commandant of the port, the navy, and the Minister of Marine himself would all be responsible for any damage done to the boat. A moment later the bosun was swearing in French at the British seamen, who were swearing back in the accents of London, the West Country and Scotland. One man, they were protesting, had tripped and brought the rest of them down, but the French bosun, not understanding a word, was threatening them with the lash, the noose, the guillotine and prison, and as he ran out of ideas, Auguste restated his warning, adding that it was not worth losing a fishing-boat for the profit on a few sacks of potatoes.

Finally, amid more shouting than Ramage had thought possible from so few men, the net and its sacks were slowly rehoisted and hauled on board the *Murex*. A run-amok choir, Ramage thought, well primed with rum, could not do better.

Auguste gestured to Ramage and the two men scrambled up the brig's side, followed by Gilbert. The bosun and two French seamen were crouched over the net, struggling to undo Auguste's knot. Ramage and Gilbert were by chance within four or five feet of the British seamen who had been hauling on the tackle.

As all the French guards hurried to help the almost apoplectic bosun undo the knot, Ramage hissed at the nearest man, who from his creased and torn uniform must be one of the brig's lieutenants: "Quickly—don't show surprise and keep your voice down: I am Captain Ramage. How many loyal men are there on board?"

The lieutenant paused and then knelt as if adjusting the buckle of his shoe. "Captain, two lieutenants, master, eleven seamen."

"And French guards?"

"Seven. They keep half of us in the bilboes while half are free."

"Who commands?"

"Lieutenant Rumsie."

"Where do the French keep you?"

"At night all of us are kept in irons in the manger."

"The guards?"

"Two sit with muskets, the rest sleep in our cabins and use the gunroom."

Gilbert suddenly called to Auguste, asking if he needed help with the knot, and Ramage realized that a French seaman with a musket was walking along the deck towards them, not suspicious but simply patrolling where the prisoners were working.

Ramage decided there was time for one last question.

"Are the mutineers coming back on board?"

"No, and the French are asking Paris what to do with us prisoners and keeping us on board until they hear."

With that the net opened, the two sacks were hauled clear, and the perspiring bosun signalled to the Britons to hoist again.

Auguste scrambled back on board the fishing-boat, followed by Gilbert and Ramage, who once again climbed down into the fish hold as the two Frenchmen unhooked the net and spread it on the deck again.

As they came to the coaming to lift out the sacks, Auguste muttered: "Did you find out anything?"

"From the English, yes."

"What do you want to know from the bosun?"

"Are they taking the job of guarding very seriously?"

"I can tell you that without asking. It is a holiday—they have jars of rum in the gunroom and one of them was boasting to me that most of them stay drunk all day and sleep it off at night. The bosun is so drunk at the moment he sees two nets, four knots and eight sacks each time we hoist."

"Good, then just find out how long they expect—here, you'd better hoist up this sack while I get the other ready."

When Auguste's head appeared at the coaming again Ramage finished the question: "—expect to be guarding these men and what the French navy intend doing with the *Murex*."

"Very well. The bosun will probably invite us all below for a drink anyway, when we've finished loading."

It was clear no one was really in a hurry: Auguste tied the net with his special knot and then as soon as the sacks were swayed on board he climbed up to help untie it.

Gilbert and Ramage went on board each time, casually sitting on the breech of a gun close to the prisoners so that Ramage could continue talking to the lieutenant, who had recovered from his surprise sufficiently to have questions of his own.

"Why are you here, sir?"

"Caught in France when the war began again. Trying to avoid capture. Are the rest of your men loyal?"

"They don't want to be prisoners of the French," the lieutenant said carefully.

"Where's the captain?"

"He's under guard in the master's cabin. Sick, I believe."

"What's his trouble?"

"Rheumatic pains. He can hardly move."

The net was being hoisted over the side and the three of them climbed down into the fishing-boat once again.

Auguste leaped over the coaming to grasp a sack and said: "Trouble with the English captain."

"So I've heard."

"Rheumatic pains. Makes him bad-tempered. Bullied the men and most mutinied."

"How long do the prisoners stay on board?"

"Who knows? They won't be short of potatoes, anyway," Auguste said.

As soon as the last sacks were pulled off the net, the French bosun mopped his forehead with a dirty piece of cloth and mumbled drunkenly: "English rum—we all deserve some. Follow me." He stumbled aft and went cautiously down the companion-way to the gunroom.

Ramage felt he was walking back in time: the *Murex* was almost identical with his second command, the *Triton* brig. There was more fancy work covering handrails, all of it well scrubbed until a few days ago, and the captain must have an obsession for turk's heads: the knots were neat but there was one on every spoke of the wheel, whereas usually there was only one on the spoke which was uppermost with the rudder amidships.

The brasswork was dulling now because it had not been polished with brick dust for several days, presumably since the mutiny. The deck was reasonably clean but unscrubbed, stained here and there by the French seamen who chewed tobacco.

He followed the others down the companion-way. The gunroom was stuffy because the French did not believe in keeping skylights open. Why did they not use the captain's cabin? Probably not enough chairs: brigs were sparsely furnished and the gunroom made a better centre for meals and card playing. It was a rectangular open space formed by a row of cabins on each side. The cabins were little more than boxes made of canvas stretched across light wooden frames, and the only substantial parts were the doors. Over the top of each door was painted the rank of its normal occupant—the lieutenants, marine officer, master and surgeon.

The table filling the centre of the gunroom was filthy now, spattered with dried soup, crumbs and crusts of bread and dark stains of red wine. The racks above several of the doors had once held the occupants' telescopes and swords, but were now empty— the first Frenchmen to board the mutinous ship must have done well, probably relieving the mutineers of their loot before they were taken on shore.

The bosun gestured to everyone to sit on the two forms beside the table, on which stood a large wicker-covered rum jar whose fumes filled the gunroom.

The bosun and three guards. Four in all, and he had counted seven, a figure confirmed by the lieutenant. So now three French-men were guarding the prisoners. There was a muffled groan from one of the cabins and Auguste, Gilbert and Ramage all looked inquiringly at the bosun, who grinned.

"The English captain. His rheumatism is bad. Saves us guarding him because he can't move."

Gilbert reached for a battered metal mug and the bosun took the hint, lifting the rum jar and beginning to pour into a sorry collection of mugs. A French seaman said: "One of the mutineers spoke some French, and before he was taken to the château he told me the captain had been in his cot since the day after they sailed."

"Why did they mutiny?"

"The rheumatism made the captain bad-tempered, so this *ros-bif* said. He used to order many floggings. Hurting other people seemed to ease his own pain. He should have tried this," the sea-man said, lifting his mug of rum. "But they said he did not drink. Prayed a lot, though it didn't seem to ease his problems." The man gave a dry laugh. "In fact praying seems to have brought him many troubles!"

"The mutineers—they are Frenchmen now, eh?" Gilbert asked as he raised his mug in a toast to the bosun.

"Frenchmen?" The bosun was shocked. He considered the matter, taking hearty sips of his rum. "No, not Frenchmen. After all, if they mutinied against their own officers, they could mutiny against us. They have no loyalty to anyone, those buffoons."

Ramage was startled to hear the man talk such reasonable sense. So, the mutineers were not welcome in Brest.

"But you are glad to have the ship!" he said.

The bosun shrugged. "For me, it is of no importance: we have enough ships now—you can see the fleet we are preparing. This brig I do not like. It goes to windward slowly."

"Surely the mutineers will be rewarded?" Ramage persisted.

"Oh yes, they'll be given a few *livres* each at the château, and thanked. Who knows, if the English navy hear that they get a good reception at Brest, perhaps they'll bring in some frigates, or maybe even ships of the line!

"We'll thank them for their ships," the bosun continued, topping up his mug from the rum jar, "but I expect we'll make sure the men leave the country after signing up in neutral ships. The Americans will be glad of them—they speak the same language. And the Dutch and the Danes are always glad to get prime seamen."

"So these men that refused to join the mutiny," Ramage persisted, managing to introduce a complaining whine into his voice, "they won't be punished? Not executed or flogged?"

"Of course not," the bosun said impatiently. "They'll be taken off to the prison at Valenciennes or Verdun or wherever it is that they keep them. The first prisoners of the new war," he added. "Come on now, let's drink to thousands more!"

CHAPTER FIVE

THE Café des Pêcheurs, halfway along the Quai de la Douane and overlooking the entire anchorage, was aptly named: at least twenty fishermen, most of them in smocks as liberally coated with red ochre as Auguste's, were playing cards, rolling dice or sipping wine at the tables outside. And arguing. Ramage listened to some of them and was amused by the vehemence that the most innocent of subjects could provoke among these bearded and rough-tongued men.

They eyed Sarah curiously: few women other than whores ever came to such a café, but because she was with Auguste she was accepted and spared any teasing or coarse remarks.

For the moment the three men and Sarah were sitting silently, looking across at the *Murex* over on their right hand and *L'Espoir* to their left. Boats were going out to the frigate, unloading casks, and returning empty to the Quai de Recouvrance, on the other side of the Penfeld river. It was from there, Auguste told them, that ships were supplied with fresh water and salt meat and fish.

The fishermen's café was a good place to talk. The few people who did not want to play cards or dice naturally went to the tables along the edge of the quay, and Ramage had already noted that no one could get within a dozen feet of their table without being seen, so it was impossible to overhear their conversation. And that, Ramage thought to himself, is just as well . . .

"*Alors,* Charles," Gilbert was saying, hesitating over the name because he was really addressing a formal question to Captain Lord Ramage of the Royal Navy. "What do you think about Auguste's proposal?"

While Ramage had sat in the gig telling Sarah what he had learned from his visit to the *Murex*, Auguste and Gilbert had

walked down the road and the fisherman had taken the opportunity to tell Gilbert that he wanted to escape to England: that
he and his brother Albert were completely disillusioned by the
Revolution and had heard enough from Gilbert to know that
England was preferable. But, he had asked, knowing nothing of
their plans, hopes and fears, how was he to get there?

Ramage knew that for the moment it boiled down to one single question: did he or did he not trust Auguste, whom he had
met only two or three hours earlier?

Obviously Gilbert did—he had known the man from boyhood, long before the Revolution. But Gilbert had been in England
for several years. Did he know what Auguste and his brother had
been doing here in Brest during those bloody years following the
Revolution?

"Tell me, Auguste, were you a fisherman during the Revolution?"

Auguste told him what he and his brother had done: they
had smuggled out Royalists, taking them half a dozen at a time,
concealed in their fishing-boat, southwards to Portugal and safety.
They had continued to do that until a few months before Bonaparte signed the Treaty with England—then they had had a
running fight with a cutter of the French navy, finally escaping.
"That was when I collected this," Auguste said, pointing to the
scar on his face.

"Our fishing-boat was so badly damaged by gunfire that we
guessed we would be betrayed the moment we put into a French
port, so we landed our refugees safely on the coast and then we
sank our fishing-boat and rowed ashore with our little skiff. We
came back to Brest a few weeks later, and no one asked questions. But we could not fish any more; instead we grew vegetables
on the piece of land our father left us."

Ramage nodded. The story seemed both likely and straightforward. Sarah suddenly asked: "What makes you approach my

husband because you and your brother want to go to England?
Bonaparte's men are hunting us, while you all have proper documents as French citizens. Surely you can steal a fishing-boat
more easily than we can."

Auguste looked first at Ramage, unused to having a woman
enter a conversation in this way, and noting the nod said: "Obviously I know you are English and if you, *m'sieu,* are caught you
will be made a prisoner of war. But you do not seem to me—
nor you, madame—the sort of person to let yourselves be taken
prisoner. I think you are planning to get back to England. Gilbert
has said nothing—and his silence," he added with a grin, "bears
out what I think."

The man *looked* a scoundrel: a once handsome rogue. The
type of person you did not trust without a lot of checking.
Auguste had trusted him and Gilbert and taken them with him
out to the *Murex,* and while they were drinking with the French
bosun, Auguste had spotted the trend of Ramage's and Gilbert's
questions, and asked some of his own.

If a man trusts you without question, then you can trust him.

Ramage found himself thinking that with the same clarity as
if he was reading a printed text. Auguste had got them out to
the *Murex* and back safely: obviously he was a man of ingenuity. At this moment Ramage knew only too well he needed the
help of a man of ingenuity who knew his way around Brest.

It was too risky telling Auguste and his brother to come out
to Jean-Jacques' château: *gendarmes* might be suspicious, and
later might remember them passing the *barrières.* Anyway, this
café was a good safe spot for what could be only a preliminary
chat.

"I have no plans at the moment," Ramage admitted. "I have
come into Brest now simply to look, and hope to get some—
well, inspiration."

"You can speak freely; I shall not betray you," Auguste said calmly.

Ramage smiled. "I would speak freely if I had anything to say. You could betray us in a few seconds by waving to those two *gendarmes* standing under the trees over there."

"True, true," Auguste said. "Well, let's start by you saying what you *want* to do. How to do it can come later."

"That is simple. First I would like to rescue the Count, then I would like to take him and Gilbert back to England."

Auguste rubbed his nose as he looked carefully at Ramage. "I am sure you would. But with a force comprising yourself, your wife, Gilbert, Louis and now myself and my brother Albert, you are outnumbered by about three hundred men."

"Only about two hundred and fifty," Ramage said dryly. "But I was simply answering your question."

"Yes, and I was teasing. But to be serious, your loyalty to the Count is admirable and what I would expect from an English *aristo* and from Gilbert. However, there is not a chance. The Count and fifty others (all of whom probably realize they are lucky to have escaped the guillotine and regard transportation to Cayenne as an acceptable alternative) are heavily guarded on board *L'Espoir*. This I can assure you. In fact, at the risk of distressing you, I can tell you that all of them are in irons and will remain so until *L'Espoir* sails in a few days' time. In fact, you may have guessed that the French government is being particularly cautious about this first voyage to Cayenne in the new war."

"Is that why boats are taking out water and provisions? I should have thought it would be quicker and easier to bring *L'Espoir* alongside at the Quai de Recouvrance so that they can load directly from carts," Ramage said.

"The commandant of the port has orders from Paris to take no risks with these exiles, so he is keeping the frigate at anchor, with other frigates round her. I think he dreams of all the *déportés* leaping over the side and swimming to the shore, or a British fleet sailing up Le Goulet to rescue them."

Ramage looked at Gilbert. "I think you realized there was no way," he said gently. "Even with fifty men."

The Frenchman nodded. "Yes, but one hopes for miracles. From what I know of you, citizen," he said, a slight emphasis on the word to indicate he was really using Ramage's title, "if any man could have done it, you could."

"Who have we here?" Auguste asked Gilbert, who looked questioningly at Ramage and, when he nodded, leaned across and whispered the name.

The Frenchman turned and looked at Ramage, his eyes bright and his lean face creased into a grin. "Captain, you are famous in Brest. If only Bonaparte knew . . . he'd give me the province as a reward for betraying you."

"You flatter me," Ramage said.

"The thought does not seem to alarm you," Auguste commented.

"You have only to shout to the *gendarmes*," Ramage said. "Mind you, your brother would get the land, not you."

Auguste raised his eyebrows. "My brother?"

"Yes, because I presume he is your heir. You could shout— but you'd never draw the breath to replace the one that you used. I have a heavy kitchen knife hidden in my right boot."

Auguste gave a sudden bellow of laughter and slapped his knee. "Done!" he said, as though he had just concluded a business deal, and Ramage saw the performance was for the benefit of any curious onlooker, but "Done" meant he had given his word; he was part of whatever Ramage might plan.

"Your interest in the—er, the potato ship. Were you looking for ideas, and did you find any?"

"I was looking. Nothing very certain has come yet. Something is hovering over my head, like a sparrowhawk in the distance."

"Fifteen prisoners on board her, if you include that rheumatic wreck of a captain. Seven French guards. Five of us, unless you include madame."

"Include madame and exclude that captain," Ramage said. "Five does not sound a very lucky number."

The *Murex*, like the *Triton* and the other ten-gun brigs, was a handsome little ship, although too small to have a graceful sheer like the frigates. Anyway, the French always designed beautiful ships, so it was unfair to compare the *Murex* with the other vessels anchored in the Roads. He thought of the *Calypso*, a French frigate which he had captured and, by a stroke of luck, been given to command. In any anchorage she was always one of the handsomest ships.

Did Bonaparte ever wonder at the contradiction that the French built the best ships but could not fight 'em? And how irritating it must be for the little Corsican that usually the British kept the original French names once they captured ships and put them into service! One of the biggest ships in the Royal Navy today was called the *Ville de Paris!* One could not imagine the French calling one of their flagships the *City of London*. And some of the best ships at present in service had been captured from the French and often the names kept—the frigates *Perle*, *Aréthuse*, *Aurore*, *Lutine*, *Melpomène*, *Minerve*, for instance. And the 80-gun *Tonnant* and the *Franklin* (which had been renamed *Canopus*), as well as the 74s *Spartiate*, *Conquérant* and *Aquilon* (now called the *Aboukir*, in honour of the battle in which Rear-Admiral Nelson had captured them). Then *Le Hoche*, 80 guns, had been a little too much for their Lordships at the Admiralty, who had renamed her *Donegal*, but *Le Bellone*, 36 guns, had been changed to *Proserphine* only to avoid confusion with the 74-gun *Bellona*. *La Pallas*, 40 guns, had been renamed *La Pique*, which showed their Lordships had no prejudice against French names! There were dozens more. And of course there were the Spanish and the Dutch . . .

He suddenly realized that the two men and Sarah were watching him. Obviously they thought his silence was because he was thinking of daring plans to get them all to England, whereas in fact he had been daydreaming over ships' names.

"Yes," he said lamely, "let's say fourteen prisoners on board the *Murex* and half of them in irons during the day. All of them are put in irons for the night, so the guards can safely sleep."

Sarah coughed as if asking permission to join in the planning, but she did not wait for anyone to nod encouragement. "M'sieu Auguste cannot get a fishing-boat—one large enough for us to sail to England?"

"No, madame, I regret I cannot. If I could, we would sail tonight. But now the commandant of the port has given fresh orders. All fishing-boats with a deck—even a small foredeck—(all except open boats, in other words) must have two armed soldiers guarding them if they are in port for the night. Apparently the order comes from Paris and is the result of the renewal of war."

"Yes," Gilbert said, "Bonaparte realizes that there are hundreds like the Count, and Charles here, who will be trying to escape if they are not already locked up."

Ramage said: "But you could get a rowing boat?"

"Yes," Auguste said cautiously, "but I do not wish to row to England in one!"

"No, but that means we can always go fishing in Le Goulet. I enjoy fishing and I am sure Gilbert does, too."

"The port commandant disapproves, though," Auguste said. "He hasn't forbidden it yet, but the sentries on the men-of-war occasionally fire a musket if they think a fisherman is too close, just as a warning."

"Any casualties?"

"Not yet."

Ramage nodded. "At night a moving boat is a difficult target, and if the fishermen keep a respectable distance . . ."

"Yes, the sentries are really only warning. And I hear that many captains of ships dislike having their sleep disturbed by random musket shots!"

Ramage nodded again. Firing muskets at anchor would certainly disturb a captain's rest, and half an hour would pass before he received an explanation and dozed off again.

"Gilbert, if you would pay for our wine, I think we had better buy some fruit and vegetables to satisfy the curiosity of the *gendarmes* at the *barrières* and bid our friend here *au revoir.*"

At the château, Louis met them with the news that a friendly neighbour of his wife's parents had told them that *L'Espoir* would be sailing in three or four days for Cayenne. The *Chef d'administration de la Marine* at Brest, Citizen Moreau, was rushing everything apparently, because the British declaration of war had taken Paris unawares and the First Consul was anxious to get this group of Royalists and priests on their way to Cayenne before the Royal Navy re-established the blockade of Brest. There was also talk of *L'Espoir*'s decision to beat out directly to the southwestward after leaving Brest, hoping to hide herself in the wastes of the Atlantic once she was out of sight of Pointe St Mathieu.

Ramage thanked Louis for the information. Since they could do nothing about *L'Espoir* and her sad human cargo, he could only note that the frigate's captain was intending to do what he would have done in the same situation. In fact, *L'Espoir* stood little risk of being intercepted because Cayenne was so far to the south round the bulge of South America that British ships of war and privateers bound for the West Indian islands would be crossing the Atlantic well to the north of her course. By staying far to the south, *L'Espoir* might risk getting beyond the belt of Trade winds and run into strong ocean currents, but she was embarking extra provisions and water, probably as an insurance against a long passage. From memory, the Île du Diable, better known to the English as Devil's Island and referred to by the French as "Cayenne," the name of the nearest town on the main-land, sat precisely on the fifth parallel of latitude, only three hundred miles from the Equator, a hot and humid hell on earth.

Louis added, almost as an afterthought, that two *gendarmes* had called to ask if there had been any sign of the Englishman, but they had been told the agreed story: he had stayed a few days before the Count had been arrested and left, as far as any-one knew, to visit friends somewhere in Provence. Why had the Count not reported that he had strangers staying in the house, as required by State Ordinance number 532, dated 1st *Vendémi-aire* year VI? Louis had shaken his head sadly and told the men that the Count, although a very law-abiding man, had not been living in France at the time of the Ordinance and probably knew nothing about it. But Louis had almost been trapped by his own inventiveness: had the Count had other visitors—not necessarily foreigners, but people "not normally inhabiting the place of habi-tation"—staying and whom he had not reported to the *préfecture?* Louis said he did not know what the Count reported. The *gen-darmes* themselves had said he had not reported the Englishman but for all Louis knew the Count *had* reported them and the *gen-darmes* had lost the record. At this, Louis related gleefully, the police had been so embarrassed that it was clear that losing papers was not unknown.

Gilbert's comment had been brief and acute: clearly the authorities were not too concerned about the Englishman and accepted that he had moved on. Much more important, they did not realize that he was the Captain Ramage who had played such havoc with their ships in the previous war; if they thought he had been a guest of the Count, then strict precautions would be taken at Brest. This had not been the case, he said with a grin, at the *barrières*.

Ramage had been momentarily startled by Gilbert's use of the word "previous," but of course he was right: that war had begun in February 1793 and ended officially with the signing of the Treaty in April last year, 1801. After eighteen months' peace Britain had now declared war, obviously alarmed by French preparations, but it was another war. What would it be called? The last one had gone on long enough, but with Bonaparte in possession of a huge army—it was said that he could mobilize a million men—how the devil could Britain alone (she had fought most of the last war alone) defeat him? The Royal Navy could only fight where there was water enough to float ships.

He cursed his daydreaming; once again Gilbert, Louis and Sarah were watching him and waiting, as though expecting brilliant ideas to spout from his mouth like water from a firehose the moment men started working the pump handles. He shook his head in a meaningless gesture and, taking Sarah's hand, led the way to their rooms. As soon as he had shut the door she poured water from the big jug into the porcelain basin on the washstand.

"I feel dirty from the top of my head to the tips of my toes," she said, hanging her coat on a hook and beginning to unbutton her dress.

Ramage sank back on the bed, wishing there was an armchair. "I am weary too. So I shall sit here and watch you undress and then watch you wash yourself from the top of your head to the tip of your toes. It is one of the greatest joys of being your husband. I'm sorry I'm too weary to undress you."

She slid the dress down and stepped out of it as once again Ramage marvelled at how natural and beautiful she looked in the coarse underwear lent her by Louis' wife. Next she undid the white ribbon—carefully-sewn strips of linen, in fact—of the shift, which was like a long apron, and unwound it.

She smiled at him and watched his eyes as she unbuttoned the bodice and slowly took it off, revealing her breasts in a movement which stopped Ramage's breath for several moments. The breasts seemed to have a life of their own; the nipples, high and large, were dark, like seductive eyes.

Still looking at him, she slid down the frilled knickers and stood naked without embarrassment. Standing naked before your husband for his inspection, she seemed to be saying, was the natural end to a day's journey into the enemy's camp.

"You approve?"

She knew he did but wanted reassuring.

"The left breast . . . is it not a fraction lower than the right?"

A look of alarm spread across her face as she hurried to the dressing-table. The large looking glass originally fitting into the frame was missing and the only one available was the small handheld glass from her travelling bag.

She held it at arm's length, twisting and turning, peering first at one breast and then the other. Then she held the glass to the side, trying to line up the nipples. Finally she put the mirror down in exasperation.

"I can't see them properly!"

Hard put to keep a straight face, Ramage said: "As you walked, it seemed to me it is actually the right one that's lower. Come over here and let me take a look."

Then she realized he was teasing. "Are you too tired to undress yourself?" she whispered.

Ramage nodded. "I shall have to rely on my wife."

Gilbert went into Brest the next day to make arrangements with Auguste and returned to say that both the fisherman and his brother would be ready and had begun collecting weapons.

So far they had six pistols and shot, two blunderbusses, three heavy daggers, a cavalry sabre and two cutlasses. When Ramage marvelled at such a collection, Gilbert had grinned. The authorities in Paris lacked popularity in Brittany, he said, so that when a drunken soldier flopped asleep into a ditch or a cavalryman riding alone was thrown from his horse and found unconscious, they were usually returned to their barracks alive but always unarmed. Occasional raids on armouries, sudden and unexpected affairs, meant that many of those not entirely in favour of the First Consul's régime had weapons hidden among the beams of old barns or concealed in sacks of grain.

On the second day, while Ramage and Sarah roamed through the great house admiring the architecture and feeling guilty at envying Jean-Jacques because of his present situation, Louis went into Brest. There was no need to take unnecessary risks and arouse suspicions, Ramage had decided, and Louis and his wife passing through the *barrières* once a week would seem normal enough while Gilbert passing along the road alone in the gig once a day might start a *gendarme* asking questions.

Many of the rooms of the château were completely bare, stripped by looters of all their furniture, carpets, hangings, curtains and occasionally complete doors. Damaged ceilings showed where chandeliers had been torn down; some staircases lacked banisters.

Yet the house, although almost empty, maintained its dignity. It had none of the delicacy and fine tracery, carefully balanced winds and imposing approaches of many of the châteaux of the Loire and Dordogne. It was four-square, and not concealing its origins—a defended home of the Counts of Rennes. The battlements of thick stone were crenellated so that men with crossbows and later muskets could hide behind them and fire down on attackers; the enormous (and original) front door, studded with iron bolts that would blunt and deflect an attacker's axe, was so massive that a much smaller door had been built more recently to one side.

Ramage was staring out of a window, one of scores and now grimy, with paint lifting from the frame in a discreet warning that rot was at work beneath, when Sarah took his arm and said quietly: "Where are you now?"

He gave a start, and then smiled without turning. "I was thinking that it's the top of the springs tonight."

She sighed and shook her head. "Springs and neaps—I know they're something to do with the moon and the tide, but . . ."

"A sailor's wife and you don't understand the tides!"

"A sailor's wife who admits she doesn't understand, and expects her all-wise and adoring husband to explain."

"The sun and the moon both pull the sea. When they are in line, both on one side of the earth or on opposite sides, they pull most and that's when we get the highest high tides, and the lowest low. They are called spring tides. They coincide with the new moon (the moon on the same side of the earth as the sun) and the full (when on the opposite side). When the sun or moon are at right-angles to each other in relation to the earth their pull is weakest and we get the smaller tides which are weaker and called neaps. So the springs are the highest and strongest around new and full moon, and the neaps are the smallest and weakest at first and third quarters."

"Nothing to do with the seasons then—spring, summer and so on?"

"Nothing at all. It is a full moon tonight so there are spring tides. The highest in terms of sea level but also the strongest in terms of current. When the tide starts to ebb, it will flow out very strongly through the Gullet."

"And that is important?"

"It would be if you were fishing from a small boat. Why, if you lost an oar you could drift to America!"

"Make sure you take plenty of bait," she said. "Am I such a stupid woman that I can't be told what you are planning?"

"I'd tell you if I knew. I'd talk it over if I thought you could help me get an idea. The fact is that *L'Espoir* sails for Cayenne with Jean-Jacques today or tomorrow and here I am, walking through his empty house, helpless and hopeless."

"My dear, how can you expect to rescue one man from a frigate?"

Ramage shrugged. "My men in the *Kathleen*, the *Triton*, and the *Calypso* in the past did what people reckoned impossible, and we did it *only* because to others it *was* impossible."

"But your men—the splendid Southwick, and Aitken, Jackson and Stafford: dozens of them—are all in Chatham on board the *Calypso*. You are"—she gave a wry smile—"in France on your honeymoon, hunted by the French."

"Not all the French; only Bonaparte's men."

"About one in ten thousand are not Bonaparte's men. You won't collect a very big army in Brittany to overthrow him."

"No," he admitted. "But I need very few. I agree we can't save Jean-Jacques, so we have to save ourselves: you and me, Gilbert and Louis (and his wife if she wants to come) and now Auguste and his brother. Five men and one, perhaps two women."

"We are a long way from England. There always seems to be bad weather in the entrance to the Channel. Why don't we travel overland towards Calais? We'd have only twenty miles or so to row or sail to England, compared with—what, a hundred and fifty to Plymouth?"

Ramage turned and pulled her towards him, and kissed her gently. "My dear, you are right in one respect: it is a much shorter sea crossing from Calais. But that's what makes it dangerous. The French *expect* escapers to try to cross there. Every rowing boat is chained up at night. There are big rewards offered—big enough to overcome most scruples. Brest is so far away from England that the French are more casual in the way they guard boats."

"But they are putting soldiers on board the fishing-boats here at night!" she protested.

"Yes, but they are the large ones with fish holds, those large enough to make the voyage to England safely in almost any weather."

"Are you proposing we all go in a rowing boat?" She was not frightened at the idea but obviously surprised and dismayed.

"No. I'm not proposing anything at the moment, beyond a couple of hours' fishing at night in the Gullet. Auguste is providing a boat for us."

"Why fishing? You hate fish and fishing. Why the sudden interest?" she asked suspiciously.

"A romantic row in the moonlight so that you can see all the pretty ships at anchor."

"Most romantic," she said with a rueful smile. "We'll have four men as chaperones. Can we hire an orchestra, and perhaps a troupe of wandering minstrels?"

CHAPTER SIX

AUGUSTE sighed in the darkness and admitted: "The price is good at the moment, but in truth I hate the smell of potatoes." He pulled fretfully at a couple of sacks, trying to find himself a more comfortable position in the little hut. "And madame, you must be very uncomfortable?"

"I had not realized potatoes could be so hard," Sarah admitted, "but if my husband is to be believed, we'll soon be sitting on the hard wooden seats of a boat and probably thinking of potatoes with nostalgia . . ."

And how long would Nicholas be? He had talked for half an

hour with Gilbert, Louis, Auguste and his brother Albert, and now he had gone for a walk along the quay. She saw now that he had been very clever. Although he had told her back at the château that he had no plans for their escape, in fact he had an idea. Certainly as he had explained it to the men, speaking softly in the darkness of Auguste's hut in the fruit and vegetable market, he had sounded diffident. Not nervous, but almost shy, so much so that first Auguste and then Gilbert had tried to reassure him. Then, as he explained his idea piece by piece, like stripping an artichoke, they had discussed it among themselves, exclaiming from time to time at its soundness, like antiquarians examining old china or an early edition of a book and agreeing on its authenticity.

The more they had exclaimed, the more diffident Nicholas had become, putting up reasons why his idea would never work and declaring he did not want anyone to risk his life in such a stupid venture. "Stupid venture," a phrase which translated well into French, was the one that definitely turned the tide, though whether a neap or a spring, she did not care. At that point, the four Frenchmen rallied together to persuade Nicholas that the plan—by now it had graduated from an idea—was not only possible but certain of success and Sarah sensed that in their own minds it had become *their* plan: one of which Captain Ramage had now to be convinced.

Then she realized that as far as Nicholas was concerned it had been a plan all the time but was such a gamble that its only chance of success was to have it carried out by men who were convinced it would succeed. What was that phrase Nicholas had once used? "Better one volunteer than three pressed men." So with four volunteers he had the equivalent of a dozen. And, of course, his wife! Louis seemed to be bearing up bravely, she thought, to the fact that his wife had decided not to come. Louis said she would go to her parents as soon as she was sure he had escaped. Between them they had prepared a likely story of Louis throwing her out of the house—of the servants' quarters of Jean-Jacques' house, rather.

Sarah sensed that both Louis and his wife had reached the stage where they bored each other. In another year it would be followed by dislike and that would turn to hatred. The wife missed life on the farm where she had been brought up, obviously preferring feeding the pigs and mucking out the cattle to feeding humans and making beds, and as she was the only child, she would inherit the farm on the death of her parents. Clearly, Sarah realized, each thought the parting had come amicably and at the right time. And, not surprisingly, the other servants had decided to stay behind.

Where *was* Nicholas? This was worse than being a young girl waiting to grow up, or a pregnant woman waiting for her hour to come. Or, she thought bitterly, a sailor's wife waiting for her man to return . . .

Ramage looked in the darkness across the Brest Roads. "Roads"— a strange name but one usually given to the anchorage in front of the port. Well, even though it was dark but cloudless, giving the stars a chance to prove themselves before the moon rose, there was plenty of traffic in the Roads; it seemed as busy as Piccadilly after the Newmarket Races, when winners wanted to celebrate and losers wanted to drown their sorrows, and the Duchess of Manston always gave a ball at which it was forbidden to talk about racehorses.

Spanish Point over there, forming the south side of Le Goulet: the château black and menacing, its walls now sharp-edged shadows. Somewhere over there in the Roads, *L'Espoir* was at anchor, and by now Jean-Jacques would be on board, a prisoner, probably awake and thinking of his home or his future in the tropical heat and sickness of the Île du Diable. Boats were going out to the frigates and ships of the line, many more than would normally be taking officers to and fro. There was no doubt that the ships were being prepared for sea in great haste.

He paused against the trunk of a huge plane tree, hidden from the sharp eyes of any patrolling *gendarmes*. The masts of the distant ships were like leafless shrubs lining twisting paths. The ships of the line were easy to distinguish, while one, two, three frigates and more were over to the right, towards Pointe des Espagnols. Further round to the left, partly hidden by the cliffs rising up at Presqu'île de Plougastel, were more frigates. Where was *L'Espoir?*

Ah, there was the *Murex* brig, much easier to spot because she had only two masts and was much closer. And it was near the top of the tide; almost slack now, and the ebb would start in half an hour or so.

Anchored ships were something like weathervanes on church steeples. If the wind was strong and the current weak, they indicated wind direction, but if the current was strong (as it would be at spring tides) and the wind weak they showed the direction from which the current was coming.

On a calm night at slack water, when the current stopped flooding in and paused before ebbing like a bewildered man on a ballroom floor, ships headed in various directions, and those carelessly anchored and usually lying to single anchors would drift and foul neighbours.

He cursed softly because at night distances were always hard to estimate, although by some good fortune the *Murex* brig had been anchored more than half a mile from the nearest ship, a frigate. And she was near enough to where he stood to see that only a single boat floated astern of her on its painter. Either the rest of her boats had been hoisted back on board or they were being kept in the dockyard. In other words, it was unlikely that the French guards had been reinforced and, more important, if they were not expecting visitors in the shape of senior officers, they would be keeping the rum jar tilted, with all the prisoners in irons.

He shivered, but was not sure if the goosepimples came from the chill of the night or the knowledge that he could no longer delay going back to the hut to start everyone moving. Sarah was the problem: she was his hostage unto fortune, although she must never realize it. When the *Calypso* went into action he had worried about Paolo, who was Gianna's heir and nephew; now it was Sarah. Would he ever go into action having given no hostages, with nothing to bother him but the fight itself? There was always something to stop him concentrating all his thoughts on the action. He shrugged and then smiled at the stupidity of such a movement alone in the darkness.

Probably most captains of the King's ships were often in this same predicament—especially, he told himself, if they were married. Yet if you had a wife, and perhaps children, you thought of them whether they were in a house in the quiet countryside or if the wife was waiting nearby in a rowing boat: in one instance you were worrying about her being widowed and the children made fatherless; in the other you were worrying about her safety. Either way, you were worrying; either way you were preoccupied. So perhaps Earl St Vincent was right when he said that if an officer married, he was lost to the Service . . .

Sarah and the four men waiting in the hut clearly expected to start off at once. He took out his watch. Yes, by now the French guards would have soaked up enough rum to ensure they were befuddled, if not in a stupefied sleep.

He gestured towards the lantern and told Gilbert: "Bring it with you, otherwise all of us stumbling along in the dark will arouse suspicion. Now, have we the fishing lines? Ah," he nodded as Auguste and his brother held up coils of thin line, "and bait?" Sarah rattled the bucket she was carrying.

Two *gendarmes* passed them on their way to the jetty and one said cheerfully: "Good fishing. It's a calm night!"

"Too calm," Auguste answered dourly. "The fish prefer some wind to ruffle the water."

Once the *gendarmes* had passed, Auguste explained: "Fishermen always grumble. I don't think the fish care about the waves; they have enough sense to stay below them."

"Unless they bite a hook," Louis said.

"Ah, no, they're biting the bait, not the hook."

"They cannot have so much sense: a meal hanging from a line is obviously bait."

"Yes," Auguste agreed sarcastically, "sensible fish eat only from a plate."

Ramage led them to the avenue of plane trees lining the quay but told Auguste to lead them on to the boat: a sentry might become suspicious of the leader of a group of fishermen who seemed uncertain which was his boat.

He dropped back to walk with Sarah who, careful to act the role of the obedient fisherman's wife, even though it was late at night, had followed the menfolk.

"Feeling nervous?"

"No, not nervous. At the moment I'm thankful not to be smelling potatoes but not sure"—she rattled the bucket—"if sliced fish is a welcome change. Do you enjoy fishing?"

"This is my first experience," Ramage admitted. "I let the men tow a hook when they want, because fish makes a welcome change from salt horse. But towing a line from a rowing boat, or casting with a rod along a river bank—no."

"You've no patience, that's why," she said.

He was saved from admitting that by Auguste stopping above

a boat moored stern to the quay. "Well, my friends," he said loudly, "I hope your muscles are all working smoothly. Now, someone haul in the sternfast so that I can jump in and slack the anchor rope: then we can get her alongside and put our gear on board."

The boat's stern was four or five feet from the dock and Louis went down the narrow stone steps to untie the sternfast from a ring that slid up and down a metal rod let into the vertical face of the quay, allowing for the rise and fall of the tide. He cursed as he nearly slipped on the green weed.

"Farmers," Auguste's brother commented unexpectedly. "That's what we are, farmers going out for a night's fishing."

No one answered as he went down to help Louis, then called up to Auguste: "All is ready for the real fishermen to board."

It took five minutes of hauling, pushing and banter for the four Frenchmen to get on board and hold the boat alongside the steps for Sarah and Ramage to climb in. The lantern set down on one of the thwarts revealed the inside of a hull which seemed to have been painted with dried fish scales and decorated with the sun-dried heads, tails and fins of past catches. The worst of the smell was for the moment masked by the sewage running into the Penfeld river from a large pipe a few feet upstream from the steps.

With Sarah seated on a thwart, the wooden bucket of bait on her knees, Ramage and Auguste counted up the oars. Four, held down by a chain wound round them and secured by a padlock. "I have the key, here," Auguste said in answer to an unspoken question. "Now, I want you two, Louis and Albert, to stand in front of the lantern: cast a shadow over the bow."

Ramage saw a pile of fishing lines and a coil of rope, and as soon as the lantern light was shadowed he saw Auguste pulling them aside and for a moment a flash of steel reflected a sudden bright star.

"They're here," Auguste muttered. "Six cutlasses . . . two, three large daggers . . . five pistols—no, six . . . a bag of shot . . . flask of powder, and another of priming powder . . . You said no muskets."

It was a remark which sounded like a reproach.

"Believe me," Ramage said, "muskets are too clumsy for boarding a ship. If they're loaded, there's always the danger of the lock catching on clothing so the musket fires just when you're trying to be quiet. A pistol tucked in the top of the trousers—that is enough. Anyway, cutlasses or knives tonight: no shots except in an emergency."

"But we can carry pistols?" Auguste asked anxiously.

"Yes, of course," Ramage assured him. "Now, let's get away from here and start fishing nearer the *Murex*. Bottle fishing— none of you ever heard of that, eh?"

Both Auguste and Gilbert repeated the phrase, which certainly lost something in translation. "No, never 'bottle fishing,'" Auguste finally admitted. "For what kind of fish?"

Ramage laughed and explained. "In the West Indies, smuggling is even more common than in the Channel, only out there it is called 'bottle fishing' when it involves liquor."

"What is it when it is silk for ladies?" Auguste asked slyly.

"No need to smuggle silk out there: no customs or excise on that," Ramage said.

Auguste unlocked the padlock and unwound the chain securing the oars. "We are ready," he said. "The fish are waiting for us."

The men took up their places on the rowing thwarts, leaving Sarah to sit at the aftermost one. They would use a tiller to avoid having to give orders to the oarsmen.

Auguste boated his oar and then scrambled forward to the bow to begin hauling in the weed-covered rope and the anchor while his brother cast off the sternfast, leaving it dangling from its ring on the quay wall. Would the boat ever return to use it again? Ramage thought not.

Gilbert tentatively pulled at his oar and nearly fell backwards off the thwart as the blade scooped air instead of digging into water.

"Don't let go of the oar," Auguste snapped. "Dip the blade deeply and just try and keep time with the rest of us."

"I know how to do it." Gilbert's voice had a determined ring. "I'm out of practice."

"And the palms of your hands will soon be sore," Auguste added unsympathetically.

"I can see the *Murex*," Sarah murmured. "She's in line with the western end of the château."

"Ah, a woman who knows the points of a compass," Albert said.

The oars creaked, the thwarts creaked from the men's weight and their exertions, and as Ramage crouched he was sure his spine was beginning to creak too. The smell of last week's fish was now almost overwhelming and seemed to be soaking into his clothes. Then he could just see the western edge of the château, stark and black against the lower stars. The only lights over there were from a high window and a few gun loops, vertical slots that, because of the thickness of the wall and the changing bearing, soon cut off the light from the lanterns inside.

Sarah put her bucket down beside the lantern as Ramage said: "We are at the meeting point of the Penfeld and Le Goulet."

"Stop rowing, men," Auguste said, and then announced formally: "Your fishing captain now hands over to your fighting captain."

Ramage laughed with the rest of them and looked forward at the *Murex* brig. She was a good half mile away and it was still slack water, with the ships heading in different directions. A frog's view of models on a pond. For a few moments the familiar shape of the brig once again brought back memories of the *Triton*. He remembered her best at anchor in some West Indian bay during a tropical night when her masts and yards cut sharp lines in a star-littered sky. Up here in northern latitudes fewer stars were visible, for reasons he could never understand, and they were not nearly so bright, as though the atmosphere was always more hazy.

To fish or not to fish? He looked slowly round the horizon. No other boats were following them out of the Penfeld; the nearest ships to the *Murex* were half a dozen frigates and ships of the line at least half a mile beyond. Various boats moved under oars (and he could see one under sail making poor progress because of the light wind) taking officers and men out to the ships. None had that purposeful, marching sentry movement of a guard-boat: the war, he guessed, was too new for the French to have started regular patrols in the Roads, and anyway lookouts along the coast (at Pointe St Mathieu, for instance) would most likely have reported that the English had not yet resumed the blockade; that no English ships were on the coast.

He coughed to attract their attention and as a way of accepting the transition announced by Auguste. "I think madame can throw that bait over the side; she must be tired of the smell."

A clatter showed Sarah had not waited to hear if anyone disagreed.

"Good, now let's get our oars on board, before someone lets go and we lose a quarter of our speed. Auguste, can you issue the weapons you have hidden up there?"

The Frenchman scrambled forward, fumbled for a minute or two, and then stood up again, clutching several objects.

"Cutlasses," he said. "Here, Gilbert, take a couple before they slip from my arms. Ah, and one for you, Captain, and one for me. I shall put mine under my thwart. Careful with your feet when you sit down again, Gilbert."

With that he bent down and burrowed under the coils of lines again. "Four knives . . ." his voice was muffled as he dropped them behind him, ". . . and the pistols."

"You have six, I believe," Ramage said. "We'll have one for madame."

"Of course!" Auguste said. "I remember Gilbert telling me she is a fine shot. I shall load it for her myself. Now . . ." he pulled the coil of lines to one side, ". . . ah, the flask of powder . . . and the priming powder . . . and the box of balls and wads. Here, Gilbert, pass things aft, starting with the knives."

For the next five minutes the men were busy checking the flints, flipping them to make sure they gave a good spark, but hiding them under a piece of cloth to conceal their unmistakable flashing. Then they loaded the pistols, putting them on half-cock.

Louis and the two brothers were wearing high fishermen's boots and slid their knives down into them. Ramage and Gilbert wore shoes and so had to tuck the knives into the waistband of their trousers. Ramage was thankful the cutlasses had come with belts, but decided against slipping his over his right shoulder and instead pushed it under the thwart.

"You were right about muskets being too bulky, Captain," Auguste commented. "With knife, pistol and cutlass, I have all the weapons I can handle."

"Yes—but everyone remember: use the pistol only to save your life: shots might arouse the sentries in another ship, or alarm a passing boat."

"Is madame content with her pistol?" Auguste inquired.

Sarah said: "Yes, it is much like the English Sea Service pistol: clumsy and heavy!"

"Yes, but remember how roughly the sailors treat them," Auguste said, beating Ramage to it, "and when you've fired, you can always throw it at the next target."

By now, Ramage was having second thoughts about his

original plan. If a sentry challenged, they could probably gain several important seconds by innocently protesting that they were fishermen; seconds which could be converted into yards, and a closer approach.

"Auguste, what would you be using out here—a seine or long lines?"

Auguste thought for a few moments. "Long lines, I think."

He guessed what Ramage had in mind and added: "One could use either, and I doubt if a sentry would know anyway! And it won't matter that we have no bait!"

Although they were not rowing, and there was very little wind, the château was slowly drawing astern and the western bank where the Penfeld ran into Le Goulet was now closer, showing the direction the boat was drifting.

"The ebb has started," Ramage said. "The rest of us can start rowing again while Auguste puts over some lines." He moved into the fisherman's seat.

Sarah took the tiller and gave occasional directions to the four oarsmen as Auguste struggled with the lines. "Hold up the lantern, madame," he said finally, "otherwise I shall be the only fish these lines catch."

"You need only two or three," Ramage said. "No one will notice."

"That's true," Auguste said and put over one and then another, feeding out the lines expertly. "Shall I sit aft and pretend to watch?"

"As long as you have your cutlass and knife ready under the thwart," Ramage said. "In fact you can take over as coxswain from madame, and start by giving me a distance."

Sarah quickly pointed out the *Murex* to the Frenchman, who exclaimed: "Why, we are close! Much closer than I thought!"

"That's the ebb taking us down." Ramage then glanced over his shoulder and was also startled to find the brig now only about five hundred yards away: already her masts and yards were standing stark against the stars like winter trees with geometrically precise branches. "Auguste, we'll row past at about a pistol shot and then, if nothing happens, turn under her bow and even closer under her stern and then if we still see no one, board this side."

Sarah suddenly murmured in English: "Nicholas, I am frightened. The *Murex* looks more like a house full of ghosts."

"I'd prefer ghosts to French *matelots*," he said lightly, while Gilbert, who had understood, gave a reassuring laugh.

"How are you going to get on board?" she asked, reverting to French. She undid the knot of scarf round her head, took it off and shook her hair free.

"I don't know at the moment," Ramage said, his sentences punctuated as he leaned forward and then stretched back with each oar stroke. "There might be a ladder hanging over the side or a rope. Otherwise, it'll probably be a scramble up the side."

Sarah was silent for a moment and then said quietly in English: "There's a light on deck. A lantern, I think. It gets hidden as rigging and things get in the way."

"Speak in French," Ramage said, trying to hide his disappointment. "We don't want our friends to think we have any secrets." He turned away towards them and repeated Sarah's report.

"A warm night, so they're drinking on deck," Auguste commented. "It would be natural. That cabin we saw—the 'gunroom' I think you called it, Captain—was very small. It would get very hot down there."

Ramage saw his ideas being thrown aside like men caught on deck by a blast of grapeshot. Five Frenchmen up on the *Murex*'s deck drinking with weapons to hand, and two more guarding the prisoners below, would be more than a match for the five of them down in the rowing boat: the *matelots* would have the advantage of height, as well as numbers. But despair, fear, alarm—all were contagious, so Ramage laughed. "It'll soon be hot on deck for them too!"

They continued rowing in the darkness at the speed set by Auguste, with an occasional "left" and "right." Auguste said he was not using the seamen's terms because not all of them understood them and anyway, facing aft, they would only get muddled.

"We are two ship's lengths from her," Auguste muttered. "How close before we begin our turn to pass?"

"One," Ramage said. That would be thirty yards, or so. Close enough for Ramage to see what was happening on deck; close enough for any French seaman to see a fishing-boat passing. Or perhaps to show whether or not rum fumes would allow French *matelots* to see that far.

"No lights showing at the stern—what does that mean?" asked Auguste.

"They're not using the captain's cabin."

Sarah said: "There are several men on deck sitting round the lantern—do you see them, Auguste?"

The Frenchman grunted and then counted aloud as an explanation why he had said nothing. ". . . three, four . . . five. Two missing. Are they guarding the prisoners?"

"They could be fetching more rum or lying drunk on the deck," Louis said. "Perhaps we should row round for another hour and keep counting. As soon as seven have fallen down drunk, we can board!"

Ramage only just managed to stop himself making the usual joke about one Englishman being equal to three Frenchmen. These men, apart from not being trained seamen, were good: they had the right spirit and they hated the régime. Do not, he told himself, underestimate hate: it drives men to show the kind of bravery they never thought themselves capable of, yet it can just as easily warp their judgement.

"She's close on our bow—we're just beginning our run down her starboard side," Auguste reported to Ramage, his voice punctuated by the creaking of the four oars, the slap of the oar blades in the water, and hiss of the stem as the boat drove on.

"Ho! *Ohé,* that boat!" The hail from the *Murex's* deck was definite: the voice was sober. "Answer!" Ramage told Auguste, whose voice carried better and had a local accent.

"Ho yourself!" Auguste shouted back. "I don't like *rosbifs* shouting at me." His voice sounded genuinely offended.

"We're not *rosbifs!*" the voice answered indignantly. "We are honest Frenchmen *guarding* the *rosbifs.*"

"You speak French like a *rosbif,*" Auguste said sourly.

"Watch your tongue: I come from Besançon. Now, why do you fish so close to us?"

"Ha!" Auguste called back contemptuously. "So you think you own the whole sea, eh? Why, you are even standing on the deck of a *rosbif* ship, not a good French ship."

"Answer: why do you fish so close?" This time it was another, harsher voice: Ramage thought he recognized it as belonging to the bosun.

"To catch fish!" exclaimed Auguste. "You're no seaman if you can't see that!"

"What do you mean? I'm the bosun; I command this ship!"

"For the time being," Auguste said contemptuously. "But you've not yet learned that fish always gather round a ship at anchor. They feed off all the weed and things growing on the bottom. They like the shade on a sunny day—"

"And from the light of the moon too, I suppose. Afraid it will drive them mad, eh?"

"And they like to eat the scraps you all throw over the side. Salt beef and salt pork may not seem very tasty to you, but to a fish it is a banquet."

By now the boat was within a few yards of the *Murex's* side.

"To save all this rowing, with my back giving me trouble again," Ramage said in a lugubrious voice, "can't we fish from your decks? Then our hooks go where the fish are thickest."

The bosun answered quickly. "Yes—but you have to give us a quarter of your catch!"

"You're a hard man," Ramage complained. "Five wives and eleven children depend on what we catch."

"You should have thought of that before you got married," the bosun sneered. "A quarter of your catch and I'll let you on board."

"Oh very well," Ramage said grudgingly, and Auguste, in an appropriately officious voice, gave the orders to the men at the oars which brought the boat alongside.

Ramage murmured: "Pistols if you can hide them; otherwise just knives."

"The bait bucket," Sarah whispered. "Put the pistols in the bait bucket and I'll carry it with my scarf on top."

Louis called up to the bosun: "I'm coming on board with the painter while they coil our fishing lines." He touched Ramage to get his approval.

Ramage turned to Sarah. "You go after Louis and flirt with the bosun. I'll bring the bucket and give it to you to hold as soon as I can."

He glanced up and saw that none of the French guards were looking over the rail. Swiftly he pushed a knife and its sheath down the inside of his trousers and made sure the belt was tight enough to hold it. It was a pity that the cutlasses would have to be left under the thwarts, but Gilbert and Albert were putting the loaded pistols into the bucket with the deftness of fishwives packing sprats. Sprat—improbably, he remembered, it was the same word in both English and French.

"Your scarf, madame," Gilbert whispered, and Ramage said loudly, "Now are we ready? Gilbert—supposing you go up, and then you and Louis can help the lady at the top."

As soon as Gilbert started climbing the battens fitted like thin steps up the *Murex*'s side, Sarah began cursing, using words which would be familiar to a fisherman's wife but which Ramage was startled to find that she not only knew but used as though they were commonplace.

"Such steps—why no rope ladder? In this skirt? Do the *rosbifs* never have women on board? It's fortunate I wear no corset. Look away, you lechers; I am tucking my skirt in my belt."

She grabbed the hem of her skirt and Ramage glimpsed long slim legs as she tucked in the cloth. "This will occupy their thoughts!" she murmured to Ramage, and before he had time to reply she had grabbed the highest batten she could reach and started climbing.

"Forgive me, Captain," Auguste murmured to Ramage, and then called in a raucous voice to Louis and Gilbert on the *Murex*'s deck: "Why you went aloft too soon! From here one sees *la citoyenne* quite differently!"

"Keep your eyes down, you old dog," Ramage said hotly in what he hoped was the correct tone for an aggrieved husband, but he found himself continuing to watch Sarah's progress. A young woman's legs in the moonlight: certainly they did not help concentration. And since the sight made his own throat tighten he could guess the effect on Auguste.

A jab in the ribs from the bucket and a casual, "Your turn, and tell Louis and Gilbert to stand by to take the lines," came from Auguste.

The lines! He had forgotten all about the fishing lines. The prospect of fishermen arriving without them was only slightly less absurd than the idea of a Royal Navy post captain on his honeymoon climbing up the side of a surrendered brig holding a bait bucket filled with loaded pistols concealed by his wife's headscarf.

He slung the greasy rope handle of the wooden pail over his left arm and began the climb. Usually sideboys held out side-ropes for the captain, and the first lieutenant waited on deck ready to give a smart salute. This time there would be a surly French bosun . . .

The bucket slid down his arm and hit the ship's side with a thud. Ramage's heart seemed to stop beating for a moment, but the pistols did not make a metallic clunk and anyway, he thought sheepishly, there's no one up there watching me. But as he slid the handle back to the crook of his elbow he saw that now there was: not the bosun but the man who presumably was the sentry.

Ramage's head came level with the deck, and in the moon-light he saw Sarah a few feet away, talking to the bosun. Amidships and sitting on forms round the grating, on which stood a lantern and a wicker-covered demijohn of rum, several seamen were watching idly.

As soon as the bosun saw Ramage he left Sarah and came over. "You came with the potatoes," he said, his voice only slightly slurred by the rum. He had not shaved for several days or washed—it seemed to Ramage for even longer. His jersey and trousers had the greasy and rumpled look that showed he usu-ally slept "all standing," the British seaman's phrase for sleeping fully clothed.

"A quarter of your catch, eh? That is agreed?"

"Yes, of course," Ramage said, continuing to walk towards Sarah so that the bosun had to follow. "Let's hope we get a good catch. My dear," he said to Sarah, "here is the bait bucket: look after it while we sort out the lines."

He held the bucket low so that as she took it she would not reveal its weight by letting it drop a few inches, and at the same moment Ramage turned to the bosun to divert his attention and said querulously: "Never get a good catch with a full or new moon, you know. Moonlight seems to frighten the fish, or put them off food."

"A quarter, though," the bosun muttered as Sarah took the bucket and turned aft, saying in the voice of a dutiful wife that she would help bait the hooks as soon as they brought the lines.

By now Albert was on board and hauling up fishing lines from a cursing Auguste, who was putting on a noisy and effective act of being afraid of being caught on the hooks.

Louis and Gilbert came up to help and Ramage, seizing the opportunity of gathering all his men close to the bucket so they could collect their pistols, called: "Hoist up all the lines—we have more room to untangle them on this ship's deck. Look, there's plenty of space aft there."

Ramage walked along the gangway and, noting that the only lantern on deck was on the grating, giving the drinkers enough light to see when their glasses were nearly empty, shouted down to Auguste: "*Merde!* Hurry up or it'll be dawn!"

The bosun watched. "You'll catch yourself on those hooks," he sneered.

"Then you won't get a quarter," Gilbert said.

"We'll see," the bosun said, and Ramage tried to decide whether or not he imagined a curious inflexion in the voice. Finally he decided that it was just the man's local accent combined with a normal sneering and bullying manner.

As soon as the lines were all on board, the four Frenchmen, led by Ramage, carried them aft to where Sarah waited. The light was poor and confusing, a muddling blend of faint moonlight and a weak yellow glow—an artist would call it a wash—from the lantern on the grating.

The bosun, Ramage noted thankfully, had remained at the gangway, and the sentry had gone back to rejoin his three fellow seamen sitting and sprawling on the forms. So the sentry had a musket—he had left it propped against the edge of the coaming—and Ramage saw there were two more within reach of the other sailors.

As Ramage busied himself with the fishing lines close to the taffrail, he managed to indicate to the men that he wanted them working with their backs to the bosun so that Sarah could give them their pistols. As the men moved casually into position Ramage suddenly thought of the fourteen Britons being held as prisoners somewhere below and the captain imprisoned by rheumatism. Eleven seamen, the master and two lieutenants—they would be in irons, probably somewhere forward on the lower deck.

Tonight the *Murex* brig, he thought grimly, certainly holds an odd collection of people, ranging from the daughter of a marquis to seven French sailors loyal to the Revolution, a post captain in the Royal Navy, and a rheumatic lieutenant, and four Frenchmen who, although perhaps not entirely Royalist, were certainly against the First Consul.

When the ingredients were mixed together, he mused as he saw Sarah dip into the bucket and give Auguste a pistol, it would be like mixing charcoal, sulphur and saltpetre, each in themselves harmless but in the right proportion forming gunpowder and needing only a spark—

"Step back from those fishing lines!"

The bosun's sudden bellow paralysed the five men.

"Woman! Come over here!"

Rape, Ramage thought: the bosun and his men intend to rape Sarah. And only Auguste has a pistol: the bosun shouted before Sarah had time to give out the others.

"Oh, lieutenant!" Sarah said, her voice apparently trembling with fear. "What do you want me for?"

"Ah, no, not for that yet," the bosun boomed, although the regret at any delay was obvious in his voice. "You'll make a good hostage against the behaviour of your husband and his friends."

Ramage saw that the bosun was aiming a musket at them. The other men were now laughing but still sprawled on the forms, two of them holding mugs in their hands.

Ramage said: "What are we supposed to do? We are poor fishermen. You gave us permission to fish."

"Ah yes, but you do not keep yourself informed, citizen. From midnight, patrols are searching all the streets and houses of Brest to find more seamen. A thousand more. The First Consul needs many more men for all these ships," he said, waving a hand towards the main anchorage. "We received orders during the day to see if any of the British prisoners in this ship want to volunteer—and then tonight the five of you row past . . ."

"My poor husband!" Sarah moaned, but Ramage noticed she still clutched the bucket to her, like a mother clasping her child.

Ramage took two steps towards her but the bosun snarled: "Halt—another step and I shoot you dead." He glanced over his shoulder at his men. "To arms, citizens! Cover them with your muskets."

There was a clatter as one of the forms tipped over, and Ramage saw the men pick up their muskets and cock them. Five muskets . . . He had not seen the others lying on the deck beyond the coaming.

Now the bosun was getting excited by the nearness of Sarah. "Ah yes, the fisherman's wife! Well, take a good took at him, my dear, because you'll not see him again for a long time. A very long time. Ever again, perhaps, if the English fight like they did before."

Ramage took another step forward but the bosun swung the barrel of the musket. "Stand still. We'll be taking you below in a minute."

With that he turned to Sarah. "Yes, look well at your man." Then, with a sudden movement of one hand he ripped away the front of Sarah's dress and as her breasts shone in the moonlight he screamed at Ramage: "Look! Look, you fish pedlar—you won't see her again for a very long time. But"—he paused, staring wide-eyed and slack-mouthed at Sarah as she tried to clutch her dress closed with one hand, the other still holding the bucket— "I'll look after her for you, won't I, my dear?"

He reached across and pulled Sarah's hand away so that the torn dress again gaped open. "Look after these wretches," the bosun ordered his men. "Now," he said to Sarah, almost slobbering the words, "you come down to my cabin!"

"No," she said, calmly and clearly, "and you put the musket down on the deck and order your men to come over one at a time and put their muskets beside it!"

The bosun stood, jaw dropped in surprise and then gave a harsh, ugly laugh.

"Be careful," Sarah warned. "Your life is in danger." Her voice was cold but the bosun was too excited to notice.

"Oh, she has spirit, this one!" he exclaimed.

"No," Sarah said, taking a step forward, "a pistol."

A moment later the bosun pulled in his bulging stomach as the muzzle of Sarah's pistol jabbed it.

"You would never dare! Ho!" He half turned to his men and called over his shoulder: "Watch me pull this hen off her nest!" He reached out and grabbed Sarah's dress again.

Ramage saw the men beginning to move, uncertain what was happening because Sarah's hand holding the pistol was hidden from them by the bosun's bulky body. Suddenly there was a bright flash and bang and a scream from the bosun, who staggered back three steps and then collapsed on the deck.

"Seize her, seize her!" one of the *matelots* screamed and then, as Sarah made a sudden movement and said something to the quartet that Ramage did not hear, the man shouted urgently: "No! Don't move! The cow has another pistol! Don't shoot, *citoyenne*—it was all in jest!"

By now Ramage was running towards the bucket, a hand groping for a pistol and cocking it as he kept an eye on the four *matelots*. In one almost continuous movement he was moving towards them with the pistol aimed. Behind him he could hear the thudding feet and then the clicking of locks as the pistols were cocked.

"My wife has dealt with the bosun. Unless you all put your muskets down I shall shoot you—the man nearest the mainmast. My friends—ah, here they are—will shoot the rest of you."

He said to Auguste conversationally: "I have the man on the right in my sights. The next is for you. Then Gilbert and then Louis."

The four *matelots* seemed frozen by the speed of events. "Muskets down on the deck," Ramage reminded them.

Sarah said with the same calm: "Shoot one of them, to encourage the others!"

The *matelots* heard her and hastily put the guns down on the deck. "Collect them up, Gilbert and Albert. Now you," he gestured to the nearest man, "come here."

As the *matelot* reluctantly walked the few feet, outlined against the brighter light thrown by the lantern and clearly expecting to be shot, Ramage wrenched his knife from its sheath and held it in his left hand.

"Closer," he ordered. "Come on, stand close to me, my friend!"

The *matelot* was a plump, pleasant-looking man with a chubby face, but now his brow was soaked in perspiration as though water was dribbling from his hair; his eyes jerked from pistol to knife and his tongue ran round his lips as though chasing an elusive word.

"Closer," Ramage said as the man stopped a couple of paces away. Then, as he shuffled forward a step, Ramage's knife curving towards him flashed briefly in the lantern light and several people gasped and Sarah dropped the now empty bucket with a crash and tried to muffle a scream.

The *matelot* swayed, vacant expression on his face, waiting for the pain to start, and everyone expected blood to spurt because clearly Ramage's knife had just eviscerated the man.

Instead his trousers fell down in a heap round his ankles.

"Next time it won't be your trousers," Ramage said. "Now, where are the keys to free the prisoners?"

The sailor stood, speechless and paralysed by fear.

Ramage prodded him with the pistol, forcing him to take a step back. The man had enough presence of mind to step out of his trousers and Sarah picked them up, checked if they had a pocket, and finding they had not, walked to the ship's side and threw them into the sea.

"It doesn't make up for my torn dress," she said to no one in particular, "but it is very satisfying!"

Auguste had taken command of his brother, Louis and Gilbert, and had them lined up with the muskets covering the other *matelots*. Auguste picked up the lantern and then, as an afterthought, put it down again, took the big bottle of rum and tossed it over the bulwark. "Madame has the right idea," he said, "no one gets fighting drunk without spirits to drink and," he added slyly, "no man is a hero without his trousers."

With that he took out his knife and cut the belts of the other three *matelots*, leaving them standing with their trousers round their ankles. "Forgive me, madame," he said to Sarah, "but I am following your husband's example."

"I am a married woman," she said demurely.

"What a wife," one of the *matelots* muttered. "She uses a pistol like a filleting knife."

"I need another lantern," Ramage said to Gilbert. "Will you get ours up from the boat? Take Louis with you and bring the cutlasses too. This fellow," he tapped the sailor on the head with the flat of the knife, "will suffer if his friends misbehave while you are gone."

As soon as Gilbert and Louis returned with the lantern and cutlasses, Ramage commented: "Time is short: that shot may bring over inquisitive people." To the trouserless seaman, who seemed to be the senior of the survivors, he said: "Now we free the British prisoners. If you want to live to an old age, you will help."

The *matelot* haltingly explained that the irons had only four bars running through them, secured by four padlocks, and the four keys were on a hook in the cabin the bosun had been using. Suddenly Ramage remembered the other two guards. Where were they?

Ramage sent Gilbert with his lantern down the companionway into the gunroom ahead of the *matelot* and himself. The lantern lit the steps and showed the *matelot's* movements clearly. Since the stroke that had cut his belt and lost him his trousers, it was clear that the man feared the blade more than the pistol, which surprised Ramage. Perhaps the wretched *matelot's* imagination conjured up a more horrifying picture of what a knife could do to a man walking about clad only in a thick woollen jersey and a pair of felt shoes obviously cobbled up by a clumsy sailmaker.

The sailor pointed to the second lieutenant's cabin and followed Gilbert into it. The two men took up all the space and Ramage stood at the doorway, with the point of the knife just resting on the base of the *matelot's* spine, so that he moved slowly and very obviously kept clear of Gilbert and the lantern.

Finally he reached round very slowly, offering four large keys to Ramage, like an acolyte at communion. "These are the ones, sir."

"You carry them. Call to the other two guards and warn them

to put their weapons down, or you'll die. Now we go and undo those padlocks."

The next cabin was empty. "The captain was here," the matelot said hastily, "but he was so ill they took him to the hospital yesterday."

Ramage felt a surge of relief. He had not looked forward to interviewing a captain who drove his crew to mutiny, whatever his state of health.

The two guards were collapsed in a drunken stupor and the prisoners were lying at the fore end of the lower deck. Iron rings protruded from the deck so that metal rods through leg irons needed only a padlock at one end—the other was too bulbous to pass through the eye—to secure each of the four rows of men. They all looked up, and although blinking and squinting in the lantern light, all were wide awake, obviously roused by the pistol shot.

Ramage decided it would be easier to ensure their attention if he left them prone on the deck for a few more minutes so he waved the *matelot* to one side, telling him to be ready.

"Gentlemen," Ramage said loudly. "I am Captain Ramage, of the King's Service. I spoke to one of your lieutenants while delivering potatoes—ah," he pointed, "it was you. Very well, in a few minutes you will all be free. I have this fellow here and three other French seamen on deck as prisoners and the bosun is dead—you heard the shot. But listen carefully: in addition to this man"—he gestured towards Gilbert—"there are three other Frenchmen up there, dressed in fishermen's clothes. Two of them do not speak English but all three are responsible for your rescue. So be very careful.

"I shall put the six French guards in the open boat we came out in, and cast them adrift so that they can row into Brest Harbour with one oar and report what's happened. That will save us guarding prisoners, and there's been enough killing for tonight."

There was some murmuring from three men who Ramage guessed were the lieutenants and the master. Very well, he would deal with them in a moment.

"The guards will report that the *Murex* has been recaptured by the English and sailed. Anyway that will be obvious to anyone standing on the beach. So, within ten minutes at the most of those irons being unlocked, I want this ship tacking down the Gullet under topsails. We'll let the anchor cable run to save time.

"Two more things. My wife is on deck." He then let a hard note come into his voice. "Any orders I give will not be questioned. I have taken command of this ship. I do not have my commission but it is dated September 1797. Nor do I have orders from the Admiralty, but anyone doubting my authority can go off in the boat with the French guards and become a prisoner of war."

C H A P T E R S E V E N

THE DESCRIPTION of him dressed in a French fisherman's smock and trousers, and standing on the quarterdeck of one of the King's ships with his wife beside him wearing a badly torn dress cobbled up with sailmaker's thread, would soon, Ramage mused, be another story added to the fund of bizarre yarns which already seemed to surround him.

At least a westerly gale was not screaming over the ebb tide and kicking up the hideous sea for which Brest Roads were notorious; at least the stars were out and the moon had risen. And if there had been no war, he would regard this as the start of a pleasant voyage. But now in an instant it could all turn out very difficult. If one of those anchored French ships opened fire and the three forts lining the cliffs along the Gullet followed suit, then in this light wind the *Murex* would be battered . . .

He picked up the speaking-trumpet and the coppery smell seemed to complete the series of memories taking him back to the *Calypso,* to the *Triton,* and then to the *Kathleen.*

"Let that cable run, Mr Phillips . . . Foretopmen there: let fall the foretopsail . . . Stand by, maintopmen!"

Strange orders, but ones carefully phrased because he had so few seamen. That delivery of potatoes had saved him—knowing how many men he would have available to handle the ship had allowed him to work out a rough general quarter, watch and station bill for two lieutenants, master and eleven seamen.

And what a bill! Seven sail-handlers: four seamen for letting fall the foretopsail, three for loosing the maintopsail. Then the foretopmen had to slide down swiftly from aloft to haul on the halyards, and as soon as the yard was up, they had to hoist the jibs and staysails. The maintopmen in turn had to race down to tend their own halyard and then help the four remaining seamen who were to haul on sheets and braces to trim the yards and sails.

Of those four, two would have been helping the second lieutenant, Bridges, to let the anchor cable run . . . The master, Phillips, would be on the fo'c's'le, making sure that the cable ran out through the hawse without snagging, and the headsails and their sheets did not wrap round things in that tenacious embrace so beloved of moving ropes. And he wondered if Swan, the young first lieutenant who was now waiting at the wheel, could remember how to box the compass in quarterpoints! It was something he would have known when he took his examination for lieutenant and, having passed, would have forgotten it . . .

Damnation, this wind was light . . . Better not too strong with such a tiny crew, but he needed enough breeze to get those topsails drawing and give him steerage-way over the ebbing tide—by the time the *Murex* was drawing level with Pointe St Mathieu he would have dodged enough rocks and reefs to sink a fleet. The first of them was just abreast Fort de Delec, the dark walls of which he could already see perched up on the cliff on his starboard hand.

Ah! At last the foretopsail tumbled down as the men slashed the gaskets. He had made sure they had knives (it meant raiding the galley) to save valuable time: untying knotted gaskets (it was sure to be the last one that jammed) could cost three or four minutes.

Two men were coming down hand over hand along the forestay! The other two were coming down the usual way, using the shrouds. A puff of wind caught the sail so that it flapped like a woman shaking a damp sheet. To Ramage's ears, by now abnormally sensitive to noise, it seemed every ship in the anchorage must hear the *Murex*'s foretopsail sounding like a ragged broadside.

Now the maintopsail flopped down with the elegant casualness of canvas in light airs.

A rapid thumping, as though a great snake was escaping from a box, ended with a splash and a cheerful hail from Phillips: "Cable away, sir!"

"Very well, Mr Phillips," Ramage called through the trumpet and warned Swan at the wheel, "Be ready to meet her—the bow will pay off to starboard but for the moment the ebb has got her!"

The brig, with her bow now heading north as though she wanted to sail up the Penfeld river and into Brest, was in fact being swept sideways by the ebb down the Gullet towards the wide entrance, a dozen miles away and stretching five miles or so between Pointe St Mathieu on the starboard side and the Camaret peninsula to larboard.

The seamen were like ants at the base of each mast. Up, up, up! The heavy foretopsail yard inched its way upwards on the halyard and then a bellowed order saw it settle and the sheets tautening, giving shape to the sail.

The wind was still west; the feathers on the string of corks forming the telltale on the larboard side reassured him about that as they bobbed in the moonlight.

"I can feel some weight on the wheel now, sir," Swan reported, as Ramage saw the maintopsail yard begin its slow rise up the mast. Damnation take the foretopmen, they had to make haste with those headsails: brigs were the devil to tack without jibs and staysail drawing, and already the *Murex* was gathering way as though she wanted to run up on the rocks in front of the château.

Ramage lifted the speaking-trumpet. He had to make them get a move on without frightening them into making silly mistakes.

"Foretopsail sheet men—aft those sheets! Brace men—brace sharp up!" Strangely-worded orders, but he had no afterguard.

Now he could see the sail outlined against the stars and it was setting perfectly, and Swan was cautiously turning the wheel a few more spokes.

"Maintopsail sheet men, are you ready? Take the strain—now, run it aft! Another six feet! Heave now, heave. Fight, belay that! Now, you men at the braces, sharp up!"

The flying jib, jib and staysail were crawling up their stays —with this light breeze and their canvas blanketed by the foretopsail, three of the four seamen were hauling a halyard each . . .

"Amidships there! Hands to the headsail sheets . . . Take the strain . . ." He watched as the sails slowed down and then stopped their climb up the stays. "Right, aft those headsail sheets . . . Foretopmen, pass them the word because I can't see a stitch of the canvas from here!"

Cheerful shouts from forward and the moonlight showing the topsails taking up gentle curves indicated that his unorthodox method of getting under way and passing sail orders to a handful of seamen, all of whom would normally be doing just one of those jobs, was working.

"Don't pinch her, Mr Swan," Ramage warned the first lieutenant. "Just keep her moving fast, and then we'll have control. We'll have to put in a few dozen tacks before you put the helm down for Plymouth."

Ramage paused and wiped the mouthpiece of the speaking-trumpet, which was green with verdigris.

"You nearly ran down the *matelots* in the fishing-boat as you were setting the maintopsail," Sarah said. "They hadn't made much progress."

"I didn't hear you reporting," Ramage teased.

"No, you didn't," she said shortly. "I didn't start the Revolution or the war."

"Remind me to tell you how much I am enjoying our honeymoon, but first we must tack."

And, he thought to himself, if the *Murex* hangs in irons we'll drift on to the rocks on the headland in front of the arsenal and opposite the château: the current sets strongly across them on the ebb.

A quick word to Swan had the wheel turning, and he could hear the creak of rudder pintles working on the gudgeons, an indication of a quiet night.

Then he gave a series of shouted commands to the men at sheets and braces and slowly (too slowly it seemed at first, convincing him he had left it too late) the *Murex*'s bow began to swing to larboard, into the wind . . .

"Not too much helm, Mr Swan, you're supposed to be turning her, not stopping her . . ." A first lieutenant should know that. Now the jibs and staysail were flapping across.

"Headsail sheets, there!"

The men knew what to do; that much was obvious in the way the sails had been set. So now he need give only brief orders, which took care of the trimming.

"Braces! Altogether now, haul! Now the sheets!"

A glance ahead showed the brig now steady on the other tack.

"Mr Swan," Ramage said quietly, walking over to the wheel, "I think you can get another point or two to windward . . ."

He watched the luff of the mainsail and then the leech.

"And another couple of spokes?"

Swan turned the wheel two more spokes but his movement lacked certainty: he was clearly nervous.

"Come now, Mr Swan," Ramage said, a sharper note in his voice. "I don't expect to have to give the first lieutenant compass courses to steer to windward. Now look'ee, you can lay the Pointe des Espagnols—that's the headland on your larboard bow."

With that he turned away and said to Sarah, "Can you see *L'Espoir* over there at anchor? I think she's gone: sailed while we were having our trouble with the bosun."

She turned and looked over the larboard quarter at all the ships moonlit against the black line of low cliffs with the town of Plougastel in the distance. Unused to allowing for a change in bearings she took two or three minutes before finally reporting: "No, she's not there. But she can only be . . ."

"Yes," Ramage said, "half an hour or so," and noted it was time to tack again: the brig was moving along well and the ebb was helping hurry them seaward. He went over to Swan and gave him the new heading for when they had gone about.

"Follow the cliff along from Brest. You see the village of Portzic? Now, just beyond that next headland—you see the building? That's Fort de Delec. You should be able to lay it, but if a messenger has reached them they'll open fire. And just beyond, on top of the cliff, is the Lion Battery. If the fort and battery begin firing at us, we'll tack over to the other side."

There was no need to tell Swan that on the other tack they would be heading for the Cornouaille Battery on the Camaret peninsula, and if the fire from that became hot enough to force them to tack north-westward again back to the Pointe St Mathieu side, they would be steering for the next fort, at Mengam, with three isolated and large rocks also waiting in the fairway for them . . .

The *Murex* went about perfectly: the headsails slapped across as the bow came round and were swiftly sheeted in; both topsails were braced sharp up on the larboard tack; Swan moved the wheel back and forth three or four spokes and then reported: "I can lay a bit to windward of the Lion Battery, sir."

Already the château was dropping astern fast and Ramage watched the irregular shape of Fort de Delec. Distance was always hard to estimate in the darkness, but a mile? At night an object usually seemed closer—so to the French gunners the *Murex* would seem to be just within range. Just? Well within range, and Sarah murmured: "I imagine Frenchmen staring along the barrels of guns . . ."

It seemed to be tempting fate to make a reassuring comment, and anyway she was not frightened. "If they're going to open fire, it'll be in the next two or three minutes," he said.

She held his arm in an unexpected gesture, and he was startled to find she was trembling. "Will it look bad if I go below if they start shooting?"

He gripped her hand. "Of course not. But it will be more frightening."

"*More* frightening? I don't understand."

"Dearest, if you stay on deck and see where the shot fall, you'll see there's no danger. If you go below you'll be waiting for the next shot to come through the deck and knock your head off!"

"I feel cold and shaky all of a sudden," she said. "Not frightened exactly. Apprehensive, perhaps."

"When you shoot a man with a pistol you usually feel shaky afterwards," Ramage said dryly, and added: "I feel cold and shaky every time after I've been in action. I think everyone does."

He looked up at Fort de Delec again. He felt he could see down the muzzles of the guns. Yes, there was the straight line of the walls; there were the embrasures. The moon had risen high enough now that he knew he would see the antlike movement of people if the guns were being loaded and trained round. It was a confounded nuisance commanding a ship which had no nightglass and no telescopes. No log or muster book for that matter—the telescopes had presumably been looted, and all the ship's papers would have been taken away by the French authorities. And charts—well, the only relevant one he had glanced at by lantern light just before getting under way, "A Draught of the Road and Harbour of Brest with the adjacent Coast," must have been copied from a captured French one, but even then gave only one line of soundings from the town of Brest right along the Gullet, stopping as it reached the first of the three rocks, Mengam, and the man at the lead could be calling out twenty fathoms amidships as the bow hit the rock.

Another couple of minutes and they would tack again and then he wanted plenty of lookouts. With luck he would be able to leave Mengam safely to one side so that on the next tack to the north-west he could pass close to the last of the three rocks, which was in fact a small reef appropriately named Le Fillettes.

The Cornouaille Battery was silent, but that was to be expected: a boat would have to be sent over to the Camaret peninsula to raise the alarm, although they would pick it up from the other forts. This next tack would bring them within range of Fort de Mengam. Was the fort named after its silent ally in the middle of the Gullet, or the other way about?

He lifted the speaking-trumpet as Sarah murmured: "Anyone raising the alarm at these forts and batteries would use the same road we rode along that afternoon from Pointe St Mathieu."

"Now my dear, you can understand my interest in the number of guns each of them mounted."

"You didn't explain," she said.

"I'm always interested in French forts. I hardly expected we'd be sailing out in these circumstances!"

She shivered and turned to look back at the town and harbour. "No, you were hoping eventually to sail your own ship in, on some wild escapade."

"Yes," he admitted, "one never ignores a chance to learn about an enemy, but I prefer having my wife beside me!"

"You are being more polite than a new husband needs to be: I am a nuisance!"

He began shouting orders through the speaking-trumpet and once again the *Murex*'s bow swung across the eye of the wind to the south-west: once again straining men hauled at the sheets and braces to trim the topsails. If only he could set the courses as well; then with more than double the amount of canvas drawing the brig would be out of the Gullet and into the Atlantic, passing the Pointe St Mathieu to starboard and the shoals to larboard off the Camaret peninsula, like a stoat after a rabbit.

He walked up to the mainmast, partly to leave Swan on his own and help him gain a confidence which had probably been badly battered by the mutiny, and partly to place extra lookouts. He called for Auguste, Albert and Louis.

"You know the Mengam?" he asked.

"Yes, Captain, I was just coming to warn you: it is very near."

"And the one beyond, and then Les Fillettes?"

"Yes, I know them all; I have fished around them dozens of times. In fact the Mengam is fine on the bow. You—yes, you can see it. Look . . ."

He stood beside Ramage, who saw they would pass clear and instructed the three Frenchmen to watch for other rocks. He walked aft to point it out to Swan, who seemed to have benefited from being left alone at the wheel. He had more life in him; he said, in the first time he had spoken except in answer to a question: "I thought it'd be the batteries we'd be dodging, sir, not the rocks."

Ramage then remembered that the *Murex* had been brought in while it was still daylight. "You were able to watch the scenery as you came in?"

"No choice, sir: we—those who had not mutinied—were all penned up on the fo'c's'le."

"What about the mutineers?"

Swan laughed at the memory. "Well, the French who came on board drove them all below. You see, sir, I was the only person in the ship who spoke any French, so when the French boarded us and asked why we were flying a white flag, I said some of the men had 'misbehaved.'"

"So they thought we—the officers and the loyal ship's company—were bringing the ship in and handing her over, and the mutineers had been trying to stop us. So for a couple of hours or so the mutineers were knocked around—until we anchored off Brest and English-speaking Frenchmen came out!"

Ramage calculated that they would be clear of the Gullet on the next tack, and Sarah joined him as he walked forward to pick up the speaking-trumpet. As he gave the first orders for the tack which would turn the *Murex* to the north-west, Auguste came up and pointed ahead.

"Sir, Les Fillettes are ahead. You will pass clear when you tack."

"Thank you, Auguste. Ah yes, I see them."

There was no reason to point them out to Swan, who was now giving the appearance of enjoying himself. The moonlight was strong enough to give a clear picture of the deck, and as they tacked the men were quicker at freeing a rope or making it fast on cleat, kevil or belaying pin.

Now Swan was steadying the ship on the new tack as sheets and braces were trimmed, and as Ramage put the speaking-trumpet down beside one of the guns and gave a contented sigh, Sarah said: "We're almost out of this beastly river. Is that—?"

"Pointe St Mathieu? Yes. It seems a long while ago . . ."

"In some ways. Certainly, as we sat up there in the sun and looked out across here and up towards Ushant, I never expected to be sailing out of the Iroise in the dead of night. Yet"—she paused, and he was not sure if she was choosing her words carefully or deciding whether or not to say it—"yet the way you looked out at the Black Rocks, and Ushant, and across this estuary to the Camaret peninsula—you were recording it, not looking at it like a visitor. You were noting it down in the pilot book in your head, ready for use when the war started again. Our ride back to Jean-Jacques'—you were more interested in the forts and batteries than anything else!"

"No," he protested mildly, "I saw as much beauty as you did. I just made a note of the things that might be trying to kill me one day, like the guns in the batteries and forts."

"But has all that *really* helped you now—as we sail out?"

"Oh yes, although I was gambling that the commandant of the port, or the commander of the artillery, or the commander of the garrisons, would all disagree about whose responsibility it was to warn the forts."

"Do you have to gamble when you're on your honeymoon?"

He squeezed her arm. "It's better for the family fortunes to gamble with roundshot rather than dice!"

Sarah laughed and nodded. "Yes, I suppose so: if a roundshot knocks her husband's head off, at least his widow has the estate. But if he gambles at backgammon tables she has a husband with a head, but no bed to sleep in!"

Ramage stood at the taffrail of the *Murex* in the darkness and mentally drew a cross on an imaginary chart to represent the brig's position. She was now clearing the gulf of the Iroise, which stretched from the high cliffs and ruined abbey of Pointe St Mathieu over there to starboard across to the Camaret peninsula to larboard.

Ahead was the Atlantic, and the English Channel was to the north, round Ushant, which stood like a sentry off the north-western tip of France. The Bay of Biscay, with Spain and Portugal beyond, was to the south. Astern, to everyone's relief, was Brest, and about three hundred miles due east of it was Paris.

So that was it: from here, a tack out to the north-westward for the rest of the night and then dawn would reveal Ushant to the north-east, so that he could then bear away. He then had a choice: either he could run with a soldier's wind to the Channel Islands to get more men (having the advantage of a short voyage with such a small ship's company), or he could stretch north (perhaps nor-nor-east, he had not looked at the chart yet) for Falmouth or Plymouth.

The advantage of either port was that once he reported and handed over the *Murex,* he and Sarah could post to London or go over to the family home at St Kew, not far from either port. On second thoughts London would be better: their Lordships would certainly need written reports, and it would do no harm to be available when Lord St Vincent read them, concerning both his escape and the size and readiness of the French fleet in Brest, and the *Murex* episode.

Anyway, the *Murex* was now making a good six or seven

knots; the courses had been set once they were safely out in the estuary and drawing well. A couple of seamen at the wheel were keeping the ship sailing fast, with Swan occasionally peering down at one or the other of the dimly lit compasses in the binnacle, his confidence restored.

Sarah was asleep down in the captain's cabin; Ramage himself was weary but warm at last, thanks to Sarah finding a heavy cloak in the captain's cabin and bringing it up to him. Dawn was not far off and the sky was clear with the moon still bright, although there was now a chill greyness that seemed to be trying to edge aside the black of night. The *Murex* was not just butting wind waves with her weather bow and scattering them in spray that drifted across like a scotch mist, salting the lips and making the eyes sore: now she was lifting over Atlantic swells that were born somewhere out in the deep ocean.

Very well, he told himself, the time had come to make the decision so that the moment daylight revealed Ushant on the horizon, he could give Swan the new course, for Falmouth, Plymouth or the Channel Islands.

Or south-westward, to start a 4,000-mile voyage to Cayenne, without orders, without much chance of success, to try to rescue Jean-Jacques and the other fifty or so people declared enemies of the French Republic?

He walked back and forth beside the taffrail and then stood looking astern at the *Murex*'s curling wake. There was one thing in the brig's favour. One thing in *his* favour, he corrected himself (there was no point in trying to shift the responsibility on to the poor *Murex*). Yes, the one thing in his favour was that he knew he was only a few hours behind *L'Espoir*. As a frigate she was much bigger, but more important she had fifty extra people on board, all of whom had to be kept under guard. So the frigate would be carrying extra men, seamen or soldiers, to make up the guard. Twenty-five? Extra in the sense that they were in addition to the normal ship's company. Whoa, not so fast; she was armed *en flûte* so she would have only the guns on the upper deck, say half a dozen 12-pounders. And that—being armed *en flûte*—meant she needed only sufficient men to fight six or eight guns, not the thirty or so which had been removed to make room for the prisoners. Against that, the French in Brest were very short of seamen: that had been the last piece of information given out by that wretched bosun before Sarah shot him. The *Commandant de l'Armée navale de Brest* would certainly favour fighting ships at the expense of transports like *L'Espoir*.

Yet the French were in a hurry to get these prisoners on their way to Cayenne before the British re-established their standing blockade of Brest, which would otherwise have made the capture of *L'Espoir* a distinct possibility. In turn that could also mean that these fifty prisoners were of considerable importance: people that Bonaparte wanted out of France at any cost and incarcerated in Devil's Island.

So apart from the importance of Jean-Jacques—which from the Royalist point of view was considerable—what about the others? What value would the British government put on them? In other words, if Captain Ramage acting without orders attempted with a brig and a dozen or so men a task for which a fully-manned frigate would not be too much, and succeeded, what then? Pats on the head, a page in the *London Gazette*, a column or so in the next issue of the *Naval Chronicle*, the grudging but heavily-qualified approval of the First Lord.

But if Captain Ramage failed in this self-appointed role of rescuer riding a (borrowed) white horse, what then? Well, the resulting court martial would make the trial establishing his father as a scapegoat for the government look like a hunt cancelled because of heavily frozen ground. At best, Captain Ramage would spend the rest of his life on half-pay. At worst? Well, at least being cashiered with the disgrace of being "rendered incapable of further service in his Majesty's Naval Service."

Yet it really boiled down to ignoring the Admiralty. By chance he had been able to recapture a British brig from the enemy, and without his activity the *Murex* would have been added to the French Navy. That was where the chance ended. Did he owe it to Jean-Jacques to try to rescue him? A debt of honour? That was using a rather high-flown phrase, but supposing Ramage had been seized and taken off to some improbable prison, and Jean-Jacques had escaped and knew where he was? Jean-Jacques would attempt a rescue. That was all there was to it, really, although the Admiralty would certainly not agree.

To make an enormous dog-leg course to call at Plymouth to get provisions, men and water would wreck everything because it would probably mean that a couple of frigates would be sent in his place, and a vital week lost—at least a week; more if there was bad weather. It would take a couple of days to convince the port admiral at Plymouth of the importance of such a rescue and pass a message to the Admiralty (though with the new telegraph, Plymouth could send a signal to London and get a reply in a few hours), then watering and provisioning the frigates would take another day or so . . . By the time they were clear of the Chops of the Channel (and perhaps driven back by a westerly storm or gale) *L'Espoir* would be a third of the way to Cayenne; a third of the way to the Île du Diable. At this moment, though, the *Murex* brig was only a matter of hours behind her. Yet without enough men to do any good and perhaps short of provisions and water. But no more than fifty miles . . . If *L'Espoir* had careless or apathetic officers of the deck, poorly set sails and inattentive men at the wheel, plus the feeling that once clear of Brest they were safe from the Royal Navy, the smaller *Murex,* sailed hard, would be able to make up the gap.

"I'm going below for half an hour," he told Swan. "Report when you can see Ushant."

Sarah was awake, unused to the swinging cot, which was little more than a large hammock with a shallow, open-topped frame fitted in it, like a box in a net bag.

"I preferred going to and from India," she said teasingly. "A proper bed is more comfortable."

"You wait until there's rough weather. Going to windward in a blow and that cot will swing comfortably, while a fixed bed tosses you out."

"How do I get out of it, anyway?"

"You don't; you're marooned!"

"Do you want to get some sleep?" she offered, sitting up with her tawny hair tousled, naked because she had only the clothes she had worn in the fishing-boat. The lantern light seemed to gild her and he turned away quickly, reassuring her and telling her to stay in the cot. Stay in the cot, he thought to himself, or the captain will not concentrate on his charts . . .

He put the lantern on the hook in the beam just forward of the desk. The charts were rolled and stowed vertically in a rack fitted on one side of the desk. Checking what charts were there meant removing each one and partly unrolling it. He sat at the desk and made a start. English Channel, western section, including the Scilly Islands; English Channel, eastern section, including the mouth of the Thames and the Medway. North Sea . . . in four sections. Ireland, the southern half. The Channel Islands. St Malo to Ouessant (the French spelling and the detail showed it was probably copied from a captured one). Ushant to Brest and south to Douarnenez . . . Those were probably the charts for her last patrol . . . Half a dozen more left. North Atlantic, southern section . . .

Ramage unrolled it. It covered from the south-western corner of Spain to the eastern side of the West Indian islands, and down to the Equator, yet giving very little detail of the South American coast. There was Trinidad—which anyway could be identified by its shape. No reference to Cayenne, though; it must be about there, just a kink in the ink line of the coast, north of Brazil.

He looked at the remaining charts. A French one of the islands of St Barthélemy, St Martin (with the southern half owned by the Dutch and given its Dutch name, St Maarten), Anguilla and well to the north, just a speck, Sombrero. Then another two of the group just to the southward, Nevis and St Christopher. And two more, St Eustatius and Saba. A detailed chart of Plymouth . . . and Falmouth . . . and, finally, the Texel, showing the north-western corner of the Netherlands.

All in all, Ramage thought wryly, he was no better off than he would be with a blank sheet of paper and his memory; in fact he was going to have to draw up a chart or two for himself. For the moment, though, he had to try to put himself in the French captain's place.

When sailing from Europe to the West Indies or the northern part of South America, the trick was to pick up the Trade winds as soon as possible without getting becalmed in the Doldrums. Which meant sailing where you could be reasonably sure of finding steady winds. Every captain and every master had his own invisible signpost in the Atlantic; a sign which said "Turn south-west here; this is where the north-east Trade winds begin."

For Ramage it was 25° North latitude, 25° West longitude. And—he took a pencil from the desk drawer and a crumpled sheet of paper which he smoothed out enough to make it usable.

According to the copied French chart, St Louis church in the centre of Brest, just north of the château, was 48° 23' 22" North, 4° 29' 27" West. That, within a mile, was where *L'Espoir* had sailed from, and she was bound first to the magic spot, 25° North, 25° West. Which . . . was . . . about . . . yes, roughly seventeen hundred miles to the south-south-west.

Then, from the magic point it was to Cayenne . . . about . . .

another two thousand miles, steering south-west-by-west. Say four thousand miles altogether, and let no one think that steering south-west-by-west from the magic point would bring him or his ship to Cayenne: he would probably start running out of the Trades by the time he reached 12° North; from then on he would be trying to fight his way south against a foul current which ran north-west along the coast of Brazil. Caught in the right place, it helped; but if the wind played about, whiffling round the compass (which it could do in those latitudes) then the current would sweep the helpless ship up towards the islands—towards Barbados, for example, where the British commander-in-chief was probably lying at anchor in Carlisle Bay.

Ramage looked at his brief calculations again and then screwed them up.

Sarah asked: "When do you think we shall be in Plymouth if this weather holds, dearest?"

"In about three months."

"No, seriously. Our families will be worrying."

"I expect the Rockleys will be worrying about you, but mine will make a wrong guess and give a sigh of relief that I am safely locked up in a French prison while they will expect you to be lodging with a respectable French family."

"Is that how it would have been, normally?"

He shrugged his shoulders. "I should think so. Anyway, my parents will not be worrying, and I'm sure as soon as they get the word they will be calling on your people."

"But we'll be back in London before then, won't we?"

He was sure she suspected the idea that was popping in and out of his mind like an importunate beggar.

She said, in a flat voice: "It would be madness to go after *L'Espoir*. You'll lose the *Murex* and everyone on board. A scout's job is to raise the alarm, dearest. Losing everything won't help Jean-Jacques, but getting help will . . ."

He nodded and was startled when she said: "You took so long to make up your mind."

She was making it easier for him, and he took the opportunity as gracefully as possible. "I needed to give it a lot of thought."

She sat up in the cot, swung her legs out on to the deck and holding one end firmly stood up. She walked over to him and, standing to one side, gently held his head against her naked body. "You had two choices, dearest, Cayenne or Plymouth. Two choices. But you know as well as I do there was really only one that you could take."

"Yes, but . . ."

"But in the same circumstances another captain would have had only one choice: he would have gone to Plymouth!"

He nuzzled against her, his unshaven face rasping slightly on her warm skin, his chin pressing gently against her breasts. "I suppose most other captains wouldn't have to choose because they do not usually meet people like Jean-Jacques."

CHAPTER EIGHT

RAMAGE had just gone on deck after Swan called that they could now sight Ushant, and the deck lookouts had been sent aloft when both men heard the hail.

"Deck here!"

"Foremast lookout, sir: sail ho! Two sail!"

"Where away?"

"Two points on the starboard bow, sir, frigates I reckon."

"Very well, keep a sharp lookout."

Swan turned to Ramage, saw that he was already looking over the bow, and heard him cursing. "Those blasted mutineers— I wish they'd left us the bring-'em-near. Even a nightglass!"

"They must have spotted us ten minutes ago, probably more. They'll recognize the rig . . ."

"And guess we're the *Murex*—perhaps sailing under the French flag?"

Ramage shook his head. News did not travel that fast. "I doubt if the Admiralty yet know anything about the mutiny. In a day or two they'll read about it in the *Moniteur:* half a page of French bombast about oppressed English seamen fighting for their *liberté, fraternité* and *égalité.*"

"Yes," Swan said bitterly, "at the price of treason and making sure that fifteen of their shipmates go into a French prison."

"That's what is meant by *fraternité,*" Ramage said laconically.

"That western-most frigate has tacked," commented Phillips, who had come on deck when he heard the hail.

"And the other one is bearing away a point or so," Ramage noted. "They're taking no chances. If we try to make a bolt for it, one can catch us to windward and the other to leeward."

"But they recognize our rig," Swan protested. "The French don't have any brigs like this one!"

"They had one briefly, until last night," Ramage said. "Remember, in wartime all sails are hostile until they prove themselves otherwise. I presume we still have a set of signal flags."

"Yes, sir," Swan said and took the hint. "I'll have our pendant numbers bent on ready."

"Deck there!" Once again the lookout was shouting from the masthead, the pitch of his voice rising with excitement.

"Deck here," Swan called back.

"More sail, sir, just beyond those frigates. Must be a couple of dozen, I reckon, and some of them 74s and bigger."

"Count 'em, blast it!" Swan shouted. "Divide 'em up and count 'em."

Ramage counted the days since the declaration of war. Yes, it might be. Indeed, if there were ships of the line it had to be, so there would be an admiral, which meant so much explaining to be done; so much persuading to be done.

"Deck there, foremasthead here . . . I'm counting as we lift up on the swell waves, sir . . . Looks like at least six o' the line—one of 'em bigger'n a 74 and seven frigates, including the first two."

"Very well," Swan said. "Report if you sight more." He turned to Ramage. "Well, sir, can't be French and I don't think they're Spanish."

"No, it'll be the Channel Fleet coming out to blockade Brest again . . . Well, they've had eighteen months' rest, but winter will soon be here."

Phillips gave a dry laugh. "The equinoctial gales will be along . . . then they'll dream of being 'Close up with the Black Rocks with an easterly wind'!"

Both Ramage and Swan laughed, but both were thankful they were not serving in the blockading fleet. The Black Rocks . . . The description really stood for the twenty-five or thirty miles from the island of Ushant in the north to the Île de Sein in the south and, covering the entrance to Brest rather than the Rocks themselves, must make up the most iron-bound coast in the world: for almost every day of the year it was a lee shore wide open to the full fury of the Atlantic.

Yet by a quirk of nature the ships of the Royal Navy, forced to blockade Brest, were fortunate. The French fleet could leave Brest only with an easterly wind. A strong wind with much west in it left them unable to beat out of the Gullet and meant that they were also blockaded by nature.

The blockading British fleet's line-of-battle ships could stay twenty, thirty or even forty miles out to sea, so that they had plenty of room when the westerly Atlantic gales turned into storms lasting a week . . . A captain with his ship under storm canvas could pull down his newly-tarred sou'wester and curse that he had ever chosen the navy, but apart from keeping station on the admiral if possible (it never was in a full storm) it was more miserable than dangerous.

As a precaution a line of frigates, each within sight of the other, linked the fleet with the French coast. But with west in the wind the admiral could be sure that nature was his ally, keeping the French penned in. France was in fact unlucky because the perfidious English had along their Channel coast large and sheltered harbours which they could enter whatever the weather—Plymouth, Dartmouth, Falmouth, Portsmouth and the area inside the Isle of Wight, Dover and the Thames estuary.

The French were plagued with much higher tides and all their main Channel harbours—Calais, Havre de Grâce, Cherbourg and Boulogne—were artificial. The first of any size which was natural was Brest—which, as the Admiralty stated it—was "outside Channel limits."

So a west wind kept the French penned in; but the situation changed immediately the wind-vane on the church of St Louis de Brest swung round: an east wind tried to blow the blockading Royal Navy out to sea and gave the French a fair wind for slipping out of the Gullet while the blockaders beat back again to close the door.

Indeed, as Ramage knew from experience, that is why the blockading fleet had the frigates—as soon as the wind turned east the British frigates moved close up to the Black Rocks: close in with the Black Rocks, a couple of miles seaward of Pointe St Mathieu. They were, he reflected, a suitable name for rocks when you were commanding a frigate on a dark night in an easterly gale and peering with salt-sore and weary eyes for a sight of the white collars of breaking seas that would enable you to give hasty helm and sail orders to save the ship.

"Close up with the Black Rocks with an easterly wind"— words written on most midshipmen's hearts, and worthy of being carved on many a captain's tombstone, Ramage thought wryly. Still, it was worse for the admirals—they might have to spend a couple of years out here, shifting their flag from ship to ship while captains and seamen had a brief rest when they returned to Plymouth for water, provisions or repairs. The wear and tear on masts, spars and cordage keeping a close blockade off somewhere like Brest was beyond belief.

With her courses furled, the *Murex* was lying hove-to, her backed foretopsail trying to push her bow one way and maintopsail to turn it the other and the pair of them leaving the brig in a state of equilibrium, rising and falling on the swell waves like a resting seagull.

"The cutter is ready to be hoisted out, sir," Swan reported. "Two of the Frenchmen, seeing how short-handed we are, volunteered as boat's crew. Six men should be enough in this wind and sea."

Ramage nodded. "Someone is standing by to help Bridges with the flags?"

"Yes, sir."

"And you can guess what the first signal will be."

"I think so, sir," Swan said with a grin.

The two frigates, one approaching from the north and the other from the north-east, were a fine sight: both had all plain sail set to the royals and Ramage guessed the one to the north-east was commanded by the senior of the two captains—the other was deliberately letting her reach the brig first.

Sarah, standing beside him and wearing her hastily repaired dress, said quietly as she watched the frigates: "Should I go below, out of sight?"

"Most certainly not!" Ramage said. "I'm anxious to show off my new bride! No," he added, "we have no signal book and very few men, so we want these fellows to guess at once that something's wrong. We don't want them to rush past hoisting a string of flag signals giving silly orders we can't read."

"Can they give you orders?"

"Yes, if they are senior. If they were made post before me, in other words."

"If their names are above yours in the *List of the Navy?* How will you know that, without looking them up in Mr Swan's copy as soon as you are introduced?"

Ramage grinned complacently. "I know the names of the thirty or so lieutenants who were above me in my year, and all those in the two preceding years, so it's not too difficult!"

"What do you think will happen now? I was just beginning to look forward to the idea of getting back to London."

"I don't know. It might be difficult to persuade the admiral that fifty French Royalists being transported have any importance."

"Who will the admiral be?"

"I don't know. Lord St Vincent commanded the Channel Fleet until the change of government saw him made First Lord. Now the war has started again, who knows . . ."

"Perhaps Lord Nelson. You know him, so it shouldn't be too difficult . . ."

"Perhaps, but I doubt it. After Copenhagen, I don't think the public—which means the politicians—would want to see him doing blockade duty. You don't have to be a brilliant tactician to blockade Brest."

"No, but you need to be a brilliant tactician if the French fleet sails from Brest and you have to stop it!"

She was sharp-witted and wide awake. Ramage had to admit that, and said: "You're right, and from what we saw in Brest, that admiral over there"—he nodded towards the British ships of the line beating up towards Ushant—"will have to stay awake."

The French coast was beginning to drop below the horizon:

the coast of gaunt, high cliffs was now little more than a thick pencil line on the eastern horizon.

Sarah gestured towards it: "I think our honeymoon is officially at an end now. Have you enjoyed it, dearest?"

"If honeymoons are always as exciting as this, I think I will get married more often!"

She wrinkled her nose at him. "I didn't care much for the company, but I enjoyed seeing France."

"Ah, yes, the French way of life. One of the most complex of life's puzzles: how can such selfish people create such an interesting atmosphere? It must be a quirk of the weather," he added teasingly. "Take away the wine and the cheese and what do you have left?"

"Lots of *gendarmes* at the *barrières!*"

Swan coughed as he approached. "The easternmost frigate, sir: she's hoisted the Union at the mizen topmasthead and our pendant."

"Very well, acknowledge and hoist out the cutter."

"Aye, aye, sir." Swan paused a moment, looking embarrassed.

"Well?" Ramage said, eyebrows raised. "Say it!"

"I was wondering, sir, if you'd sooner wear breeches—I have a spare pair left which would fit."

"No—they'll have to put up with a *sans-culottes*. They're good French fisherman's trousers, and this smock—why it smells more of potatoes than fish!"

A slatting of canvas made Ramage glance up to see the frigate tacking to the north-west. He guessed she would stand on for a mile or so, tack again until she was half a mile to windward of the *Murex,* and then heave-to.

"They've not heard about the mutiny," Ramage said loudly and both Swan and Sarah swung round.

"They haven't, sir? How can you be sure?"

"Guns," Ramage said laconically. "Neither ship has her guns

run out. Not the way you'd approach a mutinous ship."

And probably all her captain wants to know, so he can make a signal to the admiral and show that he is awake, is what ships we have sighted recently in the area, because we look as though we are on a regular patrol.

The *Murex*'s cutter was hoisted out, Ramage was on board and the men bending their backs to the oars by the time the frigate had hove-to. At the last moment Swan had shouted down that she was the *Blanche;* that the lookout had been able to read her name on her transom and one of the seamen had recognized her.

Fifteen minutes later the cutter was alongside; the *Blanche*'s seamen caught the painter the first time it was thrown (by Auguste, Ramage noted) but missed the sternfast, but even before the officer of the deck began shouting Ramage had jumped for the battens and was scrambling up the side.

At the top, the moment he stepped on deck, a lieutenant stood in front of him.

"Stand aside, blast you: your captain is the first up!"

The senior officer was always the last in and the first out of a boat, and instead of the expected young lieutenant falling over his sword and with his hat awry, here was a man dressed more like a fisherman!

"I am the captain," Ramage said quietly. "Before you—"

"Master-at-arms!" roared the lieutenant, "get this man out of my way!"

"—before you make a fool of yourself, Lieutenant," Ramage repeated without changing the tone of his voice, "I suggest you listen because I shan't tell you twice."

The lieutenant, tall and plump but with a weak mouth and chin hinting at self-indulgence, paused a moment and for the first time looked at Ramage's face. The deep-set eyes, the slightly hooked nose, the thick eyebrows . . .

"Who the hell are *you?*" he demanded.

Ramage realized that this must be the frigate's first lieutenant, and the captain would be down in his cabin.

"Most of the ship's company of that brig mutinied last week and ran her into Brest. I and a few others recaptured her and sailed her out last night. Now, either fetch your captain or take me to him."

"And who the devil do you think *you* are, to give *me* orders."

"My name is Ramage."

"Well, you can dam' well—Ramage? Lord Ramage?"

The man in fisherman's clothes just nodded his head.

"Oh my God, sir, I had no way—"

"I know that. Your captain . . . ?"

"Of course, sir, at once."

"Who is he?"

"Captain Wells, sir. Captain John Wells."

The man then ran the few steps to the companion-way, watched open-mouthed by the *Blanche*'s master and a lieutenant of Marines, who stood too far away to hear the conversation but had seen their first lieutenant move like a recoiling gun.

Wells . . . John Wells. No, that name was not in the last list of post captains that Ramage had seen, so he must have been made post after Ramage and therefore was junior to him. That was one hurdle cleared; there was nothing like a little seniority . . . And it probably meant that he was senior to the other frigate captain, too. It should not be too difficult to get a dozen men to help sail the *Murex.*

"If you'll come this way, sir . . ."

The lieutenant combined nervousness, doubt, uncertainty and embarrassment into an interesting melange which manifested itself in him taking off his hat, turning it round completely, and putting it on again.

"You did say 'Lord Ramage,' didn't you, sir?"

"You said 'Lord': I merely said 'Ramage.' I don't use my title in the Service."

"No, quite, sir: I remember in the *Gazette* . . . It is simply that we did not expect . . ."

Ramage turned aft towards the companion-way, feeling smug at his self-control: the temptation of pointing at the unmanned guns and closed ports had been almost irresistible.

Captain Wells had been given post rank late in life: Ramage guessed he was well past fifty, and like his first lieutenant he was plump, and what would have otherwise been a pleasant face with sandy eyebrows was spoiled by eyes too close together.

Now he stood at the bottom of the companion-way staring up at the apparent fisherman coming down the steps with all the assurance of a Gascon. Not, Ramage thought to himself, that Captain Wells would know the meaning of "Gasconade" or its derivation. Nor did Wells know how he was going to get any proof of the extraordinary story that the first lieutenant had just gabbled out.

Wells gave himself time by saying: "Won't you come in?"

Ramage remembered that his own cabin, couch and sleeping place in the *Calypso* frigate were larger: the French allowed their captains more room.

Wells gestured towards the single armchair and while Ramage sat down, seated himself at the desk and began taking the cap from an ink bottle.

"Ah . . . well now, perhaps you had better report to me in your own words and if you'll speak slowly, I'll write—"

"No reports, written or otherwise, to anyone except the commander-in-chief," Ramage said flatly. "My name is Ramage, and I do not have my commission but you can confirm the date from your copy of Steel's List, which I see you have on your desk. I was in France on my honeymoon—you have no doubt seen my wife on the *Murex*'s quarterdeck—when the war started again.

We escaped arrest, saw the *Murex* being brought in with a French escort and discovered that most of her ship's company had mutinied. The officers and a dozen or so loyal seamen were left on board and my wife and I"—Ramage decided Gilbert and the others would forgive the exaggeration—"with the help of four Frenchmen overpowered the guards, freed our men, and sailed the ship out of Brest. Then you came along."

"But look here, I've no proof—"

"You don't need any, Wells," Ramage snapped. "Send a dozen of your men over to help those poor souls sail the *Murex*, and make a signal to the admiral. You'll have fun with the Signal Book. I don't recall anything which quite covers this situation."

"But Ramage, I can't—"

"Tell the admiral why you can't, Wells, but I'll tell you just one more thing, after which I want a dozen topmen sending down to my cutter and I'll be off to join the fleet. Time, Wells, hours and minutes rather than days: I am desperate to save time." With that Ramage was out through the door and halfway up the companion-way before Wells had time to draw a breath.

He was calling to the first lieutenant to have his boat ready when Wells came up the companion-way, took one more look (a despairing look, it seemed to Ramage) and seeing his first lieutenant busy, called to the master to send a dozen topmen down into the boat without waiting for them to collect their gear.

"You *will* let me have them back?" he called after Ramage, as anxious as any captain to keep prime seamen.

"Yes—as soon as we're hove-to near the flagship. You can escort us down there!"

CHAPTER NINE

REGINALD Edward Clinton, knight, vice-admiral of the blue, was a bachelor and, Ramage decided at first sight, every child's idea of what Father Christmas should look like. He was plump and round-faced, the red complexion contrasting with a pair of startlingly blue eyes, which rarely moved. The admiral had a habit of swivelling his whole head when he wanted to shift his gaze. The effect, Ramage decided, was like aiming a gun.

But Admiral Clinton was decisive. He listened to Ramage's story without interruption and then asked a series of questions, starting with those referring to the beginning of Ramage's visit to France and ending with a request for the numbers and rates of the French ships anchored in Brest. After writing down the figures and the state of readiness of each of them, he put the cap back on the inkwell, wiped the tip of his quill pen with a piece of cloth and said casually: "You captured and then commanded the *Calypso,* didn't you?"

"Yes, sir. I still do—or did. She was being paid off and laid up at Chatham when I went on leave."

"Hmm. Well, she wasn't actually paid off—the war was started again. In fact I have her with me. Commanded by a fellow called Bullivant."

"Edward Bullivant, sir, son of the Navy Board contractor?"

"The same one," the admiral said, his voice flat. "What sort of officers did you have?"

"Not one I would change—indeed, sir, not one I would ever want to exchange."

"Master?"

"A man called Southwick. He'd been with me from the time I was given my first command."

"And the surgeon?" Clinton asked casually.

"A brilliant man. Used to have a practice in Wimpole Street."

"Oh? Then why is he now simply a surgeon in a frigate?"

"Drink, sir. Lost all his patients. Came to sea."

"That explains it all," Clinton said, obviously relieved.

Ramage quickly decided to risk a snub. "May I ask what it explains, sir?"

"Well, had a dam' strange signal from her at daybreak. Number 215 over her own pendant."

Ramage thought for several moments. There were more than four hundred numbered signals in the book and 215 was not one he had ever seen hoisted or heard anyone refer to.

Clinton said: "Number 215 means: *The physician of the Fleet is to come to the Admiral.* But hoisted over the *Calypso*'s pendant numbers I assume she is trying to reverse it—asking for the physician of the fleet to go to the *Calypso*."

Physician. Ramage realized the significance of the word. Most frigates and all ships of the line had surgeons, but physicians were different. There were between two and three hundred surgeons in the navy but only three physicians—Dr Harness (who had given his name to a special sort of cask), Dr Trotter (who was a friend of Lord St Vincent) and Dr Travis. One of them would be on board this flagship.

"Why would she be wanting the *physician?*" Clinton asked, although it was obvious the question was rhetorical.

"The Signal Book, sir," Ramage said. "I don't think there is any signal for requesting medical assistance."

"But why should she need it? Perhaps the surgeon has drunk himself stupid."

Ramage realized that he had not completed his reference to Bowen. "I think not, sir: his first ship was the *Triton* brig, which I commanded, and he stopped drinking."

Clinton smiled benevolently: he was making allowances for the pride of a young captain.

"Not Bowen, sir—that's the surgeon. He was cured."

"Who achieved *that* miracle?" Clinton demanded.

"Well, sir, the master and I saw him through the worst of it. As I said, he's a very intelligent man. A wonderful chess player."

"Hmm—I hope he isn't trying to make pawns of us. She has the same officers and ship's company; only Bullivant is new. What do you think is going on?"

Had Bowen started drinking again? Or been injured himself? In that case, Bullivant would have asked one of the other frigates to send over her surgeon.

"Where is the *Calypso,* sir? I did not see her."

"Some distance up to the north-west, in company with the *Blackthorne* frigate."

"So she would be close enough to ask the *Blackthorne* to send over her surgeon?"

"Yes. The *Blackthorne* is nearer to us and relayed this strange signal. Who the devil would have thought up 215 over a pendant—it's clever, if they really need the physician of the fleet."

"Or the physician's authority," Ramage said and then realized that he had inadvertently spoken aloud what was only a random thought.

"What's that you say?" the admiral demanded. "Authority? Medicine is what they want, I'd have thought."

In for a penny, in for a pound, Ramage thought, and time was passing and he still had to persuade the admiral about *L'Espoir.* "I was trying to see it from the *Calypso's* point of view, sir. Sickness, fractures—all these can be dealt with by a surgeon. I was trying to see what the physician of the fleet had that a surgeon would not have, and medically—with respect—there woud be nothing of consequence. But the physician of the fleet would have *authority*. He would be reporting direct to you, and he could act on your authority . . ."

"But what the devil does the *Calypso* want to bother me about?" Clinton growled. "I don't care if the second lieutenant has just ruptured himself: that's why she has a surgeon. Can't be scurvy or anything like that—we left Plymouth only a couple of days ago."

Southwick, Aitken, Bowen, young Paolo, Jackson, Stafford— Ramage felt a great nostalgia. The Admiralty (having no choice) had appointed a new captain to the *Calypso*, but she would always be his ship: he had captured her from the French, refitted her in the West Indies, chosen her new name, taken her into action . . . He knew every man on board and had promoted most of the officers. Every seaman had been in action with him several times and people like Jackson, Stafford and Rossi had saved his life—and he theirs, for that matter.

"Sir, whatever it is, I'm sure it's serious and unusual. I know Bullivant only by report, but I do know my officers. The first lieutenant, Aitken, thought of the signal: I'm sure of that. He's a very responsible young officer." He remembered Clinton's slight accent and added: "—and comes from an old Scots family with naval connections."

Clinton scratched his head, doubtful about something, although Ramage could not guess what. "Let me think about it. Now, are we finished with this *Murex* mutiny business? I want a list of names of the mutineers, of course, and all the loyal seamen, and the warrant and commission officers, who can give evidence against them. The brig's first lieutenant can deal with that. The Navy Board will have the last Muster Book, so they can print up some posters naming these mutinous rascals. They'll have to serve in French and neutral ships, or starve, you'll see, and we'll catch 'em and stab 'em with a Bridport dagger, just like we did those villains from the *Hermione*."

Admirals rarely used slang—at least, Ramage had not heard them—but "Bridport dagger" was very appropriate. Some of the navy's best rope, particularly hemp, came from the Dorset town of Bridport, and hemp was always used for the hangman's noose. The seamen, with their liking for the bizarre euphemism, had soon tied the town, the hemp, the noose and death into one tidy phrase.

"I'll have the list for you, sir, and that rounds off the *Murex* affair, but there is one factor: you remember I mentioned earlier that the Count of Rennes and about fifty other Royalists were being transported by Bonaparte to Devil's Island?"

Admiral Clinton nodded. "Rennes? Isn't he the refugee fellow that has a place in England? Down at Ruckinge, I seem to remember. My place is at Great Chart, and my wife and I met him several times. A friend of the Prince Regent, I think."

"The same person, sir. He came back to France at the peace. My wife and I were staying with him when he was arrested, as I was telling you, and his valet hid us. I have the valet on board the *Murex*—he's one of the four Frenchmen who helped me retake the ship."

"The others—are they people like the Count?"

"I don't know who they are, sir, but *L'Espoir* was fitted out in great haste the moment Bonaparte heard that our ambassador was leaving Paris."

"So we are too late to stop her escaping. *L'Espoir* is on her way to Devil's Island now."

"She's only a few hours ahead, sir. She left Brest about half an hour ahead of the *Murex*."

By now Admiral Clinton was lost in his own thoughts and talking to himself. "Takes a frigate to catch a frigate—*en flûte*, you say, so she'll have fewer men and few guns . . . more guards because of the prisoners . . . Yes, I'd better spare a frigate: it'd be dashed difficult if the Prince heard that nothing had been done . . . but if I could take the Count of Rennes back with me . . . the frigate'd be a prize too, and there'd be my eighth . . ." He gave a startled jerk, as if surprised to find he was not alone in the cabin.

"Ah, Ramage. Yes, well, just had an idea about that dashed signal from the *Calypso*. You've got those extra men from Wells's frigate, so the *Murex* isn't short-handed now. Supposing you take her and go on board the *Calypso* and see what the devil it's all about. You know the ship so well."

Ramage nodded and added the part that the admiral had omitted: "It will save you detaching any of your frigates, too, sir."

"Quite, quite," Clinton said, as though the thought had never occurred to him. "Give me time to think about the Count of Rennes and *L'Espoir*, so if I have any more questions later you can answer them when you get back from the *Calypso*."

"If there is any urgency, sir, a situation which I think calls for the physician of the fleet, should I repeat 215 and the *Calypso*'s pendant?"

Clinton thought for a moment. "That would also mean that this flagship had to come up to the *Calypso*?"

"Yes, sir. I was thinking only of saving time in a dire emergency."

"Very well. But look'ee Ramage, you're a sensible fellow. I've read all your *Gazettes*. Bit inclined to go your own way—that wouldn't do if you were serving under me, mind you—but you succeed. So my orders to you—I'll have them put in writing: it'll only take a couple of minutes—are to go on board the *Calypso*, and sort out whatever is the problem. I must hurry to get into position off Brest—from what you say, Bonaparte has several ships he'd like to get out before I arrive to shut the door. Now, wait on deck while I get my dam' fool secretary to write up your orders. Get the *Calypso*'s position from Captain Bennett, and anything else you need. Looks as if you'll need to visit your tailor as soon as possible."

Ramage grinned. "There's a lot to be said for trousers when you're climbing up a ship's side, sir; breeches are tight."

Clinton said: "Very well. Unless you find it absolutely necessary to hoist 215, you will come up and report to me personally. Use your discretion. I have an odd feeling about this *Calypso* affair . . . Bullivant must have just been made post . . . Influence of the father, I suppose . . ." Again the admiral seemed to drift away in a reverie, and Ramage quietly left the cabin.

Captain Bennett took Ramage into his cabin and unrolled a chart. "The fleet will be here"—he indicated a line thirty miles to the west of Ushant—"and there'll be the usual frigates here, here, here and (providing this odd signal does not mean the *Calypso* has to go back to Plymouth) here. The admiral likes a couple of frigates with him, to investigate strange sail.

"Do you want to note down any latitudes and longitudes?" he asked.

Shaking his head, Ramage said: "I should be reporting back in a few hours. How far do you estimate the *Calypso* is to the north?"

"Well, the *Blackthorne* is in sight of us and the *Calypso* can see her. Say twenty miles. This is a five-knot wind for a brig like the *Murex*—she must have a clean bottom."

"She's clean," Ramage said, "but with only a dozen hands I haven't been pressing her!"

"A dozen, eh?"

"And four landmen, only one of whom speaks English!"

At that moment a bespectacled young man came into the cabin after the Marine sentry announced him.

He handed a slim volume and a sheet of paper to Ramage. "A copy of the Signal Book and the admiral's orders, sir: he particularly wants you to read them before you leave the ship."

Murmuring "If you'll excuse me," to Bennett, he read the copperplate handwriting and stylized wording. The phrases were dignified, those used by their Lordships and admirals for scores of years. They added up to the fact that whatever happened the man giving the orders took no responsibility for the results, while the man receiving them had no choice . . . However, in this case Admiral Clinton had obviously consulted Steel's List and found that Ramage was senior to Bullivant, and the orders, which of necessity were phrased with no knowledge of what was the matter, gave Ramage authority "to rectify, make good, issue orders and otherwise do what is required for the benefit of the King's Service in relation to the vessel herein described."

Ramage folded the orders and tucked the paper down the front of his shirt. "If you'll excuse me," he said to Captain Bennett and used his pen to sign the receipt for the orders and for the Signal Book which the young secretary had been holding out.

As he climbed down into the cutter he felt himself being pulled in two directions. Up to the north, something strange was happening to the *Calypso,* a ship he had come to love and a ship's company he regarded as his own family. Out to the west, *L'Espoir* was carrying Jean-Jacques and fifty other victims of Bonaparte to Devil's Island, which meant harsh imprisonment probably ended eventually by a quick death from the black vomit.

Ramage watched as the small cutter was hoisted on board and heard Swan preparing to get the *Murex* under way again. The extra dozen seamen would mean the *Murex* could stretch to the northward under courses as well as topsails.

As soon as Swan came aft, Ramage handed him the new copy of the Signal Book. "Have someone sew up a canvas bag and find a weight to put in it. That Signal Book must be kept in the bag and the whole thing thrown over the side if . . ."

"Yes, sir," Swan said. "Anyway, now the ship isn't deaf and dumb any longer!"

"We might regret that," Ramage said. "The admiral will be changing all the signal numbers now the French probably have *Murex*'s original book."

"Oh no, sir, I forgot to tell you. I was on deck when the mutiny started and the Signal Book and private signals were on the binnacle box. I managed to throw both over the side before the mutineers got control of the ship. I'll take an oath on that, sir."

Ramage sighed with relief but said: "I wish you'd told me that earlier. The admiral is already choosing the number to add to all those in the Signal Book, and drawing up new private signals."

"Well, I know the penalties for signals, so . . ." Swan said, and both men knew the phrase usually added to them when they were issued. The new private signals handed over by the admiral's secretary, Ramage noted, had two paragraphs of warning: "The captains and other officers to whom these signals are delivered are strictly commanded to keep them in their own possession, with a sufficient weight affixed to them to insure their being sunk if it should be found necessary to throw them overboard . . . As a consequence of the most dangerous nature . . . may result from the enemy's getting possession of these signals, if any officer . . . fail in observing these directions, he will certainly be made to answer for his disobedience at a Court Martial . . ."

Which was why Swan wanted to make it clear that he had disposed of the signals. But he would certainly be tried—a court martial could clear a man of any suspicion just as well as it could find him guilty.

"You have witnesses?" Ramage said. "You may need them."

Swan said: "Yes, I understand, sir. Phillips saw me, and the two men at the wheel, who did not mutiny."

"Good, they'll be sufficient. Now, let's start carrying out our present orders. First, steer north-north-west, and warn the lookouts to watch for two frigates, one French-built. Both of them are well to the north of the fleet. We have to visit the northernmost one, the French-built."

"Like your last ship, the *Calypso*," Swan said, smiling at the thought.

"She is the *Calypso*," Ramage said, and gestured towards the taffrail. As the two men walked up and down the windward side, out of earshot of the men at the wheel and the quartermaster, Swan pausing from time to time to shout orders through the speaking-trumpet to get the brig under way, Ramage described what had happened, and why the *Murex* was being sent to the *Calypso*.

"Captain Bullivant," Swan said, "just made post, obviously. We served together as lieutenants in the *Culloden*."

"A pleasant fellow, eh?" Ramage said, realizing that Swan would be careful not to criticize one captain to another but hoping the man would realize that he needed to know as much as possible.

"He had his friends," Swan said carefully. "His father is one of the biggest contractors to the Navy Board."

"I heard about that," Ramage said. "Salt meat, isn't it?"

"Yes, sir," Swan said, unable to keep a bitter note out of his voice. "You know, a cask of salt beef, and stencilled on the outside it says 'Contains 52 pieces' . . ."

"And when the master counts them, there are only 47," Ramage finished the sentence. "And although every ship in the navy notes it down in the log—the contractor's number on the cask and the number of the pieces short—and although the log goes to the Admiralty and the Navy Board can trace the contractor in each case from the number, nothing is ever done about it."

"But the Bullivants of this world and the people they bribe

at the Navy Board get richer," Swan said, thankful that the new temporary captain of the *Murex* needed only a pointing finger, not a detailed chart.

The two men walked over to the binnacle, and after a look at the compass card and a glance up at the luffs of the sails, Ramage nodded to the quartermaster.

He was, Ramage noted, one of the original men of the *Murex*, but Swan had already said that he was only an ordinary seaman. He wondered why the *Murex*'s captain had not rated the man "able." Perhaps he had a bad record, a good seaman but a heavy drinker. All too many men disobeyed the regulations and "hoarded their tot"—instead of drinking their daily issue they kept it until the end of the week so they could get very drunk. They knew before they put aside the very first tot that if they got drunk they would probably be flogged, but all too many seasoned topers reckoned a dozen with the cat-o'-nine-tails a fair exchange for ending Saturday night in an alcoholic stupor.

With the wind almost on the beam, the brig was sailing fast. Already the line-of-battle ships making up the fleet were on the *Murex*'s starboard beam, and in half an hour they would be well aft on the quarter, their hulls beginning to sink below the horizon, hidden by the curvature of the earth.

There was little for him to do until the *Blackthorne* and the *Calypso* were sighted, so he went below to talk to Sarah. As soon as he saw her sitting on the settee, he remembered the family's London home in Palace Street. There Mrs Hanson, the butler's wife, was also the housekeeper, and Ramage had once heard her describe a disgruntled person as "on the turn, like yesterday's milk in a thunderstorm."

Sarah's expression showed that she was far from happy; Mrs Hanson would regard it as definitely curdled. No wonder the *Admiralty Instructions* forbade officers to take their wives to sea in wartime!

"So you're back," she said bleakly. "Are we bound for Plymouth now?"

"No, not yet," he said. "One of the frigates with the fleet is the *Calypso* and—"

"But she's yours!" Sarah exclaimed, suddenly coming to life.

He shook his head. "With war breaking out so quickly and the First Lord having to send out a Channel Fleet, he would have taken every ship that could get to sea. Obviously the *Calypso* had not been paid off, so as I wasn't there a new captain was sent down and he took her round to Plymouth to join Admiral Clinton."

"Clinton? The Scots family?"

"I think so: he speaks with a Scots accent. Why?"

"He was out in the East Indies once and I met him when he called on father. I think he's quite well regarded."

"Yes, we're lucky he's commanding the Fleet."

"It hardly matters, surely, if we are going to Plymouth."

"Dearest, I have no idea whether we'll be sailing for Plymouth or Jamaica or the Cape of Good Hope. All I know is that Admiral Clinton has given me orders which I am carrying out. They should take only a few hours, but"—he softened his voice—"they concern a ship, men and the sea, so nothing is certain."

She gave a ghost of a smile, as if to start making up for her earlier tartness. A start, but by no means an acceptance of the fact she was now (for the first time in their brief marriage) very definitely the moon in her husband's life; the navy was the sun. This was, of course, precisely what the Countess of Blazey had warned her about before the wedding. Sarah admitted to herself that she had thought Nicholas's mother was being too protective (of both of them) when she warned that navy wives always came second. Well, that had not prevented the Countess's own marriage being a most successful one—the Earl of Blazey, apart from being one of the navy's finest admirals until falling victim to politics, clearly loved and was loved by his wife.

"Am I allowed to know what Admiral Clinton's orders are?"

"Of course!" he said, snatching at the tiny olive branch which was being inspected rather than proffered. Quickly he explained how the *Calypso* had hoisted what seemed a bewildering signal. It took longer to explain that there were only three physicians in the entire navy, while surgeons were numbered in hundreds, but she was intrigued.

"What do you expect to find?"

"I have absolutely no idea; nor has the admiral, which is why he is sending me."

"But this new captain, Bullivant, what . . . ?"

"I'm sure he is not going to be very pleased to see me!"

"Why not? I should have thought that—"

He cut her short. "Just imagine it. The *Calypso* is not famous but people know about her. I captured her, was put in command, and took her into action several times. All the officers and many of the ship's company would be regarded by a new captain as 'my' men because normally he selects his own officers when commissioning the ship—certainly his first lieutenant and midshipmen, and probably the master.

"This wretched fellow Bullivant—I feel sorry for him. He knows that whatever he does, from how he wears his hat to the way he gives orders, everyone on board is comparing him with the previous captain. It can't give him much confidence. He must hate the thought of me—I know I should!"

"You wouldn't, you know: you'd just make sure you did everything better—and quicker, too. You are one of the lucky people who have confidence in themselves."

Ramage's laugh was bitter. She could never guess the hours before going into action when he had completely lost confidence

in himself and his plans, and would have changed them completely but for there being no time or no obvious alternative.
Even as late as two nights ago, when he led the four Frenchmen
and Sarah to capture the *Murex*—did she think he had no doubts
and fears? Well, perhaps it was better if she (along with everyone who had served with him in the *Calypso*) thought he had
not.

He heard shouting from aloft, and then Swan's question to
the masthead lookout. "Where away? . . . You are sure? . . .
French-built from the sheer? Very well, keep a sharp lookout!"

Then the shout from the top of the companion-way, "Captain, sir," but by then Ramage had given Sarah a hasty kiss and
his foot was already on the first step.

Swan repeated the bearing. "Dead ahead, sir, and the lookout says he sees her well as we lift on the swell waves. Thought
I glimpsed her sails for a moment."

"Strange how helpless one feels without a bring-'em-near,"
Ramage commented. "I should have borrowed one from the flagship."

"I can't see anyone giving up his glass, even for Captain
Ramage," Swan said jocularly.

"There!" called the master, "I glimpsed a sail then. That's her,
dead ahead!"

CHAPTER TEN

AN HOUR LATER the brig and the frigate crossed tacks,
the *Murex* passing half a mile ahead.

"No signals flying," Swan commented.

"So I see. But now we are to windward of her, so hoist her
pendant and make number 84."

Swan snapped out an order to two seamen, who began hoisting the three flags forming the *Calypso*'s pendant numbers, and told two more to hoist eight and four.

"*Pass within hail,* isn't it, sir?" Swan asked. "You have the book," he said apologetically, "but I'm presuming it hasn't been changed."

"Yes, but whether or not Captain Bullivant chooses to obey is another question. He might assume a brig is still commanded only by a lieutenant."

"I think if I was him and a brig tacked across my bow and gave a peremptory order, I'd assume she had a senior officer on board!"

"We'll see," Ramage said. "In the meantime, have 173 bent on and ready for hoisting, and have number one gun on the larboard side loaded with a blank charge. There's no need to send the men to quarters: have Bridges and a couple of men do it. Here's the key to the magazine. It was still in the desk drawer."

Swan was enjoying himself hoisting flag signals with orders for Bullivant, that much was obvious, and his enjoyment revealed more about Bullivant than his earlier comments. Ramage handed him the Signal Book, knowing that the first lieutenant could not remember the meaning of 173.

He quickly leafed through the pages, which were cut at the side with the signal numbers printed in tens.

"Ah," Swan said, "a gun and that should produce results!"

"Yes, we'll tack again; they're ignoring 84."

Ramage saw Bridges and two men running to the forward gun on the larboard side, where seamen in answer to Bridges' earlier shouted order were already casting off lashings.

Out came the tompion; a man held the flintlock in position and hurriedly tightened up the wing nut to clamp it down. The gun was quickly run in and a cartridge slid down the bore and rammed home. The gun was run out again, a quill tube pushed down the vent and priming powder shaken into the pan.

Bridges held up his hand in a signal to Ramage, who was watching the *Calypso* as she sailed on, approaching their starboard bow.

"Mr Swan, we'll pass very close across the *Calypso*'s bow . . ." Ramage gestured to the two seamen who had bent on the three flags representing the signal 173, *Furl sails.*

Ramage watched the *Calypso* out of the corner of his eye and said to the seamen: "Leave up the pendant numbers but lower 84."

By now Swan was bellowing orders and the brig's bow was turning to starboard, canvas slatting, the ropes of sheets and braces flogging, spray flying across like fine rain as the bow sliced the tops off waves. Then, with Swan giving the word to haul, the yards were braced round and sheets trimmed so the sails resumed their opulent curves. The *Murex* began to leap through the water again—right across the *Calypso*'s bow.

"Oh, nicely, nicely!" Swan exclaimed. "Less than half a cable— we'll be able to throw a biscuit on to her fo'c's'le as we pass across her bow!"

"Stand by," Ramage shouted, and saw the gun captain kneel with his left leg thrust out to one side, the trigger line taut in his right hand.

The *Calypso* was a fine sight, bow-on and just forward of the *Murex*'s beam. Men were peering over the bulwarks; Ramage thought he saw the lookout at the foremasthead gesturing down to the deck.

"Hoist 173!" Ramage said to the seamen and watched the three flags soaring upwards. He turned forward. "Mr Bridges, fire!"

The gun spurted flame and smoke, and a moment later came the flat "blam" of an unshotted gun firing, the standard signal drawing particular attention to a hoist of flags.

Ramage watched the *Calypso* for the first sign that she was altering course or clewing up sails. There was only one more signal that he could make (108, *Close nearer to the Admiral*) but if Bullivant ignored that too, what next?

Were the luffs of the courses fluttering slightly? As the *Murex* passed across the *Calypso*'s bows the frigate's masts had for a few moments been in line, but now the brig was hauling out on the *Calypso*'s beam and it was hard to distinguish an alteration of course. But . . . yes . . .

Swan exclaimed: "She's bracing her courses sharp up, sir! Yes, I can see men going up the ratlines. There, she's starting to clew up!"

Ramage judged distances and times. Better than Bullivant he knew how long it would take to clew up the big forecourse and the main course, the lowest and largest sails in the frigate; then as the *Calypso* slowed down the foretopsail would be backed, the yard braced sharp up so that the wind blew on the forward side. With well-trained crew and Aitken and Southwick, she could be hove-to a good deal faster than the smaller but undermanned *Murex*.

"She's heaving-to," Ramage told Swan. "Cross her bow again and then as soon as we're to windward, heave-to." Was there any point in sending the *Murex*'s men to general quarters? Ten guns, five each side, and only a dozen or so of the men had ever fired them. No one would know his position in a gun's crew. No, there would be chaos, and ten guns against the *Calypso*, with her well trained, experienced crew, would do about as much harm as the shrill cursing of bumboat women.

"As soon as we've hove-to, I want the cutter hoisting out to take me across to the *Calypso*."

Swan looked anxious, his eyes flickering from Ramage to the frigate. "Sir, Bridges and Phillips are quite competent to handle this ship. May I come with you to the *Calypso*? Not because I'm being nosy," he added hastily, "but I'd be happier if you had an escort."

Ramage had been thinking not of an escort but of something that might prove more necessary. "Yes—but you'll be coming as a witness. Keep your eyes and ears open. Try and remember exact phrases. I can't tell you more than that because I don't know what the devil we're going to find."

As the cutter surged down and rounded up alongside the *Calypso,* Ramage recognized several of the faces watching from over the top of the bulwark, but no one was waving a greeting and no one was standing at the entry port.

Aitken? Southwick? Young Paolo? They must be on board, and although they could never expect to find their old captain arriving alongside in a brig's cutter, surely some of them would have recognized him by now, since he had deliberately stood up in the sternsheets of the cutter for the last hundred yards. Surely *someone* would be watching through a telescope. The whole episode of a brig making peremptory signals to a frigate was unusual enough to make the cutter's arrival a matter of considerable importance.

It seemed only a moment later that the cutter was alongside and Ramage leapt for the battens just as the cutter rose on a crest. He sensed that Swan was right behind him. A rope snaked down from the *Calypso* to serve as a painter.

No sideropes, so the *Calypso* was not extending the usual courtesy to the commanding officer of another ship o' war, but perhaps there had not been time to rig them. There had, of course, and Ramage knew it, but he also knew that when Aitken and Southwick proposed it, Bullivant might have refused.

Up, up, up . . . cling to the battens with your fingers, keep your feet flat against the side of the ship to prevent the soles of your shoes from slipping . . . Yes, that gouge in the wood there was so familiar and that scarph in the plank there . . . He could remember the actions in which the hull had been damaged.

Suddenly his head came level with the deck and a moment later he was through the entry port, standing on the deck itself and staring into the muzzle of a pistol held by a man he had never seen before but who was wearing the uniform of a post captain. He had a single epaulet, showing he had less than three years' seniority, Ramage noticed inconsequentially.

"Stop!" the man bellowed. He was young, stocky, with a round face mottled with—was it anger? The pistol in his right hand was beautifully made, the barrel damascened, the silver and gold tracery of inlaid patterns catching the sun. The silver tankard in his left hand also had an intricate design worked all round it. And the man, who seemed too excited to string together a coherent sentence, took a pace forward as Swan stepped on deck.

"Stop, both of you!" He gestured with both hands as though shooing a hen back into her coop, and an amber liquid spilled from the tankard.

"You see, pirates! Look at him, a *sans-culotte!* A Republican pirate. And the other one . . ." he paused, catching his breath and then unexpectedly took a long drink from the tankard. He's wearing the . . . the *King*'s uniform . . ."

Ramage saw that the speech was becoming more slurred and the man's eyes were glazing. The man—Ramage guessed it must be Bullivant—turned and pointed. Ramage recognized the lieutenant in Marine's uniform as Rennick, now white-faced, fear showing in the way the lips were drawn back. Ramage had seen Rennick facing broadsides, muskets fired at close range, pistols from a few feet, dodging the slash of cutlasses, but the Marine officer always grinned because he loved battle. Fear? A moment later he realized why.

"Shoot these men!" Bullivant screamed. "Come on, you have

your file of Marines ready! The devil's work . . . that's what these French swine are doing . . ." His speech was slowing and Ramage glanced round.

There they all were, in a circle of men with fear on their faces: Aitken, the Scots first lieutenant; Wagstaffe; the red-haired and freckle-faced Kenton, his face red and peeling from the effect of wind and sun; young Martin, the fourth lieutenant; and old Southwick, his white mop of hair as usual trying to escape his hat and suddenly reminding Ramage of straw sticking out from under a nesting hen. And Paolo, his normally sallow face now white, his hooked nose bloodless, as though he was some young Italian model for a Botticelli painting.

Then Ramage saw that every one of the men on deck, seamen and Marines, was watching him, horrified by Bullivant's words. Rennick was making no move. The sergeant of Marines stood firm. Yes, they must be thinking, their old captain has by some magic come back, dressed as a French fisherman, and their new captain has just given orders to shoot him.

Now the signal for the physician of the fleet made sense: Bullivant had been driven mad by drink and presumably Aitken had hoisted that signal at a time when Bullivant could not see it—when he was below.

Where was the surgeon, Bowen? Even as Ramage glanced round once again, he saw the surgeon coming up the companionway, carrying a big flask. Now everyone was watching Bowen and Bullivant was smiling: it was the vapid smile of an idiot, ingratiating and welcoming.

"Ah, Mr Bowen . . . Welcome, you bring me sustenance . . . you see the demons I face." He waved both pistol and tankard towards Ramage and Swan. "Here, you are just in time." He held out the tankard and Bowen poured liquid from the flask. Bullivant took a sip, swallowed and then gulped like a calf at a cow's udders.

Swan, pressing with his elbow, caused Ramage to look down. The *Murex*'s first lieutenant had a Sea Service pistol tucked in the waistband of his breeches and was trying to draw Ramage's attention to it while Bullivant, head back and tankard to his lips, had his eyes closed.

This situation was what every officer dreaded. Relieving a captain of his command was juggling with the risk of being charged with treason. What was madness on the high seas could appear to be perfectly sane behaviour when the captain soberly described it to a row of hard-faced officers forming a court martial in the peace and quiet of a guardship's cabin in Plymouth or Portsmouth. The whole edifice of discipline was built on the authority of a senior officer—a seaman obeyed a bosun's mate who obeyed the bosun who obeyed a lieutenant who obeyed the captain who obeyed a captain senior to him or an admiral who obeyed the Admiralty: it was all in the Articles of War . . . Many covered every aspect for maintaining command—numbers XIX, XXII (carrying the death penalty for anyone even lifting a weapon against a superior), and XXXIV . . . and of course, XXXVI, the so-called captain's cloak, covering "all other crimes" not covered by the Act. None provided the means of depriving a man of command . . .

Bullivant was not just senior to all the officers and men of the *Calypso;* his commission appointing him to command the *Calypso,* signed by the Lords Commissioners of the Admiralty, and which he would have read out aloud to the ship's company when he first came on board ("reading himself in"), would have enjoined everyone to obey him, and given warning that they failed to do so "at their peril."

Only one thing could save them all from a crazed captain, and that was a more senior officer. There was no signal in the book that Aitken (as the second-in-command) could make to warn the admiral; he could only, Ramage realized, ask for the physician of the fleet and rely on him to declare the captain unfit to command.

That was the only thing unless a senior officer came on board . . . and that was why Admiral Clinton had made sure Ramage was higher up the Captains' List than Bullivant. Ramage was senior. A higher link in the chain of command . . .

Ramage pulled the pistol clear and held it out of sight behind him. All this might be of significance at a court martial charging that Bullivant was first threatening an unarmed senior officer with a pistol. To this, Ramage realized, Bullivant at the moment had the perfect defence: he did not know Ramage, who was not in uniform, and genuinely mistook him for a Frenchman.

The hell with courts martial and niggling points of law; this was the *Calypso* and Rennick had just been told by his captain to order his Marines to shoot Ramage. Now was the time to act, while everyone was paralysed by the outrageousness of the order.

Ramage waited until Bullivant lowered the tankard and then stepped forward.

"Captain Bullivant, I believe?"

"Yes, I am. Listen, Bowen, this dam' fellow speaks passable English!"

"I am Captain Ramage, and I have been ordered by Admiral Clinton to board your ship and satisfy myself on certain matters."

"Captain Ramage? Absurd. Ramage is on the Continent. Prisoner of Bonaparte. With his new wife. Ramage's, not Bonaparte's. Spy, that's what you are. Rich, Ramage is dam' rich; he wouldn't wear fisherman's clothes. That brig—I ask you, where has she come from, eh? Shoot you and sink her, doing my duty. Says he is Captain Ramage, Bowen, what do you think of that, eh?"

"He is Captain Ramage, sir," Bowen said loudly and clearly. "I have served with him for several years, and so have all the ship's officers, and they recognize him too."

"Well, I don't. I command this ship. Admiralty orders. Have

m'commission. I read it out loud when I first came on board. Death, that's what happens if you disobey me—"

Ramage said crisply: "I have identified myself to you and been recognized by all your officers. Now, I relieve you of your command, Captain Bullivant. You are a sick man. You will go to your cabin and place yourself in the surgeon's care while I take this ship to the admiral."

Bullivant flung the tankard at Ramage. It spun through the air, spilling a tail of liquor, and crashed against the bulwark. He then lifted the pistol and, his face creasing with the effort of concentration, said carefully: "You are the Devil dressed . . . as a French fisherman . . . You want me . . . to surrender this ship, Satan . . . but I shall shoot first . . ."

He tried to pull back the hammer with his thumb to cock the pistol but, glassy-eyed, it was obvious that he could probably see at least two, perhaps more, flints. And Ramage, although holding a pistol behind his back, was helpless: he could not shoot a besotted man.

It might work, Ramage thought. Suddenly he realized it was exactly the hint that Bowen was trying to give. He cursed himself for being so slow and turned and said casually to a seaman: "Jackson, pick up that tankard and give it back to Captain Bullivant."

Yes, Bowen had the idea; Bowen, of all people, the man who regularly drank himself senseless until Ramage and Southwick cured him by using a ruthlessness neither had thought the other capable of: Bowen would know. Bowen knew—or could guess—what was going on in Bullivant's befuddled mind, and Bowen had already removed the cap of the flask . . .

Jackson, holding out the tankard, approached Bullivant, whose face was streaming with perspiration, and said as though unaware that the man was wrestling with a pistol: "Your tankard, sir."

"Wha'? Wha's that? Oh, tankard, eh? I've got a set like that. No good empty."

But Bullivant's attention was now on the tankard; he had lowered the pistol but being right-handed was obviously wondering how he could take the tankard. By then Bowen was beside him, holding up the flask.

"I'll fill it for you, sir. Now, Jackson, hold it steady."

Ramage heard the suck and gurgle of the liquid as it ran from the flask and Bullivant watched with the fascination of a rabbit cornered by a stoat.

"There we are, sir, almost full. I'll have to refill this flask, though. Now, if I take the pistol you'll have a hand free for the tankard, sir . . ."

In a moment Bullivant was sucking greedily at the tankard while Bowen tucked the pistol inside his coat. He motioned to Ramage and Jackson to keep still.

It was then Ramage realized that every man in the ship seemed to be staring at Bullivant and holding his breath: it was as though there had been complete silence for an hour. Instead, Ramage knew he had been on board only a very few minutes and a frigate lying hove-to made a good deal of noise: canvas slatted, the waves slopped against the hull, the backed foretopsail yard creaked its protest at being pressed hard against the mast. It seemed that all these noises started again when Bullivant began drinking.

But what was Bowen waiting for? There was nothing to stop Ramage ordering Rennick to detail a file of Marines to take Captain Bullivant down to his cabin: he had the authority by virtue of his seniority and, much more important, the confidence of knowing that at the court martial that was bound to follow, each one of these officers would give evidence of precisely what happened: none would back and fill to save his own skin from possible reprisals from Bullivant's cronies or people over whom

Bullivant's father had influence. Aitken, Wagstaffe, Kenton, Southwick, Rennick, Martin, every seaman—they would be only too anxious to tell a court on oath exactly what had happened in these few minutes—and what had happened in the preceding few days. He had led these men in and out of action, he'd been wounded several times alongside them, he had saved Jackson's life more than once and Jackson had saved his twice as many times.

Yet why were they all standing there? It was a curious scene, unreal, yet he thought he would never forget it. Bullivant, cocked hat now awry, breeches and white silk stockings stained—from urine rather than brandy, it seemed—and face streaming with perspiration. The eyes closed now, even when he lowered the tankard and took a few breaths . . . Bowen quite calm, looking as if he was just waiting for a patient to don an overcoat; Jackson with his sandy and thinning hair tidy as usual, shaven yesterday if not today, and wearing a blue jersey and white duck trousers; Southwick like a jovial bishop unable to avoid listening to a stream of blasphemy; Aitken with colour back in his face and watching Ramage like a hawk, waiting for orders; Paolo the same—in fact, Ramage realized the boy was holding a long and narrow dagger which he must have drawn while Bullivant was fumbling with the pistol: Paolo's complexion was once again sallow, and although the boy was still balanced on the balls of his feet ready to move quickly, it was clear from his expression he knew he would not now be using the dagger and Ramage knew him well enough to gauge the boy's disappointment. Wagstaffe, Kenton, Martin . . . and the seamen, Stafford and Rossi, who were closer than he realized, and he guessed that somehow they had closed in stealthily once they recognized their old captain.

Then nearly two hundred men groaned. No, not a groan, it was a sigh, everyone breathing out after holding their breath, and a startled Ramage looked back at Bullivant in time to see him sitting on the deck and then slowly bending backwards, like a carpet unrolling, until he was sprawled flat, his cocked hat lying to one side, the tankard still clasped in one hand and the remains of the brandy spreading a slow stain across the planks of the deck.

Bowen gestured to the Marines, but before he could say anything Ramage had stepped forward. It would matter at a trial who gave the next orders, and although Ramage knew he did not give a damn for himself, the future of the officers could be damaged unless he was careful.

"Bowen, Captain Bullivant seems to have lost consciousness . . ."

The surgeon knelt beside the man, rolled back an eyelid, loosened the badly-tied stock and stood up again. "He is unconscious, sir," he said formally, "and in my opinion—"

"In your opinion," Ramage interrupted, "is he capable of carrying out his duties as captain of this ship?"

"No, sir, under no circumstances. Nor will he be for several—"

"Days?"

"—for several days, sir."

"Have him taken below to his cabin for treatment," Ramage said.

Now the formalities were over and, while Bowen called over some Marines, Ramage turned first to Southwick. As a warrant officer, the master was junior to the lieutenants, but he was old enough to be the father, even the grandfather, of any of them, and the bond between him and Ramage could not be measured by normal standards.

As Ramage reached out to shake the old man's hand he was startled to see tears running down the weathered cheeks, although the kindly mouth was smiling. "Sir . . . sir . . . when your head came up the ladder I thought I was dreaming . . . where were—"

"We'll exchange news later; now we have work to do!" He

shook hands with the lieutenants, Paolo and several of the seamen who rushed up, still hard put to believe their own eyes and anxious to touch him, as though that would make everything a reality. Then he beckoned to Swan, and together they walked aft.

"What a five minutes, sir!" Swan exclaimed. "You look down the muzzle of a pistol like a man looking in a window. My blood ran cold even though he wasn't aiming at me!"

"He saw five or six of me and wasn't sure which to shoot at."

"Even so," Swan said, "five to one are not good odds!"

"Well; it's over now. If I hand over the *Murex* to you and give you orders to rejoin the flagship, can you manage? No one will ever know if you don't feel up to it, so don't be afraid to say."

"No, sir, thanks but I'll be all right. If you'll just give me the latitude and longitude of the rendezvous."

"You can sail in company with us. I have to take this ship to the admiral. Do you want some more men?"

Swan shook his head. "No, sir, so I'll get back to the *Murex*. What about her Ladyship? Shall I send the cutter back with her?"

"No, we can't spare the time, but as long as you make sure no one else overhears, you can tell her what you saw."

"Any other message for her Ladyship, sir?"

"Tell her that Southwick, Stafford, Jackson and Aitken—no, just tell her that all the officers and ship's company of the *Calypso* send her their regards."

Swan looked puzzled. Ramage could see that the lieutenant was wondering how on earth a captain's new wife could know all the men in his previous ship. "They saved her life once, Swan. If you have time and if she's agreeable, get her to tell you about it: it'll help you pass the time as we beat back to the Fleet."

Ramage stood on the fore side of the quarterdeck with Aitken as they watched the *Murex* brace up the foretopsail yard and then bear away to the rendezvous, the clewed-up courses soon set and drawing.

"Handsome little ships, those brigs," Aitken said. "Any nostalgia, sir?" he asked, knowing Ramage had commanded the *Triton*.

"Yes and no. 'Yes' because they are handy—we tacked that one out of the Gullet with only a dozen men, and looking back on it we could probably have made do with eight. 'No' because I found it strange being in that particular one, where most of the men had mutinied and handed over the ship (and their loyal shipmates) to the enemy. It's as though treachery rubs off like soot, marking everything and leaving a distinctive smell."

"Aye, evil has a distinct smell, and all of us can recognize it. In our case it's the smell of brandy."

"It has been bad, eh?"

"Almost beyond belief, sir. We could see no end to it. There's nothing in the Articles of War or the *Regulations and Instructions* about it. Bowen reckoned medical reasons were the only safe way, but for the first day or so, when the drink wasn't in him, he was bright enough. Cunning and fawning, but shrewd. It seemed to me, sir, that if we took away his command and then he was cunning enough to keep off the liquor for a few weeks before the court martial, at the trial he could make it all look very different . . ."

"Yes, that's the danger. When you look at something from different directions, you get different views."

"And Bowen knew all about the effects of drink. That's how we came—"

Ramage held up a hand to stop him. "I'm sure the ship's officers didn't conspire against the captain, Aitken, because that's forbidden. As you know, Article XX specifies death as the only punishment for anyone 'concealing any traitorous or mutinous practice or design.' So don't mention anything resembling conspiracy—the listener immediately becomes guilty as well."

Aitken grinned. "I understand that, sir. Well, it's wonderful to have you on board again."

Ramage nodded and looked across at the *Murex*, now a couple of miles away. "I think we can get under way now and rejoin the admiral with the brig. Admiral Clinton is a very puzzled man."

They walked forward again and Aitken picked up the speaking-trumpet. Ramage realized that since he last stood here a couple of months or so ago, as they tacked up the Medway to Chatham, he had married, been to France, escaped capture when the war broke out again, recaptured the *Murex* brig, and relieved the new captain of the *Calypso* of his command. What he had not done was try to rescue Jean-Jacques.

"I'm going below to see Bowen and his patient," he told Aitken. He gave him a folded piece of paper. "Here is the rendezvous, and you'll sight the fleet before nightfall. Ignore the *Blackthorne* if she starts making signals—there's no signal in the book to describe what we're doing."

Below in the great cabin he found Bowen sitting in the chair at the desk while in the sleeping cabin Bullivant, undressed and now in his nightshirt, was breathing heavily in a drunken stupor, his lips flapping like wet laundry each time he exhaled.

Bowen hurriedly stood up as the Marine sentry announced Ramage, who gestured to him to remain seated.

"I'll take the armchair. It's good to see you, Bowen. I wish it was under happier circumstances . . ."

"Oh, I hope everything will turn out all right, sir," Bowen said vaguely. "For the moment we have about an hour before Captain Bullivant recovers consciousness and descends into the hell of *delirium tremens.*"

"Hell seems the right word: he seems obsessed with it. He recognized me as the Devil when I came on board."

"Oh yes, Satan is very real to him. For the past five or six days this ship has reeked of brimstone. The captain had all the lieutenants sprinkling the quarterdeck with holy water laced with brandy in an attempt to exorcize it, but without success."

"This conversation never took place," Ramage remarked, "so tell me the story from the beginning."

"Well, you know a good deal of the circumstances if you remember how I came to serve with you in the *Triton* brig," Bowen said with disconcerting frankness.

"There are two kinds of heavy drinkers: those who drink secretly until they are stupefied, and those who don't give a damn and get drunk openly. Captain Bullivant is a secret drinker, so no one—except perhaps his family and his wife if he is married—knows. But from my own experience I can tell you he has been drinking hard for years. Four or five years, anyway: look at the veins under the skin of his face, at his nose, at his eyes when they are open. And he looks ten or twenty years older than he is."

"But when he joined the ship," Ramage prompted.

"Ah, yes. We had fallen behind in paying off the ship because of difficulties with the dockyard, and just as well. We (that is, Mr Aitken, because of course you were on leave) suddenly received orders to commission the ship at once, and the dockyard commissioner warned us war was likely again any moment. He also said that if you did not return from France in time, the First Lord would appoint a new captain.

"We had the ship ready in what must be record time and Captain Bullivant appeared and read himself in as the new commanding officer. Very brisk, he was, and delighted with everything Aitken and Southwick had done. He made a very good impression on every person who saw him, except one man."

"And that was you." It was a comment, not a question.

"Yes, I knew the symptoms which few ever recognize. The

constant sweating, the tiny tremor of the fingers when the hands are extended, the slightly glazed appearance of the eyes and the feeling they are never quite in focus, the smell of cashews on the breath . . . the apparent temperance and lack of interest in wine and spirits. When his luggage was brought on board, I had a word with Jackson and he made sure each trunk was checked. One clinked—full of bottles, carefully packed and only two loose ones."

"And after he had read himself in?"

"All went well the next day: orders arrived from the Admiralty to proceed to Plymouth and put ourselves under Admiral Clinton's command. We were off the Nore that night and we suddenly found ourselves in the middle of the Harwich fishing fleet. Aitken sent for the captain, who came up on deck so stupefied he could not stand without holding on to something. That was the first time we heard him see the Devil."

"What did he look like?" Ramage asked.

"Well, we didn't see him since he only existed in the fumes affecting Captain Bullivant's brain, but we certainly heard *where* he was: about fifty yards on one bow and then on the other, preparing to rake us."

"With empty bottles, I suppose."

Bowen grinned as he shook his head. "No, he was on the fo'c's'le of a three-decker which was 'painted in orange stripes like a glorious sunset'—Captain Bullivant's exact words, though he didn't explain how he distinguished colour in the dark. And this took the lieutenants and Southwick by surprise, sir: I had kept my earlier observations to myself—I had not realized he had reached the stage of recurrent *delirium tremens*. I was mistaken: I should have warned Aitken."

"But the *Calypso* did not sink any of the fishing vessels?"

"No, mercifully. Anyway, eventually I quieted down the captain and got him back to bed. Next morning he was—to the layman's eyes—perfectly normal, but in the secrecy of this cabin he drank himself into a stupor every night until we arrived in Plymouth . . . There Aitken talked to me about reporting it all to Admiral Clinton."

"What was your advice?"

"Well, sir, I thought of my own cunning when you and South-wick were trying to cure me and decided Captain Bullivant was a clever man, well aware of his weakness and with enough influence at the Navy Board through his contractor father to make useless anything we could do. Admiral Clinton was busy getting his fleet to sea, so if Aitken had appeared in the flagship with a story of Satan stalking the *Calypso,* I suspect we would have been sent a new first lieutenant, not a new captain."

"So the fleet sailed. Then what happened?"

"Well, that was all Captain Bullivant was waiting for: he left the entire running of the ship to Aitken. He gave orders that he was 'not to be bothered with signals,' and that Aitken was to execute all orders from the flagship 'without troubling' him. From this we expected he would stay drinking down here in his cabin, but every now and again he would emerge raving about the Devil. He would chase him out of his cabin and up the companion-way to the quarterdeck, and would then sight him behind the binnacle, behind a carronade, trying to climb the ratlines . . ."

"Was there anything you could do?"

"Frankly none of us had the courage. If we had bundled him below and he had later remembered it, any of us—Marine, seaman or officer—could be tried for striking a superior officer, or mutiny. So we all looked for Satan, exorcized the quarter-deck . . ."

"That signal for the physician?"

"That was when his delirium was reaching the crisis. Yester-day he had the ship's company mustered aft and inspected them."

"Well, there's nothing unusual about that," Ramage commented, feeling he ought to say something, however mild, in Bullivant's defence.

"No, sir, unless you are looking for the Devil himself—and find him hiding in the bodies of three men!"

"Which three?" asked a flabbergasted Ramage.

"The seaman Rossi, the Marchesa's young nephew Paolo Orsini—and Southwick!"

"I can understand Rossi and Orsini—they have sallow complexions and black hair. But Southwick—I always think he looks like a bishop."

"That's exactly what Captain Bullivant said! He denounced Southwick because he said it was impossible for a bishop to be serving as the master in one of the King's ships, therefore he must be the Devil in disguise."

"But how did this cause a crisis?

"He swore he would hang a Devil a day until the ship was free of them. Southwick was the first and due to be executed at sunset today."

"But the men would never haul on the rope!" Ramage said. The whole thing was unthinkable.

"Sir," Bowen said very seriously, "the minute he gives anyone an order and is disobeyed, that's a breach of enough Articles of War for a death sentence at a court martial . . ."

"So . . . ?"

"So, I told Aitken that the only way out was to use 'medical grounds' to get the admiral involved. I had a plan in case that failed (the signal for the physician of the fleet, I mean) but I couldn't then be sure it would work. Luckily it did when I used it . . ."

"The tankard of brandy and the flask?"

"Yes, sir. It's the timing that is difficult. To judge how much is needed to tip the man over the edge into oblivion—well, that depends on how much he has drunk in the previous few hours, and whether he has eaten."

"You timed it perfectly."

"I thought all was lost when he threw the tankard at your head. Thank goodness you realized what I had in mind."

"I was very slow. I was surprised to see you offering him more drink. Then, quite honestly, I remembered what used to happen when Southwick and I were curing you."

"'Completing my medical education' would be a more tactful word, sir, than 'curing.'"

"As you wish. Anyway, thank you. On my behalf and the three Devils'!"

"Yes, well, Aitken and young Orsini thought of that signal. I told Aitken we should stake everything on medical grounds, and between them they thought of that signal. Aitken could only keep it hoisted for ten or fifteen minutes at a time."

"That was long enough. The *Blackthorne* repeated it and it reached the admiral."

"And he sent you at once?"

Ramage laughed dryly. "No, if the majority of the *Murex* brig's men had not mutinied and carried the ship into Brest . . . And had I not been near Brest on my honeymoon . . . And had not my wife and I had the help of four Frenchmen so we could retake the *Murex* . . . And had we not managed to sail out and accidentally meet Admiral Clinton and the fleet . . . And had the *Calypso* not been my old ship . . . No, but for all those circumstances, Mr Sawbones, I don't think your signal would have attracted the attention it deserved. Still, all's well . . ."

"But will all this end well?" Bowen asked anxiously. "We still have him"—he gestured to the door of the sleeping cabin—"in there. Supposing the admiral doesn't . . ."

"Oh, he'll do something about him, I am sure. Who you'll get in his place I do not know. Probably the first lieutenant of the flagship—that's usually the person who gets the first vacant frigate command."

"But the *Calypso*'s still inside Channel limits."

"She won't be when the admiral makes the appointment: Brest is outside the limits. He wasn't born yesterday!"

"And you, sir?"

Ramage hesitated, thinking of *L'Espoir,* which, even while the *Calypso* and the brig rejoined the Fleet, was ploughing her way towards Cayenne, towards Devil's Island. Everything depended on Admiral Clinton. Would the Prince of Wales's friendship with a French refugee have any effect? Probably not. Almost certainly not. And even if it did, Clinton must have his own favourite frigate captains, and one of them would get orders which could bring him glory or, if he failed, square his yards for ever!

"I expect I'll be taking the brig back to Plymouth and reporting what I know of the mutiny to the Admiralty."

"And your wife, sir? Is her Ladyship still in France? You mentioned her when you talked of retaking the brig."

"Yes, we escaped together and she is on board the *Murex.* She wanted to come with me to board the *Calypso,* but I was rather worried about what I might find."

"I hope her Ladyship submitted with good grace."

"Well, you know her Ladyship, Bowen. I doubt if anyone would call her submissive," Ramage said.

Bowen laughed and his memories of Lady Sarah Rockley, as she was before her marriage, were of a lively and high-spirited woman of grace and beauty who would captivate all the men in a drawing room and leave the women seeming as flat as ale drawn last week.

CHAPTER ELEVEN

ADMIRAL CLINTON sat at his desk with the alert wariness of a stag lurking in a stand of low trees at the far end of a glen. He was trying to decide whether the five men in front of him were innocent visitors or a quintet likely to board him in a cloud of smoke.

"Well now," he said finally, his Scots accent broadening, and Ramage remembered Sarah's reference to the family, "so here ye all are. Let me see . . ."

"Yes, Dr Travis, the physician of my fleet, I know *you* well enough, and so I should since I see you every day. Are ye comfortable in that old armchair?"

Travis, tall and gaunt, everyone's idea of a dour man of medicine, had obviously qualified in Edinburgh, and his brief "Aye" was all he would allow himself for the moment.

"And m'flag captain—are you comfortable, Bennett? I know ye prefer standing but with this headroom and you so tall, it worries me!"

Except for Travis, the others laughed dutifully: Captain Bennett was only an inch or so over five feet; even his hair, wiry and sitting on his head like a bob major wig, did not come within five inches of the beams.

"Then there's Captain Ramage. Lord Ramage, by rights, but he saves us any possible embarrassment by not using his title. You're a jealous man, otherwise you'd have brought that beautiful wife with you."

Ramage smiled, not at all certain whether or not the admiral was making a polite joke. "She has only a fishwife's torn smock to wear, sir, so she decided to wait for a more appropriate occasion."

Clinton gestured at Ramage's trousers and shirt. "You'd have made a good pair. I've been a sailor too long to judge a ship by the patches in her sails."

He looked round at the settee. "Well, Mr Ramage, perhaps you'd introduce these gentlemen . . ."

"Sir, Lieutenant Aitken, the *Calypso*'s first lieutenant. He has served with me in the Mediterranean and the West Indies."

"Aye," Clinton told Aitken, "he's been telling me all about you. What he doesn't know—nor do you—is that I knew all about you long ago."

He gave a laugh at the look of dismay on the young lieutenant's face. "Man, you look as though the parson's just accused you of deflowering all the young women in the village. Y'father was another Aitken, master, was he not, and he served with me in the *Ramillies, Britannia* and this ship, the *Culloden*, before I hoisted my flag. I owed a lot to y'father and I've kept an eye on you from the day y'went to sea, but you've made your own way without needing a dram of help so I've held m'peace."

Aitken was obviously startled at this news and stammered his thanks, to be cut short by Clinton. "Ye've served Mr Ramage very well, and it looks to me as if Mr Ramage feels towards the Aitken family as I do. Still, we all have the rest of our lives to live and," he added, his voice taking on a friendly warning note, "a great deal of both good and bad can happen before we go to our graves."

A sombre silence had fallen over the great cabin and in Ramage's imagination the mahogany of the desk, wine-cooler and table seemed to grow darker, but Clinton seemed not to realize the effect he had unwittingly made.

"And you must be the *Calypso*'s surgeon—Bowen, isn't it? You and Mr Aitken have had a worrying time, I imagine. Now, who starts? Perhaps we'd be better starting at the end, then Dr Travis can be about his business."

Which was another way of saying, Ramage reflected, that Travis would not have to listen to things that he could be questioned about later at a court martial.

"How did you find the patient?"

"Mr Aitken was justified in signalling for the physician of the fleet, sir. This is no reflection on the medical capacity of Mr Bowen, who I truly believe understands a great deal more about this type of illness than I do."

"Don't stop man, you've only just started!" the admiral exclaimed impatiently.

"Acting on your orders, I boarded the *Calypso* frigate as soon as she hove-to near the flagship," Travis said in a monotonous voice, obviously nettled by the admiral's remarks, "and I asked Captain Ramage why the ship had made the signal requesting the fleet's physician. He said that the captain of the frigate, a certain Captain William Bullivant, was confined to his cot unconscious and not in a fit condition to exercise command of the ship."

"Oh, go on, man!"

"Captain Ramage commented to me," Travis said heavily, "that the nature of Captain Bullivant's illness was such that not only could he not exercise command, but it led him for long periods to act in a manner prejudicial to the King's business."

Everyone in the cabin realized that Travis had spoken slowly and with great care a sentence which was carefully phrased, intended not just for the ears of the commander-in-chief but the five or more captains and flag officers who might be forming a court martial or court of inquiry.

"Did you examine the patient?"

"I was introduced to the ship's first lieutenant and her surgeon, but before discussing the case any further I went below and examined the patient. I have my notes here," he said, pulling a sheaf of papers from a leather case. The admiral watched for a moment as Travis began sorting them out, and then groaned.

"No, no, Travis, don't start pouring Latin words all over me. I'm just a simple Highlander, not one of your brilliant Edinburgh scholars."

Travis glared at the admiral, sat up straight in the armchair and put the papers back in his case. "In words of one syllable, sir, Captain Bullivant was in a drunken stupor. He has been having attacks of—if you'll permit me that Latin—*delirium tremens,* and he was proposing to have the master, a midshipman and a seaman hanged at sunset."

Clinton's face paled. It took him only a moment to connect the Bullivant family and the Navy Board, the besotted captain of a frigate and the dangers for junior officers, and another moment to realize that the whole problem had landed in his lap like a haggis sliding away from the carver's knife.

"You can testify about the man's medical condition; you don't know about the hangings."

"I do, sir," Travis contradicted, and he said with some precision: "I confirmed the captain's intentions with each of the three men and my witnesses were Captain Ramage and Lieutenant Swan, the first lieutenant of the brig."

"Very well, doctor, and thank 'ee. I'm sure you have plenty of work waiting for you."

"I have that," Travis said. "You'll be wanting a written report?"

"I'll talk to you about that later."

As soon as Travis had left the cabin, Clinton looked at Ramage. "It was as bad as that?"

"Worse, sir. Bullivant was going to shoot me when I came on board: he reckoned I was Satan, too."

Clinton permitted himself a wintry smile. "A pardonable error of identification, some might say."

Ramage gave an equally wintry smile. "With a loaded pistol at less than five paces, sir."

"Too close, too close," Clinton agreed, and turned to Bowen. "When do you think the drinking started?"

"Years ago, sir. Secret drinking. As the months pass it takes a glass or two more to produce oblivion. Finally the brain is deranged, although at first not all the time. For a long time the patient probably manages to control his drinking so that he stays this side of *delirium*, but suddenly he is put under a strain—given the command of a ship, for example. He feels himself inadequate so he has an extra glass or two, or three or four. And he passes over the line into *delirium*. A few hours later he recovers from that particular attack, craves more drink . . . and so it goes on. Fifty glasses are not enough; one is too many."

"How long will it take to cure this man?"

"That is a question better answered by Dr Travis, sir."

"I am asking you," persisted the admiral.

"You won't like my answer, sir."

"When you reach my age and rank you rarely like *anyone*'s answers about *anything*, so that's not relevant. You were cured of the same thing."

"Yes, sir, but the cause—what drove me to drink—was not the same."

Ramage was pleasantly surprised at the way Bowen was carefully making his points: the admiral was leaning forward, like the close relative listening anxiously for the diagnosis.

"What's the difference? A drink is a drink. One man's body is like another. It's the liver isn't it. Gets damaged?"

"It's really the mind, sir," Bowen corrected gently. "It's the mind that starts a man drinking, although the liver eventually kills him. The patient we are concerned with started drinking— in my opinion, of course—because it helped him forget his feelings of inadequacy."

"Inadequacy? Inadequacy?" Clinton turned the word over

like a dog with a bone. "What did he feel inadequate about?"

"Commanding a frigate, sir. He was also unlucky enough to be given the *Calypso*."

"Bowen, you are talking rubbish."

Ramage, too, was startled to hear the surgeon declaring it was Bullivant's bad luck to be given the *Calypso*, although he thought he understood the rest of the point Bowen was making.

"You asked for my medical opinion, sir, and if you'll allow me, I had one of the best practices in Wimpole Street until I ruined it all with drink. So, drink, drinking, its cause and consequences—that is a subject I know a great deal about. If I was as expert in naval strategy and tactics, I would be the admiral of the red."

Clinton nodded because for the past few years, as he had begun climbing up the ladder of flag rank, he had been surrounded by sycophants: he found that many captains brave enough in action were too quick with the fawning "Yes, sir, no sir" in this cabin: he found he still enjoyed seeing an officer's features tauten and hear him say "If you'll allow me sir" as a preliminary to flatly contradicting a commander-in-chief who could destroy his career with the wave of a hand.

"I appoint you temporarily an admiral of the red wine," Clinton said dryly. "So explain his 'inadequacy' and why he was 'unlucky.'"

"As Lieutenant Bullivant on board a ship of the line or a frigate, the patient simply obeyed orders. Sighting land, changes in wind strength or direction, tacking or wearing—every captain's standing orders set down that he is to be called, so the patient never had to decide whether that was a particular headland, whether he had to reef or furl, tack or wear. His whole life at sea was to ask a senior when he was in doubt; to report and obey."

"Yes, yes, I understand that much," Clinton said.

"Suddenly—perhaps as a result of patronage, perhaps because he had proved to be a good lieutenant—"

"Perhaps a combination of both," Clinton interrupted sarcastically.

"Yes," Bowen agreed, "perhaps. Anyway, he was suddenly made post and given a frigate in emergency conditions with no previous experience of command: with the war about to start again he was ordered to take over the frigate in Chatham, get her ready for sea immediately—remember, she was in the process of paying off—and join your fleet for blockade duty off Brest, notoriously the worst job the navy has."

Clinton nodded encouragingly. "So far we are only stating in a medical voice what we all know."

"Agreed, sir; I could have said that in a naval voice. However, I will now proceed, if I may, in my Wimpole Street voice."

Clinton grinned: he was beginning to like this whimsical sawbones. He had heard enough about young Ramage to know that by now he must be a shrewd judge of men, and had been impressed at Ramage's earlier references to Bowen and his lieutenants and the master. Bowen must have sewn him up a few times too, come to think of it, because Ramage had been wounded often enough.

"You can talk in a Wimpole Street voice, but don't send me a Wimpole Street bill because you're still a ship's surgeon!"

"And I wouldn't exchange any of it."

"Easy to talk," Clinton commented.

Ramage said quietly: "With the late peace, sir, Mr Bowen came with me in the *Calypso* on a long cruise beyond the Equator."

Clinton pushed his chair back to the full extent of the chain which secured it to the deck against the ship's roll.

"Hmmp . . . that only tells me you are loyal if not wise, Bowen, but go on. Your patient"—Ramage noted that Clinton was still keeping the episode at arm's length—"has just been given a frigate and orders to join my fleet."

"Well, sir, he's now on his own. When the officer of the deck reports a landfall, a change in wind direction or strength, the decision to reef or furl, tack or wear, the decision what to do is now entirely the patient's: he's alone in his cabin or on the windward side of the quarterdeck. Oh yes, up to a point he can accept the suggestions of the master or the first lieutenant on points of seamanship and navigation, but there are very many decisions which only the captain can make."

"Yes, yes," Clinton said impatiently.

"The problem is that our patient," Bowen said in a flat voice, "can't bring himself to make those decisions. He suddenly realizes that despite years of training and all the family money and patronage and the fact he has now been given a ship, he's not competent to command it."

"Who says so?" Clinton demanded.

"I do, sir," Bowen said promptly. "I am not competent to judge his seamanship but I can judge him as a leader—or his attempts at leadership."

"Unlucky," Clinton interrupted. "You said he was unlucky to get command of the *Calypso*. Why? Is she a difficult ship to handle? Crank, tender, slow to windward? Truculent ship's company? Leaking decks? Why unlucky, eh?"

"Had he been given command of a frigate which had been commanded by an average captain, a ship and captain which never featured in the *London Gazette*, a frigate a man served in and forgot the name a year after, I'm sure everything might have been made to serve. He would have been able to hide his sense of inadequacy. But what happened? Well, I don't wish to embarrass Captain Ramage, who wears his fame lightly, but the *Calypso* and her captain are perhaps the best known in the King's Service. Our patient knows that in everything he does on board, every decision he makes and every order he gives, he will be compared to Captain Ramage. He thinks it's a comparison made daily by the officers and men and that it's a comparison bound to be made at the Admiralty or by a commander-in-chief. 'He's not a patch on young Ramage' . . . You may not have said it yet, sir, and you may never have said it at all, but the patient can imagine you saying it."

"Very well, you've explained 'unlucky.' Now explain the *delirium tremens*," Clinton said grimly.

"You may not know the patient by appearance, sir. No? Well, he is handsome but with a weak face. By that I mean if you judge a man's character to a certain extent by his face, you would not expect this man to have a strong will. As a lieutenant he delighted in strong drink. By inclination, perhaps, because he liked the taste. However, I think it more likely he needed a dram or two to bring him abreast of the rest of the officers in whichever ship he served. So the liking for drink was already there. He may have discovered—in fact from my own experience I am sure he did—that a few drinks made him quite as good in his own estimation as the next man, perhaps even better.

"What happens if you put a weak man prone to drink into a position where he feels inadequate (and thus *is* inadequate)? Well, sir, I suggest that at first the man does what he did before—looks to the tankard or the glass to make his decisions and blunt his cares. But soon he feels he needs more proof, and the cares increase. So does the drinking in proportion.

"It has to be drunk in secret, of course, so the patient increasingly feels guilty because he thinks he would be finished if anyone (even his personal servant) knew he was drinking to make himself fit to do his job."

Clinton growled: "We still haven't got him in a *delirium*."

"It doesn't take long. Some months for a newcomer to drink; some weeks for someone who has been an average drinker; but only a few days if the man has been a secret and heavy drinker for a long time."

"You can't say what the patient was doing before he joined the *Calypso*," Clinton objected.

"I can, sir, if you'll pardon me for contradicting you. I recognized him as a heavy drinker the moment he joined the ship."

"Am *I* a heavy drinker?" Clinton suddenly asked.

Bowen looked round the cabin. "A very large wine-cooler. A rack of cut-glass decanters which a duke might envy. And racks of wine and spirits glasses. They could belong to a heavy drinker; or let us say a connoisseur of wine and spirits. A *bon vivant*, in fact. However, you asked if I thought you were a heavy drinker, so I look at you and not the glassware. In fact, sir, I had by chance made up my mind—made a diagnosis, if you would prefer it—when I first came into the cabin, before I looked round."

"Well?" Clinton demanded. "A heavy drinker or a light one?"

"I would say," Bowen said slowly, "giving it due consideration, and allowing for the responsibility resting on your shoulders, and the fact that you come from Scotland, where more whisky is distilled than rainwater collected . . . I would say you probably have a glass of wine with your dinner, and perhaps a glass of port afterwards. No more."

The admiral's face fell: he reminded Ramage of a Father Christmas recognized by the children as the butler dressed up.

"I've given up the port," he admitted, "because I was afraid of the gout. Well, Mr Sawbones, after that display, I admit I'm now more prepared to listen to you. So let us suppose your patient drinks himself into a stupor (from time to time, I'm thinking, when the pressures get heavy) because—"

"No, sir," Bowen interrupted, "he's past the 'from time to time': he needs liquor to get out of his cot of a morning; he needs liquor to get him past the noon sight. He needs liquor because he's afraid of the devils with glaring eyes and demons with sharp tongues and all the clammy, crawling beasts that are waiting to attack him: all those horrible things that come with *delirium tremens*. And don't think they're imaginary, sir. They are to the onlooker; to the victim they are terrifyingly real."

"So what do we do about your patient?"

"Are you asking from the medical point of view or are you concerned with the *King's Regulations and Admiralty Instructions* and the Articles of War, sir?"

"Damned if I know," Clinton admitted. "It's an entirely new situation as far as I am concerned."

"Medically, a captain, master and Marine guards have nursed a man through *delirium tremens* in a few days—that I know because the patient was me—but it is hard work. Yet the following days are almost more important—getting the patient interested in life again and giving him the confidence to face it without using a bottle of liquor as a pair of crutches. I like chess, and Mr Southwick, the master, played endless games with me. Captain Ramage even learned to play to help out. I was very lucky.

"Discipline is out of my field, of course, but you may want a medical opinion on the disciplinary aspect, sir. In my opinion, which I will give you in writing, the patient is completely incapable of commanding a ship: indeed, he is both unfit and incapable of leaving his cabin."

Clinton stood up and sighed. "My orders are to start and maintain a close blockade of Brest with this fleet. Provisioning and watering the ships and trying to outguess the Atlantic weather, Bonaparte and every ship's propensity for wearing out, is normally agreed to be enough to keep an admiral occupied. Your damned patient, Bowen, is going to cause more problems than the rest put together."

The phrase "your patient" was finally too much for Bowen, who stood up, white-faced and almost rigid with anger, and said

stiffly: "Sir, that he is my patient is a very unfortunate coinci-
dence. Had I any say in the matter, he would never have been
employed as a lieutenant; whoever then made him post did
something akin to treason."

And that, Ramage thought, is how Dr Bowen was court-
martialled under at least two of the Articles of War, but he was
wrong: the admiral turned to the surgeon and smiled.

"Some flag officers suffer from spasmodic deafness." He waved
a dismissal to Bowen and Aitken. "Well, gentlemen, thank you.
Mr Ramage, will you stay a few minutes with Captain Bennett?"

Sitting at the end of the highly polished rosewood table with
Bennett halfway down one side on his right and Ramage to his
left, Admiral Clinton no longer looked like an amiable Santa
Claus: the grey-blue eyes which could twinkle were now glinting like the sharp blades of two freshly honed épées.

"This conference never took place, which is why my nincompoop of a secretary is not present taking notes. But I want
privately to hear your personal opinions of this fellow Bullivant.
Bennett?"

The admiral's flag captain was only five feet tall but had
achieved some fame (and the unexpected cheers of his men)
when his ship's company mutinied at the Nore some years earlier. Some wretched man had made an insolent remark to Bennett
about a matter unconnected with the mutiny, and in front of
several hundred mutinous seamen, Bennett had taken him by
the ear to the entry port, pushed him over the side, and then
coolly told the leader of the mutineers to fish him out because
he probably could not swim.

Bennett's first words showed he had not lost his directness.
"That surgeon fellow was right: Bullivant should never have been
made post," he said emphatically.

"Salt beef and salt pork supplied by the father: that's what mattered. Thousands of casks, and plenty of cumshaw scattered among the right people in the Navy Board, and your eldest son doesn't need much ability. It's unfortunate for the seamen, officers and admirals who suffer the consequences . . . In my opinion, sir, there's only one thing to do: send him back to Plymouth in the *Murex* brig with signed reports by Bowen and Dr Travis about his 'sickness.'"

"It's a serious matter, relieving him of his command."

Ramage realized that the admiral was wavering, and he thought of the *Calypso* and her officers and ship's company. "Sir, the consequences of not doing so will be worse."

"How so? Relieving a captain of his command is serious enough!"

"You are relieving him only on medical grounds, sir," Ramage reminded Clinton. "You are not saying he is incompetent. But the consequences of leaving him in command—well, yesterday, there could have been three murders by him or a mutiny by the ship's company. There's bound to be mutiny if you leave him in command."

"*Bound* to be mutiny? You don't have much confidence in the men you've spent so long training," Clinton said sarcastically.

"On the contrary, sir: I have *complete* confidence in them: that's why I know they'd mutiny."

Bennett was watching him shrewdly. He knows, Ramage realized, but the admiral has been too remote from the day-to-day handling of a ship's company for too long.

"Do you *really* mean you're confident they would mutiny?" Clinton demanded angrily.

Ramage nodded. "Yesterday, sir, Captain Bullivant said he would hang three men, Midshipman the Count Orsini, who happens to be the nephew of the ruler of Volterra and one of our allies; the master of the ship, who is certainly the most competent seaman and one of the bravest men I know; and an Italian seaman called Rossi, a man to whom I've entrusted my life on several occasions.

"Bullivant was going to have them hanged at sunset because after inspecting the entire ship's company he identified them as Satans. I trust, sir, that any seaman would mutiny rather than obey such an order to put nooses round their necks and haul them up to the yardarm."

Ramage knew he was white-faced, and he kept his fists pressed down on the table to hide the trembling: he could feel perspiration soaking through his shirt but mercifully it did not appear on his face, which felt cold and clammy, as though he might faint.

"Quite," Clinton said calmly. "However, it seems to me the only one now left with his neck in a noose is the commander-in-chief."

"That's what he's there for, sir," Bennett said cheerfully. "I agree with Ramage completely. I know what the Articles of War say and don't say, but I'd sooner the seamen mutinied than obeyed the 'lawful' orders of a brandy-besotted madman. That's something the Articles don't allow for, and they should. Loyalty is what matters. Men who'd mutiny because of their loyalty to their officers and shipmates are the men I want round me when I go into battle."

"We aren't in battle, we're blockading Brest, and judging from the last war the only action we're going to see is dealing with a drunken maniac," Clinton grumbled.

"At least you're outside 'Channel limits,' sir," Bennett said. "That gives you more freedom."

"Leaves me short of a post captain for the *Calypso*."

Bennett glanced across the table at Ramage. "A post captain commanding a brig is a bit overweight."

Clinton waved dismissively: "Ramage has to go to England with the brig: they'll need him at the inquiry into the mutiny and recapture, and for the Bullivant affair. Commanding a *prize*-brig, don't forget." The idea raised another train of thought for the admiral. "Hmm, that's an interesting point. There's no question that Ramage *captured* the damned ship: he didn't 'retake' her because he wasn't part of the original ship's company. He, his wife and four Frenchmen. He's the only one entitled to prize-money."

"His wife will help him spend it!" Bennett said jocularly.

"So you'll be back in Plymouth in a couple of days. Lucky fellow," Clinton said, and then added: "Why so gloomy? Sailing home after your honeymoon and with a sack full of prize-money!" Then a sudden thought struck him. "What about that young Scots first lieutenant? We ought to do something for him. Make him post into the *Calypso?*"

Ramage remembered an attempt a year or more ago when Aitken was offered command of a frigate and the post rank that went with it; he had said he preferred to continue sailing with Captain Ramage. But now was not the time to mention that to a Scots admiral. Aitken could make the point later, if necessary.

Bennett rubbed his ample chins and looked down at the table. "If I was Ramage, sir, I'd be eating my heart out over the *Calypso*. And weren't you telling me earlier that he was concerned over this French count who is being transported to Cayenne—a friend of the Prince of Wales, didn't you say, sir?"

Ramage decided that Bennett was a man to whom he already owed a debt of gratitude worth more than a brig.

"Bennett," Clinton said, his voice rasping, "you have an unhappy knack of mentioning things I'm trying to forget."

"Sir, I shouldn't forget that the Prince of Wales is unlikely to forget a commander-in-chief who forgot his friend being carried off to a certain death in Cayenne . . ."

And now, Ramage thought, the repetition of "forget" and "forgot" means the ace of trumps has gone down on the table. Or it's the bait dangling in front of the fish. Or the snare carefully placed outside the rabbit hole.

"Blast it, Bennett. I've been tossing up between the Prince of Wales and Lord St Vincent ever since Ramage mentioned the Count of Rennes. And it's probably not only the Count: if there are fifty of them, half are bound to be Royalists who went back to France after exile in England and know Prinny. At least half, probably more."

"You are caught between the devil (*pace* Bullivant) of the Admiralty and the deep blue sea of the Prince, seems to me, sir."

"It's all right for you to joke about it," the admiral complained. "I'm the one who has to choose."

"Oh, I chose when you first told me about it yesterday, sir," Bennett said blithely.

"You did, eh?" the admiral exclaimed, his voice now truculent, the accent becoming more pronounced. "Surprising how easy it is to choose when you don't have the responsibility."

Ramage expected Bennett to react strongly, but instead the little man picked up the quill pen lying on the table and waved it back and forth as though fanning himself.

"I'm like that surgeon fellow, whatever his name was. I'll put it in writing if you wish, sir. As your flag captain I'm expected to give you professional advice when you ask for it."

He paused and then tapped the table with the feather of the quill. "My views are simple. Question number one, what do we do with the drunken Bullivant? Wrap him up, in a canvas straitjacket if necessary, and send him home in the *Murex* brig with reports by Bowen and Travis tucked in his pocket."

He tapped the table twice. "Question number two, who is to command the *Calypso*? There's only one possible man, and that's Ramage here. He's not needed for the *Murex* because her first lieutenant is a capable fellow, saw the mutiny and can write reports and give evidence. Also he deserves his chance of getting command of her from the Admiralty. I'm assuming Ramage here is resigned to his new wife returning to England without him."

He tapped three times. "Now, the third question, what to do about the ship of exiles. She's a frigate now armed *en flûte*. She must look very much like the *Calypso*. She'll sail like her—except, since she's French carrying exiles, she'll be short of men and will most likely shorten sail at night. And she left the Gullet about 36 hours ago.

"What you are to do, sir, brings us back to the devil and the deep blue sea. Well, consider the devil in the shape of the First Lord of the Admiralty and the rest of the Board: they're political appointments. Lord St Vincent was appointed by Addington and will probably be replaced (along with the rest of the Board) by Addington's successor. So that devil can come and go. But now let us look across the deep blue sea . . . One day the Prince will be King. He will probably have a long life—they're a long-lived family—and no doubt he inherits the long memory, too."

He grinned at Admiral Clinton. "I'll give you my recommendations in writing, sir, but you'll have to take my word for the reasoning behind them."

"Oh, you're a droll enough fellow," Clinton said, mellowing slightly. "Watch out that one day I don't drop you over the side. Ramage, call that nincompoop of a secretary for me: I seem to have a number of orders to write, and I want them all carefully copied into my order book. Especially those intended for you."

CHAPTER   TWELVE

THE ABOMINABLE Bullivant had changed nothing in the great cabin: the desk was polished, the keys were still in the locks of the drawers. The settee was the same as usual, its dark-blue cover not torn or stained. The armchair was unmarked (except by the passing years flattening the springs). The man's possessions had been stowed in his trunks and sent across to the *Murex*. Yet although he had been on board for only a few days he had left an invisible atmosphere: now Ramage knew how the owner of a house felt standing in a room which had been rifled by a burglar.

He sat down at the desk, jerking open one drawer after another. Nothing had been removed, nothing added. Letter book—that was still here, and he flipped open a few pages. Bullivant had not written any official letters or, more likely, the clerk had not copied them into the letter book. Order book—yes, the Board order giving Bullivant command of the *Calypso*, followed by the Admiralty order to him to join Admiral Clinton's fleet were here, and so was Clinton's order to Bullivant telling him to place himself under the admiral's command. Nothing else.

The "Captain's Journal" was here, started the day Bullivant joined the ship, and Ramage put it in another drawer without reading it. Yes, here was the muster book, and an entry indicated the date that Bullivant had joined the ship "as per commission." No one had noted that he was replacing Captain Ramage, who was on leave. Now there was a nice point—in noting that Bullivant had gone to the *Murex* "by order of the commander-in-chief," did Ramage now note that Captain Ramage had taken (resumed?) command "as per commission," thus having taken command twice without ever having (officially) left the ship? Or did he ignore Bullivant's brief command?

Some tedious quill pusher at the Navy Board could worry about that bureaucratic problem, and no doubt the correspondence ensuing would continue for another ten years. He noted that no seaman had been discharged and no new men had joined the ship.

He put the muster book and letter book back in the drawer, and took Admiral Clinton's order from his smock. Soon he would be back in uniform. Several officers in the flagship had offered spare uniform frocks and breeches, stockings, shirts and stocks, but Ramage guessed that his own clothes would still be in the *Calypso,* and indeed almost the first thing his steward Silkin had reported was that his trunks had been brought up from the hold and all the clothing was being washed or cleaned or ironed with a sprinkling of vinegar to get rid of the musty smell.

He opened Admiral Clinton's two sets of orders and read the second one again. The admiral and Captain Bennett had drawn them up in a hurry, which ensured brevity.

"Whereas I have received information," Admiral Clinton's orders began, "that the French national frigate *L'Espoir* sailed from Brest very recently carrying as prisoners a large group of men and women accused by the French government of disloyalty and sentenced to transportation and exile in Cayenne, you are hereby required and directed to proceed with all possible despatch in His Majesty's ship *Calypso* under your command and make the best of your way towards Cayenne and intercept the said French national frigate *L'Espoir* and free the prisoners and carry them safely to a port in England, reporting at once to my Lords Commissioners of the Admiralty the success of your mission . . ."

He slid the letter between two blank pages in the order book and put the volume back in the drawer, locking it. It was lucky that Bullivant never bothered to put a key in his pocket—every drawer in this particular desk had a different lock.

The shouting, stamping and scuffling on the deck overhead had finally stopped and Ramage listened for feet clattering down the companion-way, to be halted at his door by the Marine sentry, who would then call out the person's identity.

He sat back and sighed with sheer pleasure. It was exciting to be back—he had spent so long in this cabin it seemed like home. Indeed, it was his home. Certainly sitting at this desk dressed as a French fisherman was unusual, but there was no time to wait for Silkin's smoothing iron to finish its work.

Since boarding the ship he had used the first fifteen minutes to listen to Silkin (who regarded his sartorial report as the most important the captain would want to hear) and then come down to the great cabin and read his orders once again. He had done this while Aitken prepared the ship for the next step.

And now there were the footsteps clattering down the companion-way, and the clank of a sword-hilt held high but not high enough to prevent it catching one of the steps.

The thump of feet and clatter of a musket indicated the Marine sentry coming to attention. Two voices, a question (from the sentry, one he would have had to ask even if the visitor had been his own mother), and a reply.

Then a tap on the door and the sentry's voice: "Captain, sir— the first lieutenant!"

"Send him in."

And in came a smiling Aitken, crouching slightly because of the low headroom, his sword held clear with one hand, his cocked hat under his arm.

"Ship's company mustered aft, sir."

"Aitken"—Ramage stood up and walked towards the young Scot, his hand extended. As they shook hands, Ramage added: "I'm glad to be back and I'm glad I have the same officers."

"Thank you, sir. We held our breaths when we heard the British ambassador—Lord Whitworth, I think it is—had left Paris, but when you didn't come back from your honeymoon we guessed that the French had captured you and her Ladyship."

Ramage gestured down at his smock and trousers. "You didn't expect to meet me off Ushant in this rig! Well, you should see her Ladyship—she's dressed as a fishwife."

He led the way up the ladder and out on deck. The Marines were lined up in two ranks against the taffrail; Southwick, the lieutenants and Orsini were at the starboard end of the front file, and the seamen formed the other three sides of the square so that the quarterdeck was a box of men.

Ramage had mustered all the men not through any overweening conceit but, because of that confidence always existing among men who have fought beside each other many times, he knew that they wanted to see him and be reassured.

The drunkard who had briefly taken his place had been hoisted out lashed on to a stretcher shouting and screaming that the seamen at the staytackle were doing the Devil's work. Now Bullivant was on his way to Plymouth in the *Murex* and he could only feel sorry for Sarah. She will, he thought grimly, see and hear what we went through with Bowen. Still, it is a bare one hundred and twenty miles from Ushant to Plymouth and the *Murex* should stretch over to the north-east at a good six knots, so that Sarah will have to put up with it for only 24 hours. Then she would post to London and very soon the thought of the recent excitement would be like a half-remembered dream.

On top of the main capstan: the ship was not rolling enough to make it difficult for him to balance, and he could look round and see everyone, except for two or three Marines hidden by the mizenmast. But it was a dam' cold wind: the downdraught from the mainsail seemed to go straight through his smock. The advantage of full uniform in a northern climate was its warmth, although it was too hot for the Tropics—the cocked hat, for instance, seemed to gain a pound in weight for every ten degrees of latitude it moved south, so that near the Equator it was about as comfortable as a knight's helmet.

Now the Marines were standing stiffly to attention, the lieutenants frozen to the deck, and the seamen looking up at him, some grinning, some straight-faced, but none sucking teeth. Few captains seemed to realize that the presence or absence of the sucking of teeth revealed more about the men's attitude, happiness or discontent, than anything else.

He spoke a few words of greeting as he pulled the first of Admiral Clinton's orders from the front of his smock and the Marines and lieutenants unfroze. The seamen knew only too well what was coming next and made sure they were standing comfortably.

Ramage unfolded the paper and began the ritual of "reading himself in." Until that was completed he could not officially give any orders and expect them to be obeyed; he had purposely made "stand at ease" a gruff comment rather than an order, and the helm order to Southwick was to save time. Then he began reading.

"By virtue of the power and authority to me given as commander-in-chief of His Majesty's ships and vessels comprising the Channel Fleet, and being off Brest and outside the Channel limits, I Reginald Edward Clinton, Vice-Admiral of the Red, do hereby constitute and appoint you captain of His Majesty's ship the *Calypso* frigate, willing and requiring you forthwith to go on board and take upon you the charge and command of captain in her accordingly . . ."

Ramage paused for breath, cursing the man who had originally (probably a hundred years ago) drawn up the wording, never considering the poor captain who had to recite them loud enough so that over the sound of the wind and the sea every man in a ship's company could hear them. Well, almost all the seamen were grinning now, and he continued.

". . . Strictly charging and commanding all the officers and company of the said *Calypso* frigate to behave themselves jointly and severally in their respective employments . . . and you likewise to observe the General Printed Instructions . . . Hereof nor you nor any of you may fail as you will answer to the contrary at your peril; and for so doing this shall be your warrant . . ."

That last sentence meant just what it said: lieutenants, post captains and admirals had been court-martialled and broken for failure. The commission of course covered any orders given by superiors, and the admiral's actual orders had a vagueness about them explained partly by the lack of much knowledge about *L'Espoir,* her prisoners and her route, but also so worded that whatever happened (in case of failure) the admiral could not be blamed. Admiral Clinton had been careful to note that he and Ramage were "outside the Channel limits," because within Channel limits only the Board of Admiralty could appoint captains.

Ramage folded the orders and tucked them back inside his jersey: he had "read himself in," he was (once again) commanding the *Calypso.* As soon as he had "read himself in," Ramage reflected, a captain usually made a speech to the ship's company (threatening, inspiring, flatulent, boring—different styles). But all these men, all the names attached to the sea of faces surrounding him, knew him well: they had gone into action with him, boarded enemies beside him, pistol, cutlass or boarding-pike in hand. Some had been blown up with him, most had seen him brought back unconscious from wounds. There were no words to say to such men.

He just looked round slowly at all the men, raised his right hand in a salute that suddenly reminded him absurdly of a Roman emperor's gesture, and jumped down from the main capstan amid a swelling roar of cheers: "Three cheers and a tiger," and apparently led by Southwick.

Well, he was back. Where was *L'Espoir?*

The sea now had the is-it-mauve-or-is-it-purple? of the deep ocean, with white horses stippling the tops of a few wind waves while swell waves slid beneath them. The *Calypso* was pitching slightly and rolling heavily, the masts and their yards creaking and the bulging sails frequently flattening and slatting as a particularly quick roll suddenly spilled the wind for a minute or two.

Astern the sun had lifted over the line of distant black cloud lying low and flat on the eastern horizon like a shadowy baulk of timber floating on the sea, and quickly the last of the stars were dazzled away and the sky overhead turned pale blue and cloudless.

In a few hours they would be crossing that invisible line of latitude 23° 27' North, marking the Tropic of Cancer, and, Ramage reflected thankfully, at last they seemed to have picked up the Trade winds.

For the previous few days it had been a damp and dreary ritual. During the night the wind dropped, leaving the *Calypso* wallowing in a confused sea which bounced her up and down like a doormat being shaken and made everything movable creak, rattle or bang. In Ramage's cabin even the wine glasses clinked in their rack as though toasting each other. Two drawers full of clothes which had not been shut properly skidded across the painted canvas that served as a carpet on the cabin sole, spilling silk and lisle stockings, handkerchiefs, stocks and shirts as though a dog was making a nest in a draper's storeroom.

Dawn each day had revealed thunderstorms building up all round them, the lower clouds foaming upwards towards a higher layer which soon cut off the sun. From time to time Ramage had stood at the quarterdeck rail, picturing *L'Espoir* scores of miles ahead and sailing in different weather, the Trade winds sweeping her south and west to Cayenne, sails bulging, the French captain cheerful as he marked his chart and filled in his journal to record a fast passage from Brest.

In the *Calypso*, Ramage, almost stifling with frustration, had looked up at the sails hanging down like heavy curtains, chafing against rigging, the foot of each one wearing against the mast since the sails of the King's ships were cut with a straight foot, not the deep curve favoured by merchant ships deliberately to avoid the chafe but reducing the area of the sail, something a ship of war could not afford.

Clew up to save some of the chafe or furl and avoid any at all? Or leave them so that he would not lose a minute once the first gust of wind arrived? But when it came (this week or next) would the wind be just a nice gust or would it be a roaring blast from one of those great thunderstorms that would send topmen hurrying to furl as courses were hastily clewed up and Aitken doubled the number of men at the wheel so that four stood a chance of preventing the overpressed frigate broaching as she raced to leeward, barely under control?

Should he risk losing a mile or so of progress, should he risk that heart-stopping bang of sail torn in half by the brute strength of the wind and then the thudding and thumping of the pieces slatting, or should he furl everything and wait for the wind to set in properly?

Eventually while he argued back and forth with himself and Southwick paced up and down, a lonely figure on the lee side of the quarterdeck, or Ramage stopped and barked at the quartermaster or chatted with the officer of the deck, in this case Martin, whiffles of wind had been spotted by the lookout at the foremasthead (a man having to hold on for dear life, and Ramage would have forgiven him if he had been too dizzy to spot anything). But the dancing shadows on the water were coming from the south. Anyway, anything was better than having the ship slat and bang herself to pieces, so they had braced up the yards and trimmed the sheets and found that, with the swell from the east and the lightness of the wind, the best they could lay and keep the sails asleep was west by north. They could pinch her to west by south but she slowed like a carriage miring itself in mud.

For the rest of each of those days they had jogged along at four and five knots, with the wind falling away at night and dawn bringing more thunderstorms. And the glass had fallen a little.

Except for this morning: while it was still dark the wind had again set in light from the south but he noticed that the glass had stopped falling and went on deck to find the sky was full of stars, already a good deal brighter than usual in northern skies. As dawn had begun to push away the dark of night the wind backed slightly—the coxswain had reported it as fluking around south-east by south, and the *Calypso* would just lay south-west-by-west. An hour later it was a steady east-south-east with the *Calypso* almost laying the course.

By noon it had backed another few points so that Southwick marked the slate in the binnacle box drawer and recorded the wind as north-east-by-east, with the ship making seven knots with all sails set to the royals and laying the course. More important, the ship's company were getting the stunsails up on deck ready for hoisting. The Trades had really set in? They could only hope. The noon sight—with Southwick, Aitken and Ramage himself on deck with quadrants and sextants measuring the sun's altitude—gave the latitude as 24° 06' North. Orsini had also taken a sight, which involved only turning the adjusting screw of the sextant to get the highest angle the sun made and did not depend on the accuracy of the chronometer. The young midshipman had achieved all that without difficulty, but had stumbled over the simple calculations which involved the sextant angle and the sun's declination. The latitude, he finally admitted to Southwick, had to be wrong, as the master pointed out with mild irony, since it placed the *Calypso* on the same latitude as Edinburgh.

Ramage was allowing a knot of south-east going current but previous experience showed this was too much. However, like Southwick who was a cautious navigator, he preferred that any error put the reckoning ahead of the ship: if the ship was ahead of the reckoning she could (and many did!) run on to unseen rocks and reefs guarding the destination.

As he was taking the noon sight, Ramage felt sure the Trades were setting in with their usual abruptness. At the moment only a few of the typical Trade wind clouds—small, flat-bottomed with rounded tops and reminding him of mushrooms—were moving in neat lines apparently converging on a point beyond the western horizon.

Trade wind clouds were a never-failing entertainment in the Tropics. In fact, he reflected, weather in the Trades could also be alarming for a Johnny Newcome, whether a seaman or officer fresh to the Tropics. In crossing the Atlantic, often one would find at dawn a band of low, thick cloud to the east (to windward and therefore, one would think, approaching) which would become black and menacing as the sun rose behind it: obviously, one would think, the herald of a strange tropical storm or gale, or at least a devastating squall.

The beginning of the day in the ship usually meant that for an hour or two every man was fully occupied, and then the Newcomes would suddenly remember (with more than a stab of fear) and look astern for that low, black cloud. But a quick glance to the eastward would show a clear horizon and an innocent sun rising with all the grace and smoothness of a duchess composing herself for a portrait artist.

So by nine o'clock the sky would be clear from horizon to horizon and the sun just beginning to hint that soon it would have some warmth in it. Then the parade of the mushrooms would begin.

He called them mushrooms but they really started in the distance as rows of white pinheads on a pale blue velvet pincushion. They would gradually move to the westward, keeping in neat lines but each pinhead beginning to expand like a fluffy ball of cotton growing on its bush. On and on to the westward they would move, and the sun warming the air would make the clouds blossom larger, but they would still stay in orderly and evenly-spaced lines, like columns of well-drilled soldiers advancing across a plain. Sometimes the shapes would change: while the bottom stayed flat, the top would take up a grotesque shape, like a bun determined to alarm the baker's wife.

For Ramage the actual growth of the lines of cloud was the least of it. The fun came in looking at each of them. With flat bottom and bulging top, many were like recumbent effigies on the tops of tombs; with others the white vapour curved and twisted into the shape of faces staring up into the sky. In the course of fifteen minutes, ten chubby, long-faced, pug-nosed or long-nosed politicians familiar from cartoonists' broadsides, a dozen friends, and a dozen more bizarre but identifiable shapes would sail past on their way westward.

Occasionally, often in the late afternoon towards sunset, the western sky would slowly turn into the most horrifying scarlets and oranges, livid purples and ominous mauves, as though a child was being introduced to watercolour washes, and it seemed that within hours a most devastating hurricane must roar up against the wind and bring enormous seas to set them all fighting for their lives. But by nightfall the sky was usually clear again and sparkling with its full complement of stars and no hint of where the gaudy clouds had gone or why they had appeared.

The first flying fish always excited the ship's company: as soon as the ship slipped into the warmer southern seas most men would glance over the side as frequently as possible, hoping to be the first to glimpse the tiny silver dart skimming a foot or two high in a ridge and furrow flight over the waves to vanish as quickly as it appeared. What seemed the upper quadrant of a slowly turning and very thick wheel was the curving back of a dolphin, and always good for a yell, and sometimes a dozen or so of them would play games with the ship, racing to cut across the bow from side to side and so close that it seemed the cutwater must hit them.

For Ramage, though, there was a particular assignation in the

Tropics, and he always felt cheated if he was not the first to sight it. It was the unusual rather than beautiful white bird which could be mistaken for a great tern, but for the fact that its tail, three times as long as its body, comprised a couple of long thin feathers trailing in a narrow V. The beak of the tropic bird was red or yellow and the wings were narrow and pointed like those of the tern with the fast beat of a pigeon. Strangely enough it seemed to be a bird of the islands and headlands, one that was used to jinking and diving, and which would not stray far from land. And what was the purpose of that tail?

The birds in fact lived in colonies—he knew of several at St Eustatius and Nevis, in the Leeward Islands (each island, coincidentally, was easily identified because of the huge topless cone at one end revealing an old volcano). A passage between St Martin and St Barthélemy on one side and Saba, St Eustatius and St Kitts and Nevis on the other usually produced a dozen or more tropic birds flying across the channel.

Yet Ramage had seen them here in the middle of the Atlantic, fifteen hundred miles and more from the nearest land, flying with just the same quick, almost nervous wing beats, as though due back at the nest in twenty minutes. It seemed to make little difference whether its destination was fifteen or fifty miles away. Nor fifteen hundred: that was simply the middle of the Atlantic between the Canary Islands and Barbados. To reach one from the other (or any land) the bird had to fly nearly three thousand miles. Did it just fly day and night without stopping? He had never seen one resting on the water like a seagull. And another strange thing was that all those he had seen out in the Atlantic were always flying directly east or west, never to the north or south. On the last voyage, he remembered looking up at eight o'clock in the forenoon to see his first Tropic bird of the passage flying due east, directly over the ship. Then, at four o'clock in the afternoon, he had seen one flying due west, again passing right over the ship. The same bird? His ship's destination, Barbados, had been two thousand miles to the westward. Yet, he remembered, every tropic bird he had ever seen out in the Atlantic had passed directly over the ship: he had never seen one flying past in the distance. Nor did the bird ever dip down towards the ship, as though looking for a resting place or a tasty scrap of food.

Other species of birds often came on board, though of course they were usually much nearer land. Still, an old Barbados planter he had once spoken to said tropic birds lived on flying fish and squid, diving down for them. The planter called it the boatswain bird, and the French had several names, different in each island—*paille-en-queue, paille-en-cul,* and *fléche-en-cul.* Straw tail, arrow tail—there were a dozen ways of translating it, but the Spanish *contramaestre* was the nearest to the English boatswain bird.

He waved to Aitken to cross the quarterdeck and join him.

"Horizon looks very empty, sir," the young Scotsman commented. "Seems you only realize how big the Western Ocean is when you're looking for someone."

"We could have overtaken her. Or she could be to the north or south. Or ahead of us."

"Aye, it'll be only a matter of chance if we sight her. Ten different captains have ten different routes for making this crossing."

"So you're not very hopeful?"

"No, sir, not with the difference in time."

Ramage nodded. "Once she was a complete night ahead of us—ten hours of darkness—there was always the chance of us accidentally overtaking her. And with two or three hundred miles' difference in position, there's the weather, too. She could be stretching along comfortably with a northerly breeze while we are beating against a southerly. She could have a soldier's wind with stunsails set and we could be becalmed."

"At least we're catching up now!" Aitken gestured to the

stunsails, long narrow strips of sail each hanging down from its own tiny boom and hoisted by a halyard out to the end of a normal yard so each stunsail formed an extension of the sail, like an extra leaf at the end of a table.

"Catching up or outstripping?" Ramage mused. "I can't see Frenchmen hurrying with a ship full of prisoners: they could be treating it all as a comfortable cruise and be in no rush to get back to France—it'll be winter by then, too. They've no idea they're being chased."

The two men walked aft from the quarterdeck rail, past the companion-way leading down to the captain's cabin, then abreast the great barrel of the main capstan, with the slots for the capstan bars now filled with small wedge-shaped drawers containing bandages and tourniquets, ready at hand if they should go into action. Past one black-painted gun on its carriage, and now a second. Then came the binnacle box, like an old chest of drawers with a window on each side, a pane of stone-ground glass revealing a compass which was far enough away not to affect the one on the other side but so placed that the man on either side of the wheel had a good view.

Now the double wheel. Normally the man to windward did most of the work, pulling down on the spokes, but with the ship running before the wind as she was now doing, yards almost square and stunsails drawing, each helmsman paid attention and the quartermaster's eyes never stopped a circuit which covered the luffs of the sails, the telltales streaming out from the top of the hammock nettings, and the compass.

The telltales—Ramage was thankful to see them bobbing so vigorously. Four or five corks threaded at ten-inch intervals on a length of line, with half a dozen feathers embedded in each cork, and the whole thing tied to a rod and stuck up in the hammock nettings, one each side, might not be everyone's idea of beauty, but after those days of calm and light headwinds, they were a wonderful sight.

Now they were passing the captain's skylight—built over the forward side of the great cabin it was a mixed blessing: it provided air and light, and he could hear what was going on, but sometimes the quarterdeck was a noisy place: at night there could be the thunderous flap of sails followed at once by the officer of the deck cursing the quartermaster, and the quartermaster cursing the helmsmen for their inattention . . . The officer of the deck at night would regularly call to the lookouts (six of them, two on the fo'c's'le, two amidships, and one on each quarter) to make sure they were awake and alert . . . Then, Ramage thought sourly, there would be one of those "Is-it-isn't-it" conversations, probably between the sharp-eyed young Orsini and the officer of the deck. One would think he glimpsed a sail, or land, or breakers in the darkness. The other would be equally sure there was nothing. The muttered but heated debate would be enough to make sure that a drowsy Ramage wakened completely, and often, although he knew there was no land for a hundred miles, he would pull on a cloak and go on deck—there was always a chance . . .

Finally the last gun on the starboard side and a few more paces brought them up to the taffrail and time to turn back, both men turning inwards, a habit which ensured no interruption if they had been talking.

"This Count of Rennes, sir?" Aitken said cautiously. "You've met him?"

"He has been a friend of my family since long before the war began."

"Ah, so you feel all this personally, too, sir?"

"Yes—but he escaped to England at the Revolution and lived in England until the recent treaty. He still has an estate in Kent.

But we're chasing *L'Espoir* because he's one of the most important French Royalists alive today."

"And he won't be alive for long if they get him to Cayenne. That Devil's Island is well named, so I've heard."

"There are two or three islands. I think the French call them the Îles du Salut. One is for convicts and another for political prisoners."

"I have some notes on Cayenne and the islands," Aitken commented. "Taken from some old sailing directions from the seventies. They probably haven't changed much!"

"You have them on board?"

"In my cabin, sir. I checked as soon as you mentioned where *L'Espoir* was bound."

"We'll go over them soon, just in case."

"That's where you'll catch the rabbit, sir," Aitken commented. "A poacher doesn't set a snare in the middle of the field; no, he puts it just outside the burrow. Then you catch the rabbit when it runs for home!"

Ramage stopped for a few moments. Yes, Aitken's simile made sense: why comb the Atlantic? Three thousand miles was the distance, and assuming the *Calypso*'s lookouts could see ten miles on each beam in daylight, they were searching a swathe three thousand miles long and twenty miles wide—sixty thousand square miles. Which, to continue Aitken's simile, must be like walking across a county unable to see over the top of the grass. Cayenne was the burrow: that's where he had to set the noose.

Yet . . . yet . . . He resumed walking with Aitken.

"It doesn't leave us room or time to make any mistakes," he said. "If we're off the coast of Cayenne and *L'Espoir* heaves in sight, she only has to cover five miles or so and she's safe."

"But if we're patrolling that stretch of the coast with all our guns run out, sir," Aitken protested.

"You might just as well leave them unloaded with the tompions in," Ramage said grimly. "I can hardly fire into a ship where a quarter of those on board are likely to be those I'm ordered to rescue . . ."

"Then how are we . . . ?" Aitken broke off and came to a stop facing Ramage. He shook his head. "I've spent many hours trying to decide the route *L'Espoir* would take, so that we could intercept her, but I didn't think of . . . Yet it's so obvious!"

"Not that obvious," Ramage assured him. "Neither the admiral nor his flag captain considered it in drawing up my orders!"

"We're going to have to bluff 'em," Aitken said dourly.

"Bluff won't help much: the French will see Devil's Island close to leeward and all they have to do is make a bolt for it."

"Would they risk damage to their spars with land so close to leeward?"

"Of course. From what I've read, it's a mud-and-mangroves-and-sand coast and it's theirs, so even if we sent all their masts by the board, the ship would drift on to a friendly lee shore and the French would march their prisoners off at low water. Not quite that, because there's ten feet or so of tide, but you know what I mean."

"But *L'Espoir*'s people would know they'd then be marooned there for months, until the next batch of prisoners are sent out. Worse than that, until the next ship arrives that manages to break our blockade of Brest."

Ramage thought of the problem often facing captains: how to train their officers fully to consider all the enemy's advantages without getting too overwhelmed or depressed to think of ways of overcoming them. An overwhelmed or depressed officer was almost as dangerous as an overconfident one. Well, perhaps Aitken would get there by himself.

"The French captain may have guessed that a British frigate

is after him," Ramage said, without adding the corollary that he would have had a long time to think of his advantages and disadvantages.

"I don't see why, sir," Aitken said politely but firmly. "In fact, if you'll pardon me, I think it'll be just the opposite. He'll be treating it like an unexpected cruise."

"But he can't be sure he won't be intercepted somewhere by a patrolling British frigate."

Ramage almost grinned at the effort Aitken, usually a very patient man, was making not to show his complete disagreement with this sort of reasoning. In other words, Ramage thought, it's working: Aitken really is considering!

"Sir, no ship that he meets, not one, whether French or British, Spanish or Dutch, will know that the war has started again: the news can't possibly have reached them yet. Cayenne and Devil's Island won't know of the new war until *L'Espoir* arrives, and her captain knows that as long as he smiles and waves if he sights a British frigate, he's in no danger because the British frigate will think the world is at peace.

"The *Calypso*, sir," Aitken continued emphatically, "is the most westerly British ship that knows the war has started again.

"If we've overtaken *L'Espoir*, then we are the western-most ship in existence."

Ramage nodded agreement. "We can be thankful Bonaparte didn't send out a dozen frigates from Brest the moment our ambassador left Paris: in areas off Madeira and the Canaries they could have captured dozens of John Company and other ships all bound to and from England. But he didn't because he's a soldier and not a sailor, and anyway they're very short of seamen in Brest."

"Aye," Aitken agreed. "That Bonaparte seems to be a bonny soldier and we can be thankful he didn't take to the sea. Anyway, *L'Espoir* will have no reason to think the *Calypso* knows there's a war."

"Wouldn't she be suspicious at seeing a British frigate so far south on this coast? About eight hundred miles south of the nearest British naval headquarters, Barbados?" Ramage continued testing Aitken.

"Sir, the *Calypso*'s French-built, and apart from the fact that she's a little smarter than the usual French national ship, there's no way she'd know we're British unless we're flying our own colours."

Now Aitken was straying from the point Ramage wanted him to discover and consider.

"Yes, I agree with all that but—and it's a big 'but'—Bonaparte never forgives anyone who makes a mistake. In France there's a very complicated secret police system under which everyone is supposed to report on everyone else. One effect is that anyone failing to carry out his orders is likely to be accused of treason. Failure is frequently labelled treachery to the Revolution. And that usually means the guillotine—few brought before the courts in France are ever found not guilty."

"So you think that the captain of *L'Espoir* will have considered that among the possible risks and dangers, sir? That he won't regard this voyage as a cruise, even though he is certain to be sailing ahead of the news of war?"

"Look at it another way, Aitken: forget the naval aspect. The captain of *L'Espoir* is carrying out the orders of the admiral at Brest, but he is a realist: *he* knows that the orders really come from the Ministry of Police, from that man Fouché, in fact. His written orders may have said that he was to carry fifty *déportés* from Brest to Devil's Island and hand them over to the *préfet*, but he knows very well that those fifty men (and their women) are regarded by Bonaparte at the moment as being the fifty greatest traitors who can be transported instead of guillotined. Now do you follow?"

Aitken shook his head. "I don't think so, sir. It seems quite straightforward to me, but from the tone of your voice obviously it isn't!"

"Well, if somehow the captain does not deliver those fifty prisoners to the *préfet* in Cayenne, but instead they escape or are rescued by a British ship, so that Bonaparte and his police can't get at them, then—"

"Ah, I see!" Aitken exclaimed, his voice a mixture of triumph and disbelief. "He would be accused of treachery—of deliberately allowing those fifty to escape."

"Exactly. Ministers in power and Bonaparte himself always need scapegoats. The captain of *L'Espoir* knows that. No one commands a French national ship of war today solely because of his seamanship. Remember, in the first six months of the Revolution, France destroyed many of her best officers, so today most of her captains are former boatswains; men who've survived all those earlier régimes. The captain of *L'Espoir* has survived—for nine years. He knows how to do it; he's an expert. So you can be sure he hasn't ruled out the chance of interception."

"How does that affect us, sir? He must still be sure he is sailing ahead of the news of war."

"Come now, forget that aspect. He has fifty valuable prisoners on board—valuable particularly because they could lead him to the guillotine. Surely he must have at least one overwhelming advantage . . ."

"Well—oh yes!" Aitken exclaimed. "Fifty hostages! No one attempting a rescue would dare risk harming them! Yes, he knows no one dare fire a broadside into him. By God, he's as immune from harm as a pirate holding a nun in front of him."

"Exactly, immune from broadsides, and he doesn't have to give a damn about arriving disabled on a lee shore. If he hands over the prisoners to the *préfet* safely at the cost of losing his ship the Minister of Marine might be lenient as long as he gets a favourable report from the *préfet*. Mind you, the captain and ship's company will be marooned in Cayenne and half might die from the black vomit and the survivors be captured on their way back to France in another ship . . ."

Aitken said suddenly: "What do we do if we sight *L'Espoir* this afternoon, sir?"

"I've no idea," Ramage admitted. "We might send their masts by the board or tear their sails to shreds with langrage, but we'd still have to carry the ship by boarding and if the captain uses the prisoners as hostages and threatens their lives, we're still no nearer rescuing anyone."

"It's a worry, sir," Aitken commented, and Ramage was irritated by the Scotsman's tone: he spoke in the "Yes, well, the captain's bound to think of something" voice. However, as Aitken now knew well, this time there was no way.

Admiral Clinton was lucky, Ramage thought sourly as he turned yet again at the taffrail: if the Count of Rennes and his fellow prisoners were not rescued, or were killed, the commander-in-chief would certainly incur the disfavour of the Prince of Wales, but that was all, because his orders (as far as they went) were quite correct. But Captain Ramage, whatever the verdict of a court martial, could be sure that at best he would spend the rest of his life on the beach, drawing half-pay. No one would say anything out loud, but at the Green Room in Portsmouth, at Brooks's, White's and such places, there had been too many of his *Gazettes* published by the Admiralty for there not to be jealousy of "that fellow Ramage."

Nor would half-pay now be so boring and frustrating; in fact, with Sarah beside him it could be very lively. They would live at St Kew and running the estate would keep them busy. Yet he knew that while the war against France lasted and there were ships of the Royal Navy at sea, only half his heart would be in Cornwall. That, Sarah would know, might prove the most difficult thing to deal with.

He shook his head to dispel the thoughts: what on earth was he getting so depressed about, putting himself on half-pay when they had not even sighted *L'Espoir?*

Five minutes later, as Aitken wrote on the slate and Ramage continued pacing the windward side of the quarterdeck, there was a hail from aloft.

"Deck there—foretopmast lookout here!"

CHAPTER THIRTEEN

MESS number eight was the rather grandiose official description of one of the well-scrubbed tables and two forms flanking it on the *Calypso's* lower deck. It was on the larboard side abreast the forehatch, which ensured a bitterly cold draught in winter in northern latitudes, but as the *Calypso* under Captain Ramage's command had spent most of her time in the Tropics or the Mediterranean, the members of the mess were content.

The outboard end of the narrow side of the table fitted into the ship's side and the other was suspended from the deckhead by two ropes. Each of the forms on the long sides of the table seated four men, so that each mess in the ship comprised no more than eight men.

The mess had its own equipment. There was the bread barge, a wooden container in which the bread for the mess was kept. The bread was ship's biscuit, made in the great naval bakeries, and at the moment it was fresh, a word used to describe a square of hard baked dough which was still hard, not soft and crumbling, the happy home of the black-headed and white-bodied weevils which felt cold to the tongue but had no taste.

The bread barge was in some ways a symbol of the mess. The number eight was carefully painted on the tub-shaped receptacle and beside it was the mess kid, a tiny barrel open at one end with what looked like two wooden ears through which was threaded a rope handle. Also marked with the mess number, it was used to carry hot food from the copper boilers in the galley to the table.

The carefully scrubbed net bag folded neatly on the bread barge and with a metal tally stamped "8" fixed to it was the "kettle mess," the improbably named object in which all hot food was cooked, because boiling in the galley's copper kettles was the only way it could be done. The Calypso's cook, like those in each of the King's ships, was the man responsible for the galley in general, the cleanliness of the copper kettles and the fire that heated the water in them, but that was the limit of his cooking.

Each mess had its own cook, a man who had the job for a week. Number eight mess' cook this week was Alberto Rossi, a cheerful man who was nicknamed "Rosey" and usually corrected anyone who called him Italian by pointing out that he came from Genoa, which in Italian was spelled Genova, so that he was a Genovese. If number eight mess decided in its collective wisdom that it would use its ration of flour, suet and raisins (or currants) to make a duff, Rossi's culinary skill would extend itself to mixing the ingredients with enough water to hold them together, put them in the kettle mess and make sure (with tally safely affixed) that it was delivered to the ship's cook by 4 A.M. and collected at 11.30 A.M., in time for the noon meal.

For this week when he was the mess cook, Rossi was also responsible for washing the bowls, plates, knives, forks and spoons of the other members of the mess, and stowing them safely. And, because bread, even if not appetizing, eased hunger, he had to make sure the bread barge was full—any emptying being ascribed to the south wind. Stafford, noting it was barely half-full, might comment: "There's a southerly wind in the bread barge."

Nor were the points of the compass limited to the compass and the bread barge: tots of rum were also graded. Raw spirit was due north, while water was due west, so a mug of nor'wester was half rum and half water, while three quarters rum would become a nor'-nor'wester and a quarter of rum would be west-nor'west and find itself nobody's friend.

The seven men now sitting at mess number eight's table piled up their plates and basins. Three used old pewter plates, but four, the latest to join the mess, used bowls and looked forward to the *Calypso* taking her next prize, Rossi having explained carefully that a French prize years ago had yielded the three pewter plates in defiance of the eighth Article of War, which forbade taking "money, plate or goods" from a captured ship before a court judged it a lawful prize. There was an exception which the three men interpreted in their own way—unless the object was "for the necessary use and service of any of His Majesty's ships and vessels of war." Admittedly such objects were supposed to be declared later in the "full and entire account of the whole," but as Stafford said at the time with righteous certainty in his Cockney voice: "S'welp us, we clean forgot."

"Feels nice to be warm again," Stafford remarked, wiping his mouth on the back of his hand. "England's never very warm but the Medway's enough ter perish yer. The wind blowin' acrorst those saltings . . . why, even the beaks of the curlews curl up with the cold."

"Curlew? Is the bird? Is true, this curling?" Rossi asked, wide-eyed.

Jackson, the captain's coxswain, who owned a genuine American Protection issued to him several years earlier, shook his head. "It's just another of Staff's stories. All curlews have long curved beaks whether it's a hot day or cold."

"Anyway, I'm glad we're back in the Tropics," Stafford said cheerfully. "Don't cross the Equator, do we?"

Jackson shook his head. "Not even if we go all the way to Cayenne. What's its latitude, Gilbert?"

The Frenchman shook his head in turn. "I am ashamed," he said, "but I do not know it."

When another of the French asked a question in rapid French, Gilbert translated Jackson's question, and the Frenchman, Auguste, said succinctly: *"Cinq."*

"Auguste says five degrees North," Gilbert said.

"Five, eh? When we're in the West Indies, up and down the islands, we're usually betwixt twelve and twenty," Stafford announced, and turned to Jackson, "There, you didn't know I knowed that, didja!"

"Knew," Jackson corrected automatically, and Stafford sighed.

"Oh, all right. You didn't knew I knowed that, then."

"Mama mia," Rossi groaned, "even I know that's wrong. Say slowly, Staff: 'You didn't know I knew that.' How are these *Francesi* going to learn to speak proper?"

"Don't sound right to me," Stafford maintained. "And I come from London. You're an American, Jacko—Charlestown, ain't it? And you're from Genoa, Rosey. So I'm more likely to be right."

Jackson ran his hand through his thinning sandy hair and turned to Gilbert. "You'd better warn Auguste, Albert and Louis that if they are going to speak decent English, they'd better not listen to this picklock!"

"Picklock? I do not know this word," Gilbert said.

"Just as well, 'cos I ain't one," Stafford said amiably. "Locksmith, I was, set up in a nice way of business in Bridewell Lane. Wasn't my business if the owners of the locks wasn't always at 'ome; the lock's gotta be opened."

Gilbert nodded and smiled. "I understand."

"Yer know, the four of you are all right for Frenchies. Tell yer mates wot I said."

Gilbert translated and considered himself lucky. Just over a year ago he was living in Kent, serving the Count while they were all refugees in England. Then, with the peace, the Count had decided to return to France (and Gilbert admitted he wished now he had taken it upon himself to mention to the Count the doubts he had felt from the first). Then everything had happened at once—the Count had been taken away to Brest under arrest, Lord and Lady Ramage had managed to escape, they had all recaptured the mutinous English brig and now the four of them were serving in the Royal Navy!

His Lordship had been very apologetic, although there was no need for it. Apparently he had intended (this was when he expected to sail the *Murex* back to England) to keep them on the ship's books as "prisoners at large," and recommend their release as refugees as soon as they reached Plymouth, so they would be free to do what they wanted.

Gilbert could see his Lordship's motives, but he was forgetting that three of them—Auguste, Louis and Albert—did not speak a word of English and would never have been able to make a living. Serving in the Royal Navy, at least they would be paid and fed while they learned English, and life at sea, judging from their experience so far, was less hard than life in a wartime Brest, and no secret police watched . . .

Anyway, his Lordship had explained this odd business of "prize-money." Apparently it was a sort of reward the King paid to men of the Royal Navy for capturing an enemy ship, and as the *Murex* had been taken by the French after the mutiny, she became an enemy ship, so recapturing her meant she was then a prize.

Apparently, though, after they had recaptured the *Murex* and sailed her out of Brest, it seemed that only his Lordship would get any prize-money because he was the only one of them actually serving in the Royal Navy. That seemed unfair because her Ladyship had behaved so bravely. Certainly neither he nor Auguste, Albert nor Louis had expected any reward, but his Lordship had thought otherwise and he had talked to the admiral, who had agreed to his proposal. The result was that if the four of them volunteered for the Royal Navy, their names would be entered in the muster book of the *Calypso* and (by a certain free interpretation of dates) they would get their share.

So here they were, members of mess number eight, and Auguste and Albert were put down on the *Calypso*'s muster book as ordinary seamen while he and Louis were still landmen, because they did not yet have the skill of the other two.

And this mess number eight: although no one said anything aloud, Gilbert had the impression that while Jackson, Rossi and Stafford were not the captain's favourites—he was not the sort of man to play the game of favourites—they had all served together so long that they had a particular place. It seemed that each had saved the other's life enough times for there to be special bonds, and Gilbert had been fascinated by things Jackson had explained. Gilbert had noticed his Lordship's many scars—and now Jackson put an action and a place to each of them. The two scars on the right brow, another on the left arm, a small patch of white hair growing on his head . . . It was extraordinary that the man was still alive.

However, one thing had disappointed Gilbert: no one, least of all Jackson, Stafford and Rossi, seemed to think they had much of a chance of finding *L'Espoir*. Apparently once she left Brest she could choose one of a hundred different routes. Oh dear, if only the Count had stayed in Kent. The estate he bought at Ruckinge was pleasant; even the Prince of Wales and his less pleasant friends had been frequent guests, and the Count never complained of boredom. But undoubtedly he had a *grande nostalgie* for the château and, although expecting it, had been heartbroken when he returned to find everything had been stolen. He had—

The heart-stopping shrill of a bosun's call came down the forehatch followed by the bellow *"General quarters!* All hands to general quarters—come on there, look alive . . ." Again the call screamed—Jackson said the bosun's mates were called "Spithead Nightingales" because of the noise their calls made—and again the bellow.

Gilbert followed the others as he remembered "General quarters" was another name for a man's position when the ship went into battle. He felt a fear he had not experienced in the *Murex* affair. The *Calypso* was so big; all the men round him knew exactly what to do; they ran to their quarters as if they were hunters following well-worn tracks in a forest.

Ramage snatched up the speaking-trumpet while Aitken completed an entry and returned the slate to the drawer.

"Foremast, deck here."

"Sail ho, two points on the larboard bow, sir: I see her just as we lift on the top of the swell waves."

"Very well, keep a sharp lookout and watch the bearing closely."

Ramage felt his heart thudding. Was she *L'Espoir?* Keep calm, he told himself: it could be any one of a dozen British, Dutch, Spanish, French or American ships bound for the West Indies and staying well south looking for the Trades. Or even a ship from India or the Cape or South America, bound north and, having found a wind, holding it until forced to bear away to pick up the westerlies.

If the bearing stayed the same and the sail drew closer the *Calypso* must be overhauling the strange vessel, and it was unlikely that the *Calypso* was being outdistanced. If the sail passed to starboard, then whoever she was must be bound north; passing to larboard would show she was going south.

Southwick had heard the lookout's hail and came on deck, his round face grinning, his white hair flowing like a new mop.

"Think it's our friend, sir?"

"I doubt it; we couldn't be that lucky. She's probably a Post Office packet bound for Barbados with the mail."

Southwick shook his head, reminding Ramage of a seaman twirling a dry mop before plunging it into a bucket of water. "We'd never catch up with a packet. Those Post Office brigs are slippery."

"Could be one of our own frigates sent out by the Admiralty with despatches for the governors of the British islands, telling them war has been declared." Ramage thought a moment and then said: "Yes, she could be. She'd have sailed from Portsmouth before the Channel Fleet, of course, and run into head winds or been becalmed."

He looked round and realized that it had been a long time since he had given this particular order: "Send the men to quarters, Mr Aitken. I want Jackson aloft with the bring-'em-near —he's still the man with the sharpest eyes. I must go below and look up the private signals."

He went down to his cabin, sat at the desk and unlocked a drawer, removing the large canvas wallet which was heavy from the bar of lead sewn along the bottom and patterned with brass grommets protecting holes that would allow water to pour in and sink it quickly the moment it was thrown over the side.

He unlaced the wallet and removed five sheets of paper. They were held together by stitching down the left-hand side, so that they made a small booklet, a thin strip of lead wrapped round the edge hammered flat and forming a narrow binding.

The first page was headed "Private Signals" with the note "Channel Fleet" and the date. The first two paragraphs, signed by Admiral Clinton, showed their importance: they were, with the Signal Book, the most closely guarded papers on board any ship of war.

Ramage noted that the wording of the warning was similar if not identical to that in the document he had studied with Lieutenant Swan on board the *Murex*.

Any ship of war passing through the area cruised by the Channel Fleet would have a copy of this set of flag tables for challenging and distinguishing friend from enemy. The system was simple: depending on the day of the month (the actual month itself did not matter), there was a special challenge with its own answer.

There were four main vertical columns divided into ten horizontal sections. The first section of the first column contained the numbers 1, 11, 21, 31, and referred to those dates. The section immediately below had 2, 12, 22, with 3, 13, 23 below and then 4, 14, 24, until the tenth section ended up with 10, 20, 30, so that every day in a month was covered.

The next column had the same two phrases in each of its ten sections: *"The first signal made is—,"* and *"Answered by a—,"* and referred to the next two columns. The third was headed by "Main-topmasthead," and gave the appropriate signals to be hoisted there, while the fourth and last column headed "Fore-topmasthead" gave the signals to go up there.

Ramage noted that today was the eleventh of the month, and the date "11" was the second in the first column. The "first signal" made would be a white flag with a blue cross (the figure two in the numeral code of flags) hoisted at the main-topmasthead and a blue flag with a yellow cross (numeral seven) at the fore-topmasthead. One ship or the other (it did not matter which) would challenge first with those two, and be answered by a blue, white and red flag (numeral nine) at the main-topmasthead and a pendant over blue pierced with white (numeral zero) at the

fore-topmasthead. Numeral flags hoisted singly by a senior officer had a different meaning, but these were given in the Signal
Book and there could be no confusion.

The last page of the booklet gave the private signals to be
used at night—combinations of lights hoisted in different positions, and hails. Ramage noted that whoever thought up the
hails must have an interest in geography: the month was divided
into thirds, with the various challenges and replies being "Rus-
sia—Sweden," "Bengal—China," and "Denmark—Switzerland."

To complicate the whole system, the day began at midnight
for the flag signals (corresponding to the civil day), while it began
at noon for the night signals, and thus corresponded with the
noon-to-noon nautical day used in the logs and journals.

Ramage repeated the numbers to himself—two and seven are
the challenge, nine and zero the reply. He put the signals back
in the wallet, knotted the drawstrings, and returned it to the
drawer, which he locked.

How long before Jackson would be reporting?

The cabin was hot: he longed for the loose and comfortable
fisherman's trousers, but they had been taken away with the
smock by a disapproving Silkin, whose face was less lugubrious
now he had the captain regularly and properly dressed in stockings, breeches, coat, shirt, stock and cocked hat. That the breeches
were tight at the knees and the stock became soaked with perspiration and chafed the skin of the neck (and rasped as soon as
the whiskers began sprouting again three or four hours after
shaving) was no concern to Silkin: to him those discomforts were
the sartorial price a gentleman had to pay, and Silkin regarded
any article of clothing as "soiled" if it was only creased.

Ramage knew that by now the men would be at general
quarters: indeed, the Marine sentry had already reported that
the men who would be serving the two 12-pounders in the
great cabin and the single ones in the coach and bed place were

waiting to be allowed in to cast off the lashings and prepare the guns, hinge up the bulkheads and strike the few sticks of furniture below the gundeck. Ramage picked up his hat and left the cabin, nodding to the guns' crews as he went up on deck and pulling the front of his hat down to shield his eyes from the sun, which glared down from the sky and reflected up from the waves.

He told Aitken the flag numbers for the challenge and reply, said he did not want the guns run out for the time being, and then joined Southwick standing at the quarterdeck rail, looking forward the length of the ship. Men were hurrying about but none ran: each had that sense of purposefulness that came from constant training and which led to them using the minimum of effort needed to do a task. The decks had already been wetted and sand sprinkled, so that if the ship did go into action the damp planks would stop any spilt powder being ignited by friction and the sand would prevent it blowing about as well as stop feet slipping.

The flintlocks had been fitted to the guns. Powder boys holding cartridge boxes sat along the centreline, one behind each pair of guns, while each gun captain had fitted the firing lanyard to the lock, the lanyard being long enough for him to kneel behind the gun and fire it well clear of the recoil. A small tub of water stood between each pair of guns with lengths of slow match fitted into notches round the top edge and burning so that any glowing piece fell into the water. They would be used only if a flintlock misfired. The cook had just doused the galley fire at the order for general quarters, and the slow match were the only things burning in the ship.

Below, "fearnought" screens, thick material like heavy blankets, would have been unrolled and now hung down to make the entrance to the magazine almost a maze. Where men had now to jink about to get in, it was sure no flash from an accidental explosion would penetrate. The gunner was down inside the magazine, wearing felt shoes so that there could be no sparks inside the tiny cabin which was lined first with lathes and then plaster thickened with horsehair, and that covered with copper sheeting. The only tools allowed inside were bronze measurers, like drinking mugs on wooden handles, and bronze mallets for knocking the copper hoops from barrels of powder.

Close to each gun, stuck in spaces in the ship's side where they could be quickly snatched up, were cutlasses, pistols and tomahawks—each man knew which he was to have, because against his name in the General Quarter, Watch and Station Bill would be a single letter, C, P or T.

In less than a minute, Ramage knew, just the time it would take to load and run out the guns, cock the locks and fire, nearly two hundred pounds of roundshot could be hurling themselves invisibly at an enemy, each shot the size of a large orange and able to penetrate two feet of solid oak. Yet to a casual onlooker the *Calypso* was at this very moment simply a frigate ploughing her way majestically across the Western Ocean, stunsails set and all canvas to the royals rap full with a brisk Trade wind, the only men visible a couple of men at the wheel, three officers at the quarterdeck rail, and a couple of lookouts aloft.

Yet all this was routine: in the Chops of the Channel a frigate might be sending her ship's company to quarters every hour or so, as an unidentified and possibly hostile vessel came in sight. In wartime every strange sail could be an enemy. Admittedly, one saw a great many more ships in the approaches to the Channel and few would prove to be enemy, although so-called neutral ships trying to run the blockade were numerous. For a surprising number of people, Ramage noted, profit knew no loyalty—or perhaps it would be truer to say that whichever nation provided the profit had the trader's loyalty as a bonus.

"Deck there—mainmasthead!"

That was Jackson, and Ramage let Aitken reply. The American's report was brief.

"Reckon she's a frigate steering north, sir. Too far off to identify but you'll see her in a few minutes, two points on our larboard bow."

Aitken acknowledged and turned to Ramage, who nodded and said: "Take in the stunsails, Mr Aitken."

As soon as Aitken gave the order, there seemed to be chaos as men ran from the guns, some going to ropes round the mast, to the ship's side where stubby booms held out the foot of the sails, and others went up the ratlines.

Bosun's mates' pipes shrilled and they repeated the order: "Watch, take in starboard studding sails!"

After that it was a bellowed litany, making as much sense as a Catholic service in Latin to a Protestant, but curiously orderly and impressive.

Main and foretopmen were standing by waiting for the order to go aloft, along with men named boomtricers in the station bill for this manoeuvre. Then the orders came in a stream—"Away aloft . . . Settle the halyards . . . Haul out the downhauls . . . Haul taut . . . Lower away . . . Haul down . . ." As the tall and narrow rectangles of sail came down and were quickly stifled on deck before the wind took control, more orders followed to deal with the booms, still protruding from the ends of the yards and the ship's side like thin fingers.

"Stand by to rig in the booms . . . Rig in! . . . Aft lower boom . . . Top up . . . Ease away fore guy, haul aft . . ."

Then, to the men stifling the sails on deck: "Watch, make up stunsails." Aitken raised the speaking-trumpet: "Stand by a-loft . . ."

The quartermaster was already giving orders to the men at the wheel: with the starboard stunsails down and no longer helping to drive the ship along, the larboard stunsails, yet to be taken in, were trying to slew her round to starboard and needed a turn on the wheel to counteract them.

Then came the same ritual for the larboard stunsails, until with the canvas rolled, the booms taken in and the topmen and tricers down from aloft, Aitken gave the final order: "Watch carry on at general quarters."

At last Ramage let his brain function again. He had tried to shut it off when the sail ahead was first sighted: he wanted to store the sound of that first hail until, perhaps half an hour later, Jackson would report that the vessel was a French frigate similar in appearance to the *Calypso* and steering the same course: evidence enough that they had finally caught *L'Espoir*—although quite what he did then, he did not know.

Now, however, his lack of ideas did not matter: the ship was unlikely to be *L'Espoir* because she was going in a different direction. A frigate, yes, but following the sea roads imposed by the wind directions, probably bound for Europe but first having to go north nearly to Newfoundland before turning eastward, unless she wanted to try the slower Azores route.

Probably Royal Navy, possibly returning from the Far East or South America, but more likely the Cape of Good Hope. Anyway, she would not know the war had started again, and if she was British he was obliged to give her captain the news. Nor could he begrudge the time because *L'Espoir* could be ahead or astern, to the north or the south, so any delay or diversion could lead to her discovery. Patience, Ramage thought, as he glanced aloft at the tiny figure of Jackson perched in the maintop. It was the one thing needed by the captain of a ship of war, it was one of the virtues he had always lacked.

"Look," Stafford said, pointing at the metal rectangle of the flintlock, "you see the flint there, just like wiv a pistol or musket."

He waited for Gilbert to translate to Auguste, Albert and Louis and then continued: "Only you don't have no trigger like a handgun. Instead the lanyard—well, translate that."

He paused because he really meant that the flintlock of a great gun did not have the kind of trigger that you put your finger round, and he was rapidly realizing that a good instructor was a man who could explain complicated mechanisms and thoughts in a simple way. Jackson was good at it. The captain was fantastic.

"Yers, well, this lower bit is the trigger: when yer put a steady strain on the lanyard (yer *don't* jerk it)," he emphasized, "it pulls the trigger part up towards the ring the lanyard threads through down from—translate that!" he exclaimed, having lost both the lanyard and the thread of his explanation.

Gilbert looked up politely and said gently: "Stafford, we can see very well how it works. Your very clear explanation—it is not really necessary."

"Ah, good," sighed a mollified Stafford, with a triumphant glance at Rossi, who had earlier been jeering at the Cockney's attempts to explain the loading and firing of the *Calypso*'s twelve-pounders. "Now, here is the pricker." He held up a foot-long thin rod, pointed at one end and with a round eye at the other, and for which he as second captain of this particular gun was responsible.

He passed the pricker, which was like a large skewer, to Gilbert to inspect and waited while the others looked. "Ze prickair," Auguste repeated. *"Alors."*

"No, just 'pricker,'" Stafford corrected amiably. "Now, you saw the flannel what the cartridge is made of and what 'olds the powder. Well, now, forget that for a minute and we'll go back to the lock. That's got to make a spark what fires the gun . . ."

He waited for Gilbert's translation and noted to himself that the French seem to make things sound so difficult.

"Well, you see this 'ole 'ere leading down into the barrel—same as in a pistol, the touch'ole. Well, instead of just sprinklin' powder in the pan and lettin' it fill up the touch'ole, so that when the flint sparks off the powder and sends a flash of flame down the touch'ole to set off the charge . . . No, well, in a ship the roll or the wind could . . . well, we put a special tube in the touch'ole and sprinkle powder in the pan and cover the end . . ."

Gilbert translated a shortened version.

"Now, just remember that. But the flash down the touch'ole won't go through the flannel of the cartridge. Ho no, nothing like. That's why we use the pricker. Before we put in the tube, we jab the pricker down the touch'ole and wriggle it about so we're certain sure it's made an 'ole in the cartridge right under the touch'ole, and that means if you looked down the touch'ole you'd see the powder of the cartridge—if the light was right, o'course."

Gilbert translated but the other three men, who had already worked it all out, having seen the little tubes in their special box, were beginning to suck their teeth.

"*Now*, in goes the tube and we pour some powder into the pan and cover the end of the tube, just to make sure the spark of the flint really makes it take fire . . . The tube explodes (well, not really, it makes a flash, which goes down the touch'ole of course) and that explodes the powder in the flannel cartridge—"

"And forces the shot up the barrel and out of the muzzle," Gilbert said quickly.

"That's right! Good, I'm explaining it clearly enough, then," Stafford said smugly. "Next, now we know how to fire the gun—"

"We must learn how to load it," Rossi said triumphantly. "You forgot that!"

"I was goin' to explain the dispart sight," Stafford said sulkily.

"Only the gun captain uses that," Rossi said. "Leave it to Jackson to explain."

"Oh well," Stafford said in the most offhand manner he could contrive, but which did not reveal his relief as he realized that in fact he did not really understand how a dispart sight worked, "we'll do loading now."

Gilbert coughed. "We watched when you had gunnery practice the day before yesterday," he said. "It is the same as for a pistol except you 'swab out' the barrel. 'Swab out'—that is correct, no? And you 'worm' it every few rounds with that long handle affair which has a metal snake on the end. To pull out any burning bits of flannel cartridge which might be left inside—"

"Yes, very well, I'm glad you've understood that," Stafford said, tapping the breech of the gun with the pricker and preening himself in the certainty that the Frenchmen's understanding was due to his explanation. "The rest is obvious: you saw how we use these handspikes"—he pointed to the two long metal-shod bars, like great axe handles—"to lift and traverse the gun. 'Traversing' is when you aim it from side to side, and you say 'left' or 'right,' not 'forward' or 'aft.' Now, to elevate the gun, you—"

"Lift up the breech using a handspike as a lever," Gilbert said.

"That's right," Stafford said encouragingly. It was not as hard to explain difficult things as he had expected, even when your pupils are Frenchmen who do not speak a word of English.

"Then," Gilbert continued, reminding Stafford of his role as translator, "you pull out or push in—depending on whether you are raising or lowering the elevation—this wooden wedge under the breech. What you call the 'quoin,' no?"

"Well, we pronounce it 'coin,' but you are understanding."

Rossi chuckled and said: "Tell the Frogs about 'point blank.'"

Gilbert grinned at the Italian. "We have a *rosbif* explaining to a *frog* with a *Genovese* watching. What is a Genovese called?"

"I don't know," Rossi said expansively. "Tuscans call us the Scottish of the Mediterranean, but who are Tuscans to cast stones?"

"Why Scottish?" Stafford asked. "You don't wear kilts or play a haggis or anything."

"You eat haggis," Rossi said. "It is some kind of pudding. They make it from pigs, I think. No, Scottish because the *Genovesi* are said to be—well, 'careful' I think is the word. We don't rattle our money in our purses."

"Ah, 'mean' is the word, not 'careful,'" Stafford declared.

Rossi shrugged. "I am not interested in the word. Is not true, not for the *Genovesi* or the *Scozzesi*."

"Point-blank," Stafford said, "is the place where a roundshot would hit the sea if the gun barrel was absolutely 'orizontal when the shot fired. About two hundred yards, usually. The shot doesn't go straight when it leaves the gun but curves up and then comes down: like throwing a ball. There!" he said to Rossi. "Yer thought I didn't know!"

Shouts from aloft cut short Rossi's mocking laugh and Gilbert began translating for the other three.

CHAPTER FOURTEEN

"SHE'S HOVE-TO on the starboard tack, sir," Jackson shouted down from the mainmasthead. "Waiting for us to come down to her."

"What is she?"

"Frigate, looks as though she could be French-built, sir, but she's too far off to distinguish her colours."

Ramage turned aft and began to walk, hands clasped behind

his back, oblivious of the glances of the guns' crews on each side of the quarterdeck.

A French frigate: 32 guns or so, a hundred and fifty men or less in peacetime, and her captain with no idea the war had started again. Unless she had sighted *L'Espoir.* In which case she would know not only about the war but where *L'Espoir* was perhaps only a few hours ago. In the meantime, the fact that she had hove-to, waiting for the *Calypso* to run down towards her (like an affectionate dog rolling over on its back in anticipation of a tickled belly) meant that she had recognized the *Calypso* as French-designed and built: her distinctive and graceful sheer would be seen particularly clearly as she approached, taking in her stunsails.

Ramage walked between two guns and then looked out through a port. The Trades were kicking up their usual swell waves with wind waves sliding across the top of them. Not the sort of seas for ships to manoeuvre at close quarters; seas in which a cutter with strong men at the oars would have to take care. An accidental broach in those curling and breaking crests— which seemed sparkling white horses from the deck of a frigate but were a mass of airy froth which would not support a man's body or a boat any more than thick snow carried carriage wheels or horses' hooves—was something that kept a coxswain alert.

He turned forward again at the taffrail, cursing softly to himself. Devil take it; he wanted to concentrate all his thoughts and all his efforts on catching *L'Espoir* and rescuing her prisoners, without being bothered by another frigate, least of all French. An enemy which had to be attacked.

Yet . . . yet . . . He reached the quarterdeck rail and turned aft again, unseeing, walking instinctively, almost afraid to move or yet stand still because out there just beyond his full comprehension, like the dark hurrying shadows on a calm sea made by tiny whiffles of a breeze that came and went without direction or purpose, refusing to strengthen or go away, intent only on teasing, like a beautiful and wilful woman at a masked ball, there was a hint of an idea.

Well, at least he could see the wind shadows of an idea, and they hinted where this frigate could fit in. Taffrail, turn forward . . . So let us consider the arguments against this vague, floating idea, or anyway what little he could grasp of it. Damage to the *Calypso*'s spars . . . But they were still far enough north to make Barbados under a jury rig . . . Seamen needed as prize-crew and Marines as guards . . . Now those dark whiffling shadows were becoming a little sharper, the edges more distinctly outlined . . . Quarterdeck rail and turn . . .

No more hails from Jackson but, he suddenly realized, both Southwick and Aitken had been standing where he turned, waiting to say something but unwilling to interrupt his thoughts. He swung back to them.

"Sir," Aitken said, "the ship ahead is now in sight from here on deck. We can't make out her colours but from the cut of her sails and her sheer, she looks French all right. Shall we hoist our colours? Do you want the guns loaded now and run out?"

Ah, how one decision depended on another, but the sequence had to have a beginning. In this case the beginning was positively identifying the ship ahead as French. French-built with French-cut sails almost certainly made her one of Bonaparte's ships, because the last year and a half of peace ruled out her being recently captured by the Royal Navy.

Very well, she is French. "Don't hoist our colours," Ramage said. "She probably wouldn't be able to see them anyway because we're dead to windward. Have the guns loaded. Canister, not roundshot, and grape in the carronades. We want to tear her rigging and sails, not splinter her hull. Don't run them out, though."

He thought a moment. "Have a dozen men rig up a line of

clothes on the fo'c's'le. Laundry always looks so peaceful." He grinned. "Tell them that anything lost will be replaced by the purser."

"Pusser's slops" were never popular with any seaman proud of his appearance. "Slops," the name given to the shirts, trousers, material and other items which could be bought from the purser, who combined the role of haberdasher, tobacconist, and general supplier whose profit came from the commission he charged, were usually of poor quality. The shirts all too often came, so the men grumbled, in two sizes—too large and too small. Likewise the trousers were too long or too short. All were too expensive, as far as the men were concerned. The "pusser" was rarely a popular man, and in most ships the victim of scurrilous stories. He was, the seamen of the navy claimed, the only person who could make dead men chew tobacco. The miracle was performed when a seaman died or was killed and an unscrupulous purser put down in his books that the man had drawn a few pounds of tobacco, the price of which would be taken from the wages owing to relatives while the tobacco remained in the purser's store to be sold again. Careless pursers had even charged men who never touched tobacco.

Daydreaming . . . Again Ramage cursed his habit of letting his mind go wandering up byways when his thoughts should stay on the highway.

He waited until Aitken had finished passing the orders and watched Martin, Kenton and Wagstaffe down on the main deck supervising their divisions of guns. He looked around for Orsini and found the young midshipman waiting beside the binnacle. His role when the ship was at general quarters was to be near the captain, ready to run messages. He had once heard the boy complain to Martin that being the captain's *aide de camp* sounded a fine job in action, but Mr Ramage never wanted any messages taken anywhere . . .

Well, Paolo could hardly complain with any justification: since Gianna had first asked Ramage to take her nephew to sea as a midshipman and teach him to be an officer in the Royal Navy, the lad had been in action half a dozen times or more; he had even been given command of a prize while in the Mediterranean.

Gianna. No matter how hard he tried to shut her out, and no matter how he and Paolo had tactfully not talked about her when he had rejoined the *Calypso*, she came back. Not because of a broken love affair, because it was not really like that, and since Gianna had left England he had met Sarah and they had fallen deeply in love and married. Still, that did not mean he was not very worried over Gianna's safety or did not have affectionate memories of her.

It had been a relationship which now had a strange air of unreality about it: could it have happened to him, had she really existed? Well, she had and did because that handsome youngster over there, one of the most popular people in the ship as far as the men were concerned, was her nephew. Yes, she was the ruler of Volterra, a small state in Tuscany; yes, she had fled before Bonaparte's Army of Italy, and been rescued by Lieutenant Ramage, who had carried her to safety . . . Yes, they had both fallen in love and she had gone to England as a refugee and lived with his family, and yes it was obvious now that with such differences in religion the Catholic ruler of Volterra could never marry the Protestant heir to one of the oldest earldoms in the kingdom.

It had taken Bonaparte to end it all, though, just as he had, some years ago, then simply the general commanding the Army of Italy, unknowingly started it. Then, when Britain and France had signed that peace now called the Treaty of Amiens, Gianna had decided it was safe to return to Tuscany: that it was her duty to return to her people . . . Ramage, his father, many people, had warned her not to trust Bonaparte, that the peace would be brief, that she risked arrest by Bonaparte's police at best, assassination at worse, but she had gone. She had travelled to Paris with the Herveys while he had sailed on a long voyage with the *Calypso,* lucky to remain employed and in command in peacetime, and by bizarre circumstances he had met Sarah, returned to England and married her—and found there was no news of Gianna. No one knew if she had arrived in Volterra or not. The Herveys confirmed that she had left Paris safely, but that accounted for only the first steps on a long journey. Then, while he and Sarah had honeymooned in France, the war had started again, and with it went the last chance of knowing about Gianna.

Daydreaming again, and now the French ship was hull-up on the horizon. He looked with his glass. Yes, backed foretopsail and lying there like a gull on the water, rising and falling as the crests and troughs of the swell waves slid beneath her and carried on westward. Sails in good condition. French national colours hoisted. Guns not run out. A hoist of flags at the fore-topmasthead, probably her pendant numbers identifying her.

It might work. Surprise, that great ally, could quadruple one's apparent size (or quarter them if you're the one surprised). But he would have to do it himself: it was unfortunate that Aitken did not speak good French.

He beckoned Aitken and Southwick closer and explained his plan. He then told Southwick to call Jackson down from aloft— he was not needed as a lookout anymore. Southwick gestured down to the main deck. "Stafford and Rossi, sir? And one or two of those Frenchmen?"

They were all serving at the same gun, and the *Calypso* was not short of men. Auguste and his brother could be useful. Gilbert and Louis would be too clumsy. Ramage told the master the names and ordered him to be ready to hoist out a boat.

Formality: oddly enough, that would eventually save time. It might trip him up, too, but a boat-cloak too would be normal and hide much. "Orsini," he said, "fetch my sword and boat-cloak from the great cabin. Get your own boat-cloak too. I see you have your dirk!"

Paolo grinned and nodded as he turned to the companionway. The dirk, a short sword two feet two inches long and, as he readily admitted, little more than a broad-bladed dagger, was one of his proudest possessions, but despite that he was a realist and usually carried a seaman's cutlass as well, using the dirk as a *main gauche*. Ramage guessed he dreamed of the day when he exchanged the midshipman's dirk for a lieutenant's sword, with its elaborate hilt.

The main and forecourses were being clewed up. Seamen hurried to hook the staytackle on to the cutter, ready to hoist it out. Jackson waited until the last tie was undone and the canvas cover pulled clear before, as the captain's coxswain, climbing into the boat to check over the oars, rudder and tiller, pull the bung from the small water breaker lashed beneath one of the thwarts and confirm that it was full of fresh water, and finally put the large bung in the boat itself: it was normally left out to drain rainwater.

Stafford and Rossi were already up on the gangway with Auguste and Albert, cutlass-belts over their shoulders and pistols stuck in their belts, but Ramage guessed from their stance that the two Frenchmen were puzzled and bewildered because Gilbert's translation of the instruction to arm themselves and go to the gangway with Rossi and Stafford would have been the only orders they received.

At that moment Paolo appeared, a sword in one hand and two boat-cloaks slung over the other arm. "Put them down there, beside the capstan. Now, listen a moment," Ramage said.

Quickly he outlined what had happened so far—which Paolo had seen anyway as the *Calypso* rapidly approached the unknown frigate—and added his intentions. "Now, go and tell those two

Frenchmen what they need to know. It's time you polished your French."

After that everything happened with the speed of an impatient child shaking the coloured chips in a kaleidoscope. The ship once ahead was now fine on the starboard bow and men had left the guns to stand by at the sheets and braces controlling the foretopsail and yard. Jackson had the cutter's crew mustered on the starboard gangway. The boat would be hoisted out on the weather side, so everyone would have to work fast, but the lee side would be open to too many prying French eyes.

He lifted the glass and looked at the ship and was startled to see that she was close enough for him to notice the uniforms (or lack of them) on the quarterdeck. He glanced at Aitken, who already had the speaking-trumpet to his mouth while Southwick stood by the quartermaster close to the wheel.

The wheel began to spin and the *Calypso*'s bow started to swing slowly to starboard to put her on a curving course bringing her close to windward of the French frigate. Sails began slatting while Ramage put the telescope in the binnacle drawer, picked up his sword and clipped it on to the belt, and slung the cloak over one shoulder. He thought a moment and then flattened his hat and put it under his left arm. Paolo followed his example and, with the sails thundering aloft as the ship swung and the great foretopsail was backed, the two of them went down the steps to the gangway.

The ship slowly came to a stop, the wind now blowing on the foreside of the foretopsail, and the cutter swung out and over the side. Wagstaffe gave a brief order here and there but mostly used hand signals. In a few moments the boat was in the water, the bow held by the painter while the sternfast kept the boat close in to the rope ladder which had been unrolled over the ship's side.

Jackson was first down the ladder, the wind catching his

sandy hair, and before Rossi, who had followed him, had jumped into the boat, the American was shipping the rudder and the tiller. The rest of the men scrambled down, the last one followed by Orsini.

"Here!" Ramage shouted, throwing down to Jackson his rolled-up boat-cloak, with the hat inside. The coxswain waited until Ramage was on board and sitting in the sternsheets and then pulled the boat-cloak round him to hide his uniform. Ramage pushed his sword to one side to make the wooden grating a more comfortable seat, and then watched the enormous bulk of the *Calypso* seeming to move sideways as the men at the oars rowed the cutter clear.

Jackson eventually put the tiller over so that the cutter passed under the French frigate's stern to come along her lee side. "*La Robuste,* sir," he commented. The name meant nothing to Ramage. He counted up the gun ports. Sixteen this side, so she was a 32-gun frigate. About the same size as the *Calypso* but not built from the same plans: her sheer was flatter, her fo'c's'le was longer, and he had the impression her transom raked more sharply.

Ramage saw several faces looking down at him over the taffrail and gave a cheery wave, which the men answered enthusiastically. He glanced at Paolo sitting opposite him. The lad had a wide grin on his face: no sign of any doubts or fears.

Suddenly every damned thing seemed to be happening at once, Ramage thought, and then realized it was his own fault because he would let his concentration wander. The cutter's bowman had hooked on with his boat-hook and while men pulled and hauled to secure painter and sternfast, Ramage stood up to find that the French had also unrolled a rope ladder, so he did not have the nail-breaking and finger-twisting climb up the battens. He pushed his sword round under his boat-cloak and clutched his hat, guessing that no one on *La Robuste*'s deck would recognize it for what it was.

He leapt for the ladder and immediately started climbing, glad that Paolo was only a couple of rungs below him because his weight stopped each wooden slat trying to swing inwards. More jerks followed as the rest of the men followed and this was the moment of danger: would any of the French officers look down past Ramage and Orsini and notice that the seamen were carrying cutlasses? Ramage let his boat-cloak flow out.

Up, up, up—now his eyes at deck level; four more steps and he was on the deck itself with four men standing in a half circle to greet him—presumably the captain and three lieutenants.

Ramage paused, punched his cocked hat into shape, jammed it on his head and, undoing the buckle of his boat-cloak, swirled it off and tossed it to Jackson, who was now standing beside Paolo at the entry port.

"Captain Ramage, of His Britannic Majesty's frigate *Calypso* at your service," he said in French to the heavily-jowled and sallow-faced man with iron-grey hair who seemed to be the captain.

"*Britannic?*" the man muttered disbelievingly. He was a stocky man who had seemed taller than Ramage, but as he turned to look at the *Calypso* hove-to close by he protested: "She is flying no—" he stopped and then, arms extended and palms uppermost, he said angrily: "When she first hove-to she had no colours. She is French-built. Naturally, I think she is French."

Ramage shrugged his shoulders and smiled. "You are free to think whatever you like."

The Frenchman's shrug made Ramage's look like a feeble twitch. "Of course, of course." He introduced himself. "Citizen Robilliard, commanding the French national frigate *La Robuste*, at your service. May I—"

As he turned to introduce his officers, Ramage interrupted him calmly. "Citizen Robilliard, a moment please. You are now the former captain of the former French frigate *La Robuste*, which is now a prize to His Britannic Majesty's frigate *Calypso* . . ."

"But . . . *mon Dieu*, citizen," Robilliard protested, "the war is over. It is all finished. We are friends. Where have you been that you do not know?" He slapped his thigh and started to roar with laughter. "Ah, it is the English humour! You make a joke because—" he saw Ramage's face and his voice tailed off. He took a deep breath. "No, you don't make a joke, Captain Ramage. You come from Europe. We have just come from the Batavian Republic. You have news . . ."

Suddenly Ramage felt sorry for this amiable man, whose accent showed he had grown up not far from Honfleur.

"Yes, hostilities have begun again. Brest is blockaded—my ship is part of that fleet."

"And you are bound . . ."

" . . . for the West Indies," Ramage said. "Now, *m'sieu*, you and your ship's company must consider yourselves my prisoners."

"But this is absurd," Robilliard protested, and then looked in the direction of Ramage's pointing finger. The *Calypso*'s guns were run out while the French guns were still secured, well lashed down and ready for bad weather.

Ramage said to Paolo in Italian: "Collect papers, charts and signal books from his cabin. Take a couple of men with you."

Robilliard scratched his head, still unwilling to accept what he had heard. "I can't believe this. You have documents? A newspaper—*Le Moniteur*, perhaps? There must be a written declaration—you just come on board and tell me that you have taken my ship prize! Why no!" he exclaimed, as though suddenly losing his temper. "You are just pirates!"

"You are familiar with Brest?"

Robilliard nodded his head cautiously. "I was blockaded in there for three years."

"When did you sail?"

"As soon as the peace was signed. In fact we carried the

despatches informing the governor of the Batavian Republic."

Ramage beckoned to Auguste and Albert. "These two men can tell you the names of all the important ships in Brest three weeks ago, as well as the names of the navy and army *commandants,* and answer any questions you care to ask. They are French. I was in Brest until after the war began; I can give you a certain amount of information."

Auguste said: "It's all true, citizen. The English ambassador left Paris, war began and Bonaparte arrested all the English in France, whether officers on leave or women. Bonaparte now makes war on women."

Robilliard flushed and then said angrily to Ramage: "This is ridiculous. Why, I could seize you, and then your ship would never dare open fire for fear of killing you!"

A series of metallic clicks made him look round and he was startled to find that three seamen, Jackson, Stafford and Rossi, were standing close with broad grins on their faces and pistols aimed at Robilliard, and each man swung a cutlass as a parson might use his walking stick to knock the head off a dandelion.

"Captain," Ramage said, "we are wasting time, my ship would certainly open fire if necessary, my second-in-command has strict orders about that. But you would not be alive to hear the first broadside that might kill me. You have been tricked by the perfidious English, Captain, just as I was tricked by the perfidious French less than a month ago. There is no dishonour: no need for you to fire a broadside 'for the honour of the flag.'"

Robilliard still shook his head disbelievingly. "I have only 76 men because we were short when we left Brest and have had much sickness in Batavia and at sea, but how can you keep us all prisoner? . . ."

"That is no problem," Ramage said and signalled to Jackson. "Give me your pistol," he said in English, and then switched back to French to say to Robilliard: "We are agreed, are we not, that you and your ship are my prize?"

Robilliard shrugged his shoulders and looked round at his three lieutenants. They were all young men, their faces frozen with the shock of finding an English frigate poised to rake their ship and her captain on board *La Robuste*.

"What do you say, *mes braves?*"

"We have no choice," the oldest of them said without much conviction.

"You must remember you said that when a committee of public safety accuses me of treachery," Robilliard said bitterly. "We have no choice, certainly, but I don't want any of you claiming to be heroes if we are exchanged and get back to France."

"Don't worry," Ramage said and waving to Jackson to go aft. "My despatch will make it clear you had no knowledge of the war."

"A lot of good your despatch would do me in France!"

"I expect it will be published in the *London Gazette*, which is as good as *Le Moniteur*. Certainly, I'm sure that Bonaparte has it translated and read to him."

Robilliard was watching Ramage closely. "Yes, I believe you." He spelled out his name. "And make sure you put in the 'Pierre,' because there is my cousin, too, and although he does not command a ship he is a scoundrel—no, I didn't mean that—"

"I understand," Ramage assured him.

"But so many prisoners," Robilliard said as he watched the Tricolour flutter down as Jackson hauled on one end of the halyard. "How will you . . . ?"

"Leave that problem to me," Ramage said. "You are not short of provisions?"

"Water, but not provisions. With so many dead from sickness, I could have doubled the rations of the living."

CHAPTER FIFTEEN

RAMAGE and Aitken sat at the desk, Ramage in his normal chair and the first lieutenant opposite, trying to make himself comfortable on a chair that normally served at the dining table in the coach. Aitken was hurriedly writing notes, quill squeaking, as Ramage translated from various pages of the small pile of documents in front of them.

"Ah, here we are," Ramage said happily, "some of the answers about Cayenne. This is"—he glanced at the title page—"a sort of pilot book published three years ago, so it is reasonably up to date. Take notes as I read it aloud."

He turned over a couple of pages. "It begins with a word about the currents to expect off the coast of French Guiana. There are two—well, we knew that. The first starts close off the African coast, near to the Cape Verde Islands, and is caused by the Trade winds blowing across the Atlantic. Yes, well, we know all about that, too. It reaches to within . . ." he paused, making the conversion, "to within 35 miles of the coast, or a depth of eight fathoms, where a second current, produced by the tides, meets it. And there is the water pouring out of the Amazon and the Orinoco. Well, it's the heights not the rates that interest me.

"Hmm, numerous other rivers between the Amazon and the Orinoco carry down vast quantities of mud, tree trunks and branches . . . these accumulating along the shores have built up a border of low ground." The pilot was written in stilted French and translation was difficult. "Mangroves generally cover it between high and low water. At low water this border seems impassable: at high water there are sometimes channels accessible to vessels . . . Ah, here we are: 'The only ports are at mouths of rivers . . . there are usually bars at the entrances and shoals in the channels . . . Larger ships can anchor to wait for high water without risk because no violent tempests ever occur in this region . . .'"

"That's comforting; I dislike 'violent tempests.' The mariner 'can wait for a local pilot or send boats ahead to make soundings.'"

Aitken reached out for the inkwell. "Except for the mangroves and the lack of 'violent tempests,' it sounds rather like the east coast of England!"

"Yes. Now for the general information: the French have owned Cayenne—Guiana, rather—since 1677 . . . It stretches about two hundred and fifty miles along the coast and goes more than a hundred miles inland . . . The land is low along the coast which runs roughly north and south with a mountain chain running east and west . . . Produces and exports pepper, cinnamon, cloves and nutmegs. Nothing," Ramage noted, "that isn't used for seasoning food!"

He read several more pages without bothering to translate but finally hunched himself in his chair and squared up the book. "Here we are . . . During the summer the current runs strongly to the north-west off this coast . . . Heavy breakers generally ease at slack water . . . Tide rise just over eight feet at springs, four or five at neaps . . .

"Now, we're interested in 27 miles of coast between the River Approuague to the south and the River Mahuri to the north. The land is so flat you can see it at only seven or eight miles from seaward . . . behind it, though, are the Kaw mountains, a level ridge not very high. Now, the Mahuri river—"

He broke off, cursed and shut the book with an angry gesture and stood up. With his head bent to one side to avoid bumping it on the beams overhead he strode round the cabin, watched by a startled Aitken, who then picked up a piece of cloth and busied himself wiping the sharpened point of his quill. He knew better than to ask what was the matter. Was the vital page missing? The Scot did not trust anything French. The good luck of finding a French pilot book would obviously, he considered glumly, be cancelled by there being pages missing . . .

Ramage sat down, face flushed, and opened the pilot book again. "Cayenne . . . Cayenne . . ." he said crossly. "Wouldn't anyone in their right mind assume that any wretched Frenchman deported 'to Cayenne' was being sent to a penal colony on the island of Cayenne, which is in the middle of the entrance to the Cayenne river?"

Aitken thought for a moment but could see no danger in agreeing. "Yes, sir, that seems a reasonable assumption; indeed, a very logical conclusion."

"Yes, but any ship laden with prisoners and anchoring off the Îles de Cayenne in the Rivière de Cayenne would find herself some 25 miles too far south!

"Having no charts or pilots, I'd assumed the three Île du Salut, which include Devil's Island, were in the Cayenne river." He tapped the book. "Now I find they are three almost barren little lumps of rock seven miles offshore and 25 miles north of Cayenne, river or island. So, tear up what you've written and let's start again . . ."

"A good job we found *La Robuste*," Aitken said. "Otherwise . . ."

"Otherwise we'd have looked very stupid," Ramage completed. "Right, we start at Pointe Charlotte. The coast is low and sandy, plenty of mangroves up to the high-water mark, occasional clumps of trees behind, and isolated rocks sitting in the mud to seaward.

"By a stroke of luck, or just the kindness of nature, there is a high, cone-shaped hill nine miles inland: on a clear day you can see it for twenty miles, so you don't have to rely on the mangroves for a landfall.

"Right, now we get to it. The coast is trending west-north-west when you reach Pointe Charlotte, which is three miles north-west of the Kourou river, which is marked by three small mountains 'all remarkable objects at a long distance, and good guides for the entrance to the river.'"

"To distinguish Pointe Charlotte from a thousand other points, it has some rocks at its base," Ramage said ironically. "Of more interest to us, though: if you stand on Pointe Charlotte and stare out across the Atlantic, hoping perhaps to see Africa, you'll see instead 'a group of three small rocky islets,' and they *are* small, occupying a space of about half a mile.

"As far as I can understand from this pilot, the island farthest out in the Atlantic is the northernmost, Île du Diable, 131 feet high; the one on your left is the largest and highest, Île Royale, 216 feet; and to the right is the nearest, the southernmost, and the smallest, Île St Joseph."

"Which is the one we're particularly interested in?" Aitken asked.

"I think Île du Diable, or Devil's Island, and the blasted pilot simply says it is forbidden to land on any of the islands without the written permission of the *préfet* at Cayenne because St Joseph and Royale are 'convict settlements' while Diable is a settlement for *'détenus,'* which I'm sure means 'prisoners' but not people who have actually been convicted, although I'll check it with Gilbert because he knows better than I the finer shades of meaning in Revolutionary France."

"What about anchorages?" Aitken asked. Captains concerned themselves with tactics, first lieutenants worried about anchorages.

"The pilot makes a great song and dance that the lee of the islands provides the only sheltered anchorage along the coast—otherwise you have to go up one of the big rivers. Yes, here we are—five cables south-west of the western end of Royale, soft mud, five fathoms, well sheltered from easterly winds. Ah, Royale seems to be the headquarters—it has a fort guarding it to seaward, a church on the hill, and a jetty on the south side. Diable—well, that has only 'a fortified enclosure' for the *détenus*. St Joseph: a poor anchorage a cable to the south in hard mud—that is all it has to offer the world . . ."

"Are there any rocks and shoals?"

"Plenty," Ramage said, "and too many to mention. The positions this pilot gives are too vague to be of much use. Hmm . . . 'generally, a vessel coming in sight of the fort on Île Royale will result one hour later in a canoe with a local pilot waiting close under the north-west corner of Île du Diable . . .' He'll guide you to the recommended anchorage I've just mentioned southwest of Île Royale."

Ramage closed the book. "That's all it says about the Îles du Salut. More important, though, is that *L'Espoir* will presumably have a copy . . ."

". . . and so will wait for a pilot and anchor there?"

I hope so," Ramage said, "but I hope it doesn't mean we have to try to capture three rocky islands."

Wagstaffe walked the starboard side of *La Robuste*'s quarterdeck and reflected that commanding a ship was a satisfying experience, even if the ship was a prize-frigate and all he had to do for the next few hundred miles was stay in the wake of the *Calypso*. This was easy enough in daylight but at night it was difficult to follow the triangle of three poop lanterns. In fact, in the last couple of nights he had gone to his cot and fallen asleep to waken almost at once, certain that the three lights had gone out of sight, and the officer of the deck (Kenton the first time and Martin the second) had been startled to find the commanding officer suddenly flapping round the deck in a boat-cloak, staring forward, grunting and going below again, all without a word of explanation.

Well, Wagstaffe told himself, how on earth did one explain all that to junior lieutenants? Now he thought about it, both Kenton and Martin were sensible enough to report the moment they lost sight of the lights—indeed, there'd be enough yelling in the darkness, with the officer of the deck shouting questions at the lookouts and making a noise which would come down the skylight like a butt full of cold water.

It is easy enough to be brave and confident when the sun shines bright, he thought defensively, but hard on a dull cloudy day when it is raining. Harder still at nightfall, and dam' nearly impossible at three o'clock in the morning. Three o'clock courage, that's what he lacked. It's what distinguished Captain Ramage from most other men: he had it in abundance. It was also, Wagstaffe admitted, what kept Captain Ramage's officers poised on the balls of their feet all the time. Not because he yelled and screamed when things went wrong: perhaps it would be easier if he did. No, it was that chilly, quizzical and questioning look from those dark eyes set under thick eyebrows that was far more reproachful than words. They seemed to say: "I trained you and trusted you: now look what you've done . . ."

Wagstaffe lifted his "distance staff" and held it up. He was proud of it because it was so easy to make and to use. He had been told to keep one cable astern of the *Calypso* and in her wake. One cable was two hundred yards precisely, not one hundred and fifty or two hundred and fifty. It was a distance which anyone in the *Calypso* could check with a quadrant or sextant in a few moments because of the two simple facts: if you knew the height of an object (in this case a mainmast) and the angle it made from you, it was easy enough to work out how far away it was: the mast made the vertical side of a right-angled triangle and the angle was opposite, between the base and hypotenuse. And of course the base was the distance, in this case two hundred yards.

However, to avoid having to get a quadrant or sextant out of its box to measure the angle, it was easy enough to cut two notches in a short stick at appropriate distances apart so that when you held the stick vertically at arm's length, the lower notch was level with the *Calypso's* after waterline, and her mainmasthead touched the upper notch. If the mast appeared shorter than the distance between the notches, *La Robuste* was more than 200 yards astern: if taller, they were too close.

In fact it was not too difficult to keep station because both frigates were almost the same size and of course French-designed and built, with the sails cut by French sailmakers. Providing *La Robuste* set the same sails, and providing the men at the wheel, the quartermaster and the officers of the deck stayed alert in this sun (which was really getting some heat in it as the latitude decreased), it was easy.

What had Captain Ramage in mind? The series of rendezvous he had given to Wagstaffe, a latitude and longitude for each day, in case they lost each other during the night and were not in sight at dawn, ended up at 5° North and 52° West, which was the South American coast at Cayenne . . . The French kit of charts on board *La Robuste* did not include French Guiana, except as a half-inch square on the chart of the south part of the North Atlantic. Cayenne, Devil's Island . . . Wagstaffe shivered. It was probably no healthier than it sounded. Devil's Island was said to be the place Bonaparte sent his enemies. Well, it must be a big island because the Frenchman had a lot of enemies. And friends, too, judging from England's lack of allies.

Sergeant Ferris, the second-in-command of the Marines on board the *Calypso,* undid his pipeclayed crossbelts and unbuttoned his tunic. Sitting on the breech of one of the guns was not exactly resting in an armchair but the breech was in the shade and the breeze blowing the length of the main deck was cool, even if *La Robuste's* bilges stank so that the last foot that the pump would not suck out swirled back and forth with the frigate's pitch and roll and occasionally made the main deck smell like a Paris sewer.

Jackson walked up and sat on the truck on the after side of the gun and leaned back against the breech. "Coolest spot in the ship," he said.

"Aye," Ferris said, "count yourself lucky you're not a Marine and wearing this damned uniform."

"Trouble with the French prisoners?"

"No, not yet. A couple of them started quarrelling with each other and some of my lads had to stop them, so we've put them all in irons, each man one leg, so they're sitting in rows facing each other and staring at the sole of the other fellow's foot. Still, 46 prisoners is not too bad since I've got half the *Calypso*'s Marines, and we've got that twelve-pounder trained on 'em."

"Yes, but that's just a bluff," Jackson said. "If we have to fire it down the hatch the recoil will turn the gun upside-down!"

"The Frogs don't know that," Ferris said philosophically, "and if only half the canister catches them it won't leave many alive."

"More likely put a hole in the hull," Jackson said.

"Don't worry. Just go down in the hold and sit down with one ankle held by the irons, and I can tell you that inside ten minutes the muzzle of that twelve-pounder will seem to measure two feet in diameter and be winking at you like death himself."

Jackson's laugh was mirthless. He had fought the French for too long to have much sympathy for them. "What about Gilbert?"

Ferris puffed out his lips and then opened his mouth as if blowing out a plum stone. "Don't make a mistake about that fellow! He may be small and he may be a Frog—it's easy to forget that because he speaks such good English—but you should see him when he gets worked up!

"Before we took half the prisoners over to *Calypso* he talked to all of them below decks (this was while you was ferrying across our seamen) and gave 'em a warning. All French to me, of course, but I understood everything he said just by watching the faces of the prisoners! I think a lot of it was religion—Diable, that means the Devil, doesn't it? Well he went on a lot about him, and they shuffled about a lot, as though they were scared of the Devil. There was another chap they were scared of, too, someone called More. What with him threatening 'em with the Devil and More, and us Marines, too, we had them French twittering like frightened starlings."

"Until the two started fighting."

"Yus, but I think they are so scared that they very easily get on each other's nerves. Anyway, a day or two in irons won't hurt 'em. Given half a chance, Gilbert and his chaps would have beaten the two of them. Yet they're French too—why do they hate the fellows in this ship so much, Jacko?"

"It's not just this ship: they hate all Frenchmen who support Bonaparte. I don't know much about it myself but of course Gilbert and Louis worked for the Count of Rennes, who Bonaparte is shipping to Cayenne in the frigate we're trying to catch."

"Cayenne? That's a sort of pepper, isn't it?"

"Yes, it comes from French Guiana, which is near Brazil. It's a deadly sort of place—makes islands of the West Indies like Antigua seem as healthy as Bath. Die like flies there, according to the captain."

Ferris nodded and flapped the front of his tunic back and forth like a fan. "I can believe it. But what does the captain want with this frigate, La Robuste? Halves our strength in men, even if it doubles the number of ships. But doubling the number of guns and halving the number of men to fire them," his voice assumed the monotonous drone of a drill sergeant, "is militarily unsound, Jacko."

"Tell the captain," the American said. "He may not have considered that. Or," he added sarcastically, "he might be considering it only from a naval point of view, not a military one."

Sergeant Ferris patted his stomach. "Yes, that could be so," he agreed judicially, completely missing the tone of Jackson's voice. "Yes, I agree, he might have some particular naval plan in mind."

Wagstaffe looked at his makeshift journal. There was something very satisfying about the book, which had been made up by young Orsini stitching together the left-hand side of a dozen sheets of paper. How satisfying to write boldly across the top (normally it was only a matter of fitting names in the blank spaces of a printed form) "Journal of the Proceedings of—" he paused a moment: this was an unusual situation. He then continued, "—the former French national frigate *La Robuste*, presently prize to one of His Majesty's ships, Lieutenant Wagstaffe, commander." He had added the date and then carefully ruled in nine columns, and today, as he glanced down them, the ship's progress was becoming more obvious.

The date occupied the first two columns, the third recorded the winds (which had stayed between south-east and north-east the whole time), then came the courses (which were unchanged) and the miles covered from noon to noon, which were usually around 175. The latitude and longitude occupied the next two columns and showed to a navigator's eye the progress they were making to the south-west.

The next column, bearing and distances at noon, had been left blank, and there was only one entry under "Remarkable Observations and Accidents," which recorded putting all the prisoners in irons for 24 hours after two of them had started fighting.

Across in the *Calypso*, Ramage had just worked out the noon sight and compared his position with those of Aitken and Southwick. They tallied within three or four miles, and with the ship rolling and pitching with following wind and sea, so that taking a sight was like trying to shoot a hare from the back of a run-away horse, that was close enough.

He opened his journal and under the "Latitude" column wrote 6° 45' North; next to it was recorded the longitude, 52° 14' West. The Îles du Salut, according to the French pilot book, were 5° 17' North and 52° 36' West, so . . . they were . . . yes, ninety miles on a course of south by west a quarter west. Which meant no change in the course, but because they were making eight knots and he wanted to bring the mountains in sight soon after dawn, both the *Calypso* and *La Robuste* were going to have to reduce canvas: a little under five knots would bring the mountains in sight at daybreak so that the ships' companies would be breakfasted by the time the three islands were sighted. Providing of course the visibility was reasonable. Often there was a haze along a lee shore, presumably caused by the sea air meeting the land air, and the mistiness thrown up by the waves breaking on rocks and sandy beaches.

He wiped the pen, put the top on the ink bottle, and replaced everything in the drawer. He found Southwick and Aitken on deck.

"If the chronometer is not playing games with us, and if there's not a radical change in the speed of the current as we close the coast . . ." Ramage said.

"Ninety miles, I make it," Southwick said.

"Which means we might run up on the beach in the night," Ramage commented. "Mr Aitken, we'll try her under topsails, and then a cast of the log, if you please. Five knots will be quite enough, so we can furl the courses and get in the t'gallants and royals."

Aitken picked up the speaking-trumpet while Ramage went aft to the taffrail and looked astern at the *Calypso*'s wake. Despite the speed she was making and the wild rolling, the wake was no more than the first wrinkles on a beautiful woman's face: the French designer had produced a fast and sea-kindly hull which slipped through the water without fuss.

La Robuste was a fine sight. He could imagine how often over the past days Wagstaffe, Kenton and Martin had been measuring the angle to the *Calypso*'s mainmasthead, to maintain that magic distance of a cable. He smiled to himself because while Wagstaffe might not realize it, the next few minutes were something of a test. Wagstaffe was a fine seaman and steady, a good navigator and popular with the men. He had shown himself, in other words, to be an excellent lieutenant. He could and did carry out orders with precision. And, as Bowen had pointed out to Admiral Clinton, this is what Bullivant could do. Bullivant had only failed when he made the enormous jump from taking orders as a lieutenant to making decisions and giving orders as a captain.

How about Wagstaffe?

The *Calypso*'s bosun's mates finished the shrill notes of their calls and bellowed orders: now came the thud of bare feet as the men ran to their stations. Sails would not be furled as fast as usual, since half the *Calypso*'s men were now over in *La Robuste*, but—he took out his watch—with similar ships and similar sails set it would be interesting to compare times.

The squeal of ropes rendering through blocks, the shouts of bosun's mates, the grunts of men straining as they heaved on ropes . . . And the great rectangle of the main course, which for days had been billowing in a graceful curve, suddenly crumpled and distorted as the wind spilled when the lower corner of each side began to be pulled diagonally towards the middle.

And damnation, *La Robuste* was beginning to clew up her main course, too! Wagstaffe had plotted his noon position against the latitude and longitude of the Îles du Salut: he must have realized that the two ships would have to slow down to avoid arriving in the night, and he had his men waiting out of sight, waiting for the first wrinkles to appear in the *Calypso*'s main course . . . Yes, Wagstaffe passed the test . . .

Looking forward again and upward Ramage could see the men on the *Calypso*'s main yard furling the sail neatly and securing it with gaskets, the long strips of canvas keeping it in place. He glanced at his watch and then looked at *La Robuste* and waited for the last gasket to be passed. The *Calypso* won by under half a minute, and that victory could no doubt be explained by defects in *La Robuste*'s running rigging and the poor state of her gaskets—he had seen two tear in half, weakened by the heat and damp of a year in Far Eastern waters.

Forecourses were clewed up and then furled and *La Robuste*'s time was better, allowing for the fact that Wagstaffe had to wait for the *Calypso* to make the first move because his orders were to conform with the *Calypso*. In topgallants . . . the same. Obviously the Calypsos in *La Robuste* were enjoying themselves.

It was going to be a busy afternoon—preparations for making a landfall were, in this case, the same as for entering harbour, and as soon as the last sail was furled and the last topman down on deck again, Ramage nodded to Southwick, who was responsible for the fo'c's'le and all that went on there. The heavy anchor cable would have to be roused out while the blind bucklers closing the two hawsepipes would have to be taken off. That was always a difficult job under way with a following sea, since the bucklers were fixed securely to prevent seas coming in through the hawse holes.

One end of the first cable would then be led out through the starboard hawse and back on board again and secured to the ring of one of the two anchors on the starboard side. Then the end of a second cable would be led out of the larboard hawse and back to the ring of one of the two larboard anchors. People were often surprised that a ship the size of a frigate in fact carried six anchors and eight cables (seven of them each eighteen and a half inches in circumference and seven hundred twenty feet long). But such people had never seen a ship at anchor in a high and a heavy sea.

The covers needed taking off the boats and a couple of quarterdeck guns should be loaded with blank charges in case it was necessary to make an urgent signal to *La Robuste*. And . . . well, Ramage admitted, that was about all. All that was needed next morning was the sight of the three mountains close to the mouth of the River Kourou, Pointe Charlotte and the Îles du Salut. Still, he'd be quite satisfied if they sighted the "very remarkable conical hill" called Mont Diable in the pilot book but presumably Montagne du Diable, and which should warn in good time that he was a little too far south. *Diable, diable* . . . it had started off with Bullivant in his delirium seeing Satan; now English devils in the imagination were going to be replaced by French *diables* in fact.

CHAPTER SIXTEEN

THERE THEY WERE, three flat-topped islands still grey in the distance and overlapping so that there appeared to be only two. That would be Île du Diable just coming clear on the left while Île Royale and Île St Joseph merged to the south. As his body swayed with the rolling of the *Calypso,* making it difficult to hold the telescope steady, they moved from side to side in the circular lens as though being viewed through the bottom of a drinking glass.

He turned aft to train the glass on *La Robuste*'s quarterdeck. Yes, they too had sighted the islands; there was Wagstaffe hunched with the telescope to his eye and Kenton, Martin and

Orsini standing in a row beside him at the quarterdeck rail like inquisitive starlings.

It had been disappointing at dawn when the first light seemed to spread outward from the ship and nothing had been in sight. The traditional cry of "See a grey goose at a mile" had brought in the six lookouts stationed on deck round the ship and sent two aloft, and they had reported a clear horizon.

Then suddenly, as though a bank of fog had drifted away to reveal them (though the fog familiar in higher latitudes was of course unknown in the Tropics), they were ahead. Obviously there had been a haze hiding the coast until the sun lifted over the horizon and burned it up.

Ramage sighed, a natural reaction but one which led Southwick to ask: "You expect trouble, sir?"

Trouble? They were too far off for him to be sure. If a frigate's masts showed up behind Île Royale, revealing that *L'Espoir* had arrived (and had time to send her prisoners over to Île du Diable), then yes, they had trouble. The idea, plan, gamble—he was not sure what to call it—that had come to him several days ago like a wind shadow, and the outline of which had since sharpened, as though someone had used a quill to run an inked line round it, would have been a waste of thought if *L'Espoir* had beaten them in.

More important, Southwick's question merely emphasized that the idea was just a gamble. You could put other fancy names to it, he told himself sourly, but it was still a gamble: he was like some pallid player putting a small fortune on the turn of a dice in the final desperate throw that could lose or save a home which had been in the family for generations and was a son's rightful inheritance. So if there were masts, he had lost; if there were no masts, he had won.

Won? That was nonsense. If there were no masts, then he had not yet lost, which was a far cry from winning. No, what

Southwick's innocent and well-meant question emphasized, Ramage admitted to himself with bitterness, was that by pinning everything on beating *L'Espoir* to the Îles du Salut, he had not fully considered the consequences of losing the race.

If *L'Espoir* had not arrived, then the prisoners were still on board the frigate, and frigates were not invulnerable. But if *L'Espoir* had arrived, then the prisoners by now would be imprisoned on the Île du Diable in what the French pilot book called a "fortified enclosure," and the whole purpose of these fortifications was to keep people (rescuers, in this case) out.

Southwick was still awaiting an answer.

"If *L'Espoir* is here, yes," Ramage said.

"Because she'll have put her prisoners on shore?"

"Yes. There must be hundreds of prisoners on the island—perhaps more than one island. We can't be sure they still keep all the criminals on one island and the political prisoners on another."

"I wonder if Bonaparte sees any difference in the two sorts," Southwick commented. "He's just as likely to have put 'em all together."

"That would mean our fifty would be among perhaps five thousand others; and five thousand prisoners means how many guards?"

Southwick gave one of his famous sniffs. They came of a standard strength, but he could give each one a particular meaning. This one indicated that the whole thing was absurd and not for the serious consideration of grown men.

"Even at one guard for every twenty prisoners, plus all the camp followers and cooks and administration people, we'd never stand a chance," the master said. "To find out if *L'Espoir's* there we've got to get in sight of that fort on Île Royale, so they'll sight us and we lose surprise."

"Yes," Ramage said, and changed the painful subject, which

was thoroughly depressing him. "Now, we'd better start working out the positions of those reefs and shoals."

"Aye, I have 'em noted from the pilot book," Southwick said. "The main bank is over there, between one and two miles nor'-nor'-west of Royale." He pointed over the starboard bow.

At that moment Ramage saw Rennick down on the main deck and called him up to the quarterdeck. The Marine captain's face was as usual burned a bright red from the sun and the skin of his nose was peeling, but he gave a smart salute.

"How are the prisoners?" Ramage asked.

"Very subdued, sir. They haven't forgotten that man Gilbert. I don't know what he said before they were brought over here, but it frightened them!"

Ramage nodded. "Keep them subdued."

Supposing there were no masts. Oh yes, he had this wonderful idea, but what about the pilot? The garrisons on the islands? He shook his head and left a puzzled Rennick standing on the quarterdeck as he clattered down the companion-way to the great cabin, nodding to the sentry.

He sat down at his desk and looked at the sketch he had made of the three islands based on the information in the pilot book. Why was he looking at it? He knew the outlines and positions by heart. He pushed the sketch aside and took out the French pilot book and began reading the reference to the Îles du Salut. The words blurred into meaninglessness: he knew them by heart, so why was he reading it yet again? He put the book back in the drawer and stood up impatiently. What the devil was wrong with him? Impatience, he told himself, that's what's wrong. It needs patience to wait until we are closer to the islands so that we can be sure about the masts.

Islands! Even at this distance that was obviously an absurd word for three long lumps of rock lying like broken grindstones half a dozen miles off a flat coastline fringed with mangroves, marshy land and almost stagnant water and buzzing and whining with biting insects.

At least the islands do not suffer from a shortage of water: the rainfall must be so heavy that perpetual dampness and mildew, not drought, is the problem.

Up on the quarterdeck he said to Southwick: "Hail the lookouts. No, better still, send a man aloft with a glass."

"Yes, sir," Southwick said, but added: "You did say that Royale was 216 feet high, and Diable 131, didn't you, sir?"

Ramage glared at him. "Yes, and the truck of a frigate's mainmast won't show clear from behind 'em."

"Yes, sir, so I was thinking . . ."

"Nevertheless send a man aloft with a glass."

"Aye aye, sir." Southwick knew the strain of waiting. They had left the Channel Fleet how long ago? Nearly three weeks. For twenty days they had looked for *L'Espoir* and the captain had shown no sign of strain. Now all the tensions and anticipations of three weeks, when everyone had wondered if they would catch *L'Espoir* or beat her to Cayenne, were being compressed into an hour.

The new lookout soon hailed the quarterdeck. With the bring-'em-near he could make out some buildings on the largest island. They were low down on the seaward side, he added.

Ramage nodded: that would be the fort on Royale, and by now the French lookouts would be reporting the approach of two frigates. Was there one *préfet* in command of the three islands? Or was he a soldier, a garrison commander? It did not matter a damn, really; Ramage knew he was just trying to keep his mind occupied. He turned and began to walk back and forth along the few feet of deck between the quarterdeck rail and the taffrail, occasionally looking astern at *La Robuste* and allowing himself a glance at the islands only once every hundred times he completed the stretch.

Eventually Southwick said: "We should close the coast a lit-tle more to the north, sir. Then we know we'll be clear of that bank of rocks and can stretch down to the anchorage. Unless you want to wait for a pilot."

"Yes, we'll heave-to and wait for the pilot, if he's not there waiting for us."

"But . . . well, sir, won't the pilot realize that—"

Southwick did not bother to complete the question.

"If we don't pick him up, he'll come over to us after we've anchored."

"Yes, I see, sir," Southwick said and did not understand at all. To him, the prospect of anchoring the two frigates close in under three French islands which were probably bristling with batter-ies was something that did not bear thinking about.

The *Calypso* hove-to just long enough for the frigate's cutter to be hoisted out and rowed to *La Robuste* to collect Paolo, Jackson and the four Frenchmen, and bring them on board. Gilbert and his men had been puzzled and nervous from the moment that Wagstaffe, after reading the instructions delivered by the boat's coxswain, had ordered them away.

They were brought up to Ramage on the quarterdeck and he smiled the moment he saw their long, nervous faces. He led them aft to the taffrail and, speaking quickly in French, gave them their instructions. They talked among themselves, embar-rassed, for a couple of minutes and then Auguste nodded reluctantly.

"Me, sir. They've chosen me."

"Very well," Ramage said. "I'm sure you'll do it well. Go down to the great cabin. Silkin is there. Gilbert, you go with him, as translator."

With the cutter now towing astern—the shallower water brought calmer seas so there was no need to hoist it in again—

the *Calypso* steered for the western end of Île Royale, followed by *La Robuste*. Seen from this angle, against the flat land of the shore, the island seemed like the end of a lozenge, crowding Île St Joseph, which was much smaller and only ninety feet high. The resulting channel was wide but the water brown, obviously shallow. Here and there short branches of wood floated on the sea but did not drift, merely moving up and down. Southwick pointed out several to Ramage, who tapped the old man on the shoulder. "You're lucky to have your navigation confirmed like that—the local fishermen have put their pots down round the bank, and those bits of bough are their buoys. The only trouble is you don't know if the pots are for lobsters and therefore close to rocks, or fish, in which case they'll be further away."

"All the same to me, sir," Southwick declared cheerfully. "I don't want to take us within a mile of that bank! And these islands—I wouldn't want to stay here a week, let alone a year. If I was a Frenchman I'd take care I didn't fall foul of Bonaparte and get sent out here."

"If you were a Frenchman you might not have the choice. The Count of Rennes just wanted to be left in peace."

Southwick sniffed in agreement, recognizing that in two sentences the captain had summed it all up.

"At least we beat *L'Espoir*," he said, gesturing at the empty anchorage. "Tell me, sir, did you expect to?"

"Hopes were fighting fears. When it was dark I didn't expect to, but if it was a nice sunny day with a fresh wind—well, I hoped."

"And now, sir?"

Ramage purposely misunderstood the question. "We heave-to and wait for the pilot off the western end of the island, then we'll anchor a cable further seaward than he says. Four fathoms, soft mud, single anchor, I told Wagstaffe in the orders I sent across to anchor as far inshore of us as he dared, so the gap between the two ships is at least a cable, preferably two."

Southwick was puzzled. "I hope young Wagstaffe doesn't run on the mud. Soft mud and a lee shore. Think of the suction on that hull . . ."

Laughing at the thought, Ramage said casually: "We can always use the boats to lay out an anchor or two for him; then all hands to man the capstan. With the fiddler standing on top to set them trotting, we'd soon have him off!"

Southwick looked like a bishop to whom the suffragan's wife had just made a very improper suggestion, but Ramage saw no point in explaining everything in detail because there was a good chance he would have to abandon the plan. Which plan? There were two now and he was muddling himself. Well, he meant the one he had just explained to Gilbert and his men, the one which had occurred to him only a couple of hours ago. Call that the first plan, even though it was the last to arrive in his head. The second plan, which followed only if the first was successful, was the original idea, the one that had come like a wind shadow, and it was surrounded with ifs as thick as a blackthorn hedge intended to keep boys out of an apple orchard. The second plan did not even begin until *L'Espoir* hove in sight. Providing the first worked, and providing *L'Espoir* hove in sight, then there would be plenty of time to tell Southwick all about the second.

"Deck there, mainmasthead here!"

"Deck here," Aitken bellowed up, not bothering with the speaking-trumpet.

"There's a strange little craft ahead of us, sir: through the glass it looks like a canoe with a sail on a sprit. Four men in it."

"Very well, keep reporting it," Aitken said and turned back to Ramage. "That'll be your pilot, sir," he said with a first lieutenant's usual lofty disdain for local pilots.

"Heave-to to leeward of them so they can drop down to us. Now, our colours are stowed. Mr Southwick, tell the men no one is to speak English while the pilot boat is near. Nor is any bosun's mate to use his call. There's no need for the pilot to mistake us for an English frigate . . ."

"Mistake us?" Southwick repeated the phrase and then took his hat off, scratched his head, and ran his hand through his hair before jamming his hat back on. He took up the speaking-trumpet and bellowed the length of the ship. Without much apparent effort his voice carried Ramage's order to every man.

"Now stand by to back the foretopsail, Mr Aitken," Ramage said and could have bitten his tongue. Aitken knew what to do, and giving him unnecessary orders must be irritating.

Now he could see the pilot boat with the naked eye. Yes, it was a large dugout canoe, with a stubby mast and, like a canted boom, a sprit stuck out diagonally, holding out the square sail. And it was an old sail obviously sewn up from odd pieces of cloth. But for all that the canoe was skimming along, and through the glass he could now see there were three blacks actually handling the boat while a white man tried to sit in a dignified manner. But, judging from the urgency with which one of the others scooped water over the side using a calabash shell as a bailer, he must be sitting in a few inches of water.

The movement of the pilot canoe so intrigued him that Ramage did not notice that the *Calypso* was turning head to wind to heave-to until her bow swung and the canoe and Île Royale suddenly shifted from the larboard bow to amidships on the starboard side.

Ramage walked over to the skylight above his cabin and called down in French. He listened to the reply, laughed and looked round for Louis and Albert, who were still waiting by the taffrail.

"Wait for Gilbert and Auguste at the top of the gangway," he said in French. "You really understand what I want you to do?"

"Indeed we do, sir," Louis said. "We are proud to be able to do it!"

Ramage nodded and grinned. One Englishman was usually reckoned to be equal to three Frenchmen, but not these French-men. What had changed them? Gilbert and his three friends probably held their own political views as strongly as a Revolu-tionary sailor in Bonaparte's navy. Was it leadership? He shrugged because he had no idea: it was so, and for the moment that was all that mattered.

The pilot canoe was only a hundred yards off, and he walked back to the skylight and warned Gilbert and Auguste, but there was no reply and a moment later he saw them joining Louis and Albert at the gangway.

Ramage took off his coat and untied his stock, bundling both up with his hat and stuffing them under one of the guns.

"Mr Aitken . . . Mr Southwick . . ." he pointed at what he was doing, and each man hurriedly removed his hat, coat and stock.

Now the master, his white hair caught by the wind, could pass for—well, a rural dean, an amiable grocer, a tenant farmer who was now leaving the heavy work to his sons . . .

"You still don't look like a Republican, sir," Southwick said doubtfully. "Perhaps the hair? Too tidy?"

Ramage ran his fingers through it. "You have the advantage of me, I must admit," he said wryly.

"The breeches and silk stockings, sir?" Southwick said, his voice still doubtful. "Don't forget those whatever they're called, the *sans cullars*."

"*Sans-culottes*. No, don't worry, we don't need to dance on top of the hammock nettings!"

With that Ramage left Aitken and Southwick on the quar-terdeck and went down to the entry port where Auguste stood watching the canoe, which was now beginning to round up to come alongside, one of the men casting off the sheet and stifling the sail by standing up and clasping it to him as he reached for the mast. The other two blacks picked up paddles and began paddling the canoe the last few feet in the calm water provided by the *Calypso's* bulk.

Ramage gestured to Auguste, who took the telescope Ramage held out to him. Tucking it under one arm and straightening his shoulders, the Frenchman said with a grin: "I shall find it hard to be an ordinary seaman again, sir."

Ramage stood to one side beside a gun while Auguste went back to the entry port and Gilbert, Louis and Albert stood close to him.

There was a faint hail and Albert hurried forward with the coil of rope he was holding. From the top of the hammock nettings he threw an end down to the canoe and one of the blacks seized it. The canoe was almost level with the entry port when the pilot began to stand up.

Auguste leaned over slightly to shout down at him. "*M'sieu,* listen carefully. This frigate and the one astern have come from Brest, and a third is due any day—we lost company with her."

"Very well, Captain," the pilot answered. "There is plenty of room in the anchorage. You bring us many prisoners, eh?"

"We bring you possible sickness and death," Auguste said sadly. "Brest has *la peste.* We lost five men from it the day after sailing. The other frigate"—he gestured astern—"lost nine. I dare not think what has happened with the third frigate: I suspect we lost sight of her because she had so much sickness . . ."

"The plague? Brest a plague port? Nine—no, fourteen—dead? Quarantine! You must stay at anchor! No one to come ashore. Six weeks from the last case. Cast off!" he snapped at the seaman, who let go of the rope as though it was a poisonous snake.

As the canoe drifted away the pilot stood up and shouted: "I will report to the governor, but six weeks you stay—"

Auguste and Gilbert screamed back at him: it was an injustice, it was mocking their misery, it would leave them short of medical supplies and provisions . . .

Louis and Albert joined in. There was no wine and very little water left. Now they would get the black vomit, as well as having the plague, and anyway what authority had the pilot to give such orders?

"I'll show you!" the white-faced pilot screeched back as the canoe drifted away. "No one is to come near the shore: you stay on board. Tell the second frigate and the third when she comes in because I am not coming out again for six weeks. I know the governor will order sentries to shoot at anyone approaching the shore. That's an order; I have the authority!"

"Assassin, cuckold, pederast, Royalist traitor!" Auguste bawled and stood aside to give the others a chance while he thought up more insults.

"You wait until the Minister of Marine hears of it!" Gilbert bellowed. "Then you'll be a prisoner here, not the pilot!"

The pilot knew he was far enough away to be at a disadvantage shouting against the wind, but he took a deep breath. "Perhaps—if you live long enough to get a message to Brest. But you'll all leave your bones on the beach over there . . ."

"Your mother was a careless whore!" Auguste yelled and then shook his head. "A waste," he grumbled, "he's too far away." He handed the telescope back to Ramage. "Was that satisfactory, sir?"

A grinning Ramage patted him on the back. "Perfect. As I watched you all it was obvious the *Calypso* had at least four captains!"

"Sir," Aitken called anxiously, "we're running out of sea room!"

"Bear away and anchor when you're ready!" Ramage shouted and hurried back to the quarterdeck, passing Southwick on his way to the fo'c's'le. By now the pilot was a quarter of the way to a jetty which was just coming into view on the south side of Île Royale.

As he climbed the steps Ramage was thankful his idea had effectively ensured that no one would be coming out to the anchored ships, but he wished the pilot had not taken fright so quickly: Auguste had not been able to ask the pilot to remain in his canoe but lead the way to the anchorage.

Aitken shouted to a seaman standing in the chains, ready with the lead: "Give me a cast!" Then he gave orders to brace up the yard and trim the foretopsail sheets so that the *Calypso* turned for the last few hundred yards to the anchorage.

The leadsman reported, "Six fathoms, soft mud."

Ramage had already explained to Aitken the importance of the *Calypso* anchoring in the right place, so that *La Robuste* could position herself, and he kept both topsails shivering so that the *Calypso* had little more than steerage-way.

Ramage watched the luffs of the sails and kept an eye on the quartermaster, who would signal the moment the *Calypso* was going too slowly for the rudder to bite. He glanced astern and noted that Wagstaffe was handling his ship perfectly.

"Five fathoms . . . five fathoms . . ." the leadsman's chant was monotonous but clear. He heaved the lead forward so that it dropped into the water and hit the bottom just as the main chains passed over it. A quick up-and-down tug on the line confirmed that the lead was actually on the bottom, and by the feel of the piece of leather or cloth in his hand, marking the depths, he sang out the fathoms and feet.

The *Calypso* was now moving crabwise to the unmarked spot where Ramage intended to anchor, and Southwick's upraised arm showed that all was ready on the fo'c's'le. The anchor, stowed high up and parallel with the deck when on passage, had been lowered almost to the water. Ramage's eyes swept the luffs, saw the men at the wheel, and he said: "Down with the helm!"

Had he left it too late? Was the *Calypso* now going too slowly for the rudder to work effectively, or had the quartermaster (very sensibly) given the warning a few seconds early? In fact they could lower the anchor and, as soon as it held, the cable would swing the frigate round head to wind. Effective, but not very seamanlike, and the cable going under the hull was likely to wrench off copper sheathing.

But the *Calypso*'s bow was coming round . . . one point, two, three . . . speeding up now . . . six, seven, eight . . . fourteen, fifteen, sixteen . . . And with the wheel amidships and the foretopsail once again aback, because the yard had not been hauled round to compensate for the turn, the *Calypso* slowed.

Ramage walked to a gun port and looked over the side. The water was muddy and several pieces of palm fronds and odd branches were floating. But they stayed in the same place: the *Calypso* was stopped. Then they began moving towards the bow . . . the frigate was beginning to move astern.

Ramage signalled to Southwick and heard first the splash of the anchor and then the thunder of the cable running through the hawse. And yes, the usual smell of burning as the cable, finally dry after being stowed for weeks in the cable tier, scorched itself and the wood of the hawse-hole as it raced out.

A quick order to the topmen had the main and mizen-topsails furled, but he waited for the signal from Southwick which would indicate that the foretopsail now thrusting the *Calypso* astern had dug in the anchor.

He returned to watching the rubbish. Finally the palm fronds and broken branches slowed down and then stayed alongside. He watched a rock on Île Royale which was lined up with a headland on Île du Diable. The two remained lined up. If the rock had moved out of line that would have been proof that the anchor was dragging and the palm fronds were drifting in a current moving at the same speed as the frigate.

Ramage then jumped up on to the breech of a gun to watch *La Robuste* anchoring. She ended up positioned perfectly, and as her anchor hit the water, Ramage saw that the pilot's canoe had just arrived at the jetty.

"They're in a hurry," Aitken commented.

"I'm not surprised: the pilot has never had such a startling report to make to the governor," Ramage said.

"Now what do we do?"

"We hoist out all the boats and wait," Ramage said. "Wait and practise."

CHAPTER SEVENTEEN

SERGEANT FERRIS was, usually, a patient man. He had a rule that he would explain something three times to a Marine or seaman he regarded as intelligent and four times to a fool. But no one valuing his pride, sanity or eardrums would dare cause a fifth. If he had any sense he would do what Marine Hart was doing.

Hart made up in bulk and loudness of voice what he lacked in intelligence, and this resulted in him being, at six feet two inches tall and sixteen stone, the largest of the *Calypso*'s Marines with a bellow that sounded like a bull with spring fever.

Ferris, now commanding the Marine detachment in *La Robuste,* was thankful that Hart was an amiable man. This was due less to his nature than the fact that it was almost impossible to insult him. When he accidentally trod on someone's foot and was promptly called a "bloody great big oaf," Hart would grin and say proudly: "Ah, I am big, ain't I?" Hart had been a Marine for more than a year before he discovered to his surprise that an oaf was neither a special sort of promise nor a swear word.

"Let's have one more go, men," Ferris said, although he knew the twenty Marines in his party understood that he was using "men" instead of "Hart" because the man was liable to sulk if he thought he was being singled out. Hart, who was also left-handed, was not difficult or dangerous when he sulked but it was, as Mr Rennick once remarked, like having a stunned elephant lying at the foot of the stairs.

"The idea is this. We have one hundred and sixty Marines and seamen, an' that's dragging in every man that can wield a cutlash or fire a pistol."

To Sergeant Ferris a cutlass was always a cutlash, no matter how many times he heard Mr Rennick and the *Calypso*'s officers pronounce it correctly. On one occasion Rennick had taken him to one side and explained that it might be bad for discipline if privates heard such an ordinary word mispronounced. Ferris, a great believer in pipeclay and discipline, agreed wholeheartedly. "So," Rennick said, promptly sweeping into the linguistic breach, "it's pronounced 'cutlass.'"

"S'right, sir," Ferris agreed, "cutlash, like I always say."

Ferris looked round at his twenty men, careful not to glare at Hart. "Now the captain reckons that eighty men (that's half the total: half one side and half the other) is too many to h'act h'as a disciplined force."

Anyone except Hart who had served under Ferris knew that under stress (except of course in action), the sergeant sprinkled his sentences with both too many and too few aitches. He was not particular where they fell: a word with a vowel at its threshold was always a convenient spot.

"So h'it h'as been decided to divide the entire force, one hundred and sixty Marines and seamen, h'into eight parties each of twenty men. "'Ow h'about that, 'art, do you understand?"

"Yus, Sergeant," Hart said, nodding his head like a bear trying to disperse buzzing flies.

"Right. Now h'each party will 'ave its h'own h'objective."

Hart was not alone in sorting out the sergeant's aspiration.

"Ours will be the starboard gangway. We clear h'it. I do not want"—he spaced the words and emphasized them—"h'any of the h'enemy left alive on the starboard gangway."

"Wot about the fo'c's'le, sergeant?" Hart asked lugubriously.

"None of your affair, my man: you just confine your h'activities to the starboard gangway."

Hart digested this and then asked: "Wot about the quarterdeck, sergeant?"

Ferris took a deep breath. They were a good crowd, he had to admit that. They did not quarrel among themselves or try to dodge sentry duty in the more cramped parts of the ship, and they all agreed that Hart when possible should be the sentry at the water butt on deck, when it was in use, rather than, say, sentry at the captain's cabin, where the headroom was five feet four inches, leaving Hart with a surplus of ten inches. But why Hart? What had Ferris ever done, he asked himself, to have a Hart?

"None of your affair, my man," he repeated firmly, "you just confine your h'activities to the starboard gangway."

"But sergeant, what happens when we've done 'em all in on the starboard gangway? Don't seem fair that the fo'c's'le and the quarterdeck men and the rest of 'em get a bigger share than us. After all, we are Marines."

Ware, Ferris suddenly remembered. In Hertfordshire. That was where Hart came from. "Where?" "Ware." Yes, Ferris could remember that puzzling conversation with Marine Hart years ago.

But for once Hart was asking a good question. Once they'd cleared the gangway, were they expected just to stand there? Toss bodies over the side? Or what? Anyway, it gave him a chance to encourage Hart.

"That is a very pertinent question, my good man, and I'll raise it with Mr Wagstaffe."

"Oh Sergeant," Hart said hastily, "I wasn't trying to be perti-nent: it just seemed we was being discrimbulated against."

Not being pertinent? Ferris's brow wrinkled. He had never seen Hart so apologetic. What was wrong with "pertinent"? It was a sergeant's word, like "my man" was a sergeant's phrase. Suddenly he added two letters and saw the reason for Hart's apology.

"H'oh no, 'pertinent' and 'impertinent' are two h'utterly dif-ferent words. 'Pertinent' means—well, it's a good question. 'Impertinent' is being rude to someone of a higher station, like a sergeant, or a lieutenant."

That left "discrimbulated." Who would dare discrimbulate against Sergeant Ferris's party of men? That would risk a flog-ging. At least, it sounded as if it would. But . . . well, that word had a sort of left-handed sound about it. Then Ferris sighed.

"Hart, my good man, you mean 'discriminate.' Believe me, no one's trying to discriminate against us. Mr Rennick was there when Mr Ramage drew a diagram of the ship's deck h'on a sheet of paper, and he divided it h'up into fo'c's'le, main deck, star-board gangway, and larboard, quarterdeck and lower deck. Obviously most people are going to be on the main deck, so four parties go there, one to the fo'c's'le, one to the quarterdeck, and one to each gangway: eight parties, one hundred and sixty, plus a few under Midshipman Orsini to rescue the Royalists."

"If you say so, Sergeant," Hart said. He did not understand, he was not convinced, nor, Ferris firmly believed, did the big ox want to be convinced. Like a bull giving an occasional bellow for no reason, and not because of any bad temper, Hart had these mild attacks from time to time.

On board the *Calypso,* Ramage filled in the last couple of lines of the day's entry in his journal. He had a strange "someone-else-is-writing-this" sensation when he noted the *Calypso*'s position, under the "Bearings and distance at noon" column as "Western extremity of Île Royale bearing north by east 3/4 east five cables." Nor was it often one could be so exact, but here in the lee of the islands the sea was calm and the wind steady, and as the French pilot book gave the heights of the three islands Paolo had been set to work with sextant and tables working out the distance. His first two attempts put Île Royale eleven and then seven miles away, but by the fifth sextant reading and set of calculations his answer coincided with Southwick's.

Ramage usually left the "Remarkable Observations and Accidents" column empty, and the events of today, the first complete day after they had arrived and anchored, were so far unimportant, but if there was a court martial the record might be important. He made an abbreviated entry:

"French pilot's canoe came within hail mid-afternoon inquiring number of *déportés* on board both frigates and intended for island. Told 62 and more due in third frigate. Told that governor's orders are for both frigates and third when she arrives to remain at anchor in quarantine for six weeks after death or complete recovery of last case of cholera. Lieutenants Martin and Kenton returned on board until *L'Espoir* arrives. Ships' companies employed A.T.S.R."

He hated the initials for "As the Service required" but at this rate he would soon run out of space. There was no need to describe it as meaning scrubbing decks, setting up or replacing rigging and whippings, mending sails, and all the thousand and one jobs a sailor in a ship of war (or any ship for that matter) was heir to. And the sudden torrential rains that seemed to arrive out of a reasonably clear sky at three-hourly intervals meant that the quarterdeck awning was stretched with one corner dropped to catch water. If they could fill butts at the present rate each man would have something like a gallon of fresh water a day—something he had never experienced before. He could drink as much as he wanted; more important, he could rinse his clothes properly. Using the urine collected in the tubs in the head gave enough ammonia to bleach clothing, a rinse in salt water always meant that everything dried only to get damp on a humid day.

It would soon be necessary to send a boat to the mainland one night: the purser was complaining that he had only nineteen wreaths of twigs left for the cook to light the galley fire, and there was precious little wood left. So a wooding party would have to be sent out. And green wood needed more twigs to get it burning . . . Curious how planning the rescue of the Count of Rennes was built on the foundations of wreaths of twigs. "Wreaths" was an absurd name, yet in the Navy Board's list of "Tonnage with respect to stowage," forty wreaths of twigs were noted as weighing a ton. Out of curiosity he searched through a drawer and found the list—yes, 6 jars of oil, 40 bushels of oatmeal, 252 gallons of wine, 1,800 pounds of cheese in casks, 450 pieces of beef, 900 pieces of pork, 200 empty sacks, wooden hoops for 420 hogshead or 600 kilderkins, 240 gallons of vinegar, forty wreaths of twigs . . . each item weighed a ton. Wreaths—did the gypsies call them that when they went from door to door in towns selling kindling?

He looked at his watch. By now the *Calypso*'s parties of men should be waiting on the lower deck. Wagstaffe had just arrived on board from *La Robuste* and Aitken, Kenton, Martin and Rennick would be ready. Very well, *aux armes, citoyens*.

It was hot down on the lower deck but eighty seamen and Marines stood to attention as Aitken barked an order when Ramage came down the ladder, once again wearing his French trousers and a white shirt—with a powerful glass it was possible for anyone on the hill of Île Royale to inspect the ship's deck, so neither Marines nor officers could wear anything but what would be usual on board a French ship of war. Ramage was delighted that his stockings, breeches and coat were back in the trunks, and Silkin was now busy stitching up white duck bought from the purser into shirts and trousers. It was not seemly, Silkin had complained, that the captain should be wearing trousers cobbled up from "pusser's duck."

Ramage looked round at all the faces and found most of them were grinning. He had never before had such a large group muster on the lower deck, and the presence of the lieutenants and the ship's present position accounted for the air of excitement which was as heady as the smell of hops to leeward of a brewery.

"Fall out the officers," Ramage said, "and all of you make yourselves comfortable." Unaware of Sergeant Ferris's problem he added: "I am going through all this once. Then if there's anything someone doesn't understand, ask questions."

He looked round at the men again and said in level tones: "What is the difference between an axe and a hammer? Let's say the head of each is a chunk of metal weighing eight pounds. If you hit a plank with the hammer, you get a dent. But if you hit a plank with an axe, you get a deep cut the length of the blade.

"Why a dent with one and a deep cut with the other? Well, you've already guessed that the hammer's eight pounds when it hits the plank is spread over an area of the head likely to be twice the size of a guinea. But the eight pounds of the axe is concentrated on the blade—say four inches long by less than the thickness of a sheet of very thin paper. That's why you use an axe to fell a tree, not a hammer. Obviously you wouldn't use an axe blade to drive in a nail, either; you want the energy spread out over the flat head."

He looked round at the sailors. Yes, they understood the similes, even though they were puzzled why the captain was suddenly sermonizing like one of Mr Wesley's men.

"Now supposing you want to smash a plank of wood into kindling. You can have an eight-pound hammer or you can have an eight-pound axe—you have the choice. Or you can have eight one-pound axes or hammers.

"Supposing you were in a hurry: instead of an hour you had only five minutes to smash that plank into kindling. Wouldn't you be better off using your eight pounds of weight by chopping with eight one-pound axes rather than one axe weighing eight pounds?"

Several men immediately said yes, and the rest of them quickly muttered their agreement.

Ramage looked round and spotted Stafford. He pointed at the Cockney. "Why would we be better with eight smaller axes, Stafford?"

"Well, sir, stands ter reason, dunnit: eight blades choppin' away at eight different places is better than one big blade—that's if you want the plank as kindlin'."

"Exactly. For chopping down a tree . . ."

"Oh well, sir, the one big blade, o'course."

"Good. You all notice I am talking of a plank and not the tree: if it was a tree we'd be using the big axe to chop *in the same place;* because it's a plank for kindling we use eight small axes chopping *in several places.*"

Most of the men were nodding, reminding Ramage of a flock of pigeons. This business of speaking to them in parables was, in this instance anyway, a good one. And anything that helped maintain some sort of discipline in the heat of battle was all to the good. He found it difficult to control himself in the roar, smoke, flame and shouting of battle afloat, so he could not blame the seamen for regarding action on board an enemy ship as a concentrated group of men fighting a series of hand-to-hand actions, cutlass against cutlass, boarding-pike against pistol, tomahawk against musket. This was the hammer method, and usually it worked: the owner of any unfamiliar face was killed or taken prisoner.

"Very well, the 'plank' we might be attacking using the several small axes method is, I hope, the French frigate *L'Espoir* when she arrives."

From the satisfied "Ahs" and the way that the men wriggled to make themselves more comfortable, as though settling in for a long session, Ramage knew that only a handful of men had thought that far ahead.

"Now, capturing *L'Espoir*—providing she arrives here and providing we are still here to meet her—is going to be the most difficult job we've ever undertaken. Not the most dangerous, just the most difficult. You saw how the 'plague' trick worked: and you'll remember that Mr Orsini did a similar thing once in the Mediterranean. You were all with me when we dealt with the renegades at the Île Trinidade. But this time each of us will be fighting with one hand tied behind his back.

"There are fifty prisoners on board *L'Espoir* that we are under orders to rescue. We won't know where those prisoners are being kept in *L'Espoir*; we don't even know if the captain will be desperate enough to threaten to kill them unless we let him go free. Of course we can't use our great guns for fear of killing the prisoners. Now, listen carefully."

Quickly he outlined the plan, explaining how each group of twenty men would be under a particular leader and would have its own task. "So you see," he concluded, "the frigate is a plank of wood, and the eight groups are the eight small axes. Has anyone any questions?"

Jackson stood up. "Yes, sir. When do we expect *L'Espoir*?"

The *Calypso*'s gunroom, occupying the after part of the lower deck, was just far enough forward to clear the end of the tiller as it moved from side to side in a great arc, responding to the lines led down to it from the barrel of the wheel, but not far enough to be out of range of the harsh squeaking of the pintles of the rudder blade grinding on the gudgeons which supported them. When the *Calypso* was under way the rudder moved constantly, but the noise was almost lost in the symphony composed of water rushing past the hull and the creaking of the whole ship working as she flexed like a tree in a strong wind to ride across the troughs and crests of the waves.

The gunroom was an open space between four large boxes on one side and three on the other. The boxes were in fact cabins formed by three walls, or bulkheads, made of painted canvas stretched tightly over battens, with the ship's side forming the fourth. Each had its door, and each door had a stone-ground glass window in the upper half. Over each door was a sign bearing a carefully painted rank—surgeon, first lieutenant, and second lieutenant on the starboard side, Marine officer, third lieutenant, master and fourth lieutenant on the larboard side.

A table and forms fitted most of the remaining space, though the object like a thick tree trunk at the after end was the mizenmast, while the hatch on the larboard side, between the table and the master's cabin, and on which everyone stubbed a foot at least once a week, was the scuttle to the magazine, a reminder if any was needed that the ship's officers lived just above several tons of gunpowder.

Forward of the gunroom were two smaller cabins on the starboard side (for the gunner and the carpenter) and two to larboard, occupied by the purser and the bosun. A large cabin forward of the bosun's box was the midshipmen's berth, built to be the home of up to a dozen who could range in age from fourteen or fifteen to fifty, but at present the sole inhabitant was Midshipman Paolo Orsini, who thus had more space than anyone else in the ship except the captain.

Forward of these cabins the Marines had their tables and

forms, and at night slung their hammocks, and forward of them was what was usually called the "mess-deck," because the seamen forming the rest of the ship's company lived there, six or eight men to a table or "mess" and slinging their hammocks at night.

Right in the bow, most of the time with a leg in irons, were the *Calypso*'s half of *La Robuste*'s prisoners, guarded by a couple of Marines with muskets. For a couple of hours in the morning the French prisoners were freed for exercise but, as Ramage had told Rennick, it was unlikely they would be kept on board for more than a few days; not enough to worry about them being in irons.

In the gunroom, with the day's work in the ship completed and only the anchor watch, lookouts, and prisoners' guard to keep men from their hammocks and cots, the ship's lieutenants sat in their cabins or at the table.

The cabins were tiny and airless—there was room only for the cot, a canvas or metal bowl for washing, a trunk usually upended, a leprous mirror stuck in the best place to catch what little light squeezed through the skylight under the half-deck, and a rickety canvas chair which usually collapsed when the ship rolled violently, forcing the occupant to retreat to the forms, which were bolted to the deck.

Kenton, the red-haired and freckle-faced third lieutenant, was the smallest of the ship's officers but his chair had recently broken completely and it was only the suddenness of the collapse that saved him trapping any fingers. Now, as he waited for a carpenter's mate to make him a new chair, he had to sit on a form, munching the last piece of fruit cake he had brought with him from home, and which was edible only after he had scraped off a thick layer of mildew.

William Martin, the fourth lieutenant and son of the master shipwright at Chatham, was in his cabin behind Kenton and softly played his flute. Kenton did not particularly like the tune that "Blower" was playing and called to Aitken, who was sitting in his cabin filling in reports on provisions which should have been handed to the captain's clerk last week.

"When does the captain reckon *L'Espoir* will arrive?"

He rubbed his nose while waiting for a reply. Kenton, like Rennick, never tanned and the tropical sun meant his face was always scarlet and usually peeling. He had tried rubbing the skin with butter, goose grease (which was awful: his clothes reeked of it for days) and soap, but nothing helped.

"The captain doesn't 'reckon.' He can only guess, like you or me. He's hoping, obviously, but he's trying not to be influenced by the fact that one of the prisoners is a close friend."

"Yes, what's that all about?" Kenton asked.

"I thought you knew." Aitken was always careful to separate information that the officers should know from gossip. Sometimes the dividing line was thin.

"No, I've only heard what Southwick's said."

"Well, the captain and Lady Sarah were on their honeymoon in France and staying with this friend, the Count of Rennes, when the British ambassador left Paris. Bonaparte's police arrested many Royalists before they knew the war had started again."

"Why didn't they arrest the captain and Lady Sarah at the same time?"

"Oh, that's how we came to have those four Frenchmen on board: Gilbert managed to hide the captain and his wife; then with the other three retook the *Murex*."

"Yes, I heard some of the seamen saying that her Ladyship shot dead a Frenchman."

"She did. Saved all their lives, I gather."

Kenton sighed, a deep sigh that seemed to go on as a descant to Martin's flute. "What a lovely lady she is. The captain certainly finds 'em. I used to think the Marchesa was the loveliest woman

I ever saw until Lady Sarah came along. I'm glad I didn't have to choose between them!"

"Keep your voice down; there's no need for Orsini to hear you going on about his aunt."

"She went back to Italy, didn't she? Hey!" Kenton sat up suddenly. "Do you suppose the French arrested *her* as well?"

"Arrested or assassinated?" Aitken said sourly. "No one knows yet. She reached Paris and left for Volterra, but there's no proof she ever reached Italy."

"I don't like this making war on women."

"At least some of the women make war on the French," Aitken commented. "Think of Lady Sarah!"

"Yes. I'm sorry we missed that. That's the first time the captain's been in a scrap without us for a long time."

"Ha, a long time!" Southwick rumbled from his cabin, where he was stretched out on his cot. "You're a new boy! I've been with him since he was given his first command!"

"Yes," Kenton said. "That was the *Kathleen* cutter, wasn't it? Tell us about the first time he came aboard and what you thought of him."

"Corsica, that's where it was," Southwick said, a nostalgic note in his voice. "Bastia. Nice harbour with all those fortifications. Commodore Nelson—well, he was only a commodore then—gave orders that—"

A hammering on the deckhead had all the officers grabbing their swords and pistols from the racks over their doors and hurrying for the companion-way, Kenton muttering: "I thought I heard a hail!"

CHAPTER EIGHTEEN

THE SUN was setting, and within half an hour it would plunge below the mangrove swamps and distant hills lining the mainland. Already Île Royale and Île St Joseph seemed to have changed shape as the shadows lengthened and moved round, the sun lighting the crest of fresh hills and darkening valleys.

The captain was on deck: they all knew that because when he wanted to spend some time alone pacing up and down, he had told Martin, who was officer of the deck, that he could go below for an hour.

They looked questioningly at the captain as they reached the quarterdeck, and he simply gestured seaward.

There, like a grey swan gliding on the far side of a lake, a frigate had just come in sight round the end of Île Royale.

"She looks French-built," he said, and told Orsini: "Go aloft with a bring-'em-near and see what you make of her. You, Kenton and Martin, had better get over to *La Robuste*."

Ramage then looked again at the approaching ship, at the Île Royale which was a grey, black-streaked monster crouching close by, and at *La Robuste,* anchored abeam. From pacing the quarterdeck he knew the wind was steady from the south-east at ten to fifteen knots.

Speeds and distances. Although the approaching frigate had at first been hidden behind the Île Royale, now she had drawn clear he could see she had only three miles to reach the point where she would expect the pilot canoe to be waiting.

I command *L'Espoir* and am at the end of the long and potentially dangerous voyage across the Atlantic, he told himself. My pilot book tells me where to anchor (there, where two frigates are already anchored) and that I should find the pilot just off the western end of Île Royale.

However, there is no pilot. I curse because, apart from anything else, the sun is too low to penetrate the water enough to show reefs and rocks, and the sea is too smooth in this lee to break. And soon it will be dark. What do I do?

Obviously I assume the two anchored frigates have seen me approaching. The pilot book tells me where the bank of dangerous rocks is, and the two frigates indicate the anchorage. One or both of the frigate captains will notice that the pilot does not meet me and if I try to get to the anchorage they will have warning guns ready. So I shall creep in under topsails, and if I get too near the bank a frigate's guns will warn me, and if it gets too shallow my own leadsman will warn me.

Yes, Ramage told himself, that is what he would be thinking and doing himself, and he was damn'd sure that is what the French captain was thinking and doing. The Frenchman would be concentrating his thoughts first on the outlying rocks and reefs and then on the shallow banks with soft muddy bottoms. And at the back of his mind there would be the prospect of a good supper at the governor's house with fresh meat instead of salt tack, and fresh fruit and fresh vegetables.

Aitken was inspecting La Robuste with a telescope. "I can see Wagstaffe watching. There are a few men on deck and they look very French." He closed the telescope and looked aloft and forward to check the Calypso. "We do, too, sir." He sniffed in a fair imitation of Southwick. "And I can't wait to have the men back at work with the brick dust putting a shine on our brasswork. It's so green that the ship begins to look like those copper roofs in Copenhagen."

"I didn't know you'd ever been there."

"Copenhagen, Elsinore, Christiania, Malmö, Stockholm . . . Yes, I know the Cattegat and Skagerrak, sir. In fact every time I see some weathered copper or brass I think of Copenhagen. Those spires and towers make it a lovely city. You know it?"

Ramage nodded, and both men were aware that they were using this inane conversation to pass the time. As they watched, *L'Espoir* seemed to slow down, but they knew that it was their own reactions quickening.

Opening his telescope again and carefully lining up the focusing ring he had filed in the eyepiece tube, Ramage looked carefully at the peak at the western end of Île Royale. The church stood shadowed and the big western door closed. The flagstaff was bare and there was no movement round the building.

Obviously the garrison commander or *préfet* had listened to the pilot's story that Brest had *la peste* and that although the two frigates already arrived had lost only a few men, a third frigate still on her way was believed to have lost many more. The garrison commander would assume that this frigate was the third and that she, even more than the other two, must be prevented from bringing *la peste* to the three islands which were already crowded with convicts and *déportés*. Only one hospital, the pilot book said, and Ramage could picture it: built of stone, small windows, one or perhaps two small wards, four beds in each, and nearby a cemetery situated in a place where there was a reasonable thickness of earth on the rock. And both hospital and cemetery within a short distance of the church: one did not walk far in the sun in a latitude of 5° North, and funerals were always held within 24 hours of death.

Funerals! His mind had a macabre twist at times. Ah, *L'Espoir* was furling her courses. Quite unconsciously he began counting the seconds, which merged into minutes, and he began extending his fingers so he could keep a better tally. Finally both courses were furled and he turned to find Aitken grinning at him.

"Short of topmen, short of petty officers, or just aren't in a hurry, sir? I saw you timing them."

"Just French," Ramage said. "Latins measure time by different watches and clocks than us!"

Now *L'Espoir* was abreast the western end of the Île Royale and began turning in a graceful arc until she was head to wind and, in a few moments, hove-to just where the pilot canoe had been waiting when the *Calypso* and *La Robuste* arrived. Now only a few sodden logs marked fishpots . . .

Ramage glanced at his watch and then turned to look at the sun, which was a perfect red orb with the lower edge exactly its own diameter above the horizon. The French captain had about fifteen minutes to decide that the pilot was not coming out tonight and make for the anchorage . . .

Exactly five minutes later *L'Espoir*'s foretopsail was braced up and she bore away towards the *Calypso* and *La Robuste*.

"Send the parties to their stations, Mr Aitken," Ramage said quietly, and went down to his cabin to collect his pistols and sling a cutlass-belt over his right shoulder.

Back on deck, Ramage steadied the glass against the rigging and studied *L'Espoir,* a graceful but weather-worn ship, in the circular frame of the telescope's lenses. Certainly he had no doubt that she was *L'Espoir:* he had seen in Brest that she was, very unusually, painted a dull russet red: a red very similar to the colour of rust. And, as the last of the sun caught her side squarely, he could see why that colour had been chosen: rust weeps from dozens of bolts streaked her hull as though the tails of dull red cows had been nailed to her side. The paint almost disguised the weeps but they were as obvious to a seaman's eye as the sobs after a weeping woman dried her eyes.

Ramage walked to the taffrail and looked over the stern. Three of the *Calypso*'s boats were streamed astern on their painters and the fourth was just securing to the end of the boat boom, after taking Kenton and Martin to *La Robuste*. A rope ladder hanging down from the outer end allowed men to climb up on to the boom; a line running parallel with the boom to the ship's side acted as a handrail.

Ramage had been amused at the sight of many of the men sitting round on the main deck with "prayerbooks" (the small blocks of Portland stone used as holystones to clean the deck), sharpening cutlasses and squaring up the three-sided tips of boarding-pikes. He had forbidden them to hoist up the big grindstone on deck because it made a harsh noise and while no man, however sharp his cutlass, could resist "having a whet" on the stone, the unmistakable noise would carry to Île Royale and Île St Joseph, and make some people wonder.

Or would it? Was he being too cautious? Could anyone on the three islands ever believe that the two frigates anchored close by were British? Fortunately the Tricolour was never run up at the flagstaff by the fortress on the seaward side. He had long ago noticed that while in Revolutionary France waving the Tricolour and yelling Revolutionary slogans was very popular, it was only in Royalist Britain and on board her ships that colours were hoisted and lowered at set times.

Had the *Calypso* and *L'Espoir* been arriving at a British island with its own governor they would have fired a salute, and the fort would have replied. Had Bonaparte decreed special days on which his army and navy were to fire salutes? The Royal Navy, with its very long history, had only six, three of them for the King (birthday, accession and coronation), and the others on the Queen's birthday, the anniversary of the Restoration of Charles II, and what was called "the Gunpowder-Treason" on 5th November. Anyway, *L'Espoir* was not firing any salutes, so obviously salutes were regarded as a waste of Revolutionary gunpowder.

Yes, the captain of *L'Espoir* had chosen where he was going to anchor and the frigate was coming round in a broad sweep which would save her having to tack. And Ramage looked forward at Southwick and Aitken, who were watching from the forward end of the quarterdeck. He nodded and smiled.

The dull red hull of *L'Espoir* now seemed black as the sun finally dipped below the horizon, and Ramage was thankful that twilight in the Tropics was brief. He walked forward to the quarterdeck rail and Aitken, in trousers and a loose smock, his narrow and intense face giving him the look of a Revolutionary, commented: "He timed his arrival perfectly!"

"To suit us, yes! An hour earlier would have given him time to be rowed to Île Royale to report to the governor, and the French sentries opening fire might have led to him discovering the deception. Half an hour later and he would have anchored for the night at the pilot station and waited until tomorrow. Then he certainly would have gone over to the island."

"As it is, he might come over here expecting to be invited to supper," Southwick said.

"Oh, I'm sure he'll have supper on board here tonight. What do you propose offering him? The last of the hens had its head chopped off a few days ago."

"Gunpowder soup, a cut off a round shot, grapeshot stuffed with canister . . . Does that sound appetizing, sir?"

At that moment a slatting of sails made them look towards *L'Espoir,* which was rounding up, foretopsail aback, halfway between the *Calypso* and *La Robuste.* The new frigate's quarterdeck was perhaps a hundred yards away, and Ramage saw a man, obviously her captain, lift his hat and wave it in a greeting.

Ramage waved back, followed by Southwick and Aitken, and *L'Espoir* came to a stop and then gathered sternway as the wind pushed against the forward side of the foretopsail. An anchor splashed into the dark water as Ramage again put the telescope to his eye.

Enough men on the fo'c's'le to deal with the anchor; enough topmen waiting at the foot of the shrouds to go aloft and furl the sails. Enough, but fewer than *L'Espoir* would have had if she was not armed *en flûte*.

L'Espoir's anchor cable was making less and less of an angle with the water as she moved astern and more cable was paid out; finally she stopped, the curve in the cable disappearing as it was straightened by the weight on it, and at last her captain was satisfied the anchor was well dug in. Both topsails were furled, and while the topmen were busy aloft the rest of the ship's company crowded the side, staring at the other two frigates, the islands and the distant low shore.

"Their first sight of the Tropics," Southwick commented. "A line of mangroves and three big lumps o' rock with pretentious names."

"Not pretentious to those prisoners," Ramage reminded him. "When they sensed the ship was in calmer waters, and then heard the anchor go down . . . They know it could only be the Île du Diable. No doubt quite a few of them expect to leave their bones here."

The light was going fast now; already a dozen of the brighter stars and planets were showing through as if shy of anyone knowing they had been there all the time but outshone by the sun.

"I'll go and get meself ready, sir." Southwick excused himself and went down to his cabin in the gunroom.

"That sword of his, sir," Aitken said. "Is it a family heirloom? I've never seen anyone using a two-handed sword!"

"Two-handed and double-bladed," Ramage said. "He doesn't jab or chop with it; he whirls round like a dancer spinning with a scythe. With his white hair flying and him bellowing like a livid bull, nothing clears an enemy's ship's deck faster!"

He looked at his watch, having to hold it up to catch the last of the light. "Just seven. Let's hope Wagstaffe has his people ready."

"Your orders were clear enough, sir. An hour after sunset, if she came in during the evening."

Ramage went to the larboard side and looked through the port. Île Royale, just forward of the beam was beginning to blur at the edges, the darkening sky making a smoothing background to the otherwise stark outline. Already *La Robuste* was difficult to see against the distant mangroves, and the russet-coloured *L'Espoir* seemed to have gone to sleep, as though the flurry of activity with anchoring and furling sails had exhausted her.

On board the *Calypso* men were placing lanterns in the normal positions, as though she was greeting the night in the normal way at anchor. A sharp-eyed observer might have wondered why there was no lantern at the eentry port—but then, he might think, who was likely to come on board?

"We can start, Mr Aitken," Ramage said eventually. "Start by getting those boats still astern hauled round to the boom."

Nearly every man in the *Calypso*'s ship's company was now on the main deck and gathered in groups of twenty around the officers. There was one small group by the mainmast, one which Ramage thought of as "Paolo's Party."

Paolo stood in front of the four Frenchmen and inspected them. It was now dark and the men were almost invisible: like Paolo and everyone else in the ship, their faces, necks, hands and bare feet were smeared with lampblack, and each man had a wide strip of white duck tied round his head, covering his forehead and knotted behind, the ends left to hang down.

"Now, keep your hands from those headbands," Paolo instructed in French. "They're the only thing that will distinguish you from the French crew: remember, our people in *La Robuste,* and all the men here, have orders to kill or capture anyone without headbands—except the *déportés,* of course."

"We understand, *m'sieu,*" Auguste said. "We follow you."

Ramage stood at the inboard end of the boom. "Mr Rennick, your men should board."

Rennick, indistinguishable from a cook's mate who had spent the last hour cleaning out the galley coppers, led the way past Ramage followed by his twenty men, and Ramage was surprised how far it was possible to distinguish the white headbands. Rennick was at the end of the boom and beginning to scramble down the ladder, yet his bobbing head was clear.

"Now Mr Southwick . . . mind that meat cleaver of yours!"

Ramage felt rather than saw the master grip his hand and shake it. "Thanks for letting me go, sir," the old man said. "Me sword was getting rusty!" he murmured.

He could just see Rennick's boat drifting clear, the men lifting the oars from their stowed positions along the thwarts. Binding all those damned oars with old cloths, bits of worn sail canvas and finally new duck had caused more trouble than anything else. The duck for the headbands and the oars—ah, Ramage felt angry at the thought of it. That blasted purser, asking to whom he should charge it! Well, admittedly the purser would have to pay unless he received a written authorization from the captain to issue it, but that was hardly the moment to burden everyone with bureaucracy. Probably the wretched fellow wanted the signature on the paper before the captain left the ship in case the captain did not come back alive! Anyway, Southwick saved the wretched man's bacon by declaring there was a grave risk that many yards of duck and sail cloth, some mess-deck forms and tables, a couple of dozen worn pistols and twice as many muskets, along with fifty cutlasses whose blades were now so pitted they'd serve better as saws, were going to be written off as "damaged or lost in battle."

Eighteen, nineteen, twenty . . . That was Southwick's party. "Mr Aitken . . ." The first lieutenant looking, Ramage thought, as "lean and hungry" as any yon Cassius with blackened face, led his men out on to the boom just as Southwick's boat drifted clear and close to Rennick's.

Again Ramage counted. Yes, that was Aitken's party.

"Orsini . . ." The midshipman led his four men along the boom.

"Jackson . . ." the coxswain appeared out of the darkness, "Lead on." Yes, he recognized the outline of Stafford. A muttered *"Buona fortuna, commandante,"* came from Rossi. Nine . . . eleven . . . fifteen . . . twenty.

Then Ramage was standing there alone except for a shadowy figure. "Well, bosun, it's the first time you've had command of a frigate! Look after her until I get back!"

"Good luck, sir," the bosun said. "I'd prefer to come with you."

"I know, but tonight you have to look after the *Calypso*."

As Ramage walked out along the boom, hearing the wavelets slapping below, he cursed his own softheartedness. The man who should have been left in command was the gunner, a wretchedly weak-willed man whom Ramage had been intending to replace for a year or more, but the prospect of a long battle with the Board of Ordnance and the Navy Board had made him keep the fellow. It was said that Southwick had not spoken a word to the man for more than a year . . .

He hitched his cutlass round to the centre of his back and pushed on the two pistols in his belt, and then went down the ladder. He stepped over feet and reached the sternsheets, to find himself with Paolo and the four Frenchmen, the rest of his own group being further forward. Jackson called softly to the man at the bow, who pulled the painter through the block and the boat drifted clear of the ship. The large black mass blotting out the stars on one side was the *Calypso*: the three shapes close by were the other boats. Over there was Île Royale which, like the *Calypso*, was only identifiable because of its outline against the stars.

CHAPTER NINETEEN

RAMAGE was never really sure whether it was a hiss or a purr, but the sound of a boat's cutwater slicing through a calm sea was very restful, like going to sleep on board the ship with wavelets faintly tickling the hull. The men were breathing easily because they were rowing at a comfortable pace and the oars were groaning softly in the rowlocks instead of squeaking and clicking: the cloth lashings and the greasy slush from the cook's coppers wiped into the open-topped square rowlocks were effective.

The boat came clear of the *Calypso*'s stern and Ramage had his first glimpse of *L'Espoir* from sea level. She seemed huge, black and menacing. No, perhaps not menacing—there were several lanterns casting yellowish cones of light on deck and reaching up to the under side of the yards which poised over the ship like eagles waiting to plunge.

Beyond he could just distinguish *La Robuste* in the distance; specks of dim light showed her position. At this very moment Wagstaffe should be leading four boats towards *L'Espoir*. Ramage was not too concerned that the two groups of boats arrived simultaneously because if one attacked before the other the French would concentrate on trying to beat it off and the second would take them by surprise. Hopes and fears: at this time they ran through one's thoughts like a pair of playful kittens.

In England it would be about half past eleven o'clock at night. Sarah would be in bed. Asleep? Probably, but perhaps lying awake thinking about him. If she was awake, he knew she was thinking about him. That was not conceit. It would have been if he had thought it before their honeymoon, but since then he had discovered that she needed him as much as he needed her, and that he occupied most of her life just as she occupied what was left of his after the navy's demands were satisfied. Loneliness, he had realized, was something no bachelor really understood. Loneliness was a happily married man (or woman) sleeping alone, the absence of a loved one. Gianna . . . In Volterra it must be about half past one o'clock in the morning. Tomorrow morning, as far as they were concerned here. What was she doing? How was she? Where was she? *Was* she? He tried to drive the thought away. Was Paolo, sitting next to him in the sternsheets, thinking about his aunt? Was he wondering if Bonaparte's secret police had murdered her, or had her securely locked up, something which for a woman like her would be a kind of death—

"*Qui va là?*"

The challenge from the deck of *L'Espoir* was casual: there was no alarm in the sentry's voice. Nor, Ramage realized as his body unfroze from the first shock of the hail which had brought him back from Volterra, London, warm nights with Sarah at Jean-Jacques' château near Brest, anything but friendly expectancy.

And casually, a comforting and confident casualness, came Auguste's amiable reply, his Breton accent deliberately more pronounced than usual.

"Our captain is visiting your captain, citizen. Did you have a good voyage from Brest?"

Some night birds fussed in the distance and he recognized the squawk of a night heron. And another. They must be flying from Île Royale to the mangroves on the shore. And that squeakier note—and again. Oystercatchers? Perhaps. What about that damned sentry? Twenty yards to go. Would he be watching just this one boat he had first sighted? Or would he look beyond and see three more that, however stupid he was, would give the lie to Auguste's reply?

"One gale and five days of calm. What ship?"

"We are *L'Intrépide,* and that's *La Robuste* over there."

"Your captain's name, citizen?"

Ramage hissed: "Keep rowing: lay us alongside, whatever happens."

"Citizen Camus, and who is he visiting?"

"Who is he visiting?" asked the puzzled sentry. "Why our captain you said, citizen."

"And what's your captain's name, you mule?" Auguste asked crossly.

"Magon," said a deeper voice. "I am the captain of *L'Espoir*. But rest on your oars . . ." the voice sounded harsh yet uncertain. "*L'Intrépide*, you say? That wasn't *L'Intrépide* that I saw. And Camus—I don't know that name."

Would Auguste pull it off, delay for a couple of minutes? "Pretend you're the captain!" he hissed at Gilbert. "Interrupt in a moment!"

"I don't expect you do; we're bound for Brest from Batavia," Auguste said, repeating the story Ramage had given him earlier.

"But even so," the doubting voice said from *L'Espoir*'s deck, "I don't even remember 'Camus' as a lieutenant."

"*Merde!*" exclaimed Gilbert angrily, as though he was the Camus in question and whose patience was now exhausted. "I haven't heard of 'Magon' either, and *L'Espoir* hasn't exactly distinguished herself, has she; you probably spent all the last war safely blockaded in Brest. Took a peace treaty to get you out again, eh? Now you're at sea"—Gilbert paused a moment and Ramage thought he too had heard a shout from the other side of the ship—"you've forgotten your manners. Good night, citizen. I'm not sitting here in my boat listening to that sort of welcome when I come to pay a visit!"

"No, no, you misunderstand me, citizen," Magon said hastily, "it's—"

He broke off as two pistol shots snapped across the frigate's deck and in the distance Ramage heard the night herons squawk in alarm. "Alongside!" he shouted. "Stand by to board, men!"

It seemed only a moment later that men were tossing oars and the cutter slammed against the frigate's hull and suddenly he could smell the humid, almost sickly smell of the weed that had grown along her waterline, and there was the reek of garlic, even down here.

Ramage leapt for the battens and both ahead and astern heard shouting in English and the thud, thud, thud of the spiked heads of tomahawks being driven into the hull planking to make steps for the men to board.

Bellowing and shouting he climbed, fingers gripping the edges of the battens, feet pressing sideways for footholds and his legs heaving and thrusting him up. Suddenly he was standing on *L'Espoir*'s deck and a man he guessed to be Captain Magon was wresting a musket from the sentry, who was clearly paralysed by the shouts and shots suddenly disturbing the tropical night.

Ramage dragged a pistol from his waistband and cocked it as he aimed at Magon, but the man pitched forward as another pistol firing beside him left Ramage's ears ringing. Ramage just had time to see in the light of the lantern hanging in the shrouds that Magon was bearded, then he turned towards the quarterdeck, shouting to his men.

There was a lantern on the binnacle: as he ran up the steps towards it, cutlass in his right hand, pistol in his left, he saw the one man on the quarterdeck, probably the officer keeping an anchor watch, running towards him, the blade of a cutlass he held over his head glinting in the dim light. The man was shouting almost hysterically and from three feet away he slashed downwards.

Ramage held up his own cutlass horizontally, the parry of quinte, and the man screamed and stepped back to slash again. He must have been a butcher before going to sea, Ramage thought, noting that the man had bared his right side. A quick lunge, a gurgle, and he was leaning over the collapsed man desperately tugging his cutlass free. How many times had he shouted at men under instruction that a cutlass was a slashing weapon: using the point was a quick way of getting cut down as you tried to withdraw from a body which invariably wrapped itself round your blade.

Jackson, Rossi, Stafford and more than a dozen other men now stood round him but, except for the body at Ramage's feet, the quarterdeck was now empty. "The gunroom!" Ramage shouted and led the way down the companion-way, which would bring them out first by the door to the captain's cabin and beside the second companion-way to the gunroom.

Aitken and Rennick's boats had come alongside just ahead of Ramage's cutter, and the first lieutenant, uttering wild Scottish battle cries, scrambled down from the gangway on to the main deck where French seamen, hurrying up from the lower deck where they had been having supper, found themselves running straight into bitter fighting.

Rennick's men were dropping down on to the main deck from further forward just as Aitken, realizing the value of lanterns, seized one and held it aloft and began the desperate game of hide-and-seek among the guns.

Paolo and his four Frenchmen, who had run along the larboard gangway to the forward end, dropped down and hid behind a couple of guns as dozens of yelling Frenchmen came rushing up the forehatch ladder, some of them—Paolo guessed them to be petty officers—pausing to open up arms chests and throw cutlasses on the deck for the men to grab.

The captain had been most emphatic, so Paolo did not mind hiding behind the gun with Auguste, while Gilbert, Albert and Louis crouched under the barrel of the next one forward. "Orsini," the captain had said, and Paolo could hear the words even now, "you are not to get involved in the fighting: I have enough fighters; I want talkers!" But it was hard just crouching here and watching those men giving out cutlasses. The five of them could— but no, the captain had been emphatic.

He heard a dreadful screaming from right aft amid the shouting and cursing of a dozen men yelling in both French and English. Pistol shots, the clang of cutlass blades—*accidente,* the worst noise was coming from the gunroom: all the ship's officers and warrant officers must have been trapped there and, Paolo knew only too well, they would have swords and pistols in racks outside their cabin doors. But with all these wretches rushing up from below and snatching up cutlasses it was not a question of cutting off the snake's head . . .

Southwick had scrambled up over the starboard bow, helped by a couple of seamen and thankful that the anchor cable was thick because it was a struggle to get up on to the fo'c's'le. A French seaman emerged from the head, protesting loudly at being interrupted, but within moments he had been cut down and his body thrown over the side.

The master was just about to lead his men in a sweep across the fo'c's'le to clear out the group of men where the gangway met the fo'c's'le when the reflection from a lantern showed a white band.

"Calypso!" Southwick roared and heard a querulous Sergeant Ferris say: "Can't find any more bloody Frenchies, sir! We've cleared the starboard gangway."

"Calypso!" came a shout from the group on the other side and Southwick discovered Lieutenant Martin complaining that the larboard gangway was clear and he thought Mr Ramage and the rest of them were either aft on the main deck or down on the lower deck.

"Calypsos!" Southwick bellowed, a sudden fear catching him: the fear that there was a good fight going on and he was missing it. "Follow me!" He led the rush aft along the starboard gangway, pausing a moment to look at the main deck and find a rope ladder to scramble down, but he was beaten to it by Martin and Ferris, who jumped.

There were many writhing men but little light on the main deck: Southwick saw a couple of lanterns hooked up on the beams, and then, his eye caught by a dancing light aft, he saw a shouting and a grinning Aitken holding a lantern high with one hand, his cutlass slashing with the other.

Southwick stepped forward, both hands grasping his great sword. He paused a moment to look at the head of the nearest man, saw it had no white band, and swung. The shock of blade on bone jarred and he took a couple of steps forward to the next man.

Wagstaffe shouted to his men to get to the main hatchway but the noise drowned his voice. Wagstaffe realized too late that he and Kenton had made a mistake: the moment they had seen the starboard gangway cleared they should have secured the fore, main and after hatches and cut down *L'Espoir's* ship's company as they scrambled unarmed up to the main deck. Now dozens, scores of Frenchmen, were on the main deck, snatching up cutlasses from the arms chests. Wagstaffe led his men across to the other side of the ship.

God, that noise in the gunroom!

The fighting was now almost entirely on the main deck, with Southwick, Ferris and Martin slashing their way aft along the starboard side to meet Aitken and his men working forward, and Wagstaffe, Kenton, and Rennick slashing and jabbing their way forward along the larboard side. Right aft, one deck lower, Ramage and his men fought through the gunroom with little room to swing a cutlass and all their pistols empty. Ramage eyed the swinging lantern: the remaining Frenchmen could have saved themselves if they had cut that down, but it seemed they dreaded the darkness.

Paolo watched the fore hatch. No one had come up it for two, perhaps three minutes. *"Andiamo!"* he said to the four French-men, and then realized that with his excitement he had lapsed into Italian. "Come on!" he corrected himself, added a very Eng-lish "Damnation!" and then said: *"Allons, messieurs!"*

The lower deck was well lit: candles flickered at the tables and it took him a moment to realize that the curiously stark shadows on the deck were overturned forms. There was a great deal of shouting and cutlass clanging right aft, round the gun-room, but in his imagination Paolo could recall the captain's voice giving him orders.

He turned forward, picking up a lantern, and followed by the four Frenchmen passed the last of the tables.

"Déportés!" he called, and Gilbert, his voice agitated and crack-ing with emotion, started to shout but it ended as almost a scream: *"M'sieu le Comte!* Here is Gilbert! Please, are you there!"

Paolo held the lantern higher. They were there all right, row upon row, men next to women, each held flat on the deck by a leg iron round the ankle, and waving near the back was a man who Paolo could see was too overcome with emotion to speak.

Paolo seized Gilbert's arm and pointed and gave him the lantern, and with a gasp of relief the Frenchman stumbled for-ward, trying to avoid the other prisoners but lurching as his feet caught ankles, eyebolts and the rods linking the leg irons. Now every one of the prisoners seemed to be shouting at once, every one of them and at the top of his voice or her voice. It was absurd; of that Paolo was sure. It was unseamanlike. Ungentle-manly and unladylike, too.

"Silence!" he shouted. *"Silence! Silence!"*

He paused for breath. Yes, now he had silence down here except for the blood pounding in his ears, but right aft and on the deck above there was more shouting, screaming and clang-ing of cutlasses than he had ever heard before.

"Ladies and gentlemen!" he said, to consolidate the silence he had brought to this part of the ship. Then he could think of nothing to say. Fifty or more white faces stared up at him; a hundred or so eyes glinted in the candlelight as Auguste brought up another lantern. *Mama mia,* what would the captain say to these people if he was standing here!

"Ladies and gentlemen, I must apologize for the noise." A woman started laughing, a laugh which rose higher up the scale and ended suddenly as someone reached across and slapped her to stop the hysteria.

"I am from the *Calypso,* one of His Britannic Majesty's frigates and commanded by Captain Ramage, and—"

"Count Orsini, I think!" The voice came from the back.

"At your service," Paolo said carefully, an Italian count suspecting he was addressing a French one but determined not to give too much ground. "You have me at a disadvantage, *m'sieu.*"

"I am Rennes, and Captain Ramage told me about you."

Then Paolo remembered the rest of his orders. "Forgive me for a moment. Now, ladies and gentlemen, we shall try to release you, once we have found the keys, but please stay here until Captain Ramage comes and tells you to move: unless you are wearing one of these white headbands, you might be killed!"

At the other end of the lower deck Ramage was cursing fluently in Italian, with Jackson and Stafford providing a descant of obscene English. There was a small doorway at the after side of the gunroom and the five Frenchmen (Ramage was unsure if they were officers or seamen who had been trying to escape from the mess-deck) had managed to get through it, slashing and parrying with swords, and vanished into the darkness beyond. It was the tiller flat, a space the width of the ship across which the great wooden arm of the tiller moved in response to the wheel turning above. And now anyone going through that black hole was asking to be cut down by the men who could remain hidden behind the bulkhead.

Five men: of no consequence. With the captain dead they would soon surrender.

"You men"—he pointed to five of his group—"stay here and stop those fellows coming out. More important"—he pointed down at the thick wooden hatch cover—"that's the magazine scuttle, so guard it!"

With that he was running up the companion-way to the main deck and was just in time to see twenty or so Frenchmen retreating before Southwick, Ferris and Martin, but fighting back-to-back with twenty more who were slowly driving Aitken and fewer than a dozen men aft, trapping them against the capstan.

Aitken was still slashing with his cutlass and turned away shouting incomprehensible encouragement to his men when Ramage saw one of the Frenchmen break from the group and run towards Aitken, holding his cutlass like a pike.

There was no time to shout a warning—Aitken would never hear it—and Ramage hurled his cutlass, leaping after the spinning blade. The hilt caught the side of the Frenchman's head, he staggered, and a moment later Ramage had an arm round the man's neck and they both swayed, a shouting Aitken flicking away the cutlass of another attacker but still unaware that he had nearly been cut down.

The Frenchman was burly, two or three inches taller than Ramage, and he wore no shirt. His body was slippery from perspiration, but now, no longer stunned, he wrenched away from Ramage's grasp after punching him in the face, took a step back, and lifted his cutlass for the slash that Ramage knew would split his head in two, and for the moment he was too dizzy to do anything but stand there.

The Frenchman's blade swung up, only the sharp edge shiny;

Ramage registered dully that the blade must be rusty and only the cutting edge clean. Up, up the blade went and the Frenchman's eyes held his: the head was the target and the Frenchman was not going to be distracted.

The Frenchman's face contracted slightly, the body flexed and the right shoulder twisted an inch or two as the muscles drew at the arm. Ramage sensed rather than saw that not one of his own men was within ten feet and no one had noticed this lonely and one-sided duel.

The Frenchman was grinning: two teeth missing in front at the bottom. Unshaven. The arm coming down now. Sarah. Jean-Jacques. Such a waste, but no pain—

But the arm was still upraised and the Frenchman was looking up and tugging. In an instant Ramage realized that the man had held the cutlass too vertically as he raised it for the final blow and the point had caught in the deckhead above. As he struggled to free it, Ramage moved two paces closer, kicked the man in the groin and then picked up his own cutlass. That made seven.

He turned to join Aitken and found that in the few moments of the strange duel, which had seemed at the time to be lasting ages, his own party had combined with the first lieutenant's and driven the Frenchmen forward again, squeezing them against Southwick's party.

Ramage jumped up on to the capstan head and crouched to avoid the deck beams. It was easier to look across the main deck from here. Two, four, eight . . . twelve . . . thirteen . . . sixteen . . . All the rest wore white bands round their heads. And here were Southwick, Ferris and Martin coming along the starboard side, grinning.

"Just going to give Aitken a hand!" Southwick said and led his men in a scramble over the cranked pump handle.

So apart from a few unwounded but surrendering Frenchmen, the main deck was suddenly secure. But the *déportés?* For a moment he had a clear picture of fifty people in irons at the fore end of the lower deck, their throats cut by some rabid Revolutionary.

Jackson was beside him now, with Stafford and Rossi. "Lost you for a moment, sir," the American said.

"It was a long moment," Ramage said, "but come on!"

He jumped off the capstan and snatched up a lantern lying on its side, flipped open the door and straightened the wick. Fortunately it could only just have been knocked over because the wax had not run. He shut the door and clattered down the companion-way to find himself outside the gunroom again. What the devil had made him go up on the main deck after leaving those five men on guard? The whole reason for the voyage and this attack was waiting at the forward end of the lower deck, and he remembered with sick fear that Paolo had not reported, nor Gilbert, nor Auguste.

He was past the after hatch; there, like a vast tree trunk, was the mainmast. Now the main hatch and past these forms lying over the deck, an indication of the way the Frenchmen had been surprised.

Candles alight on the tables. There was a lantern, two lanterns, moving about right up forward, and now he could see a mass of bodies lying on the deck. And two or three men moving among them—murderous Republicans cutting the throats of the *déportés?*

He was concentrating so carefully on not tripping in the half-darkness that he was almost among the slaughtered *déportés* before he realized it, and he looked up with his cutlass raised to find that the nearest rabid Republican killer with the lantern was in fact Paolo.

"Your friend is in the last row, sir," Paolo said calmly, not realizing how close to death he had been. "I understand that the key to unlock these irons is in the captain's possession. A Captain Magon, I believe."

Ramage stepped over the prone people to where Gilbert was kneeling. There, his ankle held by a leg iron, was Jean-Jacques, who looked up and grinned and said: "I hardly expected to see you here. Is Sarah with you?"

CHAPTER TWENTY

RAMAGE stepped out on to the jetty where the group of Frenchmen stood with a white flag on a staff, and the wind tugged at the similar white flag being held up in the cutter's bow. Gilbert and Paolo followed and as Jackson stood a French officer held up a hand and said in French: "Only one man, the captain."

Ramage stopped. "Where is the island governor?"

"At the fortress, waiting for you."

"My letter suggesting a truce said we meet and negotiate on this jetty."

The French officer shrugged his shoulders. "It is not my concern. My orders are to escort you to the fort."

Ramage turned to his men. "We go back to the ship." He then said to the French officer: "I shall return in half an hour. If the governor is not here, *L'Espoir* will then be blown up."

"But her crew!"

Ramage raised his eyebrows in what he hoped was a cold and callous glare. "*What* about them?"

"They will all be killed!"

"The survivors, yes. Many were killed last night. The rest . . . well, that depends on the governor. Half an hour then. If he is not here, we shall sail at once, and *L'Espoir* will vanish a few minutes later." He looked across the anchorage and laughed.

"Perhaps not vanish: you will see plenty of smoke and an abundance of wreckage!"

"A moment," the French officer said hurriedly, "we can reach an accommodation."

"I assure you that we cannot," Ramage said stiffly. "I talk only to the governor. No one on Île Royale, the Île du Diable or the Île St Joseph—or for that matter down in Cayenne—is performing a favour for me. I am offering him the lives of 64 French seamen from *L'Espoir*. They treated the *déportés* so shamefully they will never be exchanged from England. The wounded certainly will not survive the voyage . . ." he paused and composed himself for another cold-blooded laugh. It came out quite satisfactorily judging from the look on Jackson's face. ". . . And I have grave doubts about the unwounded. My men have no sympathy . . ." He gave an expressive shrug and waved a hand towards the broad Atlantic on the other side of the island, a gesture which he saw achieved its purpose in conjuring up a picture of shark fins cutting through the water.

The Frenchman pointed towards the seaward end of the jetty. "*M'sieu*, you speak French like a Frenchman. Walk a few steps with me—"

"Tell your party to stay by the boat," Ramage snapped as he saw a couple of lieutenants begin to follow.

The officer snapped out an order which froze the men. Lot's wife, Ramage thought, and looked curiously at the officer. He did not recognize the man's uniform, which was well cut in green cloth. It had black buttons with a design or initials on them. If his rank was a captain or major, one would have expected . . . His thoughts were interrupted as the man tried to smile, indicating that they should walk the few paces which would take them to the end of the jetty and out of earshot of everyone else.

When they stopped, Ramage turned to the man and guessed the answer before he said: "Well?"

"There is no need to go to the fort; we can negotiate here."

"You command the garrison?"

"I command all three islands."

"And you are?"

"General Beaupré."

"Prove it."

He was a solidly built man with a flowing black moustache and brown eyes that were friendly. Not at all what one expected of a jailer, Ramage decided.

"Lieutenant Miot!" Beaupré called.

"Oui, mon général?"

Ramage nodded. "All right—you are a general. We negotiate. I have three French frigates, not two—the two farthest from us I captured recently, one last night and the other last week. The nearest I captured a couple of years ago and she is now commissioned into the Royal Navy."

"You want to exchange something for the two frigates?" General Beaupré was incredulous.

"No, I was simply introducing you to the situation. *L'Espoir,* the frigate that arrived last night, was bringing you more than fifty *déportés.*"

"Yes, I guessed that. They would be kept on the other island." He pointed. "The Île du Diable is for *déportés,* who are of course political prisoners. The criminals are kept on Île St Joseph and here, on Île Royale."

"I am not interested in the criminals," Ramage said. "I will exchange my prisoners, the men from *L'Espoir* and *La Robuste,* for all the *déportés* you have on the Île du Diable."

The general's face fell. "But I don't have any *déportés!*"

"Where are they?" Ramage demanded.

"With the treaty that ended the war, they were all sent back to France. Why should we detain them in peacetime? I have only criminals now. And what people they are. Every one of them, men and women, think nothing of murder! But *déportés* now, why that is absurd."

"Because we are all at peace, eh?"

"Yes, of course," the general said. "When you mentioned *déportés* in *L'Espoir*—that was a slip of the tongue, was it not? You meant 'convicts.'"

Ramage shook his head slowly, angry with himself for not realizing. His note sent on shore earlier had merely said that the ships did not have *la peste* on board, that the shooting and shouting of the previous night had been caused by the capture of *L'Espoir* by men of the Royal Navy. Ramage had suggested a truce to discuss the disposal of French wounded and prisoners; he had forgotten the most important item of news.

"No, *déportés*. The war has started again."

The general paled. "War," he muttered. "I thought it was piracy. War . . . I suppose *L'Espoir* also brought despatches giving me the news."

"I expect so," Ramage said. "We have not gone through all the papers yet. However, what about the exchange?"

The general faced Ramage squarely. "I have no *déportés*. If you wish, we will visit the three islands and you can question any one you like. Convicts—yes, scores, and you are welcome to them. The *déportés* in *L'Espoir* would have been the first for a year, and the buildings for them on the Île du Diable are falling down— termites, white ants, the rain . . . Nothing lasts, be it buildings or men. Termites or the black vomit," he said hopelessly. "We're all exiles here . . . the convicts are locked up at night. But are their jailers free?"

He suddenly shook his head, apparently startled that he should have been confiding in not only a foreigner but now, apparently, an enemy.

He said: "Shall we inspect this island first and then go to Diable and St Joseph? Once the sun gets up . . ."

Once the sun gets up these islands must be among the hottest, most unpleasant and unhealthy in the world, but that was not the reason Ramage shook his head. The general had obviously been speaking the truth about the *déportés,* and when the man rambled off on that brief soliloquy it was because he knew that a new war only prolonged his stay on the islands, where the sun, sea, the fevers and the swamps ensured that the jailer was as much a prisoner as the jailed.

"I accept your word," Ramage said. "Our boats will start landing the French wounded as soon as I return on board and give the order. Then we will land the French seamen we hold as prisoners, first from *La Robuste* and then from *L'Espoir.* All this under a flag of truce, eh?"

"A flag of truce," the general echoed. "You are being generous," he admitted, "since I have nothing to give you in return."

Ramage was not about to tell him that prisoners were a confounded nuisance in a ship of war. "Very well, then we are agreed."

"Your name," the general said. "I read it on the letter. Of course you know it is a French word, too. But I know you by reputation. I can only hope you go back to *La Manche:* my countrymen would not welcome your arrival to Martinique or Guadeloupe . . ."

Ramage stood up from behind his desk and smiled at Aitken and Wagstaffe. "Very well, then, each frigate is to keep a couple of cables apart by day, and one cable by night, and the rendezvous is Carlisle Bay, Barbados."

"Thank you, sir," Aitken said. "Being *L'Espoir*'s temporary first lieutenant is going to be good experience for Kenton."

Southwick, who was staying in the *Calypso* with Ramage, laughed and commented to Wagstaffe: "And young Orsini will learn a lot being your second and third lieutenant!"

Ramage said to Wagstaffe: "Are you happy with just Martin and Orsini? Until we get up to Trinidad the wind can chop about."

"We'll be all right, sir. Do you think the admiral there will buy 'em in?"

"Two frigates in good condition with no damage—except for a few nicks from pistol balls in one of them? I should think he'll be only too glad. You'll all be rich men!"

"They haven't done too badly up to now," Southwick said. "Enough in the Funds to retire as knights of the shire!"

"And you!" Wagstaffe exclaimed. "Since you began serving with Mr Ramage, you've made enough money to buy ten taverns and ten breweries to supply them!"

"I'm not complaining," Southwick said, and turning to Wagstaffe said seriously: "You could let young Orsini think we shall be depending on his positions."

Wagstaffe nodded. "I'll let him *think* that, but I expect he'll come along with some workings that put us in the middle of the sugar cane in Demerara!"

As the two lieutenants left the cabin with Southwick, Ramage walked through to the coach, where a Frenchman was busy writing. "Jean-Jacques, we sail in half an hour. Judging by the way that quill is bobbing, you've now recovered enough to tell me what happened when they arrested you in Brest."

"Yes, yes," the Frenchman agreed. "But first you must tell me the—how do you say, 'the butcher's bill'?"

"Yes, and it makes a sad story. *L'Espoir* had 127 officers and men on board when she anchored here last night, and 54 *déportés*. The captain and two of the three lieutenants were killed in our attack, and 27 petty officers and seamen. Thirty-three more were wounded."

"More than half of them killed or wounded," Jean-Jacques said. "They fought hard."

Ramage was silent. The French had fought hard, but they

knew they were fighting to survive. Most men tried to stay alive. The bravery came when you risked your life just to save others or obey orders. Jean-Jacques looked up at Ramage.

"Because we *déportés* were the cause, I hardly dare ask your casualties: it is like asking a man how many of his family have just been killed."

"Eight killed and nineteen wounded. Three of the wounded won't see another sunset but the others will be standing a watch before we land you all at Portsmouth."

"Sarah. You said last night that she was safe and well. I prayed that she would have come to no harm under my roof."

"Gilbert and Louis . . ."

"Yes, they obeyed my orders. These other two, Auguste and Albert, tell me about them. I was too excited and too exhausted to understand about a ship called the *Murex*. A British brig, Gilbert said, and Sarah shot the man in command. Tell me," he said anxiously, "was that not . . . well, rather drastic?"